THEIR DISCOVERY

LEGALLY BOUND BOOK 3

REBECCA GRACE ALLEN

Rebecca Grace Allen Enterprises

Their Discovery

Copyright © 2019 by Rebecca Grace Allen

Digital ISBN: 978-0-9992066-8-3

Print ISBN: 978-0-9992066-9-0

Print ISBN: 978-0-9998004-0-9

Editing by Jennifer Miller

Cover Design by Romantic Book Affairs

Exploring their fantasies could save their marriage...or push it over the edge

Legally Bound, Book 3

Samantha Archer's life has hit a wall. Her world is housework, homework and reminding her husband—the biggest kid in the family—to help out at home. Once she felt confident, powerful and sexy, but Brady doesn't seem to notice her anymore, and now all she feels is invisible.

Brady has tried being the goofy guy who stole Sam's heart, but it's not working. He's losing the woman he loves and doesn't have a clue how to fix it. He's keeping his darkest fantasies hidden, too, sure they're not what Sam wants, and his inability to please her cuts him deeper than she knows.

When Sam lands a new job at a law firm, Brady still won't pick up the slack, and one night giving him orders unexpectedly reignites their missing spark. Sam discovers the Femdomme she didn't know she was, kindling Brady's submissive desires.

But while things heat up inside the bedroom, life outside it starts unraveling. Brady's need to call the shots at work complicates his hunger to kneel for his wife, and Sam has longed to experiment in more ways than one. Their exploration of dominance and submission goes a step too far when they invite Sam's sultry switch coworker into their bed, and the fallout could cost them everything.

Warning: Contains a six-foot-five, ex-football player geek and a ballsy, badass redhead who's learning to unleash her inner Domme. Scenes depicting humiliation, pegging and threesomes could disturb, or stimulate a thirst for adventure.

Praise for *their discovery*

"I have been on the Legally Bound journey from nearly Day 1, and Their Discovery was the perfect way to end this series."
—4 star Goodreads review

"I wish this had been the first novel of this genre that I had ever read."
—5 star Goodreads review

"Wow! This book was way more than I expected...This was my first time reading this author's work and will definitely be reading more."
—5 star Goodreads review

"A tender, hot and real romance."
—4 star Goodreads review

"Super exciting and steaming hot."
—4 star Goodreads review

Praise for *her claim*

"As emotionally fulfilling as it is blistering."
—RT Book Reviews, 4 star review

"I love Allen's voice! This story is a sexy twist on readers' favorite erotic tropes."
—Cara McKenna, author of *Willing Victim*

"HOLY SEXY, BATMAN! ...Her Claim is a fabulous addition to the Legally Bound collection."
—5 star Goodreads review

"Hot like you've rarely read, frustrating and so so sweet."
—The Book Hammock, 5 stars

This is the end of my Legally Bound series, and was perhaps the hardest to write out of all my books. It asked me to dig down and dredge up some really difficult emotions, and to put on the page things not seen in a typical romance novel.

In many romance books, marriage and babies equals happily ever after. And in a lot of romance books, especially ones involving BDSM, the Dominant knows exactly what to do, executes everything almost perfectly, and knows how to fix things when they go sour.

This is not one of those books.

This is a story about marriage, and how after a while, you can forget to see the partner you've chosen—how love gets lost in the hectic and sometimes humdrum pace of life. It's also a story about beginner BDSM, where people make mistakes. They try new things, and while those things occasionally go over smoothly, they can also sometimes crash and burn.

Sam makes mistakes. So does Brady. You're going to be mad at them. Your heart may break for them. But stick with them. They'll win you over in the end.

On a separate note, some reviewers who received advanced reader copies of this book pointed out issues with the story regrading Sam's weight loss journey. I wish to thank them for their honesty.

1

$\mathcal{S}$amantha Archer was disappearing.

Not in the literal sense. People *saw* her—saw her as a wife, as a mom, and she was still visible in her redheaded, five-foot-six form. But here in the passenger seat of her family's car, her evening gown smudged with wedding cake and a husband beside her who'd barely looked at her all night, Sam felt herself fading away.

"Mom?"

Sam glanced over her shoulder. Hope was fast asleep, her head lolled to the side on the headrest, legs barely visible beneath her dress. But Allegra, of course, was wide awake. "What is it, honey?"

"I still don't know where my pink gloves are."

Sam closed her eyes for a second and took a breath.

She's not defiant. Just distracted.

"I told you before we left that we'd look when we got home. It was part of your plan tonight, remember?"

The Plan was one of Allegra's behavior-management tools—a check-in with reminders, whenever they left the house.

Tonight it hadn't stuck.

"Daddy is going to help you find them," Sam added as calmly as she could. "And you can wear them to school tomorrow."

She glanced to the left, waiting to catch Brady's eye. His gaze remained fixed on the road, more dazed than distant. He'd been like that since they left the reception, his mind someplace else again. Sam willed him to speak up, to pitch in, to do *something* to prove he was still present in their marriage. Today had been a long day for everyone, but would it kill him to respond?

"But what if we can't find them?" Allegra whined, and Sam knew what was coming next. She had to manage this meltdown before it started.

"We'll find them," Sam replied, forcing every ounce of motherly soothing vibes she could into her words. The psychologist had said they needed to be patient. Allegra's impulses weren't always within her control. "As soon as we get home. Daddy will help you, right?"

When Brady didn't reply, Sam elbowed him across the armrest. Jolted from wherever he'd gone in his head, he glanced in the rearview mirror.

"Right," he said. "We're gonna find it, honey. No problem."

It was the *it* that made Sam cringe. "Them. Two gloves. We're going to find *them*."

A heartbeat passed before he responded.

"Right. Of course, two gloves. One glove would be silly. Who'd walk around with one glove on?"

Allegra giggled, mollified by her father's response. Sam, however, was not. Brady would need a reminder about the gloves when they got home, as well as the babysitter job posting she'd asked him about on Friday. He promised he'd do it by the end of the weekend, but between yesterday's snowstorm, Jack's wedding today and Brady's propensity to forget everything she said, Sam was pretty sure he hadn't done it. At least football season was over. Brady's attention was even harder to get when the Patriots were playing, worse if they were winning. Impossible when they were in the Super Bowl. She would've taken care of the posting herself, but she'd been busy entertaining their children during their midwinter break. And it was the only thing she'd asked him to do.

"I'm sorry about your dress," Allegra said.

Sam looked over her shoulder again. That was her eldest child, flipping from infuriating to sweet on a dime.

"It's okay, sweetie." Sam knew the wedding would overstimulate her, not to mention all the decadent food. She hadn't wanted Allegra to have any cake at all—the fondant was enough to spin her into overdrive—but she'd allowed it against her own better judgment. Allegra's powerful temper had flared anyway when Hope had gotten a bigger slice than she did, triggering yet another *it's not fair* meltdown. One slam of her no-longer-little fist on the table had sent a forkful of Sam's own dessert straight onto her black velvet gown. "You didn't do it on pur—"

"Aunt Lilly looked pretty tonight."

Sam sighed, and not just at Allegra's inability to stop herself from interrupting. "She sure did."

The bride *had* looked lovely, but no one in this car had noticed how Sam had looked, or the fact that she'd finally fit back into this dress. It was selfish, to want to be the center of someone's attention on her brother-in-law's wedding day. She shouldn't have felt this way.

But she did.

Allegra grew quiet, distracted once again by the iPad Sam had given her in one of the many attempts to keep her calm. Screen time was a lousy cover for Sam's less-than-stellar parenting, but she needed a few moments of silence. She looked out the window as Brady took the exit off the Mass Pike to the quiet, tree-lined streets of Newton.

Ten miles west from downtown Boston, it was a patchwork of villages, an old mill town turned suburb. The schools were good, and it was close to her parents and to Brady's job. Adjacent to Brookline and Cambridge, it was a stone's throw from the Harvard campus and housed the famous Heartbreak Hill—the spot known to Boston Marathoners for hitting a wall.

Sam knew the feeling.

The brakes shuddered a bit when they came to a light, but Brady's car handled it. They both drove strong, sturdy cars built for weather like this. The thaw they'd seen on Valentine's Day had been nothing more than a tease, and now fresh powder from last night's squall rested atop a layer of frozen slush.

The Northeast in February wasn't fun, but like their cars, Sam valued her toughness on being able to handle it. She liked to say she was a born-and-bred New Englander, hardy and unfelled by the frequent blizzards and the average high of just above freezing. She'd even joke about the winters she'd spent in DC, and how the city was crippled by the lightest snowstorm. Those were moments of bravado though, when she put on her *I'm fine* mask. The one she wore so much she forgot it wasn't her anymore.

Most people tonight had no idea Sam was barely keeping it together. That Allegra's anger over her younger sister's existence made her downright mean sometimes, and that Hope never asked why Allegra got rewards for doing day-to-day things, never mimicked her sister's disruptive behavior or sought revenge. People at the wedding had said Hope was the best behaved seven-year-old they'd ever seen, but the truth was she'd become overly passive in the face of Allegra's paths of destruction, and Sam had no idea what to do about it.

The truth also was that she and Brady were barely connecting at all.

By the time they'd pulled into their driveway, Allegra was as dead to the world as Hope was. Brady cut the engine, and Sam reached up to finger her necklace, a nervous habit she couldn't shake. Those first few moments of sleep with Allegra were precarious, and having her pass out minutes before they got home was only going to make her crankier. Sam tried to anticipate potentially explosive situations, but it almost never worked, and would be even less likely to tonight. Spending Sunday evening at Jack's wedding was enough of a catalyst to get Allegra out of whack, and after the cake incident and the pink gloves lost to the void of the house, waking her was going to be a nightmare.

"Can you carry her?" Sam whispered. "Keep her asleep as long as possible?"

"I can."

He turned Sam's way, a boyish smile behind his dark, full beard.

It was crazy how her heart could still flutter at his baby face and silky brown curls. Even in this dim light, she could see amusement playing in his eyes, a bright blue that turned nearly turquoise sometimes. She hoped that smile meant he'd noticed she'd reached her pre-baby weight, that he was finally going to tell her how nice she looked.

"Or I could throw her in the sled, aim for the door and hope for the best."

Nope. Not the reaction she'd wanted.

Brady's smile paused, a question mark hanging in the air that was now growing cold between them. Or maybe it was their marriage, devoid of anything resembling heat.

"What?" he asked. "I was kidding."

He was always kidding. If her husband wasn't lost in his own thoughts or working, he was trying to be funny.

Sam didn't need funny. She needed a partner. Someone who picked up the slack at home and shared the mental workload of parenting with her. Someone who noticed her and made her feel wanted and interesting again.

She grabbed the handle and shoved the door open. "Just carry her, please?"

Brady let out a defeated sigh. Sam's chest pinched at the sound, but she pushed it aside. His bruised ego could manage, and it wasn't as if he wasn't going to joke around again.

She closed the door and tightened her coat around her body. Christ, it was cold—the kind of frigid that burned your face and hurt your teeth when you opened your mouth. The shock of the icy night air was going to startle Allegra if being pulled from the car didn't, and Sam braced herself for the impending screaming fit as they opened the back doors.

Allegra didn't so much as blink when Brady lifted her from the seat. Her head slumped on his big shoulder, and her legs dangled limply along his sides. Exhaling in relief, Sam unbuckled Hope's seatbelt and picked her up, but struggled to close the door with her hip the way she usually did, heels slipping on snowy pavement. Brady quickly walked around the car, shifted Allegra onto one arm and reached the other out. Sam passed Hope over, amazed at how he could hold both of them with ease He was still built like a linebacker, even if he didn't play anymore.

He nodded at the house with an unspoken, *"You get the door."*

It was his silent apology for the place their marriage was in, and Sam immediately regretted being so sharp with him.

She closed the car doors and followed him up the walkway, carefully picking through the snow in her heels. Sure, Brady hadn't shoveled, the Christmas decorations were still up and she feared for the shape of their gutters, but he was trying, and seeing him carry their children softened her. It reminded her of his strength, of the tremendous arms hidden beneath his winter coat. The crisp black suit he'd worn tonight showed them off, the clean lines accenting thick forearms connected to sinewy shoulders.

Brawny build, eyes and smile—they were the holy trinity that had knocked Sam over when she'd met him at age nineteen. At six-foot-five, he towered over her, and the solid wall of muscle he'd been had stirred some kind of cavewoman impulse. He hadn't *seemed* stronger than everyone else—he *was*. But he was docile with her. And having someone that masculine follow her around campus like a puppy dog had been intoxicating. She'd felt adored and exalted. Worshipped, even.

She shouldn't have liked it as much as she did, but something inside her had needed his attention, *demanded* it when they'd dated in college and when their paths had crossed again years later. But they'd lost that spark in the time since, and it was like a fire burned out, a smoky carcass left behind now that it was gone.

Stepping past him on the stoop, she unlocked the front door and flipped on the foyer light, flattening herself against the wall to make room for Brady's massive frame as he passed her. Standing there, she couldn't help but imagine how this scenario would've been different years ago. If they were in one of their dorm rooms instead of this house. Alone instead of with kids.

Back then, she wouldn't have hesitated.

She'd have pushed him against the wall. Undone his tie and unbuttoned his crisp, white dress shirt. Smoothing her palms over his arms, she'd have waited for his breath to catch. For him to lose control and beg for her touch.

The only thing Brady lost was his balance, tripping over the snow boots Allegra hadn't put away and cursing loudly. It shook both girls awake and doused any inkling of Sam's desire.

"Language," she snapped.

He mumbled an apology as he lowered the girls to the floor. Frustration twisted through Sam's jaw, soldering it shut as she bent to hastily unzip their jackets. Why were things like this? Two seconds ago she was mentally undressing him, and now she was angry all over again. At one point, Brady's crass behavior and fun-loving attitude hadn't bothered her. If anything, it had drawn her in even more. But that playfulness and immaturity was fine in college. Now the concept of being an adult seemed as foreign to him as remembering not to say *motherfucker* in front of their children.

Allegra started to cry. Disoriented and cranky with her meds worn off, her words were barely decipherable.

"I—want—my—pink— gloves!"

Hope said nothing as usual, going mute to stay out of the crossfire. Her eyes half closed, she swayed unsteadily on her feet. Sam reached out a hand to stop her from toppling over, then freed her from her coat before yanking off her own.

"Daddy will find the gloves. We're going to bed."

"But I want to *see* the glo—"

"You'll *see* them in the morning."

She shouldn't have spoken so sharply, but she was done, just fucking done. She hung up their coats, then took both girls' hands before turning to Brady.

"Set the coffee machine, take the trash out and find Allegra's gloves, please. I'll put them to bed."

Sam didn't wait for his response. She led her daughters upstairs and went about the business of putting on pj's and overseeing tooth-brushing. Hope was out as soon as her head hit the pillow, but Allegra was too worked up to wind down—first squirting toothpaste all over the countertop, then refusing to wear her striped pajamas because the ones with the pink hearts were dirty—and Sam was ready to snap again.

She didn't want to be like this. Not if motherhood was going to be her only career. She wanted to be calm, patient, to be the earth mother she read about in the parenting blogs who never got mad and fed their families Paleo diets and put pictures of everyone healthy, smiling and suntanned on the Internet. But she wasn't that woman. Sam's bizarrely popular Instagram account looked cheerful, but for her it had been nothing more than a place to keep her accountable to her workouts and healthy eating, and to feel like she was connecting with the outside world. Despite how great her life looked in tiny four-by-four filtered pictures, her patience was a threadbare rug. A straggly thing that had gone thin and tattered.

When Allegra finally drifted off after three chapters from the book they were reading, Sam could barely drag herself downstairs. Sam took a breath at the landing, hoping the things she'd needed done were finished so she could go crash, but Brady was in the living room, still in his coat and sitting on the couch. A frown pinched his face, his eyes on his phone.

She needed to count to ten. To not freak out. To *not* bark at him again.

"Did you take care of the trash or find the gloves?" she asked.

He didn't look up. A moment passed before he responded. "No, sorry."

One. Two. Three... "Why not?"

"There's an emergency at work."

Four. Five. "Couldn't you have helped me before you started on your emails?"

Six. Seven.

Eight.

"Brady."

He lowered his phone but didn't meet her eyes. "I'm sorry. One of the servers went down. I've gotta handle this. Besides, you're better at finding things. You always know where everything is."

Fuck nine and ten. Sam had to grind her teeth to fight back the shout that lodged in her gut. There was always a server down.

Always some emergency. Always something distracting him, and the insistence that he shouldn't do something because *she was better at it.*

"Fine. I'll do it."

She stormed into the kitchen and set the coffee machine. Hauling the garbage to the door, she retrieved her coat, put on her winter boots and went out into the inky dark cold. She dropped the bag in the bin and rolled it to the street. Needing a minute, she looked at the sky and tried not to feel so bitter, angry and resentful.

She loved her husband. Loved her kids. But that was her entire world, when once upon a time, she'd been someone. She'd spent her days surrounded by people who were diverse and worldly, who wanted her opinion on things. She'd stay up late having deep conversations about policies and committees and legislative agendas, and she'd felt important. Noticed. *Seen.* She'd turned heads when she walked into a room, a redheaded bombshell who'd said things that were smart and done things that were wild, and the only stains on her clothes were from spilled champagne or the marks of passion.

These days, passion was something she only read about in books.

Sam heaved a sigh into the darkness. She should've been happy. She had a comfortable life. They were financially stable on a one-parent income. But *she* was missing in that equation, huge chunks of whoever she'd been left out on the curb like the trash. The life she'd given up was an unfinished sentence, a regret she could never shake.

But this was her life now. She'd chosen it, and her *woe is me* crap needed to stop.

Back inside, she opened the coat closet. She *did* know where everything was, from the last five years' tax returns to all their carefully labeled boxes of baby photos. And she was going to find those damn gloves. Locating them beneath a pile of scarves on the floor, Sam stuffed them into Allegra's jacket pockets. She re-hung her coat, took off her boots and went to the living room. Brady hadn't moved. Fixated on the screen in his palm, he was oblivious to the fact that she was standing there.

"I'm going to bed," she said.

His reply came slowly. "Okay. Be there in a minute."

Treading up the stairs and into the bathroom, Sam felt a weight on her. A decade of parenting had dumped them in a dry spell to end all dry spells. Between that and the fact that Brady worked so much, they hadn't done anything sexual in a long time.

It was as much her fault as it was his.

She'd been physically uncomfortable with her body for years. Some moms felt beautiful when they were expecting, but she'd been miserable. And while other women rocked a curvy figure and had amazing sex lives, Sam hadn't felt attractive since before childbirth, before the weight gain and stretch marks, the breastfeeding and sleepless nights. Before the fights over who got to be carried and who held Mommy's hand. Even before the calls from school and doctor visits and Allegra's eventual diagnosis, Sam had stopped wanting to be touched at all, especially once her metabolism slowed to a crawl at age thirty. That was a year after Hope was born, and by then she'd packed on so many pounds none of her clothes fit her anymore.

Brady had remained mostly unaffected by hitting the big three-oh. He no longer sported the flat abs he'd once had, but he could still eat a pile of nachos every week and fit into the same size jeans while Sam had spent the last decade wearing elastic waistbands and baggy shirts. She'd finally shed the weight, but now she and Brady barely talked anymore, and the bedroom had stopped being a place for intimacy. It was a place to snatch a moment of privacy, a few hours of sleep before somebody was grabbing at her again. They'd fallen into a pattern, a rut she didn't know how to get out of.

After taking off her makeup and splashing water over her face, Sam downed her birth control pill and flipped off the light. Not that she needed the insurance policy against having another baby. They'd doubled up on protection after Hope was born because Sam was *not* getting pregnant again, but she had a feeling fishing out their probably dusty box of condoms wouldn't be necessary. When she found Brady, his giant frame was sprawled across their bed. The TV was on, his coat had been thrown God knows where, his suit in a pile on the floor and replaced with a graphic tee and flannel pants.

So much for stripping off his dress shirt.

Maybe all he needed was some encouragement. Facing the dresser and the mirror above it, Sam pulled out the pins holding up her hair. The locks slipped softly down her shoulders, landing beneath her shoulder blades. Reaching around to unzip her gown, she let it glide to the floor. When she was naked except for a bra and panties, she found Brady's reflection in the mirror.

Their eyes met in the glass, held there, but then he quickly skirted his gaze away.

Disappointment landed in a hard punch to her gut. She'd killed herself to get her figure back, and now he wouldn't even look at her. Maybe he wasn't attracted to her anymore. Or he was happier with his hand.

He reached for the remote and switched channels aimlessly. Sam yanked open a drawer and pulled her pajamas out. She threw her gown in the hamper, gathered Brady's suit to join it, then got into bed. The mattress was massive—extra long and wide to accommodate Brady's height. Once they'd squeezed themselves into one of their twin-size dorm-room beds, not minding how little room they had. Now, this bed large enough for three was filled with temper tantrums, homework and an ocean of empty sheets between them. She could take her iPad from her nightstand, open one of the many dirty books she had stored inside it and indulge in the fantasy they provided, but she'd left the damn thing in the car, and tonight she couldn't bear it anyway.

Brady's channel-changing landed on the national news. The White House correspondent was on. He paused, then lifted his arm, remote poised at the TV again.

Sam shot a hand out, catching his wrist. "Wait."

Brady froze, and Sam tried not to read too much into his tension at her touch. She listened instead to the report, and, for a minute, pretended her parents had never asked her to come home, that she hadn't gotten stuck here and lost out on the most amazing opportunity she'd ever had.

Guilt burned like acid. She should've been thankful Mom had recuperated. Happy she'd run into Brady again. Grateful that she'd gotten married and had two beautiful children. But she'd wanted *more* for her life. And watching the glittering lights of the Washington Monument on the television, all she felt was invisible.

She let go of Brady's wrist. "You can turn it off."

Moving to her side, she wiggled off her wedding and engagement rings for the night. They pinged against the heart-shaped dish on her nightstand, and Sam closed her eyes. The TV's sound stopped, and then there was darkness behind Sam's eyelids as he shut off the lamp. Hearing him shift beside her, she silently asked for his touch. She yearned for those huge arms to pull her in, for his chest to press against her back, to know he'd noticed her sadness and it mattered.

He turned away from her instead. Sam didn't bother to stifle her tears.

Crying silently, she waited for sleep to claim her.

2

What the *hell* was that noise?

Brady reached out for the blaring sound. His phone alarm, that's what it was, but why was it going off so freaking early?

He smacked around his nightstand until his cell was beneath his palm. Squinting his eyes open, he looked for the word *snooze* on the screen and tapped it. No, definitely not time to get up yet. It was dark out, for Christ's sake. But something stuck in the back of his mind even as his eyes drooped closed. He had something to do today. Was it Tuesday? Friday?

"Sam, what day is it?" he mumbled. "Do I have to go to work today?"

He probably did, what with the alarm and all. But, seriously. Too damn early.

"Sam?"

No answer.

He rolled over and found the space beside him empty. Not a shock, even though he didn't like it. She was usually up before him, the girls always needing something, but Brady wasn't sure that was the reason he woke up alone lately.

Could two years be considered *lately*?

He turned back to his nightstand, reached for his phone again and tipped the screen so he could read it. Monday. Six a.m. And clearly a school day, because Allegra was shouting down the hall. But his eldest child was always shouting these days. She was a hurricane in a ten-year-old's body, the Tasmanian Devil on the wrong dose of Ritalin.

Sam had it covered, though. Her voice carried upstairs in that tight tone that proved she was aggravated but trying to keep her shit together.

She often used the same tone with him, especially when he asked what day it was or what he needed to do. It was a good thing she hadn't heard his question this morning or she'd have bit his head off. It wasn't that he didn't like his job. He loved it. It was the only place he felt fucking competent. He just legit couldn't recall information like what day it was sometimes—there was too much going on in his head to keep track of stuff like that—and relying on Sam to provide him with the answers was easier than figuring it out himself.

Sitting up, Brady flipped through emails to fight off the grogginess. He had two client meetings today and a server migration to check. The Apps Team was late on three projects, two sites were going live, the Web-Dev Group was about to push a new release and the offshore-hosting-support department had been working all night on those damn failed servers.

Time to get up.

He swung his legs over the side of the bed, wincing when his bare feet met the hardwoods. Their house was old, but they'd chosen it because of its character, and because his parents gave them the down payment for it before Dad sold his legal practice and they moved to Maine. It had three bedrooms, a finished basement and a backyard they could use when it wasn't in the single digits outside, but the floors didn't hold heat for shit and the ceilings weren't built for someone as big as he was.

Brady towered over most people and had since about the fourth grade. He was so tall they'd needed a specialty size mattress and frame—California King, it was called, extra wide and long enough that his feet didn't hang over the edge. He could've pretended to be an NFL player if he were in the kind of shape he used to be. He wasn't sporting a dad-bod—he hadn't gotten *that* bad—but his abs weren't as hard as they'd been. And yesterday's appetizers, pasta and wedding cake were a "treat-yo-self" indulgence he'd treated himself to a bit too much.

The gym was definitely in order today.

Heading toward the bathroom, he had to duck under the doorframe to get inside. He was like a wizard in Hobbiton in here, or the Giant in *The Princess Bride*, clumsily fumbling through his life. He'd certainly fumbled last night.

Flipping up the seat, he did his business and sighed. He should've told Sam how incredible she'd looked, or at least asked her to dance. He'd meant to say something, but he was on information overload—making sure he had Jack's ring in his pocket. Not forgetting to email himself his speech, which he did, then scrambled right before the toasts and found it in his drafts. His brain didn't have enough operating power; like a single-core processor, he couldn't do that many things at once. By the time they'd gotten home and he'd dealt with that damn server error, Sam had been so pissed it seemed smarter to keep silent, even when she'd undressed in front of him.

Had it been a hint, or not? She hadn't been interested in sex in ages, and Brady needed things simple. It was easier when Sam spelled things out, like in college when she'd call him over to her dorm. Her mouth open in that half smile, she'd hook her finger into his shirt and whisper exactly what she wanted him to do to her.

She asked, he did it. Simple, and near goddamn perfect, because Brady was not the initiator. Something visceral inside stopped him from making the first move. Something primitive he had no desire to talk about.

Brady got the shower going, twisting his wedding ring around as he waited for the water to heat. Sam always took her rings off at night, something she'd started when her fingers got swollen from pregnancy and she was afraid they'd get stuck. At least she never removed her necklace—the ten-year wedding anniversary gift he'd given her a year ago.

Pulling his ring off, he ran his thumb over the inside, felt the comforting sensation of the inscription there.

"I take care of you, you take care of me."

End of story. It was a cheesy line in a card he'd given her once, and since he'd been the one to buy their rings, he'd put it there, too. It was his promise on their wedding day. Sam had stayed, so he was going to take care of her.

He was still trying, all these years later, but he worried the actual end of their story was here.

He pushed his ring into place, pulled back the curtain and got under the hot stream. The nozzle didn't go high enough to fit all of him, so he had to crouch in order to douse his head completely. He would've preferred a bath. The tub didn't fit him any better than the shower, but it was more relaxing, and better than freezing his bare ass while attempting to rinse out shampoo.

He didn't have time to sit in a tub, though, not with a family to take care of, two kids to send off to college eventually and a business to run. And real men didn't take baths, right? Real men ripped their bathrooms apart and redid them with their bare hands, installed gleaming countertops and mega-sized tubs they said were for their wives but they secretly wanted for themselves. But Brady's skills were with code, not construction, and Sam hadn't wanted to spend money on a reno.

He rinsed out the shampoo, crossed his arms and watched the bubbles pool at the bottom of the tub. He hated how unhappy Sam was, but he couldn't blame her. She'd had dreams—big ones she put on hold for her family, then abandoned for him. It was why he'd tried to change the channel so quickly last night. But she'd wanted to keep watching, and he hoped she hadn't noticed how he'd tensed when she'd grabbed his wrist and given him an order.

If she did, she hadn't said anything. She'd turned over and disconnected from him instead. He'd known she was crying, and he'd wanted to...what? Apologize? Kiss her? Anything to make her feel better, but he'd felt defeated, unable to close this gap. It was like there was an invisible force field down the middle of the bed, keeping them apart. He missed her, though, even with her right there next to him.

When had they stopped saying they loved each other? A year ago? Two? It was probably longer that things hadn't been good, but it was the last time he could remember them being anything more than roommates. He tried to fix things by being the same goofy guy she fell for, but she didn't like his jokes anymore.

It sucked, 'cause he was never good at talking. Making people laugh was easier.

Humor was how Brady functioned, how he dealt with his size. Most people were intimidated by his sheer mass, so he smiled as often as he could—the whole gentle-giant thing. Most of the women he'd dated before Sam were disappointed to discover he was just a big softie, but she hadn't minded. She had control over him despite being over a foot shorter and had him wrapped around her finger as easily as their daughters did from the moment they were born.

He shut the water off, and the screeching pipes sounded like reality crashing in on him, like one of those cartoon anvils falling from the sky. He couldn't pinpoint the exact cause, couldn't hit it the way he worked a line of code, but somewhere along the way, he and Sam had fallen apart. And he didn't have a clue how to fix it.

He dried off and trimmed his beard, then high-tailed it through getting dressed. Good thing he had his trusty collection of superhero T-shirts to layer under his assortment of flannel shirts, because it was Ice Planet Hoth-level cold out there. Throwing on his *Empire Strikes Back* one in homage to the weather, he threw his wallet and phone in his jeans pockets and went downstairs for his coat. Shoveling the front walk before the bus came would make Sam happy, but by the time Brady was inside and stomping snow off his boots, Allegra and Hope were already having to be separated.

"It's not fair," Allegra shouted from the front hall. "Why doesn't Hope have a behavior chart?"

A lot wasn't fair to Allegra, the first of which was having a younger sibling at all. It wasn't fair that Hope got to be carried. It wasn't fair Hope had so little homework. Wasn't fair that she didn't need a time-out while Allegra was in one more than basically anywhere else.

"Hope doesn't have a chart because you're both different," Sam said.

Very politically correct. Hope didn't need to be reminded to brush her teeth while Allegra was so distracted that if Sam reminded her to brush, she'd lose track of what she was doing by the time she got to the bathroom. Not a big challenge to figure out which parent she'd inherited that from.

"Now finish getting ready."

Allegra tore through the house, not even seeing him as he walked down the hall. Hope, however, was sitting on the living-room couch and flipping through flashcards.

"Morning, Daddy," she said placidly.

"Morning, munchkin."

He bent to kiss the crown of her head, a fiery red that rivaled her mother's. Their faces were almost identical but that was where her similarities to Sam ended. Hope had his blue eyes and was like him in all the ways Allegra wasn't—silent in the face of confrontation and good at math. At four, she'd mastered number recognition and was now problem-solving on a second-grade level. A big bone of contention for her big sister. It was more than your run-of-the-mill sibling rivalry. All kids butt heads, but their arguing was one-sided.

He got why Hope acted that way though. Brady knew a thing or two about being lost in a sibling's shadow.

When Brady entered the kitchen, Sam was making a plate of food for him.

"Man, it's wicked cold out there," he said. "Lucky Charms for breakfast?"

She paused and looked up. It was a joke from college, a game they used to play when they'd ditch the dining hall, eat sugary cereal and watch bad TV. Crammed into his twin-size bed, they'd dig their hands into the box and see who came out with a four-leaf clover marshmallow first. Sam's grin would be wild when she did it, and Brady became addicted to that smile.

"Since when do we eat that?" she replied. "Frosting rots the kids' teeth."

"Right. I forgot."

And bad thinking to open the morning with a joke. His attempt at humor last night had bombed like the *Batman vs. Superman* movie. Better to avoid an argument and soothe her ruffled feathers.

He took the plate of eggs and toast, poured himself a cup of coffee and sat.

"Thanks for making this," he said, because he did appreciate what she did. And wasn't there something else? "And for taking care of everything last night."

He didn't remember everything, specifically. Something about Allegra's scarf and the trash that had been shoved aside in his mind once the support tickets started blowing up his phone. Having one of his clients hemorrhaging money hijacked his concentration.

"Finding the gloves on my own was easier than interrupting you."

Gloves. That was it, gloves. "And faster," he said, sipping his coffee and offering her a grin. "You always know where everything is." It was a feat that truly amazed him. When he put something down, there was a fifty-fifty shot he'd never find it again.

She wiped off the counter and leaned back against it. She was tired—her warm brown eyes showed signs of exhaustion—but she still managed to look sexy in an old Boston University T-shirt and flannel bottoms.

"And you?" she prompted. "Did you take care of everything you were supposed to this weekend?"

Brady blinked. "Everything?" She was staring at him expectantly. Shit.

Sam crossed her arms. "The sitter posting."

"Crap, I forgot. Sorry."

"At least you're not cursing in front of the kids."

Brady frowned. It wasn't like he used that language on purpose. It was how they talked at work, and it wasn't easy to switch gears. Trying to head off a fight, he went with logic. "Your parents haven't put their apartment on the market yet. We've got time."

Sam pinched her lips and exhaled heavily. It was a combination he'd learned to dread.

"My parents are the only steady babysitters the girls have ever known. This is going to be a hard transition for them, Allegra especially, in case you've forgotten *that*, too."

"I haven't," he mumbled, his cheeks heating.

Once, Sam's reaction when he got things wrong turned him on in ways he couldn't explain, like in college when she'd spend an hour helping him with some book or historical fact and he couldn't retain it. She'd smile and say they'd have to start over, and he'd need to shove his football jersey on his lap to hide the more-than-semi he'd be sporting.

Now her annoyance had turned into all-out exasperation.

Sam turned to the side and braced her hands against the counter. "I'm sorry," she said. "I don't want to fight."

His chest tightened, then loosened. "Me neither."

She shook her head in that way she often did—the way that let him know she hadn't meant to be so abrupt but was too worn out to stop herself. "You're working. I shouldn't expect you to do more on top of it."

The sadness in her voice cut through him. She should expect more. She should expect the goddamn world from him.

"I'll get the post done tonight. Promise," he said, even palming his phone and putting a reminder in his calendar for it. "If not, you can put me in a time-out."

She laughed softly, and a flare of happiness went off in Brady's chest. No matter how shitty things got, hearing the sound of her laughter lightened everything. It was a drug to him—her happiness—and he'd do anything for another hit.

He glanced at the clock. Five minutes before the bus came. Five minutes to try to fix things. "What are you doing today?" he asked.

She rattled off her list, a host of chores including everything from stopping by her parents' place to laundry to groceries to picking up Allegra's new dance shoes. Brady marveled as he listened. He might run a business, but he had a whole team to help him there. She made this family run all on her own. She knew if they were low on toilet paper, when everyone's doctor appointments were and how to make their favorite foods while somehow keeping them healthy.

She went up on her toes, stretching her supple body to put an unused juice glass back in its place. The move pulled her nightshirt away from her back, offering Brady a slice of skin in between the cotton and the edge of her pajama bottoms.

He adjusted himself and tried to think about something else, and not just because his kids were nearby. Even if they weren't, he'd bet nothing would happen. Sam's lack of interest in sex had been from the baby weight she'd gained. Brady never minded when she was heavier—he'd joked that there was more of Sam to love. To him it was a reminder of the years they'd spent building this family, the lives they'd lived. Her hips had seemed more lush back then, too, her breasts fuller. She'd stopped letting him play with them when she was nursing, and now that she'd lost the weight, he'd been waiting for the green light to go back there again.

She'd never given it.

They'd become platonic, disconnected in a sexless marriage. He'd taught himself to shut down his impulses, trying to find satisfaction with his right hand. But now, watching her move around, her messy red hair up in a bun, he wished he could get her even messier, wished he could reach for whatever she was trying to get, and after he'd given it to her, she'd hop up on the counter and take off her shirt. She'd tell him to kiss each tender nipple, then order him to the floor. Laughing, she'd comment on how desperate she'd gotten him, how she'd bet he couldn't wait until his face was between her thighs.

Brady tore his gaze away from her, his cheeks blazing. He wasn't supposed to fantasize like that. A real man didn't want his wife to order him around, to let her take what she wanted and to revel in whatever pleasure he could give her. He was the ex-football player, the breadwinner, the dad of two little girls. He was supposed to be strong. Dominant. Like the men in her books.

He'd peeked at them once when she'd left her iPad open. After months of saying she felt fat, that the kids would hear, or one of the dozens of other reasons she'd given him, he never imagined she'd be reading, well, *smut*. And the men who filled those digital pages gave orders and grabbed fistfuls of hair. They were rough and aggressive, took what they wanted and commanded obedience.

That wasn't him. And if that was what Sam wanted, there was no point in reaching for her at all.

It was ironic. A real flaw in his DNA. He knew a few strands different and he'd be more like the kind of guy Sam wanted. The kind who was forceful in bed and didn't miss half of what she was saying because he had so much on his mind he couldn't focus. It was like the information got stuck between his ears and his brain, which often had him standing stock-still and trying to recall what she'd asked, lowering his head in embarrassment when she had to repeat it.

Like right now.

"I'm sorry, what?" he asked.

Sam sighed and shut the cabinet door. "Never mind."

"No, Sammy—"

"It's fine."

The roar of the bus yanked their gazes toward the window. Sam turned to the living room.

"Time to go," she hollered, and then it was all hands on deck, Brady swallowing the remainder of his breakfast before shoving his arms back in his coat. He turned to look at his wife as she zipped their daughters' jackets and whisked on their backpacks.

I want to make you happy. I'm sorry I suck so much at it.

He rushed the girls out the door, barely making it to the curb in time. Once they were on board and seated, Brady's shoulders slumped with relief. He walked toward his car and glanced back at the house. Sam was standing at the kitchen window looking at the bus, but her phone was in her hand.

He took out his own phone. Typed the words *"I'm sorry,"* and hit send.

Her face shifted into a faint smile. A message came up on Brady's screen.

"I'm sorry, too."

His breathing went shallow—a sharp pinch that wasn't from the cold. He wanted to type that he loved her, that he could still take care of her, but he was doing a piss-poor job at it anyway, and he was terrified she wouldn't say it back. Even if she did, those feeble words weren't going to stitch them back together. So he chose other words instead.

"*Sitter posting today,*" he typed as he got into the car. "*I promise.*"

"*Thanks. Have a good day.*"

He started the engine, then backed down the driveway, repeating a chorus of the words "sitter posting" in his head. He was going to fix this. He'd make things better for Sam.

He had to.

3

*S*am watched the bus chug down the road and prayed she wouldn't get a call from school today. She'd gotten up extra early to make a hearty meal, because Allegra managed better if her belly was full of good food, but it hadn't helped at the breakfast table. Every day since Hope was born had felt like an apology. At least the hair-pulling and biting had stopped. Allegra couldn't always manage her verbal aggression and emotional immaturity, but Hope sat there and took it, and Sam's heart ached for both of them.

Being a stay-at-home mom didn't mean she knew what she was doing. Sometimes she thought she was doing more harm than good.

Her smaller, doppelganger self, Hope was a smile wrapped up in skin. Born with Brady's gentleness and bright blue eyes, she was soft-spoken and unwilling to fight back. Allegra was like her father in a different way—she had his golden-brown hair and was a bull in a china shop, crashing through everything around her. But she'd also inherited Sam's eyes, as well as Sam's tendency to speak her mind without thinking about the consequences.

And Sam had done exactly that this morning, snapping at Brady and being nothing short of mean.

He backed out of the driveway. Sam turned from the window and sighed. Another shitty morning when she was too tired, too impatient to be nice. He'd even shoveled without her asking, and she hadn't even thanked him. Her fuse was so short, her cup so full, it took almost nothing to knock it over. It was so frustrating when he zoned out. He'd been in his own world again, blanking out when all she'd asked him to do was pick up Allegra's prescription refill on his way home.

She knew she was only seeing the negative. It wasn't worth fighting about. She could stop at the pharmacy herself later. But she was already feeling so invisible. Couldn't he at least listen to her for five minutes?

He couldn't, though, and there was a time when she'd been more patient with it. But having a child with severe ADHD was hard enough. Having a thirty-six-year-old husband who made jokes instead of dealing with his own shit made it even harder.

She got dressed, grabbed her gym bag and headed out into the cold. The air was teeth-grittingly frigid, and she burrowed into her winter coat as she waited for her car to heat up. At least the gym was only a short drive away. The local YMCA had plenty of classes, a decent workout area and a dedicated childcare space, which had made it easier when Hope was home with her.

A December baby, Hope had missed the kindergarten cutoff and had been home a year longer than planned. Junk food had become a staple by then, and Sam had been shocked to discover at a routine physical that she'd almost doubled her body weight. Certain her doctor was wrong, she'd gone to her closet only to realize she no longer fit into any of her pre-baby clothes. After sobbing on her bedroom floor, she picked herself up, dusted off her gym pass and started eating better. It had been a hard habit to get into, but she'd finally gotten herself back to the shape she'd once been in. Thank you, kettlebells.

That was why she never kept stuff like Lucky Charms in the house anymore. Not only was that sugary stuff not good for Allegra, but Sam was in constant fear of how easily she could literally tip the scale back in the other direction.

The gym was fairly empty, so Sam did a quick warm-up, then went to the weights floor. Lifting was her jam, the only place where she felt like she had any kind of power. At home she could put in all the effort she wanted and it wouldn't change anything. Here, effort put in yielded results. Squats. Lunges. Deadlifts. Here she was in control. Here she was surrounded by other adults, even if they were mostly the stay-at-home moms she'd tried to befriend but quickly discovered she had nothing in common with.

The women she'd met had never seemed to *get* her, or her children. They'd go on about how wonderful motherhood was, how peaceful and fulfilling, how much Sam should cherish these days when her babies were young. But then there were the side-eyes when Allegra refused to follow directions at mommy-and-me Gymboree. All judgy and self-righteous, they'd whisper when Sam had to corral Allegra back to the routine. And don't get her started on why Sam had named her Allegra. No, it wasn't because she liked the allergy medicine. The name meant joyful, thank you very much, not that she'd seemed all that happy during library storytime. Other kids would listen quietly while Allegra tried to rip pages out of books and screamed when Sam stopped her. The moms would glare, and Sam would glare back, too sleep-deprived to care.

Yeah, she cherished those days. Fuck other moms. That was a meme she should post on her Instagram.

She finished her routine, racked her weights and went to the locker room. The Momzillas were chattering about the next book they'd become obsessed with, the only thing Sam had mildly bonded with them over.

"Mommy porn." That's what they'd called it. Sam had never read romance before, but she couldn't help her curiosity when they were all gushing about it. She grew fascinated by the power dynamics—which characters took the lead and which ones didn't. Who gained satisfaction from the obedience of the other. The intricate world of protocols, safewords, limits and consent.

It had been a decent escape, for a time. A flimsy substitute for sex, because if she wasn't having it, she might as well read about it. But those women were almost always bossed around in a way she never got on board with. And they all had amazing jobs and never had cake on their clothes, weren't exhausted because there hadn't been a night in ten years when a child wasn't hollering for them in the middle of it. Plus, every book concluded with over-the-top, wildly perfect scenarios where they got the job *and* the guy, and saying "I do" automatically meant happy ever after.

She showered and got dressed. Catching herself in the mirror, she grimaced at the sight of her four-leaf clover charm lit up by a red spot at the base of her throat. It wasn't the necklace—she'd loved the anniversary gift Brady had given her, wore it all the time. But her skin always got splotchy after a workout. Her fair complexion often got her leaving the gym looking like Hope after she'd caught Fifth Disease, and the heat from the hair dryer was only going to make it worse.

She flipped her head over and dried the strands in the back. Sam went from pale to lobster in the sun, had none of the trademark freckles redheads so often had, and could never find the right shade of concealer, but her hair was her calling card—her secret weapon and her best feature. It wasn't flame bright but a classic rich red, vibrant and deep.

Her hair was also her Achilles heel, her Kryptonite. She loved having it played with, her scalp so sensitive it tingled. Brady used to play with it in college, discovering it was the best relaxer, and foreplay.

Another thing he'd forgotten.

Finished drying, she flexed a bicep, took a mirror selfie and uploaded it to Instagram.

#MondayMotivation #FitGirl #HealthyIsTheNewSkinny
#IsThisAllIHaveToShowForMyself?

Yeah, skip the last tag. She hit share and her phone started buzzing with likes, people who followed her weight-loss journey and found her inspirational. She enjoyed the attention, but they were accounts online, clicks on devices scattered across the globe. The one person she wanted to notice never seemed to.

Back on the road, Sam stopped at the pharmacy to pick up Allegra's pills. It didn't seem like they'd found the right mix, but despite the outbursts of the last two days, they were in a better place than they'd been.

First there was the can't-sit-still and on-a-whim behaviors that started when she was three, then the out-of-control hyperactivity and academic underachievement in kindergarten. Sam had been the one to fill out the paperwork to get Allegra diagnosed. She'd wanted Brady's input, and to suggest they do the same for him, but he'd of course made jokes about it, and Sam hadn't had the energy to push it. He didn't come to the appointments Sam was always shuttling Allegra to, either: the pediatrician for the meds, individual counseling for Allegra and family therapy to map out the behavior plan. They'd started Allegra on a low dose of a stimulant, but the first medication had amped her up so much she couldn't fall asleep, while another threw her into a zombie-like trance. Now she was on a short-lasting, four-hour drug, but when it wore off she got hangry, so she always needed nutritional snacks on hand in between the morning dose and the second one she took in the nurse's office before lunch.

The bad days were when Allegra ditched those snacks for something full of food dyes at school, or when it was a schoolmate's birthday. Sam steered Allegra clear of those foods at home, and they'd already had to discuss what kind of food she could expect at her own party in a few months, but Sam couldn't control what happened when she wasn't there. Even the school support team wasn't much of a help. Allegra qualified for Section 504, which got her assistance with writing assignments into her planner, a seat far from distractions and a quiet area for test-taking, but even that wasn't helping. And as Allegra spun in more circles, Hope stood so still it was like she was trying to disappear.

It was almost comical, what a bad job Sam was doing raising them.

Prescription filled, she headed toward her parents' place. Fifteen minutes east on Beacon Street, it was prime real estate, with a brick-and-stone exterior and steps from the T. They were going to make a killing from it, whenever they ended up selling.

She used her key to open the door. "It's me," she said, then nearly tripped over a giant box. "What's this?"

"Oh, I signed up for one of those meal delivery services," Sam's mom said, one hand on a kitchen chair as she tried to reach for a screaming tea kettle. "Thought we'd see if we liked it."

Sam stepped quickly over to her mother. "I've got that, Mom. Sit."

Once her mother was safely in a chair, Sam removed the kettle from the stovetop. "So my cooking isn't good enough for you now, huh?" she asked with a smile, gesturing toward the box.

"You won't be cooking for us in Arizona," her mother said.

Sam paused as she poured two cups of tea. Her parents had bought a condo in Sedona months ago on a whim after visiting friends out there, but they hadn't made any decisions about moving.

She brought the tea to the table. "How are you feeling?"

Her mother waved a hand. "The cold always makes it harder."

"That's why I'm here."

Sam returned to the counter and began straightening up. The rheumatoid arthritis her mom had developed when Sam was in high school made housework difficult. They'd downsized into this apartment after Sam went to college—a second-floor building with an old elevator. They weren't helpless, certainly not now that Dad had retired, but cleaning, helping with meals and keeping everything organized was what Sam had done when she lived here, so she'd kept on doing it.

"Where's Dad?" she asked.

"He's peering through his bookshelf, trying to pick out which books to give away." Her mother huffed out a sigh. "Leave the counter be, will you? Sit here and talk."

Sam held out a block of cheese with mold on it. "You know this is bad, right?"

Her mother took it from her hand and put it on the table. "It's fine. How was the wedding?"

They'd been invited—Jack had known them for ages—but they'd said no because Sam's mom didn't want to "overdo it." She was in much better shape now, but the paranoia of having more problems had settled in long ago.

"It was nice." Sam scavenged through a cabinet for more expired products. "Allegra had a few meltdowns."

"Poor girl. I don't get why she has it so rough."

Neither did she.

"Was it a fun night, though?" her mom asked. "Did you and Brady dance?"

"It would've been nice if we had."

"So why didn't you?"

Because only couples who talked and touched danced at weddings. "We're not getting along right now."

"That makes me sad."

Sam shut the cabinet and turned around. "Well, you taught me to be honest."

Her parents had been college professors, and both at UMass Amherst. They valued education, and had raised Sam to be moral, ethical and straightforward.

Maybe she'd become a bit too much of the last one.

Her father came in with a smile, dressed in the same sweater, shirt and tie he'd worn when he was teaching, a pile of books in his hand. "There's my scholar."

He kissed Sam on the cheek. Sam rolled her eyes with a smile. "I haven't been a scholar for a while now."

"You'll always be one to me." He put the books he was holding on the table, a tattered old hardcover of the complete works of Franz Kafka on top of it. "These are going."

"You're giving away Kafka?" she asked in surprise.

"I thought we always agreed he was incredibly overrated."

"We did." She'd found the grotesqueness and utter hopelessness of his work to be more like neurosis than art, but one of these stories had a special place in her heart. She wasn't letting this one get donated away.

"I'll take care of it," she said, and slipped the volume in her purse.

"It makes me *sad*," her mother said, emphasizing the word like

Sam needed the reminder, "because you two have so much history. Seventeen years is a long time."

Funny, how everyone glossed over when Sam and Brady weren't together. They'd met seventeen years ago, but the time she'd spent in DC was forgotten like it was something negligible, easily written off.

The unfairness of it made her want to scream like Allegra having one of her temper tantrums. After dominating her high school model congress and spending her summers volunteering for local politicians, Sam had charged headfirst into B.U.'s Political Science program, tacking on a double minor in French Studies and English Lit. By her junior year she was running a four-oh, was a member of student government and a peer tutor, making her a shoo-in for the DC Internship Program.

It had taken her away from Brady for a semester, but they'd only been casually dating at the time. She wasn't serious about him, not the way she'd been about her studies. And Washington had been a dream come true: the culture, the pace, the politically charged atmosphere of a town that ran on power and favors. She fell in love with life on The Hill, and with being assigned to Representative Arnold Dawes, a Democrat from California who was a ranking member of the House Committee on Oversight and Reform.

Brady had probably figured she wouldn't be sticking around when she returned to school the following semester, even before she'd received the call from Dawes saying there was a position waiting for her after graduation.

"He's a good man," her father added, taking a sip of his tea. "Takes good care of you and the kids. That's not something you throw away."

"Yes, he's a good man," Sam said. It didn't mean things were working though. Didn't mean she was happy. "And no one is throwing out anything." She retrieved the block of moldy gouda from the table. "Except for this cheese."

She threw it into a large black garbage bag, then went into the other rooms to begin gathering up what was in the trash.

"Did you tell your doctors about your decision yet?" she hollered from the living room.

"Oh yes, they're supportive," her mother yelled back. "My physical therapist said I can exercise more regularly in a warm environment."

"Did he say changing locations would make a long-term difference?"

"No, but I'm not willing to risk my health anymore before *this* hip replacement wears out."

Sam kept her eyes on her tasks. That had always been a fear, for all of them. Her mother's condition had progressed when Sam was in DC, requiring total joint replacement. Sam came home without a second thought—Mom was having surgery, so she was on a plane, no questions asked. But then one of her implants dislocated, her body rejecting the hip, requiring a second surgery. A one-week trip home turned into two, then a month, and then having to call the congressman and say she couldn't come back for a while because her family needed her.

Turned out rock bottom was sitting in a PT waiting room watching C-SPAN.

Sam became the one to take Mom to her appointments, sleeping on her parents' couch because there was no bedroom for her, and she wasn't planning on staying long. Now they were trading the Massachusetts chill for the warmer, arid climate of the Southwest and a summer-camp-style retirement community, leaving Sam without their support and wondering what she'd come home for in the first place.

"How soon is this happening?" she asked. "Today? Tomorrow? Next year?"

"We don't have a definite date yet," her mother said.

"It would be nice to know, so I could prepare myself." The ambiguousness of it made the need for a sitter more urgent.

Her father must've heard the sadness in her voice, because he was suddenly in the living room next to her. "We'll miss you, too," he said. "But think of it this way: without us around and the girls in school, you can start working again."

Sam forced a smile. "I'm not sure it'll be that easy. But I'm happy for you guys."

She didn't begrudge her parents the right to enjoy their retirement. And without them here, there'd be less caretaking in her already chaotic and exhausting life. It was a good thing.

Sam bagged up the trash, dumped it by the door, then gave them both a kiss on the cheek. "Gotta go. Lots of errands to do."

"Give the girls a hug for us," her father said.

"And Brady!" her mother added.

"I will," she said, and headed out the door.

4

By the time Sam did the rest of her errands, which included purchasing a new pair of hip-hop dance shoes for Allegra—hot pink with sequins, of course—there were only a few hours left before the bus came back and the afternoon bedlam began. Sam started the dishwasher, then walked through the house, collecting toys and clothes and video game boxes as she went. This place was pure anarchy by the end of the weekend. She'd clean up on Mondays, but before she knew it, it was a disaster again, overrun with her children's and husband's stuff. Barely any space in this house felt like hers, which she supposed made sense. It *wasn't* hers.

The down payment had been a wedding gift from Brady's parents. Extravagant, but Brady's business was taking off at the time, and she was temping around Mom's appointments. No steady income meant Sam couldn't be on the mortgage, just on the deed. It was a beautiful house, but as she heaved a bin full of dry clothes up from the basement and dumped the contents on the couch, she couldn't help but feel defeated.

This was what her life had amounted to—separating piles of fabric in an empty house.

She'd planned to be more, to use the education and skills she'd worked so hard to get. But she'd gotten pregnant quickly after she and Brady got married, and since she was still Mom's Appointment Taxi it made more sense for her to stay home. She'd looked at jobs again when Allegra was in pre-k, but then she'd discovered Hope was on the way and was back in the same boat again.

The positive pregnancy test had been a shock. It was during the small window of time when she'd taken off some of the pounds she'd packed on with Allegra, and she and Brady were having sex again. Somehow she'd managed to forget to take her pill for a few nights. Usually so regimented, she'd gotten out of her routine, exhausted from dealing with a badly behaving three-year-old while shuttling Mom to appointments. And then, boom—she was doing all that, plus morning sickness.

It was why she'd sworn never to have sex without two forms of protection again.

She was more nauseous with Hope than she'd been with Allegra, and put on twice the weight. Add to that a more difficult birth, resulting in a longer recovery and two children under the age of five while Brady zipped back to work after two weeks of paternity leave.

That was the US healthcare system for you.

She balled up a pair of Hope's socks and tossed them in the basket. She wasn't blaming anyone for this. Lots of women made the choice to stay home. She supported Brady's career—he was a genius with all things tech, and even when his work took over their lives, it was what put food on the table. But eventually, never being around adults had become suffocating. Daycare cost a small fortune, and for as much as her parents were good sitters, Mom could only take the girls for a few hours on her own. She'd sit for longer when Dad was home but steering clear of a flare-up meant avoiding exposure to infections, so she'd only babysit when the girls didn't have any signs of a sniffle.

How often were school-aged children germ-free?

At least they were both in school now. She wanted to go back to work but it was another thing she felt powerless over. Who was going to hire her? She'd been out of the workforce for so long she felt paralyzed to get back into it. The one phone interview she'd had in December had been through luck and connections alone, but two months had gone by and she hadn't heard diddly-squat.

Finished folding, she went to her purse, got the Kafka novel and brought it to the bookcase. She'd show Brady it was here, but she doubted he recalled that particular memory. Her own recollections called to her, although from a different time. She traced her fingers over her scrapbook in the top corner—the mementos she'd kept from DC.

Opening its dusty cover, she paged through the items she'd kept —articles, photos, her acceptance letter into the program, a letter of recommendation from Congressman Dawes. She'd made several copies, even sent one in when she'd applied to that job. His marks of high praise and signature were all that remained of her short stint as a member of his staff.

Being a staffer wasn't exactly the greatest gig. It was the lowest rung on the totem pole, and her salary was absolute shit. But she'd loved it, and Dawes had been her dream boss. An old, balding man with warm, steady eyes, he was gentle on the outside but ruthless when he needed to be. Whenever she was lucky enough to spend some time with him, he'd given her advice on a life in politics. He'd instructed her to learn the landscape, to figure out who had power and who didn't, to find out what people wanted. They'd trade Machiavellian quotes. She'd say it was better to be feared than loved if you couldn't be both. He'd answer that politics had no relation to morals.

It was true. Because when the boss was wheels-up back to the district, that was when things got wild.

If she were a different kind of woman, she'd be having a cigarette or a drink right now.

Sam paged through photos of her younger self, holding drinks, thin and beautiful, smiling with people whose names she didn't remember and had lost track of over the years. Her life there had been all-consuming and exciting, a frenetic pace that ran around the clock. There were parties and fundraisers, drinks when no one could wind down. Every night, there was that edgy feeling that anything could happen, that a conversation could yield you a powerful ally or a sweaty night in bed. It was a constant power game, in a world of public service. There were people who liked to serve, people who liked to be served, and others who liked the hunt.

She'd learned how to play those games, though, had been so confident she'd earned herself the staffer nickname of the Boston Bombshell. She was always surrounded by overly ambitious men in suits; charming, witty men who flouted their power and took what they wanted without apology, but they didn't intimidate her.

She wasn't interested in any of them either—her heart was in her job. But she had enjoyed flirting, the attention she'd received, enjoyed the nights when she'd kissed more than one person, and one night more than one gender.

Sam's skin went hot. She'd never gone that way before, never had a threesome or been with a girl. She'd been curious that night, and wanted to indulge in that curiosity, but backed out of the chance.

She put the scrapbook away with a sigh.

Brady didn't know much about Sam's life there. She had a feeling he didn't want to.

She took the basket upstairs and into the girls' rooms. Brady had been happy for her when she'd gotten the Washington internship, even emailed her daily. He hadn't been as enthusiastic when she'd made the decision to go back, his bright blue eyes cast away when he wished her all the best. It was his eyes that caught Sam when she'd run into him again in a bar years later. His beard had filled out—he was more of a man than the boy she'd left behind, but those eyes hadn't changed.

They picked up where they'd left off. He'd asked if she was seeing anyone, and her "no" had been enough. She'd edited out the things she'd done in DC, because she'd never *dated* anyone and hadn't wanted to hear about Brady's sexual exploits either. She just wanted the ease of being with him. He'd been an amazing support when she was taking care of Mom, showing up with takeout when she was too tired to cook. Flowers because it had been a long week and he'd wanted to see her smile. He'd noticed her then, and it wasn't long after that when he got on one knee, held out a ring and said if she stayed, he'd take care of her the rest of his life.

She'd wanted to take care of him, too. That was the inscription inside their wedding bands. She felt it now between her finger and the handle of the basket, the words pressing into her skin.

But she hadn't only stayed because he'd asked her to. She'd stayed because she loved him. Because she knew he would always be there for her, a protector, a fierce defender of her no matter what.

He certainly had been back at school.

Everyone had known what happened. The incident in the locker room when Nick Sterling, Boston Terriers' star quarterback, had been attacked by his teammates. The campus paper had covered the beating, but only whispers among students had divulged the reasons behind it. Nick was gay, a dangerous thing to say out loud back then, when queer youth were getting beaten up or killed.

Nick hadn't cared. He'd had the courage to be honest about who he was and had been beaten to a pulp because of it. As had Brady, Terriers' linebacker and Nick's best friend, for trying to defend him.

Brady had still been on crutches when Sam was assigned as his tutor, and she'd wanted to tuck him away someplace safe, to hunt down those bigoted rednecks and claw them to shreds. But all Brady had wanted was her attention, and he'd hung on her every word, from her teaching him about literature to the basics of American government to her last gasping moans in bed.

The memories popped like firecrackers. How she'd been able to feel his gaze, a sparkling blue heat that had tracked her across the library floor. The way he'd try to convince her into going for coffee after their session was up, finally sweet-talking her weeks later into a date. How he'd stood outside her dorm room after that first kiss, his body on a razor's edge, vibrating with the need for more. They were desperate for each other then, tearing one another's clothes off whenever they got the chance. But they'd never recovered that kind of crackling desire, and there didn't seem any way to rekindle things. They barely even said *I love you* to each other anymore.

She put the rest of the laundry away, then went back to her bedroom. She didn't know what to say to Brady these days. Of course she still loved him, but it was hard to remember that when she was a control-freak planner in an out-of-control existence, stuck between impulsive parents and an even more impulsive child, one child who barely talked and a husband who barely listened to her.

Was it possible to love your husband but hate your marriage? To love your kids but hate what motherhood had turned you into?

Sam dropped the empty basket onto her bed, flopped onto her back next to it and stared at the ceiling. She didn't want to hate anything. She wanted to be happy. To be desired by her husband. To not fall down on the job as a parent. To feel like she was *someone*, instead of the Finder of All the Things, The Kisser of Boo-Boos, the Resident Responsible Adult. She'd been someone once, but that someone was gone.

The once striking, once passionate, once brilliant, and now invisible, Samantha Archer.

Her phone rang. Sam pulled it from her back pocket and accepted the call with a smile.

"Lilly Sterling-Archer, why are you calling me the first day of your honeymoon?"

"I'm not on my honeymoon yet. The flight doesn't leave until tonight."

"Flight shmight. Shouldn't you be in the throes of wedded bliss?"

Lilly laughed. "No bliss at the moment. I'm reading my emails and packing, and Jack is napping."

Sam had to smirk. "You tired him out last night?"

"The wedding tired him out, not me."

"Uh-huh."

Sam wasn't intentionally giving her brand-new sister-in-law a hard time. They'd become friends over the last year, and Lilly's presence in Jack's life had given Sam one less person to look after. It helped that the girl was a fantastic cook. Sam had brought over trays of food in the months after Jack's first wife's death, when he was too mired in grief to care for himself, but Lilly's youthful, freckled face had brought him back from the grave. And if Brady and Nick hadn't stayed as thick as thieves, it might never have happened.

Lilly was Nick's younger sister, and despite a hefty age gap between her and Jack, they were starting their own happily ever after.

"You'll have plenty of time for bliss in Aruba," Sam said.

"Yeah, I don't think Jack's gonna let me out of the room much."

It was the word *let* that had Sam stifling a laugh. Lilly had never admitted it, but Sam hadn't needed an announcement to pick up on the newlyweds' dynamic. It was obvious from Jack's attentiveness, how he always seemed intrinsically aware and protective of her. It was like the characters in her books come to life—the way Lilly blushed when he stared at her, and the bratty way she sometimes toyed with him.

The heart-shaped padlock necklace Lilly wore was a dead giveaway, too.

"Will you need his permission?" Sam asked. She was nothing if not curious, and it didn't hurt to push a little to get at the truth.

"I have a feeling Jack might be a bit—" Lilly breathed in, "—*controlling* this week."

Sam snorted. "And *I* have a feeling you won't mind at all."

"Not really," Lilly said meekly.

That was the confirmation she'd been looking for. Sam smiled in triumph. Lilly's necklace was a collar, something that showed her deference and submission to Jack. Sam had often witnessed Jack brushing his fingers over the locket in a tender, yet possessive move as well.

"Well that's the point of honeymoons, babycakes. You're not supposed to see anything but each other."

A pang of sadness tugged at Sam's heart. But she wasn't jealous. Lilly might've been living out something Sam had only read about, but Sam had discovered she preferred the stories when the tables were turned. When the men were the ones on their knees and the women wielded instruments of pain and pleasure.

She'd considered showing Brady the scenes she liked. She'd even thought of taking charge herself, of pinning him down and *making* things happen. But that hadn't been possible with two kids in the house and fifty extra pounds around her middle. Besides, her husband barely relinquished the remote, let alone power in the bedroom.

"Anyway," Lilly said. "You know that position you applied for at the firm?"

"You mean *le phone interview that went le nowhere*?" Sam asked grimly. Lilly was an attorney at Forrester, Schaeffer and Pierce, the biggest law firm in Boston. She'd been the one who let Sam know about the receptionist opening there. "I recall it."

"They didn't end up hiring anyone."

"So?" Wow, she'd succeeded in sounding disinterested.

"So didn't you tell Cassie and me that you couldn't do full time?"

Cassie was a former associate at the firm, now working for the governor. She was the only other friend Sam had, and was dating Jack's best friend, Patrick. Cassie and Patrick had fought constantly but had finally gotten past their *I-hate-you-I-want-you* tug-of-war that had gone on for the better part of the last year. They also had their own brand of kinky shit going on between them, something Sam had sussed out of Cassie before the holidays as well.

She wasn't jealous of Cassie either. She *wasn't*.

"That's what I said. I can't do a nine-to-five. Someone's gotta be home to meet the bus." And to shuttle Hope and Allegra to dance and appointments, and help with homework afterward.

"What about eight to two?"

A buzz started in Sam's gut. "What aren't you telling me?"

"I called HR. They made it into a part-time job-share position."

The buzzing got louder. "Why would they have done that?"

"I dunno. I think someone might be gunning for you."

"Gabe?" Nick's husband was a partner at the firm, but Sam didn't think he had that kind of clout.

"Nah. Gotta be someone higher up."

Reaching for the charm at her throat, Sam rolled it back and forth along the chain. "Still, they didn't call me."

Ugh, where was her confidence? The part of her that had barreled into Dawes' office and told him she was going to be the best intern he'd ever seen?

"Things move kinda slow at that place," a different, lower voice unexpectedly chimed in. "They haven't even found a replacement for me yet."

"Cassie!" Sam dropped her hand and scowled. "Why didn't you tell me you were both on the phone?"

"Because then you'd feel like this was an intervention," Cassie said. "Which it is. You're calling the firm. We just wanted you to come to the decision on your own."

Sam's scowl went deeper. She was at the same time annoyed at them for not being honest with her, grateful they cared enough to do what they were doing and embarrassed she hadn't picked up on it beforehand. Stupid mute button.

"I haven't made any decisions yet."

"Yes you have," Cassie said. "You have no reason not to."

"How about I've never worked at a law firm before?"

"You worked in Congress. And phones work the same everywhere."

"Have you looked at the receptionist's phone there?"

"No—"

"Then how do you know they're the same?"

Cassie laughed. "Jesus, Sam. You argue like a lawyer."

"She does," Lilly added. "You sure you don't want to be an attorney?"

"Laws change the world, not lawyers," Sam said.

It was something Dawes had said, one of the pieces of wisdom she'd collected and repeated to sound important. That was all she had now—outdated quotes from a mentor who'd lost his seat, retired and passed away.

"We're not changing the world. We're getting you a job," Cassie said. "Lilly, get off the phone and go to Aruba. Sam, call the firm. We know you want to."

Sam didn't know what she wanted. She'd let go of her career goals around when Britney Spears shaved her head, stopped keeping track of the news because it depressed her, and hid her depression behind a veneer of pithy comments. But there was no reason she shouldn't at least find out if she was still in the running. It fit in her schedule, and it was a chance to get out of the house. To *be* someone again.

"Okay," she said. "I'll call."

5

"*Excuse* me, Mr. Archer?"

Halfway up the ramp, Brady turned around. One of his newer programmers jogged up behind him, out of breath with pit stains on his shirt.

"Paul, we use first names here, remember?"

"Right," Paul said on a laugh that turned into a wheeze.

"You okay?"

Paul nodded, then doubled over to catch his breath. Brady wasn't sure if he should be dialing 9-1-1 or not, but Paul held up a hand waving that he was okay. This was why there was a workout area in Helios' basement—part of their employee benefit package. Most developers spent too much time sitting on their asses, and Brady wanted his people both well-paid and healthy.

Paul righted himself. "So, Mr.—"

"Brady."

"Brady," Paul repeated. Another thing about Helios—no one was superior to anyone else. They were a team. It was part of the company dynamic, and keeping everyone on a first-name basis backed that shit up.

"That's me." Brady crossed his arms and smiled. "What's up?"

Paul had to crane his neck to look Brady in the eye. Then again, so did almost everyone. "I think I know why the customer info is missing from those test orders."

"Oh yeah? Shoot."

Paul launched into an idea on the project he'd been assigned to, words crashing together in his excitement to have one of the bosses' ears. Brady smiled. He'd been a CTO since they opened this place, but it was still entertaining to be treated like this. He'd been a junior programmer too once, before he'd gotten past his hacker phase.

Sam had been in DC then, gone for good as far as Brady had known. The dot-com bubble had burst, and he couldn't get a job, so he freelanced as a web developer and tried to break into small business sites to see if he could. One night when he was up late and bored, he found the security hole in a local ecommerce site and backed off fast. He'd done it on a whim; he never expected to succeed.

He also hadn't known what he'd done could've been a crime.

Dad was furious. They went into the company together, and Brady explained the relatively low level of effort it had taken to gain unauthorized access. The owners were shocked they'd been outdone by a kid and offered him a job as a developer specializing in cyber security. Penetration testing, they called it. A funny-ass name for poking at a user interface and seeing what areas had flaws or holes.

Who knew people got paid for that shit?

Turned out there was such a thing as ethical hacking. White hats, they were called. Black hats did the bad stuff, and discovering that shored up Brady's ethics. He wasn't doing that again without permission. Or money. While he was getting his feet wet as a developer, he started winning hacking challenges. Companies set up servers with vulnerabilities, awarding money to people who got in. He made a bit of an underground name for himself, went to a DefCon hacker conference and met Myles and Wendell.

Bostonians themselves, Myles was a whiz in phone apps, and Wendell was a game-designer legend. After a lengthy discussion about the *ThunderCats* and the realization that they knew more than their bosses, they decided to join forces. A healthy investment from their fathers and over a decade later, they were the Super Friends of the New England Internet-based business scene.

They called themselves Helios, mostly because it sounded cool, although Wendell had come up with a great PR reason: Helios was the personification of the sun, bringing light to the earth. Anything could be done when the right light was shed on it, and that's what they put out there—ingenuity, imagination. If what a client wanted wasn't built, they would create it. And if there was no way to create it, they would *create* the way to create it.

They were gods here, Titans of the web, app and gaming world. Brady's experience with mythology was limited to watching Disney's *Hercules* with his kids. But when it came to work, he didn't feel like a giant bumbling through his life. At Helios, his ability to be a superhuman lifesaver amounted to more than his collection of shirts. Here, he could sit in on a Dev Team meeting and fill the whiteboard with new ideas. He could go to the gamer den, play the games they were making and fix things when they'd run into a wall.

Here he *was* a superhero.

He stopped Paul before the guy ran out of air.

"I think you might be right." There was a bug on a site they were building for a big client, an auto-fill issue on the shopping cart, and Paul might've cracked through the problem. "It means we'll have to rebuild using a different checkout extension. Think you can get on that before the next team meeting?"

Paul looked like he'd won the lottery or discovered free porn on the Internet.

"Yes! Thank you, Mr. Ar—Brady. Thank you. I'll get on it right away."

He turned and jogged down the ramp. Brady treaded the rest of the way up to the main floor, then climbed three flights on the wire, open-air staircase that led to the offices. The twelve-thousand-square-foot industrial complex that had once housed a textile mill was cheap as shit to buy and a good space for the business to grow in. It was also close enough to home that he could work late or early when he needed to, which was often.

That was part of being the boss. He was often up around the

clock monitoring site launches or doing damage control. He'd spent vacations glued to his emails and had nearly missed an entire Red Sox game last spring because he'd been dealing with client complaints. To be honest he was exhausted, but he needed to work this hard with Sam not bringing in any income.

It was why he'd gone downstairs to lift an hour ago. It wasn't just to shed some of yesterday's meal. Every once in a while he needed a reboot—to shut down and recharge.

Reaching his office, Brady closed the door, stripped off his sweaty T-shirt and exchanged it for the Batman one he had hanging on a hook on the back of his door. Sometimes he felt like too much of a geek—like his love of Marvel movies, Twitter list that followed the films' actors, and comic-book character shirts made him a giant nerd, a six-foot-five dork who didn't play football anymore to beef up his testosterone, but whatever. He liked the tees, and this was the last clean shirt from the load Sam had done for him, something she probably knew without having to check. Every other week, a bag of freshly folded tees was by the door, waiting for him to take in without him having to ask.

He didn't know how she did it.

Sinking into his chair, Brady stared at the site he'd been on earlier. It wasn't a Helios project, and not one he had to test for bugs. No, he was testing for his own issues. The title itself sounded like a bad download for virus detection.

"Self-Quiz: Do You Have Adult ADHD/ADD?"

Brady twisted his wedding ring, rubbing it between the thumb and forefinger of his other hand. Diagnosing shit online was never a good idea. But since no one else had ever done the job, he'd asked Google.

He grabbed the mouse and scrolled to review the questions he'd answered.

"Do you often lose track of what you're supposed to be doing? Forget dates or make mistakes because you're not paying attention?"

The last twenty-four hours was a friggin' case study on that.

"Are you distracted by noise or activity around you? When people are talking, do you drift off or tune out?"

Affirmative, especially when it came to Sam.

"Do you have a hard time remembering appointments or obligations?"

He almost had to snort. Double yes on that one.

"Do you misplace things, or have difficulty finding things at home or at work?"

At work, never. He had a support ticket system to keep track of stuff, things he could search or review if he needed. At home, his brain was like a junk drawer—everything got thrown into it, and he could never find anything when he wanted to. But he'd had to pick an answer, so he'd gone with yes.

It was hard to make a call with some of these questions. They ranged from things he did so often it was ridiculous to things he almost never did—*"Do you often make decisions and act on them impulsively? Do you procrastinate? Fidget and squirm?"*—so he was second-guessing himself with every yes or no box he checked.

He brought the cursor over the submit button and clicked. The page refreshed, and the results came out in bold at the top of the screen:

"Your score suggests INATTENTION is a problem for you."

Really? Ya think? No shit.

He frowned at the screen. The results were rebroadcasts of things he'd heard from teachers as a kid: he was forgetful, distracted, a poor listener overwhelmed by hectic situations. He glossed over the part that talked about ADHD as a spectrum disorder. He'd seen those words over Sam's shoulder back when she was getting Allegra tested. He hadn't wanted to deal with it then. He didn't want to now.

He looked out the window and toward the direction of home. He let Sam deal with Allegra's issues, not because he didn't want to help but because it killed him to see it. It made him feel like he'd passed on something defective to her and not just the Archer curls.

He didn't have a clue how to help her, either.

Brady closed the site after reading how ADHD wasn't an illness, because that shit wasn't helping. An illness came and went. You could cure an illness. ADHD was ongoing, and if he couldn't be cured, what was the point of going to a doctor?

He'd seen firsthand what the process of finding the right meds had done to Allegra. Brady couldn't risk that for himself. Not with everything that rode on him at work.

And he could always focus when it came to computers.

That was why his father bought him a laptop back when the Internet was brand new. Dad declared it a toy, no better than his Nintendo 64, but Brady had been fascinated with the Internet and barely left his room for anything other than JV practice because of it. Good thing Jack was already out of the house then, or Brady would've felt even more inferior.

He'd worshipped his big brother as a kid; nine years Jack's junior, Brady had wanted to be like him in every way. But Jack was the genius, the one Dad sent to Harvard and invited to be a lawyer in his own firm. The youngest hotshot attorney to be offered partner, Jack turned it down for a professorship at Harvard Law. No wonder it had barely mattered that Brady could code a website as easily as he could tackle a running back, or that his talent on the field had gotten him recruited to play at B.U.

Football had been the only thing he had over Jack—that and three inches of height. The game gave Brady confidence, too. Made him feel his size was good for something, and he'd liked being on a team. He'd had hopes of going pro—a pipe dream of being drafted to his beloved Patriots. Sure, he liked computers, but his major was background noise to his focus on the Terriers and their all-time record year. Then the team was terminated, the ninety-first year of B.U. football coming to a painful end.

More painful for him and Nick than a few others.

Brady ran his fingertips along the scar above his right ear, the line fifteen stitches had left behind. It didn't hurt the way his knee did sometimes—aching when the weather got bad or when he kept it in one position for too long—but the scar was still there, a reminder etched in his skin.

One move. One body slam that drove his skull against the

concrete and his knee to the floor, blowing it out in one shot and ending his athletic career.

He'd never regretted that day. He'd stand in traffic for his friends, and he hadn't given a crap that Nick was gay. The guy could run plays and throw like it was his X-Men mutant skill, and always laughed at Brady's jokes. Why should he care what turned Nick's crank?

Their teammates cared. It had only taken one second with Brady's back turned before they were pummeling Nick's head.

He'd jumped in, trying to be the peacemaker. He hated fights. It was why he never fought with Sam. He was more like Hope—passive and wanting to please.

His football career was a casualty of that event. Dad said he was too passive, not wanting to press charges, but lawsuits had a tendency to be long and drawn out, and if Nick wanted it all in his rearview mirror, then Brady was sticking by his buddy's side.

The guys who'd done it got expelled, the team disbanded, even though the administration's party line on banning the game was financial issues and "the changing needs of the institution."

Brady knew bullshit when he saw it. The university was saving its ass, dumping the sport to hide the fact that half the team had beat up their star quarterback because he liked boys instead of girls. But losing football stuck with Brady, made him feel like he'd lost a limb even after he'd ditched the crutches. Without sports, what was his size for? Instead of making him stronger, it made him vulnerable.

Which was the state he'd been in when he met Sam.

His grades were slipping, and the last thing he'd wanted was to lose football *and* flunk out, so he'd signed up for peer tutoring. He still remembered how it felt to watch her crossing the room and coming to his table, his bad leg propped up on the chair next to him. Sweaty palms. Heart palpitations. And a more-than-obvious boner that made him swear he'd never wear track pants to a tutoring session again.

But it wasn't just her gorgeous red hair and phenomenal body that had him hobbling back to his room and rubbing one off. Even at nineteen, she'd radiated a sense of intellect and superiority, and something in him had loved the feeling that she was smarter, higher than him somehow.

He hadn't known what that meant, then.

When he'd finally won her over, she'd taken him out to meet her friends and fawned over him like he was a new toy—a shiny object to be shown off. He'd been embarrassed, but then she'd looked at him with a gaze so pleased and approving, he was rock hard and ready to worship her in seconds.

Now she only looked at him with impatience and disappointment.

Brady fiddled with his ring again. It had been good for a while when the girls were young, when he could still make her laugh and they'd be too tired to cook so they'd have Lucky Charms for dinner. That was before Sam changed her eating habits. He was thankful for it—they were all healthier because of it—but sometimes he missed that sugary cereal, so sweet it made his teeth ache.

It was her who'd come up with the green marshmallow thing. She'd believed in him, told him he could do more than football, and when his grades improved he'd called her his good luck charm. She left a box with him on exam days, and it became a private joke he loved. It was why he'd given her that necklace. A white-gold four-leaf clover, it had two closed petals for the girls, one covered in diamonds for Sam, and an open one for him, symbolizing how empty he'd be without her.

He hadn't said that at the time.

He didn't say a lot out loud, like the fact that he was always walking on eggshells, that he was petrified to forget the next damn thing or the crippling fear that one wrong step would end his marriage forever. He'd watched Sam walk out of his life twice and hoped putting that ring on her finger meant she wasn't going anywhere again. Now he wasn't so sure.

If only he could hit some kind of magical Ctrl-Alt-Delete on her life, or find her something to do up here. His suggestion last year that she turn her Instagram posts into a published book had been a colossal failure. He'd wanted her to have something of her own, but

Sam didn't belong hidden behind the pages of a book. She belonged someplace exciting, doing something important.

He blamed himself, blamed the fact that he'd been two feet deep into this place when they'd found each other again. If she hadn't run into him in that bar, she could've gone back to Washington. It would've meant they'd never have gotten married or had the girls, but maybe she would've been happier.

God, he hated the idea that she'd be better off without him. The fear that it was true made it hard to breathe. Was there a test online to see if you could fix a crumbling marriage? He'd search for one, but he wasn't sure he wanted to see the answer.

If only it could be the way it was back in college, when things were fucking *simpler*. When she'd help him with the stuff he'd forget, writing reminders on little heart-shaped Post-it Notes. When she'd call him to her room and tell him what he was allowed to touch and what he wasn't until he was so twisted up with wanting her, he couldn't think straight.

She'd let him have her in bits and pieces then, sometimes sending him back to his dorm without any relief at all. The anticipation of wondering when he'd get to be with her again was almost better than coming himself.

He'd always enjoyed giving pleasure, liked it better when he was told what to do. Football was like that in a way. The coach gave instructions, he listened—pass, tackle, defend. But with Sam it had always been different. She doled out orders, and he craved her satisfaction. He'd never pieced together what that meant until she read those books and BDSM became a thing everyone talked about. One night searching the web had him staring at a list of kink terminology and breathing uncomfortably hard.

Submission and humiliation were keywords that hit at him, turned him on and made him queasy and on edge all at once. He'd let himself think about it the last time he and Sam had sex—a time so long ago he didn't want to think about it—and it had been like a light bulb turning on, like the whole damn B.U. stadium floodlights blinding him right in the face.

But he couldn't tell her the idea of her controlling him, of her laughing at his desperate thrusts and pointing out how close to orgasm he was had made him come like a damn rocket, or why he'd turned away in shame afterward.

Brady didn't doubt his masculinity, but he couldn't shake the feeling that it wasn't manly to willingly forfeit power. It felt like a sign of weakness, to want to be on your knees for your wife instead of the other way around. Sam was frustrated enough with his shortcomings, so he bottled up those fantasies and desires, kept them a secret, convinced they'd push her away even more. The fact that he'd kept her from her dreams was bad enough. The shit he wanted in bed? That made it even worse.

His computer chimed with an incoming chat. Brady lifted his head.

"So, I did a thing today..." Sam's message began.

Brady's heart sped up.

"A thing, huh?" He could see her typing in response but raced his fingers over the keys to get ahead of her. *"Wait, let me guess. You robbed the bank on Federal Street. No, wait—you signed up for the Iron Man Challenge."*

Sam stopped typing. An emoticon with rolled eyes popped up in his chat window.

He grinned. Maybe that test was right and he was a bit impulsive. But humor was the best weapon to combat feeling awkward.

"They still want me at Forrester. I have an in-person interview tomorrow."

His brows shot up. *"The reception gig?"*

Had Gabe helped with this? Had Lilly?

"They changed it to a part-time role. I'd start early but be home by three."

"That's great," he typed, but a million questions crackled through his mind, a string of explosives on a line. Was she nervous? Were they telling the kids?

The kids—crap. Brady moused over to his browser and typed *care.com* into the address bar, because of course, he'd forgotten about the stupid posting. He'd hit the snooze button on the calendar reminder he'd set that morning, turning it off by accident during a meeting and never got back to it.

"How do you want to celebrate?"

The dots beneath her name bounced in his chat window. He stared at them even as his phone buzzed with notifications about his three o'clock meeting.

"Let's save celebrating for if I get the job. But maybe we could get takeout tomorrow, so I don't have to cook and do the dishes, too?"

Brady frowned, confused. *"I thought you liked cooking."*

She'd taken it on like the next Food Network star when she'd started losing weight, making healthy and delicious things he never imagined eating, like kale chips and zucchini fries.

The last one still shocked him.

"I do..."

More dings. More emails. But he needed to focus on her.

"It's the cleaning up I hate."

Well, if something as simple as that would make her happy, no problemo. *"Takeout tomorrow night it is,"* he typed. *"And I'll do all the dishes."*

He couldn't do it the way she did. Sam had a system for stacking the bowls and containers that he blanked out on every time she showed him. How important was it to know how to load the dishwasher properly when he had sixteen projects and thirty developers to juggle? Just throw the plates in there. They'll still get clean.

"Hell, maybe I'll even do the laundry, too."

That eye-rolling emoticon appeared again. *"I won't push my luck."*

Brady grinned and closed the chat. Standing, he left his screen open to the childcare site, then headed out to his meeting. He could do what she needed. It was just remembering a few things.

If he could manage to do that, things between them might magically get better.

6

The conference room Sam was sitting in was spotless.

Not sterile like a doctor's office, but perfectly organized, not a speck out of place. The gleaming glass table didn't have a single smudge. Legal pads and pens sat neatly in the center. Fresh flowers were in the corner. Bookshelves framed the walls, filled with legal volumes in matching colors, and in the middle, a span of windows looked out over the Boston skyline.

The firm's lobby had been as pristine, with the names Forrester, Schaeffer and Pierce on the wall in bold red letters and a portrait of the three name partners beside it.

Her resume on crisp paper in front of her and the firm application already filled out, Sam fingered her necklace, thumbed the bottom edge of the clover's stem before stopping herself and smoothing down her blouse, skirt and matching wool crepe blazer.

She'd been anxious pulling the outfit from her closet that morning. She hadn't worn it since Allegra was in diapers, but it slid on like a glove. Classic, too, so it wasn't out of style. Paired with cream-colored pumps that were black at the toe—Hope had them dubbed Sam's Barbie-doll shoes—and her hair loosely curled, she looked put together, professional.

The Boston Bombshell by dress, even if her brain hadn't caught up yet.

She'd felt like a fraud walking toward the building from the parking garage. Standing outside, she'd craned her head up to see all of it, a reflective blue glass that stretched high into the sky. Who the hell was she? What shot did she have? Jobs in places like this were reserved for people with more experience than temping and two years as a congressional staffer. But standing in the elevator, Sam had dredged up her former self—the young girl who'd gone to Washington without a doubt in her mind.

That version of her yelled from the past.

Suck it up, buttercup. I handled DC. You can handle a damn interview.

The door behind her opened. Sam stood and turned around, immediately recognizing the man standing there from his profile on the company site. She'd made a point to peruse it before today's interview. He walked toward her with a smile and a hand extended for her to shake.

"Samantha, thank you for coming in."

She responded with a firm grip of the man's hand. "My pleasure, Mr. Phillips. It's nice to meet you."

Sam's initial phone call had been with one of the HR assistants. Now she was dealing with the big guns—Johnson Phillips was the Director. Grabbing a legal pad from the pile, Phillips unclipped a packet of information and plunked it on the table. She resumed her spot in her chair as he sat across from her

"Let's get right to it, shall we?" he asked.

Sam nodded. "Fire away."

"Tell me about your most recent position."

Most recent was a decade ago.

"My last job was temping. Filing, typing, minor office work. Before that, I was a congressional staffer for Representative Arnold Dawes."

"I saw that on your resume. What were your responsibilities there?"

Sam did the mental equivalent of cracking her knuckles. "I started as an intern during college but was invited back after graduation. I was the first point of contact for the office. I managed the front desk, answered phones, directed people to the right staffer, often taking over myself during late-night hours. I sorted the mail, too, which doesn't sound like a lot, but trust me, it was."

"I imagine. We get overloaded with mail, too."

She'd seen that when she walked in. The person covering the desk seemed overwhelmed.

"I'm not easily felled by a heap of envelopes."

Phillips grinned. "Good to know."

"Some letters required immediate action," she continued. "Knowing what needed a personalized response and what didn't was essential. Sending a constituent a form letter was a recipe for getting your ass booted out the door."

Sam almost covered her mouth. She'd cursed. In an interview. Jesus, was she channeling Brady or something? But it made Phillips laugh.

"Sounds like the way things are here. You don't want to piss off the wrong client."

"Or the wrong attorney, I'd guess."

"Correct."

"Eventually I was given more important tasks," she added. "Research, sometimes working on policy drafts. Almost everything had a same-day deadline, so I assure you, I know how to work in a fast-paced environment."

Fast-paced was an understatement. Everything depended on momentum there, on being awake more than you slept, on being everywhere at once. Bars were as much the arena for debate as the House floor. Truces were often called in private rooms for elected officials, deals struck over drinks when the sun was coming up. Sam still remembered the jittery mishmash of being hungover and overcaffeinated.

She felt a bit that way now.

"Why politics?" Phillips asked.

She hated that question, because she wasn't up to date on current legislation. Reading about it now was the equivalent of her nose pressed against the glass. But he needed an answer.

"I was always fascinated with federal and state issues. The idea of grassroots lobbying, building coalitions. I watched *West Wing* religiously when I was in high school. When other kids were playing house, I was pretending to be President."

That earned her another laugh from Phillips, who scribbled notes on a pad. It made her think though. Maybe that was why she struggled as a parent—she'd dreamed of teaching her children French, reading them books about American politics, but Allegra didn't have an interest in either one, and Hope was either going to be a silent movie star or a math genius.

"What would you consider your biggest success?" Phillips asked.

"We started getting calls from a politically important businessman who wanted to become a major donor."

This was the real reason Dawes had dubbed her the Boston Bombshell. It wasn't because of the way she'd torn through his office and turned it into a perfectly run machine. Sam could tell that the caller was shady right off the bat. One large donation and he tried to take advantage of his position—demanding meetings, being inappropriate with the staff. Money didn't always equal power, not when you talked down to the wrong redhead.

"Something about him seemed off, so I did my homework. Turned out this guy had been brought up on charges of money laundering and bribery. He'd been acquitted, but accepting contributions from him could've turned into an ugly corruption scandal."

Phillips' gaze flicked toward a space behind her. Sam glanced over her shoulder. A man was standing in the doorway with his hands in his pockets.

"So you're the one who got Arnie out of that mess," he said.

His grin was smug, teeth showing with a slightly uneven gap in the front. He was a bit on the short side but that didn't matter. With his hands in his pockets and one leg crossed casually over the ankle of the other, he oozed confidence nonetheless.

That confidence was well founded. Sam recognized his face from his portrait.

He was Reginald Pierce.

"Mr. Pierce," Sam said quickly, standing. "It's a pleasure to meet you."

He sauntered into the room. "Likewise."

"You knew the congressman?" she asked.

"He was a buddy of mine from grade school." Pierce pulled his hands from his pockets, balanced his elbows on the top of a chair and leaned forward. Sam refused to be rattled by his lack of handshake. She'd been around men like this in DC all the time. It was a power struggle in the making—he was the alpha, but he was testing her, seeing how strong she could be. "I miss that son of a bitch."

Sam hadn't been able to go to Dawes' funeral, too busy with the girls and taking care of her mom. "Me, too. I loved working for him."

"Why did you leave?"

It seemed Mr. Pierce was leading things now, so Sam directed her answers toward him.

"My mother needed surgery," she explained. "Her recovery time kept extending, and my father wasn't handling things on his own. I needed to be here, so I used up my sick days, then my vacation and FMLA. There was no Paid Family Leave then. Eventually I ran out of time."

"That's too bad," he said.

"It was." She'd sobbed when she'd gotten off the phone with Dawes, who'd said when she could come back, he'd find a place for her. "I'd planned to return to Washington eventually, but then the congressman lost his seat and there was no job to go back to. I got married, had kids, and staying home was the right choice for my family. But I'm extremely organized, good at multitasking, and I'm ready to get back out there."

"You sure?" Pierce asked.

The question irked her. As if having children had somehow infected her and he had to be certain she wasn't going to have a relapse. It was like this in politics, too—a boys' club. A landscape somehow not suitable for women.

She gave Pierce a firm look in response and simply said, "I am."

"Well," Phillips interjected, "you're currently on the top of a very short list of candidates. Do you have any questions for us?"

"Just one." She was toeing a line she probably shouldn't have, but she was genuinely curious. "Why am I your top candidate?"

Pierce gave her a cocky smile. "Not everyone has a recommendation letter from Arnie Dawes. If you're the same girl that got him to write that letter, then you'll run my reception desk like he'd run a war room."

Girl?

He may have been the one who was pulling for her, but she wasn't letting him win this battle of wills. Sam pushed back her chair, stood and gathered her things. "I hate to break it to you, Mr. Pierce. But I'm not the same girl."

"You're not?"

"Oh no." She took a step toward him. "I'm a much, *much* smarter woman."

Pierce broke out in laughter, head tipping backward, and Phillips followed suit. Finally, Pierce extended his hand.

"Samantha Archer," he said as they shook. "I look forward to seeing more of you."

7

———

Sam looked around her dining room in disgust.

Hours ago, she'd felt at the top of the world. She'd walked out of the firm like a boss. She fucking *owned* that interview. Once she got home, however, it was back to her regularly scheduled programming.

Her pulse pounding, Sam stacked the abandoned plastic plates and cups that had been left on the dining room table and brought them to the kitchen. No one's coats had been put away either, dumped unceremoniously in the living room. The dishwasher was full from last night, today's dishes were in the sink. And no one had asked her how the interview went.

She rinsed out the containers, tossing them one by one into the recycle bin. She'd spent the remainder of her afternoon running errands, the roads slick with a coating of snow and people driving like Mass-holes. She'd barely made it in time to meet the bus. At least, Brady had followed through on his promise to get takeout, arriving home with two large bags from Panera she'd ordered in advance online to make sure it was all correct, and announcing he'd take care of everything—clean-up included.

So much for that.

Dinner had been the standard bedlam—Allegra complaining

that her sandwich didn't taste right, Hope barely speaking and Brady glancing at work emails on his phone and oblivious to it all. She'd gone upstairs to change her clothes afterward—something she'd been unable to do before dinner because *Mommy I need, Mommy I can't, Mommy will you*—banking on Brady's insistence that he'd get everything done. She'd come back down, however, to discover everything had been left exactly where it was.

Shrieking laughter came from the basement. Sam ground her jaw. One thing, that was all she'd asked of him. But no, he'd abandoned it to play with the girls, horsing around instead of being an actual parent.

Sam inhaled and exhaled, trying to control her temper. She didn't want to be mad, but this was always how it went: Brady forgetting what she'd asked him, the things she wanted or needed ignored. The house left for her to deal with while everyone else did what they enjoyed. She was disappearing again, when today she'd felt seen.

There was a crash followed by a thump, then the sound of Brady cursing.

That. Was. It.

Storming to the basement door, she opened it and hollered, "Girls, bedtime. Now."

Allegra's voice came first. "Aw, Mom. Can we have five—"

"Now!"

Silence followed. If there was one thing her children had learned, it was when not to mess with their mother. They trudged quietly up the steps. Brady remained behind, probably to deal with whatever mess he'd made. When Sam returned to the kitchen after the usual bedtime circus, the table had been cleared, the remaining plastic containers jammed haphazardly in the recycle bin, and Brady was standing by the open dishwasher.

He turned around, his hands full of bowls and a smile on his face. "I'll give you five hundred dollars if you tell me where these go."

She stomped past him to the fridge. "Don't joke, Brady."

"I wasn't joking. I don't know where they belong."

Seriously? How was he so good at his job but so damn lost at home?

"Second cabinet on the left," she muttered. "Bottom shelf." This was why she never asked him to help with housework. It was more trouble than it was worth.

She stomped over to the fridge, telling herself to let it go.

But she always let it go. "You said you'd help today."

"I am! I just—" His words broke off on a sigh.

Sam looked over at him. He'd changed at some point into pajama pants, taken off his long-sleeved button-down to reveal the faded, worn-in Spider-man T-shirt he had on beneath it. The pale blue fabric clung to his ropy back muscles, but Sam was too annoyed to be turned on.

"Why are you so pissed?" he asked.

His tone was quiet, not demanding. As if he truly didn't know.

"Because you said you would do something and you didn't."

"I got dinner, didn't I?"

"Yes, but you said you'd clean up. You said you'd do the dishes." A list formed in her mind, a goddamn clown car of complaints. "You said you'd do the sitter posting and you didn't. You said you'd help find the gloves and you didn't. You're always telling me you'll do things and then you don't do them."

"I'll do the dishes," he offered. "I didn't forget. I was planning on it. I just started playing with the girls and time got away from me."

"We won't have the luxury of *time getting away from you* if I get this job, Brady."

His reaction to her words was visceral—eyes cast downward, mouth pinching into a wince, like she'd punched him in the stomach. "I know we won't," he said softly.

Fuck, she hated this. She didn't want to be angry at him. But this argument was a train wreck, barreling too fast for her to stop.

"Good, because I'm gonna need you to step up. I need you to help me take care of the house and not check out all the time."

"I'm not checking out." He sighed. "It's just that..."

"It's just what?"

He shook his head but didn't respond. It was times like this, when he refused to participate, that Sam felt her marriage falling apart.

She didn't want this.

She didn't *want this.*

"Talk, Brady!"

He snapped into focus, a racecar driver who'd seen a checkered flag. "I feel like I can never do anything right!"

Sam recoiled in surprise. Brady didn't yell. Ever. "That's not true."

"It feels like it. No matter what I do, I do it wrong. And you act like I want to piss you off!" He stared at her. "I want you to be happy, Sammy. That's all I want."

He felt he could never do anything right? He wanted her happy? It was hard to believe, since he'd been horsing around instead of helping like he promised.

"If you want me happy, then put away the dishes *and* do what's in the sink while I get off my feet for five goddamn minutes."

He stood still and held her gaze. "That's what you want," he confirmed.

"That's what I want."

She shifted her weight uncomfortably as the seconds ticked by. For a minute it felt like they were back at B.U., when not only had he seen her, but she was the only thing he *could* see.

"Okay." He went around her to the breakfast table and pulled out a chair. "Please sit?"

Sam paused. Was this another joke? It didn't seem to be as he stood there, expectant and waiting. He wasn't being sarcastic. His request had been soft and low, and his face was calm, his eyes filled with a deference she didn't understand. One that made her feel elevated and catered to.

It was unnerving.

"All right."

She immediately felt better—she wasn't used to that many hours in heels—and her breath caught when she felt his hands at the bottom of her hair.

"May I?" he asked.

She was caught off guard. He was just brushing the ends, but each soft tug stimulated all the nerve endings on her head. "Okay."

He continued combing the last inch of the locks, rubbing them between his fingers. She'd assumed he'd forgotten how much she enjoyed this, but then he ran his fingers through her hair, lifting it from her face and gently easing out any tangles.

It was the most intimate they'd been in years.

He did it again, deliberate and slow. Brady had large hands, and she missed what he could do with them. He was even better with his mouth. It had taken time and direction, but once he'd figured out her spots, his tongue had been fucking magical.

He moved in closer, starting at her temples and combing at the roots before running his fingertips down the strands. The sensation was hypnotic. Jesus, if he'd done this instead of joking, the fight never would've started. With him standing so close, Sam got a hit of his scent. It was the same heady combination he'd always had—wood spice deodorant and peppermint soap mixed with an earthy bit of sweat.

Years ago, she'd worn that smell on her like perfume.

He gathered her hair and put it over one shoulder.

"Better?" he asked.

She paused, unsure about the dynamic between them. The fight seemed to have dissipated, but there was a strange vibration now—a different kind of energy. Like the charge in the air before a snowfall. "Yes, better."

But she hadn't asked him to stop. She didn't like that he had.

He went back to the counter. Sam watched as Brady put away the rest of the dishes, then stepped toward the sink and turned on the water.

"Thank you," she said. "For helping."

"It's not that I don't want to," he replied softly. "I'm just not sure how to do it right. Like your system for putting things into the dishwasher."

She did have a system. A way to stack everything for maximum efficiency. She didn't know he'd noticed.

"And I don't know how you know where everything goes in the cabinets without looking. It's hard for me to keep track."

Sam frowned, guilt stabbing. He'd always had issues recalling things. It was why they'd met in the first place. Why was she never patient with it?

Staring at his profile, she threw out some sarcasm to lighten the mood.

"Well, silly. If you can't figure out where things go, I'll fucking tell you."

She wasn't sure if he'd missed the lightness in her tone, or if he'd caught it and was embarrassed regardless, but from this angle, she could see his chin lower slightly as a swallow constricted his throat. It was a small tell, something he used to do when she was tutoring him, ashamed because he'd gotten an answer wrong.

Back then she'd soothe him, put a hand on one of his giant arms and tell him it was her job to help him get things right. He'd blush and smile up at her, eyes sparkling and hopeful.

He wasn't smiling now. But a strange part of her…liked his discomfort.

"I don't mind telling you what to do, you know," she added. "Being your wife is like training an excitable puppy."

Brady went rigid, his muscles tensing beneath his T-shirt as color rose on his cheeks. It had been a long time since she'd seen him react like that, even longer since she'd seen his brow wrinkle and his head sink down more, a surefire sign that he was turned on. It was what he'd do back in the day, when she'd taunt him for wanting her so badly. What he'd done every time she'd ordered him to her dorm room and teased that he must've sprinted across campus to have gotten to her so fast.

When she'd *ordered* him over.

Was that it?

She stared at him. He was waiting, barely moving.

"Maybe that's all you need," she said. "To be given a little—" she paused, testing out the effect of her words, "—discipline."

A noticeable shudder went through him.

Holy shit. She'd read moments like this in her books. Scenes when the Dominant would give his submissive a command, and everything would change. Was that happening now?

She wanted to push Brady harder. To see if she was right.

Sam stood and padded slowly over to him, but he remained frozen, as if he were a helpless animal and she was a lioness stalking her prey.

"You want to see me happy?" she asked, and even she was surprised at how soft and seductive her voice sounded.

Brady didn't look up from the sink. "You know I do."

Moving in behind him, she put her hands on him. His T-shirt was soft beneath her palms. His breathing went shallow as she caressed all those bunched muscles in his lower back. God, he still was a specimen, his torso thick, a dip at the base of his spine leading to the ass she'd once loved to grab and squeeze.

She pressed herself against him. Her chin barely cleared his shoulder blades, but she rubbed her upper body back and forth, testing to see if he could feel her tightened nipples through her tank top and robe. There was the slightest buck of his hips.

Humming softly in approval, Sam went up on her toes, got her lips as close to his ear as she could and whispered, "Then you go back to washing while I have a little fun."

Sam lowered her hands until her palms met the hem of his tee. She raised the fabric up with her fingers. Brady let out an unsteady breath when she found warm, bare skin.

"I'm going to play," she said. "And you're not gonna miss a speck of food on those plates, understand?"

He swallowed audibly. "Yes."

The word came out strained. Like he was trying not to beg.

"And you'll have to be quiet so the girls don't hear. Can you do that?"

Another swallow, with a quick nod of his head tacked on after it. This wasn't real. It wasn't *them*. Or maybe it was them, some ghostly past version coming back for one repeat performance. Mentioning it seemed dangerous though, as if it could break the spell, so Sam waited until Brady reached for a plate. He began scrubbing, and there was a slight tremor in his limbs as Sam moved her hands around to his belly. She had no idea if this was anything more than Brady being turned on, but the idea of making him her plaything sent heat rushing through her, made her skin tingle and her heart pound.

She caressed that spot for a moment, enjoying the sensation beneath her fingertips. Brady's skin had always been smooth, baby soft under the hair that ran a trail into his boxers. And what was at the end of that trail was a goddamn pot of gold.

She etched a nail along the cotton waistband of his sweats. Brady's breathing hitched, his belly rising and falling. Why he was suddenly so responsive when they'd had months of nothing sexual at all was beyond her, but she wasn't going to ask now. What she was going to do was dip her hands beneath the elastic, beyond that patch of curls and to the prize beneath it.

"Stay quiet," she reminded, and slid her hand downward until she found rigid flesh.

Brady held himself still. Body poised. Waiting. Obedient. Silent. The muffled shudder that came out of him was almost as rewarding as the feel of him in her fist.

"Look what I found," she teased, singsong, and gave him a long, languid stroke.

He was hard. Harder than she could ever remember him being, and that was saying something. She'd been shocked at the size of his erection the first time she'd seen it. He was thick enough for her fingertips to barely meet when she wrapped a hand around him. He always got bigger the closer he got to coming, too.

Sam grinned, a faded memory coming back—a night years ago, after a winter-break separation. Their reunion had been all hands and very few words, and she'd worked him until he was on the brink of orgasm, then stopped to marvel at his size. He hadn't complained. He'd just grunted and stared at her. At her mercy, he'd waited for her to take the lead, obedient and silent.

Sam blinked. Was she reading this right?

"You want that again?" she asked, her voice low.

He nodded—a quick, desperate move.

"Say please."

His shoulders shook. "Please."

She blinked again. Was Brady a submissive? Could he always have been? He'd behaved like one in college, but somehow she'd never connected the dots. She'd never entertained the idea that she was a Domme either, for all that she'd been turned on reading about BDSM, but here she was, her own breathing sharp and short as she watched Brady shake with need. She could be imagining all this, pretending that some inherent, unspoken need in him was answering some unrealized, intrinsic need of hers.

She needed to find out.

Experimenting, she slowly stroked that gloriously rigid flesh, fingers slippery with pre-come as she skated a thumb over his tip. She found a rhythm, and his breathing quickened. He put down the plate he'd been rinsing and gripped the sides of the sink with shaking arms. Sam immediately stopped stroking.

"I thought I told you to finish those dishes," she said, somehow pulling off harsh and playful in the same breath.

His head bowed, and his cock pulsed in her grip. "You did," he gritted out.

"Well if you want more of this—" Sam stroked him again. His head sank back. "—then you'd better do what I say."

"God." Brady's voice broke on the word. Hands trembling, he retrieved the plate, rinsed it, and placed it in the dishwasher. As he reached for another one, Sam felt an insane, giddy rush. Power crackled through her like a snapping set of fireworks. It was electrifying, seeing him weak like this.

She wasn't imagining a damn thing—not his reaction, nor her own.

She waited until he'd rinsed off another dish before sliding her other hand into his boxers. As she resumed stroking him with one hand, she reached the other one lower, cupping his balls and tugging gently.

He huffed out a breath. Struggling to keep quiet. But he was behaving.

"Good boy," she whispered.

Brady's entire body went taut. "Oh, fuck. Sammy."

The breath rushed out of him. He pumped his hips, then held painfully still. The high it gave her was almost too much. She needed to be touched, too, but there was another problem that needed to be addressed first.

"Oh fuck?" she asked mockingly. "Brady Archer, something's gotta be done about your mouth."

He groaned, listing slightly. Sam pushed the cotton of his boxers out to make room for her palm and flattened it over the tip, rubbing circles against his slit. He was positively drenched, and she shivered at the slickness she found there. His hips moved in time with her hand, his movements hungry, eager.

Desperate.

"I didn't tell you to move."

She released him, pulling her hands out of his boxers and letting his waistband snap against his tummy. His tiny whimper of disappointment made her grin widely.

"There you go again," she said. "Whining like a little puppy."

A heavy exhale shook his frame along with a low groan. What *was* this? She had a million questions, but it was a struggle to think beyond the haze of desire, past the throbbing in her clit and the need to come herself.

"Shut off the water and turn around," she said.

Brady did as he was told. When he moved to face her, his eyes were bright blue, focused and steady, a hulk of a man panting and waiting.

For her.

How had she missed this? Was it because she'd been looking everywhere but at them? Looking at their friends' kinky dynamics instead, at fictional characters instead of her husband and herself? She wanted to ask Brady if this had always been there, but she didn't know how. Not now anyway, with both of them on the edge of whatever this was. Her chest rose and fell, his only movement the opening and closing of his fists, arms close by his sides. She wanted him. Wanted his hands on her now, doing her bidding until she shattered.

"Brady—"

"Mom!"

Sam froze. Allegra's night terrors didn't come as often as they used to, but when she woke up and her anxiety kicked in, it meant another repetition of her bedtime ritual was needed.

"Coming, honey," Sam yelled.

Sam blinked hard, attempting to rid herself of the longing that was still coursing through her. She had to shift from sexpot to mom, from this temptress she'd suddenly become into the person who messily attempted to solve her daughter's problems.

She didn't want to. Not yet.

And Brady was twisting his wedding ring around, not looking at her.

"I'll finish the dishes," he mumbled.

Sam's stomach dropped. Whatever they'd recaptured moments ago, it had vanished, and she didn't know how to reclaim it.

"Okay," she said. "Come up when you're done?"

He nodded, but he didn't appear upstairs, not even hours later. Lying in the dark until she couldn't keep her eyes open anymore, Sam fell asleep waiting for him.

8

Watching the action on each end of the air hockey table, Brady leaned over and readied his striker. The puck was slingshotting from one player to the next, lightning quick. As soon as it flew his way, Brady took his shot. It ricocheted off the opposite corner and straight into Wendell's goal.

Brady didn't need to shout out his score. The sound of the alarm and the noise of applause did it for him. He tossed his striker on the table in victory and grinned.

"You suck," Wendell said.

"You're just jealous of my epic hand-eye coordination skills."

Wendell gave him the finger. "How's this for hand-eye coordination?" He motioned for someone to turn the lights on. "Brady Archer, ladies and gentlemen—your undefeated champion for three weeks running."

Nick set down his striker. "I think I should get a runner-up prize."

"Runner-up?" Brady asked. "You don't even work here."

"I jumped in when you were short a player. Best-friend status makes me a legal substitution." He gestured toward the table. "Besides, for this, I'd learn some friggin' computer shit. This thing is awesome."

Brady grinned. "Hell yeah, it is."

The new four-player Galaxy Collision QuadAir table had been a worthwhile business expense. The work-hard, play-hard environment at Helios was the closest thing he'd had to a team since his Terrier days, and the basement weight room, gamer den, and newly minted hump-day air hockey tournaments made their employees more productive and just plain happier.

Air hockey was the only game Brady played on his feet these days. He tried to stay active, did as much as he could with dumbbells and a bench, but he was basically a recreational athlete with a creaky knee. The sewn-together ligaments bothered him when the weather was bad, and the snow today was getting his old injury as worked up as his brain was.

He was still wrecked by what happened with Sam last night. Half a day later, he still hadn't figured it out.

Paul looked at his score—a solid electronic zero—and frowned. Brady walked over to his side of the table. "Don't be bummed. There's always next Wednesday."

"Thanks Mr. Arch—Brady. Thanks."

The onlookers broke up, heading back to their desks or lunch. Nick grabbed his coat. He'd slung it over a chair when he'd shown up, offering to step in and play since Myles was out sick. "Ready for lunch?"

"I'm starved. Burgers?"

Nick wrinkled his nose. "They got anything with actual vegetables?"

Brady rolled his eyes. "Yes, health freak. Let's go."

A few minutes later, they were squinting against the wintery mix pelting the ground and crossing the street. Brady's stomach growled when they got inside the gourmet burger bar. He'd skipped breakfast and gone into work early, not ready to face Sam. It was a shitty thing to do after avoiding her last night, playing video games in the living room until he was sure she'd gone to sleep, but he'd had to.

Brady walked up to the tablet on the counter and punched the box next to a triple patty. With cheese.

Nick looked over the counter toward the kitchen. "Does anyone even work here?"

"Of course. Somebody's gotta cook the food." Bacon. He needed bacon, too.

"But it would be nice to, you know, talk to a person."

"Why? People screw things up. A computer can't."

Brady wished he'd been a computer last night, with a simple on/off switch. Then he could've rebooted his sex drive. He slid his credit card into the slot on the tablet, signed with his finger and grabbed a cup. "You need a soda?"

Nick pulled a water bottle from his jacket pocket. "I'm all set."

Brady nodded and went to the electronic drink machine. He stared at the fountain as it poured the sugary liquid into his cup. What the hell had happened last night? First he and Sam were arguing, then he was trying to do the things she wanted, and the next thing he knew, she was setting his body on fucking fire.

He couldn't remember the last time she'd touched him like that. It wasn't so much her touch as it was her words, or maybe it was both—the mocking, the ordering him around, speeding him up and crashing him back down again. Then she'd called him good boy and he'd lost it.

Had she known what she was doing?

She couldn't have. He'd kept this part of himself hidden, stunting his desire at any cost. He was sure bringing it up would be the final nail in the coffin—the thing that would end their marriage and drive her away for good. But last night she'd teased him. Taunted him. Tortured and humiliated him. Why would she have done that if she hadn't known?

Fuck, he had to stop thinking about this. Not only was he getting a boner in the middle of a burger joint, but he'd also stopped paying attention to the drink machine and soda was about to spill everywhere.

Nick was sitting at a table and scrolling through his phone when Brady sat across from him. "You wanna go out tonight?" Nick asked.

"Dude. It's Wednesday."

"So?"

"So, I've got a job and kids and responsibilities and shit."

"I've got responsibilities, too, dickface."

"You're a photographer. You run your own business." And had free time at odd hours, like the middle of the day on a Wednesday.

"So do you," Nick replied. "Your argument is invalid."

"Well, it was easier before."

"Before what?"

Before my wife grabbed my dick while I was washing the dishes and nearly made me come in my pants.

Brady stared at the kitchen. How long did a freaking burger take?

"Before things got tough with Allegra," he answered.

Not the truth but not a lie either.

"I thought she was doing better. With the new meds and all."

"Depends on the day."

And most days, not so much. He'd tried to introduce her to coding in the hopes it would help her focus the way it had for him, but she wasn't interested. Football was even less of a draw. The one time he'd tried to get her to watch a game on TV she'd declared it boring and left the room.

The kitchen door opened, and Brady glanced up, hopeful. A server carrying a triple bacon cheeseburger and a veggie patty wrapped in lettuce walked to their table.

"Thank God." He ripped into his sandwich and eyed Nick's lunch. "Why you gotta be so damn nutritious?"

"'Cause we're not that far away from forty and I don't want to die of heart failure." Nick nodded toward Brady's food. "You could stand to do the same."

"What are you mother-henning me for?"

"Practice."

"For what?"

"Nothing. I'm just saying, we can't eat like we used to."

Brady chewed through another mouthful and glared. He could only fuel his burger-and-pizza addiction when Sam wasn't looking. His lunch was probably three thousand calories, but whatever. He'd burned a ton whooping everyone's ass at air hockey. And he'd been able to eat like this when he'd been tossing a ball every day.

"You ever miss it?" Brady asked.

"Eating like we used to?"

"No, dumbass. Football."

Nick shook his head. "Nah. It was just a game."

Brady went back to his food. Nick had moved on from the Terriers in a way Brady hadn't. Football was where Brady felt the same as the other guys, on the outside at least. And it helped that he loved the sport. It was half about the game, half about the good times. He got to play like a monster and eat that way, too. He missed that camaraderie.

"What did you have in mind for tonight, anyway?"

"There's a basketball game on. We could watch at Barrel 'n' Flask."

Brady made an *eh* face. He'd be into the pub they liked by Fenway, but he wasn't much of a basketball fan. He'd watch a game if the Celtics were playing, or hockey if the Bruins were on the ice, but it wasn't like watching the Pats. Sports were tied with Marvel movies in Brady's head, save for football which superseded everything. It was sacrilege, to be a Native New Englander and not worship the team that had dominated the NFL the last few decades. He was still glowing from their last Super Bowl win, but that also meant there were no more games until September, and they were weeks out from baseball season, when watching the Red Sox would get him through till the fall.

Nick took a bite of his lettuce-crap. Brady scowled at it.

"Sam would sell a kidney to get me to eat like you do."

"You should listen to her. Speaking of Sam, would she be up for joining us? She was going out with us for a while there."

Brady stared at his food. Sam *had* joined them for a few nights out, but for the most part he'd been going out without her. She'd always said she preferred staying home rather than ask her parents to babysit last minute. That he should go. Have fun.

He'd thought it was because she hadn't wanted to be around him.

"I dunno." He popped another bite in his mouth and wiped his messy hands on his napkin. Truth was, he didn't have the first clue what Sam was up for.

A beat of silence passed. Nick put his food on his plate. "You two okay?"

"Sure." Lie. "Why?"

"No reason."

For the most part, Brady had put up a front with his friends and family, keeping the problems with him and Sam on the DL. He didn't like to burden other people, and honestly hadn't wanted to tell his best friend with his perfectly stable marriage anything about it. But Nick clearly knew something was up, so Brady had to say something.

"Sam had a job interview yesterday."

"I know. Gabe told me."

"Oh. Yeah. Duh." Because the two of them talked, like normal couples did. "She needs work. To get out and do something for her."

"Yeah." Nick's eyebrows were raised. Brady raised his back at him.

"Dude, I know I'm hot, but we're both taken and I'm straight. No need to stare at what you can't have."

"You're such a fucking pain in the ass."

"That's what *he* said."

"Oh my God."

"That's what *he*—"

"Brady, will you be serious for a second?"

"Why would I do that?"

"Because you and Sam were barely speaking at the wedding and you're gonna joke around until someone forces it out of you."

He couldn't argue with logic. Brady spun his ring around. "Things aren't...good right now. We keep fighting. And we haven't had sex in forever." Except last night had been the start of a thing. Hadn't it?

He looked up at Nick, who hadn't spoken. "TMI?"

"Dude, I saw you sweaty, smelly and gross in a campus locker room. I think we passed TMI a decade and a half ago."

He talked about locker rooms so easily. Like he hadn't been beaten to a pulp in one.

"You talking to Sam about it?" Nick asked. Brady shook his head. "You talking to *anyone*?"

"I'm talking to you now, aren't I?"

"That's not what I mean."

"I talked to Jack and Patrick, a few months back."

"And?"

"And...it sucked," Brady replied.

It had been his own personal Spanish Inquisition, and not the fun Mel Brooks version. It was emasculating as hell, being taken out to lunch by his perfect big brother and his big brother's friend who Brady had looked up to since he was five. Ten minutes in and he'd felt like he was on one of those old *ABC Afterschool Specials*—except those shows never ended in bedroom advice from two men in their forties. It had been Patrick's bright idea, and Brady discovered that not only was he not as smart or as good looking as Jack, but he'd ended up on the shallow end of the gene pool with sex, too.

He wished he'd never said anything to them about his marriage being in trouble in the first place. At least Patrick was the only one he'd admitted the truth about himself to. He'd mostly avoided both of them since.

Nick folded his arms on the table. "I'd have thought Jack would be good at offering direction."

"Why? Because he's so old?"

"No, because he's a Dominant."

Brady's mouth dropped open. "Wait, how do you... Why do you know... What?"

Nick laughed. "I know about Lilly being a submissive. It wasn't hard to figure out that if she was one half of the equation, Jack was the other."

His jaw just about hit the floor. "How do you know about Lilly?"

"She told me."

"She *told* you?"

How did siblings talk to each other like that? How did anybody talk to *anyone* like that?

Actually, Lilly was the only person Brady could talk to about this. He'd practically been her and Jack's matchmaker, and his mad database skills had helped her win a case last year. But talking to your brother's wife about the fact that you both liked to kneel was fucking weird, and every time he'd been around her lately, he'd worried she could smell it on him, like some BDSM sixth sense.

I see kinky people. They don't know they're kinky, but they are.

"Dude, we can't talk about this," Brady said. "It's my brother and your sister."

"We're not talking about your brother and my sister. We're talking about you. That's what people do. They talk about shit with each other."

But talking about *this* shit made him feel as small and knocked around as the puck he'd just slammed across the air hockey table. And he couldn't tell if Nick was saying Jack could help because he had experience calling the shots, or if it was because his best buddy knew Brady liked having his shots called.

He chose to ignore the elephant in the room. Brady gnawed off a piece of his burger and purposely talked with his mouth full. "I guess I'm not people."

"I give up." Nick finished the rest of his crap-wich, balled up the wrapper and tossed it in the trash. Whew. Saved by the lack-of-table-manners. "Maybe if Sam gets the job it will help."

He'd keep his fingers crossed.

Back in the office that afternoon, Brady's concentration hit a wall. He tried to focus, but his thoughts kept going in circles. Nick was right. He should try talking to Sam. Not about their relationship, but what had gone down last night. At least then she could confirm what he'd thought had happened hadn't, and put him out of his misery.

His knee ached. Brady looked out his window. The sleet had changed to snow, the sky darkening even more than it already was at four o'clock. He wasn't one of the bosses for nothing. He opened a chat to Wendell.

"What do you say we call it a snow day and close up shop?" Brady typed.

"You're just trying to avoid an air hockey rematch."

He laughed. *"You want to get your ass beat twice in one day?"*

Wendell followed up a second later. *"I'll play caboose and lock up. You get home safe."*

His heart thudding in his chest, Brady packed his things and left.

* * *

There was another car in the driveway when Brady arrived home. One that belonged to Sam's parents.

He didn't mind his in-laws. They were good people, he saw them more often than he saw his own folks, and his fear of getting post-traumatic osteoarthritis was a bond he shared with Sam's mom. It wasn't that Brady and his parents *didn't talk*, they just... didn't talk. They FaceTimed with the kids when Dad could hold the phone up right, but Brady ended up looking up his mother's nose half the time. Sam's parents lived here, which meant his daughters spent more time with them, and Allegra contained her outbursts a little better when her favorite grandparents were around. But it meant he wasn't likely to talk to Sam about anything.

It was probably for the best. Stomping through the half foot of snow that had begun to stick, Brady pushed the door open.

"Daddy!" The sight of Hope's little body hurtling toward him was the image he was sure he'd remember when he walked her down the aisle.

"Hey, munchkin." Still in his coat, he picked her up. "How was school?"

"Good. Nana and Pop are here. They're helping Allegra with her homework."

"Isn't that nice of them. Who helped you with yours?"

"Nobody. I did it by myself."

"All by yourself? No way." She nodded. Kid had inherited her mother's brain, all right. She'd probably be doing calculus this time next year.

He put her down, toed off his shoes and shook off his coat. He slung it over the banister, then stopped himself and put it in the coat closet. That would make Sam happy. Hope took him by the hand and towed him into the kitchen.

"Daddy's home!" she said.

Sam turned around from the stove. Her hair was doing some kind of magical bouncy shit, soft and curling around her shoulders. She was wearing that sweater thing she loved, the one with the hood and the pockets, skin-tight leggings and slippers beneath it. But it wasn't her body, her clothes or her hair that got his attention.

It was her smile.

"Hope," Sam said. "Go and tell everyone it's time to wash up. I need to talk to Daddy."

Hope dutifully ran to the living room, and Brady stood awkwardly while Sam stirred something green and stringy in a pot.

"I have something to tell you," she said.

"What's that?"

The three beats of silence made him worry his lunchtime burger truly was giving him a heart attack.

She put down the ladle. "I got the job."

"For real?" He wanted to pick her up, to twirl her around in celebration, but he wasn't sure she'd appreciate the advance. "That's great!"

She laughed, looking almost giddy, and that was good enough. Man, she shouldn't have been stuck at home all this time. The woman in front of him seemed like the Sam he used to know.

"I can't believe they decided so quickly," he added.

"It turns out they always wanted me. One of the partners knew Arnold Dawes."

"No shit." He winced, then remembered the girls weren't in the room, and she didn't make any comments about his language anyway. Sam didn't talk about the congressman she'd worked for often, but Brady knew he'd been like a second father to her. "When did you find that out?"

"Yesterday. In the interview."

A weird tension coiled up in Brady's chest. She'd known and hadn't said anything? "That's cool. How come you didn't call me at work and tell me you'd gotten the job?"

She shrugged and went to the fridge to retrieve a jar of tomato sauce. "I was busy."

The tension wound tighter. "Oh. Okay."

Sam put the jar on the counter and paused. She took a step toward him, hesitant. Almost experimental. "And I wanted to tell you in person. I thought it would make me...happy."

There was a weight to her last word, like she was trying to tell him something.

Brady's thoughts slowed. He stared at her. "Did it?"

No longer joyful, Sam's smile morphed into the sly one she'd worn so often in college, the one that said she knew what he was thinking but didn't care to share it. "It did."

"Oh." His pulse was practically strangling him. "Good."

She went back to the stove, and Brady watched her move, the sway of her hips. He wanted her. Wanted permission to touch her.

Permission. Fuck if that didn't send shudders up his spine.

"I start on Monday," she said, her back to him. "My parents offered to come over to help with stuff, since HR sent me a boatload of paperwork."

He ignored the stab of jealousy that she'd told them first. "A boatload of paperwork for a part-time job?"

"They do everything by the book there. They even needed a photo of my diploma. But I'm going to have an early start from now on. I'll need you to get the girls out the door in the mornings."

Point taken. "Will do."

"I'd planned on telling them about the job at dinner. Allegra might freak less with my parents here."

"Right." He couldn't tear his eyes away from her ass. Her hair. Her everything. "So you like it?" he asked. "The job?"

It seemed silly to ask her now, after she'd already accepted it. But Sam didn't seem to mind. She moved the pot to the sink and dumped what was in it into a strainer.

"I do. It's mostly phones, mail and filing, but that's what I did in DC. And it won't disrupt the girls' schedules much."

"That doesn't matter if it makes you...happy."

He was testing his words now, too, looking for a reaction, but he'd also meant what he said.

He meant it in a way he didn't know if she'd understand.

Sam put the pot down. Her gaze was intense, a little quirk to her smile. Was something going on here? Or was he making shit up, seeing things he wanted to see?

"I can reach out to the sitters who responded to the ad after dinner," he added, because he'd finally gotten to that this morning. "See if any of them are free in the afternoon. In case you get stuck at work or something."

Her eyes remained steady. "I'd like that."

Lightning shot through him. Brady almost couldn't breathe. It seemed like something different, something *more* was buzzing beneath their words, but neither of them was acknowledging it, like some strange kinky version of Russian roulette.

"Okay. I will then."

Allegra came crashing into the room, Sam's parents behind her, the two of them waving around the homework they'd helped her with and going on about how much more work kids had to do these days. Brady greeted them, thanking them for coming by. They bookended Allegra at dinner, who didn't freak out at Sam's announcement. She wanted to know what on earth they were eating and if she'd still be able to go to dance class after school.

Crisis averted. Sam caught Brady's eye and smiled.

Once dinner was finished—a surprisingly good meal of edamame noodles that he hoped cleansed his system from lunch— Brady excused himself and went to the basement. It was part laundry room, part family room, part at-home workspace for him. He left the light off when he reached the bottom, not wanting anything to drive out the image of Sam's smile. It made him wired. Edgy.

It was dangerous, what they were dancing around. Dangerous how happy he wanted to make her.

Dangerous to expose the secret he'd kept from her.

Not so much a secret as he'd thought, but how? He'd been

positive she wanted one thing since those stupid books came out—an aggressive man in a three-piece suit.

Unless *she* wanted to be the one in the suit.

He fell into the chair, his whole body tingling. Was it possible? If so, he was sunk—turned on beyond belief, and absolutely fucking terrified. He'd kept a stopper in this bottle for so long, he didn't know what uncorking it would do to him.

But the idea of her coming home in fancy work clothes, tying him up and ordering him to please her had him rock hard at his desk. Closing his eyes, he plucked fantasies like candies from a jar, thinking of all the lewd acts a Dominant Sam could perform. Her dressed up in leather, demanding that he kneel. Tying him up and teasing him with that mouth of hers. He hadn't felt it in a while, but his wife's skills at oral were mind blowing. There were dozens of ways she could drive him into subspace, that drunken high feeling he'd read about in chat forums on FetLife before nerves had driven him to cancel his account. He imagined her introducing him to the prostate orgasm, wielding toys that would bring the kind of pleasure he'd only dreamed about or seen in porn.

The door at the top of the steps creaked open. Brady instinctively shot forward, hiding his hard-on beneath the desk. Sam appeared at the top of the steps. She was hidden in shadow, the hallway light silhouetting her, and didn't question why he had the lights off.

"Cassie texted." Her voice was different. Stronger, yet softer somehow. "She wants to celebrate my getting the job. So we're going out with everyone on Friday."

Brady swallowed. These sounded like commands, ones he had no problem obeying. "Okay."

"And my parents are taking the girls for the weekend."

"The whole weekend?"

"All of it."

Did that mean what he thought it meant? He couldn't see her face, but she didn't say anything else, and her words hung there like a warning or a promise.

"Okay," he said again. Sam waited a moment before closing the door.

Brady exhaled heavily. Part of him wanted to lock that door, wrap his fist around his dick and take care of things right now. But the rest of him wanted whatever opportunity she was offering him, wanted Sam's hands, Sam's words, Sam ordering him to the edge and allowing him to go over it.

Something new and crisp was crackling between them, something finally uncovered after all these years. He still wasn't sure that was where they were at—if she truly knew—but if she did and didn't hate him for it, then he could wait.

A weekend alone with her. It could be the opportunity he'd waited for.

And he wasn't going to wreck it.

9

"**W**hat are we drinking?"

Sam shimmied onto the barstool next to Cassie. "I'm not sure. The last time I had a drink was when we went out for Lilly and your birthdays."

"In September?"

"Sad, isn't it."

Five months since she'd had a night out. They'd gone to a strip joint, then met up with Brady, Jack and Patrick at a dance club. The night had ended with an argument with Brady, one that had spilled out in front of their friends. They'd gone home early because of it and didn't speak the rest of the night.

Hopefully tonight would be better.

She'd Ubered here after her parents picked up the girls—armed with instructions on Allegra's plan and a cooler packed with meals for the weekend—and met Cassie in front of Barrel 'n' Flask. The sports pub next to Fenway was decently packed, the bar top filled with people. She used to find places like this impossible, back when she was overweight and unemployed. But as Sam looked at the high-tops leading to the pool tables in the back, the exposed brick walls and TVs everywhere, conversations loud and boisterous, it felt like she'd come out of hiding.

"We have to do that again," Cassie said. "Gabe's been talking about making a gay bar night happen. Lilly is dying to see him and Nick in drag."

"I'd pay to see that."

"How have you *not* seen that by now?"

"What? Nick in drag, or been to a gay bar?"

"Either."

"Honey, in all the years Brady and Nick have been friends, not once has my husband stepped out of his manly comfort zone far enough for that to happen."

Although what was in Brady's comfort zone might be a whole new ballgame now.

She'd spent the last two days when she wasn't getting ready for work poring through her dirty book collection, trying to figure out what the Dominants in those stories did, what step to take next. Brady had been different, too. Off, but not distant, not lost in his work or unaware. He seemed *more* aware than usual—hanging up his coat, paying more attention when she talked—which she loved, but he was also quiet. Like he was intimidated by her, or waiting for something.

She wished he would say what he wanted. Fiction only helped so much.

"I vote for blood-orange cosmos," Cassie announced. "They're my fave."

Sam laughed. "I'll have one, but cut me off after that." A little liquid courage was good, but she wanted to stay sharp. Sloppy drunk was not her plan for tonight. Her plan involved the bikini wax she'd gotten today, and seeing her husband's reaction.

"Patrick joining us tonight?" Sam asked as Cassie waved down the bartender.

Heir to Dunham & Strauss, a local publishing empire, Patrick had been the worst kind of womanizer, a playboy to the fullest. It was a shock, to see just how much falling for Cassie had changed him.

"Eventually," Cassie replied. "He's promised not to act like a douche."

"That doesn't sound like much fun for you."

Cassie hid her laugh behind a curtain of her short, shiny brown hair.

"What?" Sam asked. "Isn't that what you said last year? He's a dick sometimes, but you liked it?"

It was before Thanksgiving, when she'd run into Cassie at Faneuil Hall Marketplace, and they'd had thirty seconds of adult conversation before Allegra was at it again.

"That's what I said."

Sam wanted to press the issue, but she and Cassie had only been friends a few months, certainly not long enough to ask if her hunch about her and Patrick was true. She'd figured their arguments were nothing more than foreplay—that their kink was having it more than a bit rough, something she'd read about in one particularly dirty book. Consensual non-consent, it was called. Finding out if she was right could mean she had a shot at someone to get advice from on her current situation with Brady. As much as she wanted what was building between them, she felt like a fawn in new stilettos walking into it. She'd thought about calling Jack, but he was on his honeymoon and it was weird anyway, to ask a man how best to dominate his baby brother.

Cassie ordered their drinks, winked at the bartender, then turned back around.

"Do you..." Sam began, then twisted her necklace, "...ever read romance novels?"

"Since I got this new job, I don't have time to read anything that isn't legislation or new regulations, but I watched my share of *telenovelas* with my sister and mother growing up."

Cassie was half Cuban, born in Miami, and Sam loved it when she flipped languages, switching easily from English into Spanish. "They're like Spanish soap operas, right?"

"Yup. They get pretty racy."

Racy, like hot and heavy? Or racy like I want to chain my husband to the bed tonight?

Yeah, she couldn't ask that.

"I've only read a few—" liar, liar, pants on fire, "—but I always found it crazy, how in the end the women got it all. The guy, the job, the sex. All those grand, perfect happy endings."

"It seems to me that you've got that now. The guy, the kids and the job." Their drinks arrived. Cassie raised her glass. "To working woman with their own real-life happy endings."

They clinked glasses. "To working women."

"You look fierce, by the way," Cassie said. "I want those shoes."

Sam dangled a foot out. "Allegra calls them my bandage heels."

It was because of how the black bands crisscrossed to midway up her calf. Open-toed with a three-inch spike heel, they'd been sitting in the back of her closet for eons. They weren't the best choice of footwear in tonight's icy weather, but she'd put them on anyway, along with the jeans she hadn't believed she'd fit back into.

"Well," Cassie said. "You might do some *damage* with them tonight."

Sam had to laugh. Damage wasn't what she wanted, but maybe inflict a tiny bit of pain?

Was that how a Dominatrix thought?

She'd certainly gone through pain herself in preparation for tonight. Once the sting of the wax job had faded, she had to admit she got why women did this. Having that thin strip of hair and bare skin beneath her clothes, with cleavage peeking out from under a leopard-print blouse and her hair in a high ponytail, made her feel sexy. Fearless. Wanton.

She'd been waiting forever to feel this way—like a butterfly, or Dorothy leaving Kansas, shedding an old, cracked, black-and-white skin. For so long she'd been uncomfortable in her body, working on fumes without a good night's sleep, cleaning up after her children and feeling guilty for taking a few minutes to shower on her own. She'd watched the world go by without her, everyone else moving forward while she was staying still.

Not anymore.

Her phone beeped. She took it out of her purse and read Brady's text.

"Just parked. Found Patrick, Nick and Gabe walking up from the T. Be there in a few."

"Looks like our boys are about to arrive."

They settled up, gathered their things and made their way to a table. "How are things with you and Brady, by the way?"

I almost got him off standing up in our kitchen the other night, but then he ignored me, so I dunno! "Okay, I guess. Why?"

"Patrick noticed he wasn't his usual self at the wedding."

"You mean how he didn't eat half the cake on his own?"

"No, because he wasn't joking around."

They found a table, pulled out their chairs and sat. "I think we could all use a break from Brady's jokes once in a while."

"Fair point. But you guys are okay?"

Across the pub, the front door opened. Four men walked in—Nick first with his blond hair and dimpled smile, Gabe behind him looking like a Calvin Klein model. Patrick entered next, all crisp suit and dark hair and goatee. And then there was Brady, pulling up the rear in his favorite leather bomber jacket and Buffalo Plaid shirt, beard full, curly hair mussed from the breeze. They were all laughing, but then his gaze swept the room, like he was seeking her out. Blue turned to turquoise, eyes bright and beaming as he gave her a sheepish smile.

"Brady is kind of like a puppy sometimes," Sam said. "Goofy, loveable and full of energy." She crossed her legs and took a sip of her drink. "But sometimes puppies need to be reined in."

* * *

Jesus Christ. Was Sam trying to kill him?

Seeing her in a dress last week was incredible, but this, tonight, was unreal. Tight jeans. Shirt that dipped low enough to tease. Her hair all swooped up and pretty, showing off her neck and shoulders. And heels he'd had far too many thoughts about when she'd bought them years ago. She looked the part he'd wanted her to play, his wildest fantasy come to life.

Breathe. He needed to breathe. There was a good chance she was dressed up to celebrate—he would *not* get his hopes up—but something inside him whispered she was wearing all that for him.

"There's Forrester, Schaeffer and Pierce's newest star," Patrick said as he, Brady and Gabe neared the table, Nick staying behind to grab a round of beers. "Congratulations, Samantha."

Patrick put a hand on Cassie's shoulder as he said it. Brady was glad the guy's touch remained on his girlfriend. While he'd never done anything more than kiss Sam's hand in the past—a thing he'd done more to show off in front of Cassie than anything else—tonight Brady didn't want Patrick touching his wife. Him or anyone else.

"Thank you," Sam said, raising her glass. "I'm rejoining the working world."

"And I," Gabe said, "can't wait to see your smiling face when I come in every day."

"Aww, Gabe. You're gonna make me blush." But Sam was looking at Brady when she said it.

Was she calling out his blush from the other night? He'd never been good at reading subtext. But his pulse was hammering like Animal from the Muppets on a drum solo.

Nick returned with a round and they all sat. Sam wasn't touching Brady—she was keeping her body more than a few inches away—but that was okay. He could wait. He could wait all night for her to make a move, if it meant that later she'd drive him trembling over the edge.

Fuck, he needed a drink. Brady reached for his beer and took a sip. Was it possible to be nervous as shit but incredibly turned on at the same time? He looked at Sam, feeling like he was in quicksand and she was his rope and anchor, but she'd rejoined the conversation around them.

"So," Patrick said, "let's hear about this job."

Brady drifted into his own thoughts as everyone talked, glanced at the games on the TV. Going to this pub had become a bit of a tradition, starting back when he and Patrick were trying to get a grieving Jack out of the house.

Seeing his brother get remarried was a massive relief, and a bit annoying. It was one more perfect thing he'd done. Jack had worried how people would react to the sixteen-year age gap between him and Lilly, but he should've known he'd have the full Archer Clan support. Mom and Dad loved her once they'd had a taste of her cooking, and Jack's son, Josh, had come around after a while. They'd all been visiting this weekend, and as much as Brady loved his nephew, watching everyone fawn over Jack was too much for Brady, and he wasn't too upset they were all gone.

He was glad Lilly and Jack weren't here tonight either, although being around Patrick was no picnic. It was during the lunch in this very bar that Patrick had declared Jack the "authority on getting smacked around," then followed Brady outside when he'd needed an escape. Stupidly, he'd told Patrick what was going on—the first time he'd gotten the mangled words out. Just like Nick, Patrick had asked if he'd talked to Sam, which of course he couldn't, and Brady was sure since then that Patrick could see weakness stamped all over him. He'd had two ways of being around his group since that day— full-on comedian, or completely silent.

He didn't want to be either tonight. All he wanted was for Sam to give him that smile again, the one that had been in his head all week.

He kept waiting as the night went on. For a solid hour, everyone was talking, and Brady twisted his ring beneath the table, stuck between being focused on Sam and not really listening. Cassie mentioned how demanding the firm could get, how busy Sam was going to be, and Brady checked the time. Maybe Sam had no intention of anything happening tonight. Maybe she was just enjoying the attention.

He couldn't take the disappointment. *He* wanted her attention. And he wasn't getting it.

"How busy are you gonna be?" he asked. "It's just reception."

Sam turned on him, eyes flashing. "Is that what you think?"

His cheeks heated. It wasn't the smartest thing, to poke fun at her new job, but he stood a better chance of getting what he wanted if Sam was a little angry. It certainly worked that way the other night.

"Sure, you'll have stuff to do," he said. "But you won't be as busy as *I* am at work."

Nick snorted. "Dude, I was at your job the other day. You spent half of it playing air hockey. You're nothing but a glorified webmaster."

Brady grinned wider, not minding the way his joke was backfiring if it got Sam's attention. She was still staring, her chin raised in challenge.

Take the bait, Sammy. Put me in my place.

"Air hockey takes skill," he said to Nick. "And that word is from like 1998."

"And why just master?" Gabe added. "Girls can be computer programmers."

Nick laughed. "Truth! What do they call female web developers? A web—"

Sam cut him off. "Mistress."

She looked straight at Brady as she said it, perfectly cool and calm. Her tongue came out to moisten her lips, and she finally gave him that hint of a smile, her mouth open in that *gotcha* way she used to.

God. That word and look confirmed everything. She knew, and this was happening, and oh fucking God.

Sam reached for her purse. "I think it's time for Mr. Funny and me to go home."

Mechanically, Brady obeyed, his ears ringing as he threw on his coat. Cassie pouted, saying it was too early, that they should stay, but Sam shook her head politely and slipped on her own jacket. "We need to get to bed."

Bed. Not sleep. *Bed.*

Brady was suddenly way too turned on to be in public. He fumbled for his wallet, ready to pull out some cash for the single beer he'd had, but Nick waved him off.

"My treat," he said. "You guys are a cheap date."

They made it to the car without speaking. Sam said nothing as he opened the door for her, the smile still on her face. When they hit the Pike, she placed a hand on his thigh.

Brady glanced down to see her slim fingers across his leg and gulped. Legit *gulped.*

"Eyes on the road," she scolded. "Keep your hands at nine and three."

"Yes, ma'am." There. He said it. Finally said it. Although it wasn't the name he really wanted to call her.

She slapped his thigh lightly. "Behave."

It nearly made him swerve into the next lane.

Brady focused on the road, getting dizzy as Sam made lazy strokes over his jeans, nails drifting with the occasional scratch. He was so damn hard, erection pressing against his zipper through his boxers as her hand got closer and closer. He wanted to ask what brought this on, why she was being like this when she hadn't wanted anything in ages, but he was so relieved to feel it that he didn't want to risk mucking it up with a question.

He banged a left into the driveway, his breathing impossibly fast as he cut the engine. Sam shifted in her seat and replaced her left hand with her right.

"You looked like you were about to combust tonight," she said, soft and sexy.

"I was."

Two of her fingers tiptoed upward, until she found his hard-on and mapped it through his jeans. Brady's hips shot forward into her touch. Jesus. She made that humming noise from the other night, the one that was like jet fuel to his libido, and Brady braced a palm against the steering wheel to steady himself as she unbuttoned his fly.

Unapologetic. Fast. Like she owned what was beneath it.

"Did you get yourself all worked up?" She shoved his pants open and snaked her hand into his boxers. His breath shuddered out of him when her fingers met the slick tip of his dick. "Oh, yes you did. Poor thing. We'd better fix that."

She began stroking him, right there in the front seat. The sound of her fist on his flesh was too much. Brady huffed out a breath. Pinched his eyes shut.

"Such a good boy," she cooed, and his entire body went hot. No, he couldn't handle this. Couldn't handle her seeing through him when he'd kept this wall up for so long. His thoughts went in spirals, words he was unable to choke out as she jerked and twisted, pleasure so blinding it hurt.

Sam stopped stroking. Brady groaned but held himself still, head mashed against the seat.

She clucked her tongue at him. "Are you dying to come?"

A strangled noise came out of him. She was taunting him, teasing him again. The mockery in her tone was humiliating, but it felt good and was true, so he nodded.

"Good." Sam tucked him, throbbing and desperate, back in his pants. She zipped his fly, then leaned in close and whispered, "Then I guess you'd better unlock that car door and take me inside."

Brady opened his eyes and looked at her. His brain, so often all over the place, centered on three little words:

Take her. Inside.

Complicated turned simple. Suddenly he knew exactly what to do.

"May I take you?" he asked quietly. "Inside?"

A lifetime passed before she answered. "I thought you'd never ask."

10

Brady barely registered the cold as he followed Sam into the house. She pulled her keys from her purse and let them in, the front entrance silent and dark. The emptiness without the kids there was as eerie as it was thrilling. Sam closed the door, then reached out to finger the buttons on Brady's shirt. His heart pounded as she toyed with them.

Did she know the power she had over him already?

She popped a button open and smiled up at him, fiendish like a cat. "I like you like this."

He looked down. Another button came undone. "Like what?"

Sam flattened her hand on his chest and shoved him backward. Brady could've easily overpowered her—he had eleven inches on her and over a hundred pounds—but he gave no resistance, grunting when his back collided with the wall. Sam put a finger over his mouth.

"Quiet," she said. "I like you quiet."

His eyes damn near rolled back in his head.

He wanted to touch her, but the fierceness in her expression kept him exactly where he was. Sam reached for his coat collar, tugged off the sleeves until his arms were free. She dropped it on the floor, and Brady nearly made a crack about it belonging in the coat closet but cut himself off in time. The wrong word could snap this in two like a twig under his boot. Sliding one jean-clad leg between his, she clasped his hands and drew his wrists upward until she'd captured them above his head.

"Kiss me," she ordered.

He leaned in, and suddenly it felt brand new between them again. Like their first kiss in a dorm hallway, like they were both young and uncertain, exhaling shaky breaths until he closed the distance between them and his mouth crashed against hers.

He kissed her like she liked to be kissed, the way he'd somehow memorized back in the day. Open mouth. Lower lip searing over hers. Hot. Messy. Like they were trying to consume one another. He danced his tongue out to meet hers, and a charge went through him when she quickly took the lead. Her teeth drove over his bottom lip in a sharp bite, everything going fast and aggressive. She released his hands and drove hers into his hair, gripping madly. His body bucked off the wall when her hips met his.

How long had it been since she kissed him like this? Years, probably. But this kiss was different.

He wasn't sure she'd *ever* kissed him like *this*.

She broke off and looked at him, eyes blazing. "I love that you kept your hands above your head."

"You didn't tell me to move them."

She hummed, a noise of approval that practically vibrated through him. Her hands fell to his chest again, blunt thumbnails rasping over his nipples, which were surprisingly tender beneath his shirt. "What an obedient little pet you are."

Brady grunted again. His hips arched toward hers.

"You like that?" she asked.

He nodded, and Sam smiled wildly. He was sure some kind of horrible joy rushed through her at the flash of heat on his cheeks.

"Well then, let's treat you like a proper little puppy." She stepped several paces back. His body ached at the space she'd put between them until she crooked a finger and said, "Come."

Brady didn't waste time moving over to her. Sam turned around, and he remained a step behind her as she walked up the stairs. He didn't mind—the view was spectacular. Her ass in those jeans, the magnificent roll of her shoulders as her jacket came off, hooked on the banister on the landing.

When they crossed the threshold of the bedroom, Sam flicked on a lamp and turned to face him. Brady remained immobile, waiting for her command.

"Shirt off," she said.

He did as he was told, removing his button-down. He grasped the tee he had on beneath it, but Sam put a hand up to stop him.

"Did I tell you to take off both of them?"

He froze. "No, ma'am."

"Hmm," she said, but it wasn't that pleased little noise that made his skin buzz. "I don't think I like that name. But for now—" She made a fist in the tee he'd layered beneath his shirt. "Arms up."

Brady raised his arms until they were once again above his head. She pulled his shirt up, ruffling his hair as it came off.

"I like you quiet *and* messy," she said. "Pants off next. Boxers and socks, too."

He scrambled to do her bidding, shoving them off and kicking everything to the side. He hadn't been naked in front of her in a while, but any self-consciousness he might've had evaporated when she ran a finger along his chest.

"So pretty," she murmured.

Brady blushed and beamed. It was the Sam he remembered from college, approving and accepting, like some goddess allowing him into her service. She ran a palm up one of his thighs, over his belly and down the other leg. His dick twitched at the nearness of her touch, greedy and pulsing. His balls ached. How long was she going to keep him like this?

"Your legs are like tree trunks, pet," she said. "I want to climb them. I want to ride your powerful, beautiful body like a Ferris wheel until I've wrung every last shaking drop of pleasure from the both of us."

Oh, Jesus. It wasn't just the promise of what she was offering—it was hearing that nickname again.

Pet.

Being called that so easily by her was too intimate. Too terrifying. It implied safety and vulnerability and being taken care of, and he wasn't sure he was safe here yet. Safety meant honesty. Openness. And they hadn't discussed a thing. Not that talking was his top priority right now, but still. How had she known he wanted this? If she knew, why hadn't she said anything?

How long had she kept this part of herself secret from him, too?

"What?" she asked, pulling her hand back.

Brady didn't know what she'd seen in his eyes, but it meant she'd stopped touching him.

He shook his head. "Nothing."

He was breathing too fast to think anyway. He was shaking now, this crazy need to kneel no matter what it did to his knee pulsing through him. He wanted to serve her. To close his eyes and let her command him.

His thoughts derailed even further when she stepped toward the bed.

"Stay," she said. "Watch."

He did, eyes glued to her as the top came off. Her bra next. She undid the straps on those pointy heels, slipped them off and shimmied her jeans down her waist. She shed her panties, and then he saw it.

"When did you do...that?"

Sam stroked a finger over the landing strip of soft, downy red. "Today."

Brady stared. He'd never minded the hair, just like he'd never minded her heavy or in the mornings without makeup. Sam in her natural state, in a way no one but him ever saw her, was what he liked, but this was another sign that she'd planned for tonight. He wanted her to know how happy that made him.

He was also curious as fuck to know how smooth she felt.

"Like what you see?" she asked.

He nodded. Sam sank to the bed and spread her legs. "Then come here and touch."

Brady staggered a few steps forward, ignoring the incessant pulse between his legs. He kept one hand clenched in a fist while reaching the other toward his wife's body. The fist was necessary. He was sure once he touched her, once her bare thigh grazed his, nothing would stop him from grabbing his dick. But when he traced a fingertip along her silky skin, Sam hissed in a breath, and Brady forgot everything except her pleasure.

"Feel different?" he asked.

Her mouth opened, then she smiled. "Feels more...intense."

Well that was a fucking win. He drifted his touch, feather soft, on the outside of her lips until her head fell back and she winged her legs wider. Her clit peeked out, pink and wet. Brady grazed it with his pointer finger and paused when she jumped.

"May I?" he asked.

She hadn't given him permission, but then again, she never had before. He didn't know the rules here, didn't know how to play this new game. Sam gazed up at him, not at all less dominant because she was sitting while he stood. He was her slave, always had been, and she knew it now, knew it in ways that flipped their world upside down. Right now though, he wasn't her husband. He wasn't her equal.

He was her submissive. Her pet.

"Do you remember what I like?" she asked.

Oh, Brady remembered. He remembered she was more sensitive on her right than her left, remembered that she liked to be pounded after she came, liked *harder* and *more* to ride out the pulses until the sheets got soaking wet. "I do."

"Then you may get a condom."

Disappointment and excitement crashed together. He wasn't sure if she wasn't letting him touch her because she didn't want him to, or if she was as close to the edge as he was and needed to wait.

Wrenching a nightstand drawer open and digging his hand under the layers of pajamas and underwear he'd hid the box under, Brady pulled out a foil package. He didn't mind using one. They'd used condoms and the pill for a while, and as worked up as he was, the barrier would help him not be a two-pump chump. But he had half a mind to check the expiration date on the damn thing.

"They're still good," Sam said. "I looked."

Brady nodded quickly, ripped it open and sheathed himself. He didn't know how far they were taking this, didn't know if they were ever going to talk about safewords or limits or any of the things he'd read about online, but Brady chose to rely on seventeen years of history with Sam and trust her.

He was safe here, with her.

She stood, came over to him and caressed his tip through the extra space in the rubber. That smile of hers returned when he shuddered.

"Excited?" she asked.

Did she need to ask? "Out of my mind." If she didn't let him inside her soon, he was going to die.

"On the bed," she said. "Face up."

He collapsed backward onto it, clumsy in his eagerness and giant size. The mattress bounced and Sam sniggered and shook her head. Something about her laugh was a sharp contrast to the lust flooding through him. He liked it, though, liked her contempt in a way that made him feel small instead of the colossal beast he was.

Sam climbed on top and bracketed his chest with her palms. It took every damn ounce of willpower he had not to thrust up when she lowered herself onto him. So hot. So tight. It was all Brady could do to palm her hips and hold on. She pulled him in deeper, then winced and held still.

"You okay?" he gritted out.

She bent her head and laughed, a sound that was more frustration than anything else. "I forgot how big you get."

He had to smile. But this wasn't a moment for his ego. It had been too long, and her body needed to acclimate. "Here." He shifted his body down slightly, changing the angle. "Better?"

Sam nodded and closed her eyes. Her ponytail slipped over her shoulder, the ends tickling his chest as she moved again. Slower now, she let him ease inside, waiting until he was fully seated before opening her eyes.

"Much better," she said, eyelids heavy.

It was the drowsy, full look he remembered being shocked by when she'd asked him once to hold still and let her feel. Her hands drifted up to his neck, and then she was kissing him, tongue seeking and teasing. Brady lifted his head off the pillow to catch more of her kiss, but she pulled away, rasping her open lips over his.

"Such a good boy," she whispered.

"God, S—" He wanted to say Sammy, but the name didn't feel right now. She wasn't his Sam, not here, not like this. "So good."

"Mmmm," she hummed softly, then rolled her hips, and Brady's pleasure spiked. She repeated the motion, making a circle he felt every inch of. His torso jerked involuntarily. "That good, too?"

"Fuck, yes." His words were a hoarse whisper.

"What about it?"

She rolled on the upstroke again and his hands lifted sharply. Christ, had that been something she'd read in a book? Because if so, he was sorry he'd hated on them. "All of it."

She laughed and did it again, swiveling faster, and Brady gasped, his release dangerously close.

"Poor thing," she said. "So close to the edge you can't stand it. I feel you shaking."

He flinched, needing to look away because those words struck at him in that uncomfortable, powerful way, but she wouldn't let him. Two hands on his neck, she dragged his gaze back to hers. Bending forward, she brought her sweaty cheek to his, talking in his ear.

"So sad. So close. You want it so badly. You're gonna lose it any second now, aren't you? I can tell."

Her words were singsong, teasing, delicious and cruel. Brady had to pinch his eyes shut. He was smiling and he wasn't. He liked it and he didn't. She rocked her hips harder, and he squirmed beneath her, loving this and hating this and *God*, she was going to make him come.

"Please stop," he begged. "I can't..."

"Please stop what?" Her words were sharp. She swiveled again. "Stop this?"

"No...*shit*...I—"

"You don't want me to stop. You want to come. You want to feel it happen."

She had to stop talking. If he had a shot in hell of pleasing her, she. Had. To. Stop.

"Say it, pet. Say you want to come."

"I wanna come," he moaned. He sounded pathetic. Pushed to a place deep in his head. In his body, deep in the pleasure. And he was about to blow.

"No," she snapped. Brady's eyes flew open. "Don't you dare come. Watch me first."

But it was too late. His body took over, his senses obliterated by the sudden crush of his release. His orgasm tore through him, and Brady gripped the sheets as his eyes slammed closed. He turned his face to the side, cutting himself off from her even as their bodies were still joined, because it was the only way he could withstand the mortification.

Sam's hands were on his chest when he recovered. Brady couldn't meet her eyes, but looked between their bodies instead, one palm at her thigh, urging her up. She swung a leg around, moving off him. Thank God. The condom was full, and the last thing they needed was two years' worth of pent-up jizz breaking it open, birth control pills or not. He tied it off and threw it in the trash, but kept his back to her, not sure what to do next.

It took a few moments, but she finally spoke first.

"Did you like that?" Sam asked quietly. "Me taking control?"

His throat went dry. "Couldn't you tell?"

"I think so."

Her voice was soft. Curious and forgiving. Relief poured through him, but he hadn't done what she'd asked. He'd come when she'd instructed him not to, when she should've gone first. He turned around to find her on her side, nipples tight, looking like a calendar model, his own personal porn star.

"Let me," he said shakily. "Let me please you."

Sam didn't say a word. She simply shifted onto her back, and the look on her face was something that hovered on amazement.

He hadn't done anything to deserve that look yet. He needed her praise, but first he needed the euphoria of making her come. To prove he could still rock her damn world.

He lumbered over her, shimmied between her thighs. Nuzzling her slippery, nearly bare skin, he kissed, then parted her flesh with his thumbs. One glancing touch over her clit, and her body jerked. He did it again. And again. He wasn't teasing her. She'd taught him one steamy night years ago that she liked to wait, that she held herself off sometimes for hours to give herself a more powerful release.

He did it two more times, then stopped, knowing she liked that agony. She lifted her head and growled. Actually fucking growled.

"You do still know what I like," she said.

He did. He bent his head and licked, first lightly, then more firmly, then buried his nose against her. His first purposeful suck had one of her hands slamming against the blanket while the other found a home in his hair. Brady kept at it, pouring out his apology and adoration with the movements of his lips and tongue. Good Lord, he remembered her taste, remembered getting drunk on it in college. Who needed a keg when he could get inebriated off Sam? Brady flicked his tongue endlessly until he found what he was looking for.

"There—right there—*Jesus*, yes."

Yeah, he still knew all her spots, even if she hadn't let him near them in a while.

He banished the thought when her thighs began to shake. He placed one palm on her lower belly, used the other to slide two fingers inside. She was scorching hot, so sloppy wet he was hard again in an instant, but there was nothing else, no thought other than Sam's collision with release.

It was always violent when she came, a goddamn firestorm of gasps and shudders and her back arching off the bed. Her belly tensed beneath his palm, she squeezed his fingers and her clit pulsed against his tongue, then she cried out and thrashed so much he had to go up on his elbows to stay with her. He eased off with his mouth, then fucked her harder with his fingers, pounding as her clutch in his hair grew sharp enough to hurt. She wasn't going to come a second time—this was more a way to bring her down when she was flying too high—and he grinned as she drenched his hand before she sagged against the bed, spent.

She let go, exhaling into a smile as she scratched the top of his head. Brady glowed with pride in having served her.

There was so much to say. So much to talk about.

"Did—"

"Did—"

They both said it at the same time. Brady laughed. "You go first," he said, wanting the *Did you like that as much as I did?* to come from her.

"Did you reach any of the sitters yet?" she asked.

He froze. They were still naked. Still breathing hard, and that's what she was asking?

"I'm sorry. I forgot." He'd lost track of the task over the last few days, too absorbed in what was going on between them.

"No, I'm sorry," Sam replied quickly. "Wrong thing to say. It's just...on my mind."

That helped ease the sting, but he hated the sudden fallout. Without warning, they were back to *them* again. No longer a glorious Domme and her pet. They were back to Brady and Sam, Mom and Dad. Back to the husband who was disappointing his wife.

She stroked his head, fingers gentle. "I liked tonight."

Her words were as soft as her touch. He settled against her, head relaxing on her warm belly. "Me, too."

She kept petting him, and that was something, at least. Brady sank into the sensation and let his eyes drift closed. He wasn't satisfying her out of the bedroom, but if he could do it here, maybe it would be enough to save them.

11

———

Sam woke up on Saturday morning groggy and alone.

She hadn't fallen asleep right away the night before. She'd dozed while Brady slept, naked on the bedspread until she'd realized she hadn't taken her pill. She'd managed to get up without waking him and went to the bathroom to down it, then cleaned herself up. When she glanced at her reflection, she'd barely recognized the person she saw. Her ponytail was loose and unkempt, her eye makeup smudged to all hell. She looked freshly fucked, and shocked beyond belief.

Something had happened between her and Brady, something big they couldn't ignore. When they'd been playing at Dominant and submissive, those roles and what they meant so clear, she'd felt like a magnet snapped into place. And she'd never been as turned on by her husband as she had last night.

They needed to talk.

But Brady looked too peaceful, cocooned beneath the blankets when she'd returned. She'd eyed him, all cozy, sleepy and warm, remembering a moment when they'd first brought Allegra home from the hospital and she'd only stopped crying when she fell asleep on Brady's chest. It was one of the things she loved, too, curling up in his big burly arms. How long had it been since they'd cuddled?

Since she'd woken in his embrace? She wanted that more than she wanted to break this silence, and she'd been too enamored at the prospect of a night without being needed by a screaming child to do anything but sleep. So she dove in beside him, got as close as she dared and closed her eyes.

Apparently that was a massive mistake.

Sam reached over and picked up her phone from the nightstand. Brady had sent her a text.

"Problem with the servers again. Gotta go to the office."

It had a timestamp of 6:42 a.m.

She should've tried harder to wake him up. Only now in the light of the day, rubbing her eyes as the sun streamed in through the windows, did she think about all the ways she'd fucked up last night. And she had the sneaking suspicion he'd gone into work to avoid her.

"Hope everything is okay," she typed, then fell back against the sheets.

That question about the sitters had definitely bothered him, but she'd done worse than that. There'd been no discussion of safewords, nothing about limits and certainly no aftercare. She knew better than that—she'd read enough books to know that was a thing, one *she* held the reins on. It was her job to initiate stuff like that, but she'd been too wrapped up in the moment, infatuated by what was happening.

Having Brady do her bidding was a rush like she'd never experienced. The way he'd kept his eyes on her as her clothes fell to the floor, his hands clenched by his sides. She'd always had a thing for his legs, his carved, muscular calves. He might not be nineteen anymore, but he was still an Adonis as far as she was concerned. And she'd loved the sound of him gritting out words when he was stretched out beneath her, trembling and needy, all that masculine strength tethered for her.

How had she not known this about herself?

She'd always been a dominating personality. It was why she'd been into politics in the first place, and why she'd chosen Brady. He'd practically rolled over and begged for belly rubs when she complimented him in college. Calling him pet had been a surprise, but it rolled off her tongue so easily, and it seemed to suit him, especially when she'd made him stand still. There was something so attractive about a strong man leashed to the spot, and she'd loved seeing her husband strain for her, the lean of his body as she moved away, a puppy struggling to obey his master.

She'd thought he hadn't wanted her anymore. That they'd lost this spark. But they'd reclaimed it last night, lit that fire that used to fuel them and turned it into an inferno. Something fierce had gripped her when she'd taunted him about how close to coming he was. She'd wanted to push him more, to subject him to the torture of her words.

But she'd fucked up. She'd pushed him too far, ordering him to hold off when it was obvious he was on the brink. She hadn't asked what he needed or taken care of him afterward, either, and now he'd shut himself away from her because of it.

Her phone buzzed with a reply.

"It's going okay," he texted. *"I've got a finger in the dam, for now."*

Sam stared at his words. Maybe she could get him to talk to her if she made up some kind of technological excuse first.

"Can you chat? I'm having trouble with the computer."

Brady was slow to respond. *"In like an hour?"*

"Okay."

That gave her time to gather her thoughts. She had things to do, too. The grocery list had to be written. She had a week's worth of the girls' lunches to plan, not to mention laundry and getting herself ready for work. But for now, she was in a daze, wandering through the house in a bathrobe after a long, hot shower.

It was strange to not have any demands on her, no cleaning or acting as kitchen staff or answering constant questions. Her parents were taking the girls to a movie today as part of their sleepover weekend, which amazingly was going well. They'd stated they wanted more quality time with their grandchildren before they moved, whenever that was going to be, and Sam had zero problem with that.

She hadn't told the girls her parents were moving yet. The

change could send Allegra into a downward spiral. But not having an actual date meant Sam couldn't plan for anything, and what Allegra didn't know yet wouldn't hurt her. So for the moment, Sam relished the rare silence and read *The Washington Post* feed on her phone.

She swiped through articles, skimming through the stories about the Left and the Right, the battle for power in government.

"People are attracted to power," Dawes had told her one morning when they were racing across The Hill. Hoping he'd be with her for the next midterm elections, he'd educated her on the Ps of Primary season: projected returns, percentages, precincts. But the one that was most important was power.

She'd listened closely as he'd explained that power existed everywhere—in nature, in the food chain, in every organization and relationship. "Figure out what people need from your power, then learn how to wield it."

She hadn't felt powerful in over a decade. She did now. So what did Brady need from her? How could she give it, and were there times she could decide not to?

If only she had someone to talk to. In her books, the characters had a person to ask questions, an older, wiser guide. She needed someone like that for herself. A kinky fairy godmother.

An hour later, she was dressed and settled at the computer in the basement. She logged in to her user account and opened up chat. The icon next to Brady's name was green.

"Hi," she typed. *"Still a good time?"*

"Yeah. What's wrong with the computer?"

Shit. She'd forgotten to come up with an excuse. *"I'm trying to pay the bills, but the bank site isn't working."*

"Did you clear your cache?"

She hadn't, of course, so she let him talk her through the process. Fictional problem notwithstanding, Brady was always good with stuff like this. Even at school, he'd fix her laptop when it wasn't working, and seemed to intrinsically know how to work every device they owned.

"All fixed?" he typed.

"Yes. But..." How should she approach this? Might as well be straightforward. *"I'd like to talk about last night."*

A pause followed. *"Okay..."*

Was he nervous? If so, she wanted to shield him from that, to drive out any feelings other than him knowing she'd loved every minute of it.

"I can't stop thinking about it," she wrote.

Her heart pounded as she waited for his response. The little dots that showed him typing finally bounced.

"Neither can I."

Sam's body tingled. She sat up straighter. *"I want you to tell me something."*

"What's that?"

Immediate obedience. She liked that. *"When did you start wanting me like that?"*

"I never stopped."

Her heart stuttered. *"Even when I was pregnant and fat and exhausted?"*

"You're always beautiful to me, Sam."

Her insides pinched together—a tightening in her sternum. *"I thought you'd stopped wanting me."*

Her confidence was wavering. But she had to be honest.

"Not the case at all."

"Then why—"

She stopped typing before hitting return. Then why what? Why had he never tried anything when she didn't want to be touched? What had she expected of him?

"—didn't you ever say anything?"

"I'm not good at talking. Or...initiating...stuff."

It hit her, clear as day. Brady was not the initiator, never had been. Every time they were intimate, it was because she'd struck the match. And now, after last night, she finally understood why.

Sam tapped her fingers once, twice, then started to type.

"How long have you wanted me to dominate you?"

Maybe this was a new beginning for them, or maybe it was the beginning of the end. Either way, she had to know.

A good minute passed before he keyed a response.

"I always have."

God. Her legs swung open of their own will. She sat forward in the chair, watching those bouncing dots stop, then start, then stop again. Clearly he was trying to get words out, but something was holding him back. She put her hands to the keyboard.

"You can ask me questions, too, you know."

"I thought—" His typing abruptly cut off. Sam waited. *"—that wasn't what you wanted."*

She frowned. *"What do you mean?"*

"I thought you wanted what's in your books."

"You know about my books?"

"You left your iPad out a few times."

She wanted to hide under the table. But she had nothing to be ashamed of.

*"You mean you think I wanted **you** to dominate **me**?"*

"Bingo."

"No way. I get more turned on when you're the one who's all edgy and begging."

He didn't reply, but she could picture him sitting in his office, chin tipped down, pupils dilated. He started typing, then stopped again.

What did he need? She could read her friends without even talking to them, but her husband's emotions were something she needed a damn password for.

"Brady, if you want something from me, all you have to do is ask."

The dots bounced. *"Can we do it again?"*

She had to laugh at his sudden eagerness. *"As a matter of fact, I want you on your knees in front of me as soon as possible."*

"God."

It was like stepping out of reality. Like they were slipping into new roles that allowed them to break out of their old ones and be different people for each other. *"Tell me what you liked about it."*

"I liked making you come."

Sam inhaled slowly. She'd forgotten the ache that spread

through her after an orgasm, sated only by a good hard fucking. Clearly, Brady hadn't.

"*I liked that, too,*" she wrote. "*Know what else I liked?*'"

"*What?*"

"*Watching you force back your pleasure until you couldn't take it anymore.*"

"*Sammy...*"

She smirked at the screen. She'd bet he was adjusting himself beneath his desk. But she wanted more of that, more of seeing those muscular hands twisted into fists on the sheets, wanted him hungry for her, begging.

"*When can you leave work?*"

"*I can finish faster if we stop talking about this, LOL.*"

For the first time in a while, his joking nature made her laugh. Sam responded with a winking smiley face. "*Get your ass off chat, then.*"

"*Okay.*"

She'd thought he'd say *yes ma'am*, but she'd said she didn't like that. She hadn't hated it, but it didn't fit as well as calling him pet did.

Something to discuss later.

He arrived home shortly after lunch. She opened the door for him. Shoulders huge in his winter coat, he looked massive and intense—a Herculean ex-linebacker geek. A blast of arctic air blew in with him, but she didn't think it was the cold that had gotten his cheeks so red. He was silent as he took off his coat, gaze never breaking from hers even as he stomped off the snow and unlaced his boots. He unzipped his hoodie, and those colossal arms stretched the sleeves of his gray Captain America T-shirt. It felt like the Brady she'd met in college was in front of her, the one who'd wanted her so desperately, and she wanted to ask where he'd been all this time.

She tugged him to her by the front of his shirt and kissed him instead. A hard, wet, breathless kiss. His hands inched up, but they remained motionless until she placed them on her waist. He skimmed his palms along her hip bones, his breath came out hot, and when their bodies collided, a moan escaped him.

Sam grinned when they came up for air. "I have something to show you."

"Okay."

She turned, knowing he would follow. When they stepped inside the bedroom, Sam swiped to unlock the iPad she'd left on the bed, putting it back down so Brady could see the site she'd left it open to.

"Sex toys?" he asked.

"Very specific ones."

They were all BDSM toys, things she'd read about but only imagined using. But Brady remained immobile, staring at the bed, quiet as he fiddled with his wedding ring.

"Does this make you uncomfortable?" she asked.

He shrugged.

"What does it make you?"

"Horny," he replied, then laughed. But that ring was still turning.

Brady barely talked most of the time, when he wasn't cracking a joke. Now he seemed almost mute. Not that she could blame him. She hadn't done things correctly. Half because she wanted to soothe him, and half because she wanted to touch, Sam came up next to him and ran her palm along his back. He responded with a short, sharp inhale.

"I know we moved too fast last night," she said softly. "We didn't talk about safewords. You know what those are?"

"Yes." How he knew, she didn't ask. Maybe he'd read more of her books than he let on.

"That was my mistake. I was too wrapped up in this. In you." Slipping her hand under his shirt, she scratched lightly. "Forgive me?"

Brady shivered and nodded. "Of course."

"Thank you," Sam said. "Now, go. Look. Show me what you like."

He inhaled again, this time longer, but still shakily. "Okay."

They settled into bed, the iPad between them, and Brady leaned over it, swiped and tapped. Instead of watching the screen, she watched his hand, his buffed nails and strong fingers. There was so much she liked about his body—the fine hair on his arms, the dip between his shoulder and neck. Why didn't she ever tell him that?

She glanced up at his hairline, at the scar that was still beneath it, and gave it a kiss.

He leaned into her. "This is weird."

"What is?"

"Looking at this with you."

She didn't like that, but she didn't stop nuzzling. "I don't want it to be."

Out of the corner of her eye, she watched his fingers pinch in and spread out. What did he need? What would make him comfortable? She nuzzled lower, bit lightly at his earlobe. Brady sucked in a breath.

"Are you nervous, pet?"

He nodded. Heat spun off his cheeks. She kissed his neck. "You don't need to be. As a matter of fact, you're exactly what you should be."

"And what's that?"

She put her lips to his ear. "A submissive, showing his Domme what he wants."

His grunt was low and dirty. "It's insane hearing you say that word."

"Submissive?" she asked. Brady groaned and nodded again. "That's what you are, isn't it?"

Another deep inhale. An even deeper exhale. "Yes."

The admission thrilled her. She wished she'd figured this out sooner, that she'd always known. She wished he knew how to talk and she'd never felt uncomfortable with herself and they hadn't lost a decade when they could've been exploring this.

She nuzzled his ear again, watched his shoulder curl up in a twitch. "And what should a good little sub do when his Domme asks him to do something?"

"What's that?"

Sam drove her hand into his hair, grabbed a fistful of his curls and tugged. "He should behave."

He drew in a hiss and shuddered. Smiling, Sam released his hair.

"Now. Show me what you like."

He lifted his head. Looked at the screen and tapped definitively. "That," he said.

Sam turned to look. "A vibrating cock ring? Very nice."

He tapped again. "That, too."

It was a set of chains for the bed. She hummed softly. "That's lovely. Expensive though."

"I know."

She might not be able to read Brady well, but she knew when he was crestfallen. Tousling his hair again, she said, "It might be a worthwhile expense. After all, I love the idea of you helpless."

Brady licked his lips, and Sam let her mind roll with the fantasy. "I could chain you up," she said. "Turn on that toy and leave you there, all strung out from pleasure."

He stared at her. He was hanging on her words, like he used to.

"We could find one with an app," she suggested. "Put it on you and send you off to work. Or even better, make you wear it when we go out. That'd be fun. To see you playing pool with Patrick, and turn the vibrations up, watch you miss your shot and double over."

Brady flinched. One massive shoulder going up, he turned back to the iPad.

"I don't want to do this in public," he said. "Definitely not around everyone else."

"Okay," she replied soothingly. She didn't need to broadcast this to the world if he wasn't comfortable. "Just at home then."

They were quiet for a moment. Sam wanted them back where they were. *Be a Domme. Be sexy.* She kissed his neck. "Anything else you want to show me?"

He nodded, and Sam felt him stiffen as he swiped again. The flash of red on his cheeks grew brighter. "Something for that."

He'd brought them to the page for anal play.

"Butt plugs and strap-ons and dildos, oh my," she teased. "I think you've been to this site before."

"I have."

He wanted to be chained up and pegged? Jesus, call her an idiot for thinking Brady wouldn't be into shit. He was even kinkier than she was.

"You like...all of this?" she asked, shocked.

She'd only tiptoed toward his back door once, and that was in college. He'd bucked away like she'd struck a match back there, which, given this new information, it seems she had.

"Yeah." His blush deepened. But he didn't look aroused anymore. He looked ashamed of himself.

"Don't be embarrassed." Sam tapped on one of the items and pictured Brady on all fours. Imagined stimulating his prostate, the noises he would make. "Do you have any idea how hot that is?"

A little laugh. A little moment of incredulity. "You think?"

"Me fucking you? Yeah. God yeah."

His shoulders sank with relief. "Okay. Good."

It was more than good. "We're buying it," she said, nudging the iPad out of his hands and putting it to the side. "All of it."

She wanted to reward him for his honesty, to show him she appreciated it. Sam slipped her hand beneath the front of his shirt. Brady's eyes sank closed.

There were so many things she wanted to do to him, so many ways she could bring him pleasure. She licked her lips, remembering his taste, the heavy weight of him in her mouth. She stroked his belly, built but not perfect, soft padding over muscles that were already leaping and straining for her. Her panties went damp, a desire so sharp she wanted to snarl and attack, but she wasn't making the same mistakes as last night.

This time she would do it right.

"Is there anything else you want?" she asked. "Anything you're not telling me?"

His breathing went shaky. If there was anything she'd learned in the last few days, it was that he was the most honest when he was turned on.

She leaned over, lifted his shirt and kissed his belly. Spread her fingers wide and gave a little lick. He jumped.

"I loved what you did in the kitchen the other night," he said.

Still kissing his soft skin, she reached over to the iPad, and, one by one, dragged things into the shopping cart. "What did you love?"

A heartbeat passed before he answered. "Your hands. I like your hands on me."

"Uh-huh," she prompted. She added a bottle of lube to their growing number of toys. "Anything else?"

Tap. Touch. Tease. Lick.

"I'd kill to see you all dressed up. A corset or leather or something."

Sam smiled against his belly. "We might be able to work something out." And refinance the house in the process. This shit didn't come cheap.

"Anything you *don't* want?" she asked.

Brady went quiet, so she answered his silence with a pause in her shopping and a pass of her palm over his jeans. He was like steel under there, and she squeezed at the same time as she glanced up at him. "If you want me to touch, you have to talk."

That got them somewhere. He looked straight at her.

"No gross stuff," he said. "Like, bathroom things."

Sam laughed. "That's a hard limit for me, too."

It was lingo she'd picked up in her reading—the absolute hard line of what two people were willing to do together when they engaged in a power exchange.

Sam stroked him through his jeans. His mouth dropped open, eyelids going drowsy with lust. She did it again, just to watch his reaction. "Anything else?"

Brady swallowed. His cheeks went the color of flame.

"No, but there's something else I do want. Something...different."

"Tell me."

He placed a palm over hers to stop her ministrations. "I miss the way things used to be. With us. In college."

"You mean when we'd eat Lucky Charms until our stomachs hurt?"

He laughed, slightly. "Isn't it my job to make the jokes?"

"It is." But despite the calories, she missed those days, pressing their bodies together on that tiny dorm-room bed, fingers covered in powdered sugar from hearts, stars and moons. "Sorry for interrupting."

Brady blew out a breath. "I miss when it wasn't a sure thing I could have you, and what you gave was like a privilege."

"What do you mean?"

His sheepish smile appeared, sweet and boyish, eyes glittering.

"You remember that morning I had an exam but stopped by your room first?"

The memory came back like the sun coming out from behind a cloud. "You were really fired up." He had been. Heavy breaths and shoulders filling her doorway and all but pleading with her.

"It seemed like a good idea—blow off some steam before the test, help me think straight. But you wouldn't say yes." He laughed again, but then his face changed. "You got on the bed, lifted your legs, shimmied your panties up and let me lick. That was it, just the one taste."

"I remember." The lust-drunk look in Brady's eyes had made it nearly impossible for her to say no, but she was his tutor. He couldn't miss a test because of her.

That look was back now, and there was nowhere he needed to be.

"Your flavor was on my face all day, a trace left behind in my beard. It drove me crazy, wanting you."

"And you liked that." She was half asking, half stating.

"I did."

It was a shock, to discover they'd been longing for the same thing all along—a past she thought they couldn't recapture. Sharing these desires built a tenuous bridge between who they were in the bedroom and outside of it.

"I did, too," she said. "Know what else I liked?"

"What's that?"

"Calling you pet."

His eyes changed. Darkened with desire.

"Did you like that name?"

His voice dropped to a low rumble. "Yes."

"It's how I think of you, when we're like this. My eager—" She fingered the collar of his shirt. "—hungry—"

Stroked her fingertips down it.

"—little—"

Ran her palm beneath the hem.

"—pet."

His breathing was quick and shallow. Sam grinned.

"Is there something you'd like to call me?"

Brady's throat worked. He licked his lips. "May I call you... Mistress?"

She hummed happily. "You liked that last night."

Brady nodded slowly, as if in a trance. She'd thrown that word out on purpose, needing to sate this curiosity, to see once and for all if this fantasy was real.

"I like that title. Much better than ma'am. So yes, you may call me that. But there's one more word we need to discuss." She put the iPad on her nightstand. "Your safeword."

"It would be bad if I used Beetlejuice, right?"

She wanted to flick him for breaking the mood, but she'd done that herself moments ago. And it was funny. "Only if you say it three times."

Brady chuckled out a nervous breath. Sam crawled over him, hovered her body a few inches away, and waited.

"Metamorphosis," he said.

Sam paused, everything in her going soft and sweet. "Kafka?"

"It was the first thing—"

"I tutored you on, I know."

That book had been a challenge to help him with, especially with his constant jokes about giant cockroaches, but he'd done well on his paper and she'd been proud of him. Damn, she hadn't thought he'd remembered.

Sam bent over him, kissed his lips, licked into his mouth until his tongue danced along hers. "Now, pet, time to get that pretty body of yours all messy."

Brady made a noise she couldn't define after that. The choked sound of an animal being caught by its prey, giving in to its lovely death.

He gave his consent in the fluttering of his eyelids, his head tilting back as she unzipped his pants and slid them down. Sam pushed his pants over his feet, then his boxers, then tossed it all to the side.

"What about you?" he asked.

"You mean I should come first?"

He nodded, then shuddered helplessly as she circled her palm over his slick tip. She'd been cruel last night, making him hold back when he couldn't.

"I'll want that, most of the time. And I won't want you to come without my permission, either. But not right now." She stroked his straining erection, and he stuttered out a moan. "Right now is for you."

Pleasure, that's what she wanted—to give it and let him take it freely.

Sam stretched out beside him. Brady turned his face toward hers, mouth open, beard brushing against her cheek as his eyes closed. She watched him give in, watched the kick of his hips and the tightening of his belly as he took what she offered and shattered beside her.

* * *

When the girls returned home the next morning, Brady had trouble shifting gears.

He and Sam had spent the rest of Saturday in bed, her fiery red hair tumbling over her shoulders as she took what she wanted from him. And this morning was like waking up in some foreign world. Ironic, considering what he'd chosen for a safeword.

The Metamorphosis was a book he'd fallen behind on after that day in the locker room. A weird-ass story about a guy waking up as a bug. But he had an idea of how the main character must've felt. When he'd woken up in the hospital knowing his knee was shot, it was the same. Brady couldn't move his body the way he used to, didn't feel about himself the way he had before.

Today was similar. His knee worked, and he certainly wasn't a bug, but it was like he wasn't sure he fit into this new skin he was wearing. It was more like a layer peeled back, exposed and uneasy.

He only felt comfortable in it when he and Sam were alone. Transitioning out of whatever place she'd gotten him to in his head when the girls were dropped off wasn't easy, and a part of him resented having to do it. They'd only just discovered this thing between them—or *re*discovered it—and he didn't want to let it go. He'd gone outside to work out his frustrations by taking down the Christmas lights, but he was still short-tempered, especially when he'd tripped over a pile of Allegra's things when he walked back in the door.

"Goddamn it," he shouted, immediately regretting it when Sam came around the corner. Her fury over his language wasn't something he could handle after this weekend. But she wasn't mad. If anything, she seemed…scheming?

She came up close. Pulled him aside.

"I have an idea," she said with that smile, that damn smile that melted his reasoning, short-circuited his thinking and made him unable to focus on anything but her. "Know all those lovely things we bought last night?"

His gaze darted to the living room where Hope sat, then back to Sam. "Yes?"

She kept her voice low. "As punishment for that mouth of yours, you don't get to come at all until the delivery arrives. And every curse in front of our children will earn you one day more of denial after it does."

Oh, Jesus. He needed to lean into her. To hide his heated flush. But he wasn't her pet now. He was Brady. Husband. Daddy.

Wasn't he?

"If you behave, however," she continued, "I'll reward you with the toy of your choice when it gets here. Understood?"

His chin lowered. He shouldn't have been this turned on with the kids in the house, but Sam was leading the charge, taking him down this path, and he was helpless to do anything but follow.

"Yes, Mistress," he whispered.

Sam's grin was wild. "Good boy."

12

"You sure you're okay?"

Sam waved off Lilly's concern. "I'm fine, I promise."

Lilly wrinkled her nose. Fresh from her honeymoon, all blond and tan, she hovered over Sam, unconvinced.

"It seems unfair to throw you into the fire on your first day."

Sam put both hands on her desk. She'd been trained on the phone lines and the copier, learned who all the attorneys were and memorized the staff roster before Lilly and Gabe took her out to a quick lunch, on the firm's dime, no less. It was a lot to absorb, but she'd always been quick on her feet and able to multitask, and she needed to calm Lilly's fears.

"I've got a handle on the mail. I understand the switchboard." Despite the years that had passed, it wasn't that different from the one she'd worked in DC. Sam held up the firm's handbook. "And if I get bored, I can read this."

Lilly laughed. "If you're okay, I have a client meeting to prepare for."

Not long ago, Lilly had been a timid paralegal, too broken from a past Samantha knew little about and lacking enough confidence to take the bar exam. It was nice to see her sister-in-law standing there, a woman in her own power, feeling her own success.

"Get after it then, girl," Sam said.

Lilly hurried off and Sam surveyed the reception area. Her desk was a C-shape behind a hutch. Ahead of her were the double glass doors of the firm, the lobby and elevators beyond it. Sam didn't feel as solid as Lilly seemed to, but this was a space for her, without games or toys or dirty dishes for her to clean up. Even her bag finally felt like her own. Instead of being filled with candy wrappers, snotty tissues and mini plushies, her purse had been cleaned out and now carried her cell, a folio notebook, several pens and a protein bar.

Which honestly was a goddamn miracle. It hadn't been an easy morning.

Allegra had enough trouble switching from the weekend to her weekday routine as it was, so not having Sam to help her didn't go over well. Hope was surprisingly clingy, refusing to speak and hanging on to Sam's coat when she'd tried to leave. And of course, Sam's parents had chosen this morning to let her know they were finally putting their apartment on the market. It was enough to make her nearly lose her shit while pulling on her pantyhose, but Brady had handled the girls, coaxing them away from her so she could get to work on time.

A warm feeling of appreciation skated over her. Things had shifted with them since Friday, and being dominant with Brady had her seeing power dynamics everywhere. When Johnson Phillips walked her around the building this morning, she'd observed people's behaviors—who'd shaken her hand with confidence and who hadn't. Who walked with a sense of authority and who looked at the floor.

Who was dominant, and who was submissive.

It was unreal, that she was getting to live this life. A week ago, she had no career, and a DOA sex life. Now she had a spot at the helm of a huge company, leading and in charge. And maybe she'd get to be *in charge* more tonight.

"Looks like you're settling in nicely."

Sam glanced up. Reginald Pierce was at the doorway, watching her. "I am. Thank you, Mr. Pierce."

His gaze flicked about two inches south of her collar. "Please, Samantha. Call me Reg."

"Oh, I think titles are more professional, don't you?"

She held his eye and stood her ground.

"They are." He gave her a slow grin and took a step toward her. "So, *Mrs. Archer*. Everyone been treating you right so far? We haven't overwhelmed you?"

"Not yet. Like I told Mr. Phillips in the interview, I'm not a skittish person."

"I doubt Arnie would've thought so highly of you if you were."

Sam took the compliment with an appreciative nod. But he remained there, a target she kept missing. "Is there something you need, Mr. Pierce?"

Pierce balanced his arms on the hutch. The little gap between his two front teeth was humanizing, as was his slightly unkempt beard, but she couldn't help thinking he looked like a serial killer lying to the cops.

"I hoped I could assign you a project to do in your spare time."

"A project?" She couldn't get a read on this man. Was he being slimy, or straightforward? "What kind?"

"You know I work on estate planning."

"Yes." She'd learned that this morning. "Mr. Forrester runs the litigation and intellectual property practice groups while Mr. Schaeffer handles bankruptcy and labor."

"I'm impressed." He glanced lower again. "You've clearly read your handbook."

Slimy. Definitely slimy.

"Anyway, I'm the trustee of the estate of a longstanding client. Mildred Quincy Choate."

"Quincy, as in *the* Quincys?"

"Correct."

Sam knew her New England history. Quincy, Massachusetts. John Quincy Adams. This woman was from Boston's founding family.

"And the Choate family," she said. "I know that name, too. One was a senator in the eighteen-hundreds, and another was a federal judge."

"Also, correct. I'm seeing more and more why Arnie liked you."

Slimy or not, Sam couldn't help it—she liked the praise.

"Sadly," he continued, "Mildred is in hospice care now. I've been responsible for managing her investments, paying her bills, and for the eventual distribution of her assets. I'd like you to do a final organization before we close out the file."

"Won't I have to ask Mr. Phillips for permission? As you said, I did read the handbook. HR manages my role."

Pierce's smile turned into something Sam could've called benevolent if she wasn't fairly certain there was menace behind it.

"Who do you think the boss is here?"

The shift from genuine to a power play was dizzying. Must've been what made him such a great lawyer.

"Understood. I look forward to helping out."

Two light raps of his fist on the hutch followed. "I'll get you access to the file."

He headed in the other direction, and Sam tried to refocus. A phone started ringing though, and it took a moment of staring at the switchboard before she realized it was her cell.

"Shit, shit, shit," she whispered, reaching into her bag to silence it.

Snatching it from the compartment she'd tucked it into, she immediately hit the button on the side to turn the ringer off. How had she forgotten to do that? But her stomach clenched and her heart raced at the number on the screen. It was Hope and Allegra's school. The most likely thing was that Allegra was having another behavior issue, best case could be the nurse calling to say one of them was sick. The district had a text notification system for things like bomb threats and lock down drills, so she could squelch that particular moment of panic. But as the call went to voicemail Sam stared at her phone, certain listening to the message at her desk on her first day would be a bad idea.

"You okay, love?"

The question came from a soft, feminine voice with an accent

Sam couldn't place. She glanced up to see a shockingly beautiful woman in front of her—green eyes, her skin such a warm brown tone it almost looked like she glowed.

"My kids' school called. I don't know what's wrong."

"I'll take over your spot for a tick."

A tick? Where was this woman from? She sounded British, but not quite. Australian, maybe? Wherever she was from, she had cheekbones like a model and lashes Sam would be jealous of forever if they were real.

"Are you sure?"

The other woman came around the desk and ushered Sam out of her seat. "Go on. I've got you covered."

Relief caught Sam on an exhale. "Thanks. I'll be right back."

She scurried into the staff kitchen, standing in a corner to listen to the message. Once she'd heard the voicemail and could breathe again, she called the school and informed them that no, Allegra's extra snack wasn't missing. It had probably been put in the left side pocket of her backpack rather than the right where her daughter expected it to be. It was one of the instructions Sam had rattled off to Brady the night before.

Clearly he hadn't been paying attention. She'd deal with that later.

Problem solved, Sam walked back to reception. The woman who'd helped her was smiling as she took a call, all red lips and striking brows. With her blond-brown ringlets pushed back with a headband and diamond studs in her ears, she was flashy in a way Sam hadn't been able to be in years.

She hung up the phone. "All sorted now?"

Sorted. Definitely not American. "Yes. Minor drama with one of my daughters."

"You don't have to tell me. Mine are always giving me hell."

"You have kids?"

"Two daughters. Eight and four."

"Mine are ten and seven."

"Then clearly we feel each other's pain." The other woman

stood, and Sam's gaze darted to her left hand. No wedding ring. "I'm Hanna Clay, by the way. Reginald—"

"—Pierce's secretary. I know," Sam finished for her. She'd read her name and position on the company roster. "It's nice to meet you. I'm—"

"Samantha Archer." Hanna grinned brightly. "Everyone knows. It's lovely to meet you, too."

That was unexpected, and rewarding. After so long feeling invisible, a whole company of people knew who she was.

"I'd better get back to it," Hanna said, stepping around Sam's chair and walking past her. Sam marveled over the other woman's sense of fashion. Black turtleneck dress, stunning knee-high boots, and where did she get her concealer? Her skin was so smooth, it looked like it was airbrushed on.

"Thanks again, by the way," Sam said. "For covering me."

"No problem, love. We moms gotta stick together."

Something lit up inside Sam, a sense of belonging she hadn't felt in ages. No other mom had made her feel a part of something—they'd made her feel like an outcast instead.

The phone rang. Sam reached for the receiver.

"Forrester, Schaeffer and Pierce," she said, waving as Hanna walked off. Like Hanna, like Lilly and Cassie, Sam was starting to feel like a woman in her own right, taking her place in the world, untapped power at her fingertips.

And she was ready to grab it.

13

y the middle of the week, Brady was a shaky mess.

His concentration issues were a nightmare, his brainwaves scattered between work and home. He'd been up early every day, taking care of the girls while Sam got ready for work. He'd herded them successfully out the door each morning, but not without reminding himself aloud what they needed or where things should go.

He was desperate not to disappoint her—his wife. His Mistress.

There was no clear line between when she was one or the other, no delineation between when she wanted to dominate and when she wanted him to remember things. It was stressful, switching from one role to the other, but he didn't bring it up. It wasn't just the fear of his punishment or the reward for his good behavior. It was the fact that he was making Sam happy.

The smile she'd given him each morning as she walked out the door was enough to make him feel like a god, but today she'd emerged from the bathroom with a different look on her face. She'd locked the bedroom door, dropped her towel and ordered Brady to his knees.

He'd been uncertain—the girls were running around downstairs —but he'd obeyed anyway, sinking to the floor at the foot of the bed.

It was something he'd only dreamed about, and the reality of kneeling before her was better than his wildest fantasies.

"Is your knee okay?" she'd asked.

His knee had been the last part of his body he was thinking about. "It's fine."

"Good." She'd settled herself on the edge of the mattress, spread her legs and petted the back of his head. "One taste."

Suddenly he was nineteen again, face between the luscious thighs of the hottest girl on campus. He'd put his lips to her smooth skin, rubbed them back and forth, dipped his chin forward until his beard tickled her clit. Opening her up with one gentle move of his thumbs, he'd sparked his tongue along her flesh until she gasped.

That sound, and the flavor of her on his beard, had driven him crazy all day. So much so that he'd been mentally fucking absent at Helios' programmer team meeting that afternoon, his head somewhere not at all "SFW" when Paul presented the new payment application.

It was not a good scene.

Paul's solution worked, but it meant the one-step checkout application they promised the client was going to be late. Brady felt lousy that he hadn't been the one to find the bug, even lousier that he hadn't been on the ball in the meeting. With so much going on between Helios and home, he felt like a hard drive running out of memory space; there was only so much data he could hold.

But he didn't want to be Brady the boss right now. He wanted to be Sam's pet, wanted to be on his knees until she was wrung out with pleasure and smiling at him.

And he definitely didn't want to talk to his brother on the drive home.

The call rang a second time, chiming loudly through the car speakers. They hadn't talked since Jack came back from his honeymoon. Groaning, Brady pushed the button on his steering wheel connecting his car to his phone and picked up the call.

"Hey." He squinted through the pellets of freezing rain hitting his windshield. The roads were icy, the sky pitch black, something he could use as his excuse to hang up if he needed to. "Happy to be back?"

"I wasn't missing this weather, that's for sure. How've things been with you?"

Great. My wife figured out I like to have her control me, and I've had a hard-on for a week.

"Fine."

"Things at work good?"

"Same old. Can't complain."

There was a beat of silence, the only sound the road noise and his wipers squeaking across the windshield. Brady's heartbeat kicked up. Please, *please* let Jack not ask any questions about him and Sam. He didn't want to lie, but the last time he and his brother had talked about his marriage had been bad enough. Exactly zero percent of him wanted to talk about it now. How Lilly and Nick discussed this shit was beyond him.

"Well, I wanted to check in," Jack said. "Sam enjoying working at the firm?"

He could've been imagining the undertone of competition here —the weird sense that at least Sam had gone into law. Helios was a massive success, but Brady felt second-rate when compared to his brother.

"She loves it."

"Lilly mentioned she seemed happy."

"She is." And not just because of the job. *He* was making her happy. Brady slowed and turned onto his street, his body both relaxing and winding up knowing she was close. "I'm home. Can I talk to you later?"

"Yup. Take it easy."

Brady knew he was being distant, but his mind was on one thing. Like a moth to a flame, he hurried inside, called to Sam and this thing they'd found between them.

Later that night, after dinner had been cleaned up and the girls had been bathed and put to bed, Sam sat on the edge of the bed brushing her hair. Stretched out behind her, Brady watched the rubber-tipped bristles run through her long red strands, watched the small of her back and the curve of her ass until he couldn't stand not being the one touching her.

She looked over her shoulder. "Are you thinking how much this resembles a paddle?"

Brady chuckled. "No." But good to know she was. "I was thinking something else, though."

"What's that?"

He sat up. Scooted forward. Put out his hand. "Can I?"

"Can you what?"

"Brush your hair."

Sam held his gaze for a breath, then offered him the brush. He moved forward until he was behind her, slid his legs along either side of her until he'd enveloped her, his front to her back. When he passed the brush gently over her head, she sighed softly and sank into him.

"I love that you remember how much I like this," she said.

"How could I forget?" The first time he'd randomly done this one night in college, she'd closed her eyes and told him if he wanted any that night, he wouldn't stop what he was doing until she said so.

The rubbery tips made a soft hush as they moved against her shiny strands. He ran it through her hair over and over again until all knots were gone and the brush slid through it with ease. It was good, comfortable, but having her butt nestled between his legs had him wanting more. He wanted her gasping, wanted her pointing out what a mess he was with that hint of playful irritation.

But how? He still couldn't initiate, so how did he get what he wanted?

"Can I brush...all your hair?" he asked.

Smooth, Archer. Smooth.

There was another tilt of Sam's head as she looked over her shoulder. "All of it?"

"Yeah." He'd been dying to get closer to that little patch of red all day. "All of it."

She smiled, laughing. "Is that what you want?"

He shrugged. "I think it could be hot."

"I think it's weird," she said. Before Brady's heart completely plummeted into his stomach, she added, "But you've been a good boy, so I'll let you watch me. And buy me a new brush when we're done."

His disappointment faded, lost in the echo of the words *good boy* and in the shape of her body as she stood and took the brush from him.

"Lock the door," she said.

Brady was on his feet in an instant, crossing the room and ensuring their privacy with an audible click. Returning to the foot of the bed, he watched as she sat against the pillows, sexy as hell in her tank top and tiny shorts. She maneuvered the brush between her spread legs, passed it over the cotton, and Brady's breath caught at the same time hers did.

"That's an interesting sensation," she said. "Never done this before."

"No?"

She shook her head. "Never thought of my hairbrush as a sex toy. But I guess you have, dirty boy."

He hadn't, but he grinned anyway. "Do more with it."

She slanted an eyebrow, and Brady immediately backpedaled. "I mean, please do more with it, Mistress?"

He swore his heart stopped completely until she said, "Better."

Jesus. Was it normal for a sub to be so worried about displeasing their Dominant?

Was any of this normal at all?

Sam lifted the waistband of her shorts and tucked the brush beneath it. All Brady could see was the rectangular shape of it moving under her shorts and the flex of her hips as she rocked against it.

"God," he whispered, needing to palm himself, to stifle the ache.

"You like to watch?" she asked. "My great big bear of a voyeur?"

"I like to watch *you*."

She shuddered, eyes heavy lidded. "It's the hottest thing ever, the way you're looking at me."

"What do I look like?"

"Like you want to be this brush. Like you can't stand that you're not."

She wasn't wrong. Her hand wrapped around the handle, and she moved it faster. Her head fell back, and she widened her legs farther.

"Tell me about the toys you want me to use on you, pet," she said. "You've pleased me with how good you've been, paying attention to your language. I want to think about how I'm going to reward you."

His brain stopped at the words *you've pleased me*. So simple, and yet they had the power to undo him, to build him up and fluster him as he imagined what was happening beneath her shorts. Imagined her pleasure mounting, imagined being the cause of it, the vulgar things she could do to him until he was crying out in desperation.

"Hello?" she asked. No irritation, just a smile on her lips as her breath quickened. "Did you forget what I asked you already?"

Fuck. He had, but he couldn't answer, his own hips thrusting in time with hers.

She chuckled. "So turned on he can't recall a single question."

That made him uncomfortable, but his cheeks burned and his erection stiffened further. He didn't like bringing his attention issues in here, but her pointing it out reached that tender place inside him, the place that enjoyed her mockery.

"Tell me, pet." She was breathless now. "What do you want?"

"I want you to come," he said.

"You're gonna get your wish."

She quickened her pace, the brush making sharp up-and-down motions under the cotton, and then her back was arching and her toes were curling and Brady was lost to the look on her face, to her fist twisted in the blanket, her gasps silent as she rode out her release to the end.

"More?" he asked, already moving closer, ready to bring her what she needed.

She shook her head. "You didn't do what I asked."

"Do what?"

Sam's head dropped back in mock-frustration. Was she surprised he was blanking? He couldn't have remembered his own name right now if she'd asked him.

Sam slipped the brush free. Putting it on her nightstand, she shifted forward, crawled toward him and licked the shell of his ear. "You didn't tell me what toys you wanted."

"Oh." He'd been thinking about those today, too. "The...vibrating ring," he said, his eyes cast downward.

"That's not what you want."

"How can you tell?"

Sam moved around in front of him, stood at the edge of the bed, put her hands on his chest and spread her fingers. Brady could've resisted, but it was so much better when she took control, when she threw that lasso around him and coiled it tight.

He let her press until he was flat on his back on the bed. Her hands found the waistband of his pajama bottoms, fingers teasing back and forth over his skin.

"Your cheeks aren't red enough," she said. "That's how. When you're turned on your face turns crimson."

"Oh." Was it not blazing now?

Back and forth her fingers went, until he thickened up and tented the flannel and she made that damn humming noise again.

"That sound makes me crazy," he said.

"What sound?"

"When you hum."

"Hmm." She smiled, like the seductress that undid him at nineteen and tied him to her for life. "I do it when you've made me happy."

"I think that's why I like it."

Her fingers dipped lower, teasing at his pubic hair. "I want to play." Her gaze flicked up. "May I?"

She was asking *his* permission?

"Yes," he croaked. Like he was going to say no.

Sam was slow, tantalizing as she hooked her fingers into his boxers and pulled them along with his pj bottoms down to his knees, leaving them there. There was no warning—no teasing or stroke of her hands before she took him deep into her mouth.

"Jesus." Brady's hips lifted involuntarily, head digging back against the mattress. "I thought...*fuck*...I wasn't allowed to come until the toys arrived."

She popped her mouth off him—"You're not."—then went back to sucking.

A stroke of her tongue had him panting. "So you're gonna torture me?"

"Mmm-hmm."

The vibrations in her mouth made him moan. He couldn't breathe, couldn't think. He'd been waiting ages for this. Her total lack of gag reflex was insane. "Please don't. I'm not gonna...*shit*."

She opened up on the upstroke. A lick around his tip was a power play, one she definitely had the upper hand in. "Guess you'd better tell me which toy you want then."

He shivered. This wasn't only pleasure. It was a test. To see how much he could take before he snapped. Wet suction enveloped him again. So good. So damn good. But a harder suck was a warning.

"The butt plug," he choked out, not wanting a repeat of last time. "I want that."

She popped off him. "Really."

It was the toy he'd thought about the most, and fuck if that didn't embarrass him even more. Logically he knew it shouldn't. There was nothing wrong with being interested in anal, aside from his constant fear of seeming weak.

But weak, apparently, was right where Sam wanted him.

She tugged his bottoms until they were off. Kneeling, she palmed his shins, wrapped her hands around his calves—as best she could anyway.

"Didn't your coach once call your legs powerhouses?"

Brady nodded. And she was moving them like they were feathers, until his knees were up and his feet were on the bed. One loud crick of his bad knee gave her pause, but when he shook his head, she dipped hers down. The last thing Brady saw was the mischievous glint in her eyes until the crown of her head was all that was in his view.

The shock of her tongue along his back door was electric.

"Oh, *fuck*."

His head fell back, and he made fists out of the sheets. A small, teasing circle followed, her lick gentle yet confident. Brady could feel his pulse in his dick.

"You want me here?" she murmured. "You want me to play with your ass?"

He slammed his eyes shut, his jaw ground tight. "Yes."

She began a rhythm, little laps that blew his goddamn mind. He wanted to tell her he wasn't ready for that yet, but he wasn't sure it was the truth. And whatever his brain was saying was demolished by the pleasure she was bringing him anyway. The power she had over him when they were like this was unreal.

She reached up, stroked him, drove her tongue inside, and the combination was too much.

"Oh fuck, stop," he said on a gasp.

"Mm-mmm." The sound of her *no* came out against his heated flesh.

Shit. *Stop* wasn't what hit the damn pause button on this, and that teasing reminder from her was gasoline to the fire. She was poking at that raw spot inside him, showing him how helpless he was, and how much he liked it.

She stroked faster. Tongued harder. What was his fucking safeword?

"Kafka. Bug." He twisted around, too close, too close, *too damn close*. "Metamorphosis!"

That stopped her. She pulled back with an amused smile. Brady's heart pounded, and his dick twitched. She'd worked him up, checked his control, and he'd passed the test. She was beautiful, smirking at his pitiless desperation and Brady tried to catch his breath as he gazed up at her. She'd edged him to that uncomfortable place, gotten him helpless and humiliated, and he'd liked it. He'd been flat on his back with his wife's tongue up his ass and he wanted more, wanted her mimicking his crazed hunger and reflecting it back at him.

How could feeling so messed up feel so perfect?

"I've missed this," she said. "You looking at me like that."

"I never stopped."

The mockery in her expression melted away. Now she was looking at him the way *he'd* missed—eyes soft, smile gentle. The way she'd looked when she'd agreed to go out with him, when he'd asked her to marry him, when she'd said, "I do."

"Thank you," she said.

"For what?"

"For telling me what you wanted."

He wanted so much more than that. He wanted to tell her he loved her, but he was already too exposed. No matter how dirty they'd been together, she hadn't said it, and him saying it first meant the risk of getting shot down, of her not saying it back.

He used his boxers to clean himself off, grabbed some new ones and climbed with Sam beneath the covers. She shut off the light, and they cuddled for the first time in forever.

"The toys will be here on Saturday," she told him, head nestled on his chest.

Three days until they were like this again.

Three days to get his head on straight.

"I can't wait."

14

Friday arrived swiftly. Sam should've been exhausted after her first full week of work, at least two nights snuggling with Allegra when she couldn't sleep, never getting to the gym and the awful, frigid weather, but instead she was energized, giddy like a kid on Christmas.

"Your package is on the way!" her email notification had read that morning.

"You're damn straight it is."

Sam laughed at her own joke. She'd been tracking the toy delivery online, scheming and preparing. She'd created a list of errands Brady would need to run on Saturday, and the girls were scheduled for separate sleepover dates. She'd needed to plan with Allegra, and the mom-guilt had hit hard. Sam compensated for the fact that she was sending her children away for a second weekend in a row by ordering whatever they wanted for dinner and having a Disney movie marathon.

Brady kept his distance while they watched, silent on the other end of the couch. He'd hidden in the basement after the movies ended, too, saying he had to work. His distance could've been from the continued orgasm denial, but it was more likely because of the fight they'd had last night.

She winced, hating the memory of Brady's crestfallen expression. But seriously, was it that hard to remember to put the girls' homework folders in their bags? Allegra was old enough that she should've remembered it herself, but sticking to routines was part of her problem, and Hope had just started having homework. She couldn't be responsible for remembering to pack it, a thing Sam had reminded Brady of. She'd even told him *again* the night before how she prepped the girls' bags. It hadn't helped. He'd remembered Allegra's snacks, but neither of their homework folders, and it had landed Allegra in a lunch with no recess and made Hope even more silent than usual.

He hadn't replaced Sam's hairbrush, either.

It was so frustrating to have to tell him what to do, but he'd looked like a puppy who'd been kicked when she yelled, which of course made her feel even worse. Was Domme-guilt a thing, too? Where did these lines cross? How did people who did this know when to turn it on and off, how to come back when they'd hit one end of the spectrum and wanted to return? She enjoyed bossing him around in bed, but when they were outside it, he still lagged behind. All she wanted was for him to share the load at home without her having to remind him about stuff all the time.

Maybe there was no line. Maybe she had to spell everything out. If that's what he needed, then wasn't it her job to provide that for him? He didn't want to let her down—she knew that. And she didn't want to be unkind in response. When he brushed her hair the other night, she'd seen Brady's worshipful side, and it had been lovely and sweet and intoxicating. She needed to be careful with him, but how could she do that twenty-four seven? How did anyone in a BDSM relationship balance this?

It was what she'd wondered about when she'd found not one but two new brushes waiting for her in the bathroom this afternoon. She'd thought about calling Lilly or Cassie again, then decided against it once and for all. Neither of them was in the same role she was, and besides, Brady didn't want anyone to know. She'd thought about going online for answers, but she wasn't sure what kind of weirdness she'd find there.

"Hey Google," she said out loud just for fun to her empty bedroom after putting the girls to bed, "explain BDSM."

No, the only answers she could find were in her books.

She shut herself up in the bath with her iPad. Tabbing through highlighted sections, she reread scenes of the Dominant staying in control, taking their pleasure but creating a scene that was wholly for the submissive, and afterward, moments with characters lying in bed and opening up to one another as they shared their deepest secrets.

That was nerve-racking. Sam's biggest secret was that she'd kissed a girl, that she'd almost had a threesome once, but there was no reason to tell Brady that now.

What kinds of secrets could Brady be keeping?

She'd thought they'd known each other, but it turned out they didn't at all. They'd discovered this new world together, uncovered desires he'd hidden and she'd never known she had. It didn't feel like a betrayal though. It felt like she was finally getting to know her husband. They hadn't talked a lot, but sex broke the walls they'd both had up and let them be closer to each other.

No matter what Brady had forgotten in terms of the girls, he *had* done what she'd asked. He'd watched his language, and for that, he was going to be rewarded.

She just needed to make sure she knew what to do with the damn thing.

Climbing out of the tub, Sam grabbed a towel and locked the door. Wrapping the terrycloth around her, she sat on the closed toilet seat lid. After lowering the volume on her iPad, she opened a browser and studied dirty videos about prostate orgasms the way she'd once studied foreign policy. The guys in those short scenes made noises of pleasure like she'd never heard, and she imagined Brady's gaze focused relentlessly on her, the pinch of his lips as he bit back a moan. She'd devour him with her eyes first, cruel and erotic, then gently push the toy inside him when he was at the brink. Tilting it until she rubbed that button inside him, she'd roll it in circles until he got them both sticky and slick.

God. She wanted this as badly now as he did.

But curiosity lingered after she'd watched several scenes, her eyes darting up to the category entitled threesomes.

She loved the big burliness of Brady, loved the feel of his beard against her face and his cock in her hands. And he was the only person who'd ever captured her heart. But she'd always wondered what it would be like to add something feminine to that strong masculinity, what it would be like to be with a woman, and a man.

She stared at the category tab. Her heart beat a little faster.

Checking the sound was off, she hovered her finger and tapped.

Countless little boxes popped up, scenes with options of positions and combinations of couples. She chose one and waited for it to start. It felt illicit—a bit dirty, a bit wild and a bit like looking into the past.

It had been late. Last call after a pretty crazy night at a bar on U Street. Leaving, she'd been approached first by the guy, then the girl she'd kissed that night. It was so goddamn cliché—he was a hot freshman congressman and the girl was a staffer on the other side of the aisle. Sam had been with them at separate moments during the course of the evening. The guy hadn't been her type—blond, rich, the kind of guy who'd grown up going to his Daddy's country club and was accustomed to getting his way. She'd only kissed him for the thrill of walking away after. The girl, however, had lips that had grabbed Sam's attention—full and bright red, and she'd been curious what they'd feel like against her own. Neither of them had a problem that she'd kissed both of them, and it was the girl who'd suggested they all go somewhere together.

Sam had thought seriously about doing it, and she'd be lying if she said she hadn't been insanely turned on. But Dawes had warned her about getting messed up in a scandal. The last thing anyone needed in that business was dirty skeletons in their closet.

Her advice had saved him from one scandal. She'd needed to heed his.

Professionally, she was glad she'd said no. But, like everything that had happened in DC, it remained a regret—an opportunity she'd missed.

A noise outside the bathroom startled her. Sam quickly closed the window. Guilt and nerves made her heart race even faster. But no harm had been done. Porn wasn't real life, and now that she'd watched a few videos, she knew how to give Brady what he needed.

And have some fun herself.

* * *

By Saturday afternoon, the house was silent. Outside the sun glinted on the snow, the yellow-gold light already waning. The girls were gone, on their way with their sleeping bags and overnight duffels. Sam had made sure everything they needed was tucked away before Brady drove off with them, her mom-guilt dissipating in the face of the girls' excitement.

Brady looked excited, too, a light in his eyes when she'd tucked a to-do list into his pocket. She'd given him explicit details, hoping it would keep him on-task and busy.

She couldn't be answering the phone, after all. She had work to do.

The doorbell rang, and once the UPS truck had driven off, she hurried to retrieve the two large boxes from her front stoop. Sam staggered with the giant packages, bringing them inside the house to the kitchen. She'd bought a bit more than she and Brady had discussed.

It was a good thing she had a job now.

The bed restraint system had been pricey, as had the upgrades she'd bought for it—a set of shiny black cuffs with chains. Sam sliced the box open and took them out first, listened to the tinny sound of metal against metal, and breathed in the leather scent. Digging deeper into the box, she found the rest of her toys, then opened the other container. Inside was the lockable, UV sanitizing storage chest she'd purchased.

She wanted to be a Domme, but she'd be damned if these toys were gonna be more things she had to clean.

Tossing the boxes in the trash, she carried the lot upstairs. A half hour later, she was sweatier and more disheveled than when she started, but at least everything was set.

"Easy to install, my ass," she muttered at the restraint packaging as she threw it out. And not a minute too soon. She stood to the sound of the front door opening, heralding Brady's return.

Sam hurried to greet him, stopping a few stairs from the bottom.

"Hey," she said. "Did you complete your tasks?"

He took his jacket off and actually hung it up. "The girls are safely at their friends' houses. Allegra's refill has been picked up. And takeout—" he held up the Panera bag, "—is right here."

"Good," she said softly. "Put it in the fridge."

Even from this distance, she could see his eyes blaze. He went into the kitchen. She heard the sound of his obedience with the fridge door opening and closing. When he returned, Sam went down a few more steps, stood on the bottom one in front of him.

He towered over her, all brawny, broad-shouldered man. Despite his size, he looked uncertain, the fingers of his right hand twisting the ring on his left. She'd seen him do that before, last week when she'd asked him to look at the toys. She did the same thing to her necklace, twisting it back and forth along the chain. Had they always shared the same anxious habit? Funny, the things that could escape your attention over the years.

"You're turning that ring around like it's gonna vanish if you stop."

"Yeah," he said quietly. "I guess I am."

"Why is that?"

"Grounds me, I guess."

Was that what he did? Reach for the thing that bound them together? The reality of that made a fist around her heart and squeezed. She wanted to tell him she loved him. That she always had. That nothing had changed. But it didn't seem like the right time. She had to be someone else right now—not his wife, because that woman didn't steady him, didn't calm him the way his Mistress did.

He didn't need love. He needed control.

"Hey."

He met her gaze, his brows pushed together, worry in the dip between them, in the line of his frown. Cupping his face in her palms, she whispered, "You don't need to be nervous. I'm here. And I'm not going anywhere."

Brady exhaled and leaned forward, like he was falling into her, like she was his safety net. She kissed him, still needing to go up on her toes from her vantage point on the steps. It was an easy, brushing kiss at first—lips passing over lips, a wet, soft, quiet exchange of breath—until her tongue touched his.

Sparks. That was the only way to explain it. The kind of electricity they'd had standing in front of a dorm room as nineteen-year-olds. Sam pulled back, her hands still on his face. Brady rested his forehead against hers.

"I want to keep kissing you," he said.

"I want to do more than kiss you."

He shuddered. Sam inhaled, too, deeply. He was wearing a long-sleeved crewneck his shoulders looked delicious in. He'd trimmed his beard and showered that morning, too, and she could smell the woodsy peppermint scent, all clean and masculine and *him*.

"Will you come upstairs with me?" she asked.

It hadn't occurred to her to ask before today. She'd walked, expecting him to follow. Now she wanted to be certain she had his consent.

Brady's eyes opened, sharp and blue. "Yes."

She turned and led him up the stairs. His steps halted when they reached the bedroom.

"Whoa." He blew out a breath. "We're using everything?"

Two large nylon straps were now wrapped around the head and footboards, connecting to four tethers with O-rings at the end. She'd linked them to the chains and cuffs for Brady's wrists and ankles, the silver and black a stark contrast against the white sheets. Waiting in the middle was the smallest plug from the anal training kit, a bottle of lube and one vibrating cock ring.

"Not everything." She strode over to the bed. "Just enough so that you get your reward and I—" she lifted a cuff and dropped it, "—get mine. Any objections, pet?"

His eyes sank closed on a strangled grunt. "None, Mistress."

"Good. Now, come here and undress me."

Everywhere else she hated having to give him orders, but here, right now, she loved it.

Brady stepped toward her, began unbuttoning the little black button-down she had on. It was tucked into her favorite jeans, easy to take off. No muss, no fuss. One by one, he popped the buttons free.

"You know, pet. We never discussed aftercare."

"We didn't."

The shirt open, he fanned the edges aside, slid them free of her jeans. They were both already breathing hard, but she had to slow this down. Her mistakes had become an albatross: making the comment about the sitter that first night, not asking him about safewords and limits, forcing him not to come when there was no way he could stop. But today, she'd fix that. She'd be like the good Dominants in her books. The ones who stayed in role, who stayed in control, making sure their submissives felt safe enough to let go.

"What do you need?" she asked. "After?"

"I don't know." His fingers inched back up, the fabric slowly coming loose. Sam shivered when he rolled the sleeves down her arms.

The shirt gone, he fingered the button on her jeans, glanced at her face.

"Keep going," she said.

He popped it open.

"You must need something," she urged. She was already picturing what she was going to do to him, how his big body was going to heave and tremble. She needed to know how to reattach his pieces once she'd blown him apart.

"A shower?" He slowly unzipped her fly. A little shudder escaped her, belying her composure. Brady cracked an impish grin. "A cigarette?"

No Mr. Funny. Not now.

"I want an answer, pet."

His face went serious. "I don't know what I need," he said softly.

"Okay." At least that was a response. "We'll figure it out together."

He pulled her jeans down, lowering himself to the floor along with them. He looked at her bare feet, palmed one foot, helped her balance while he tugged off the denim.

"You like me barefoot?"

"I like you everything."

Sam laughed and slid the jeans away with her toes.

"I bet you like knowing you're gonna come soon."

He licked his bottom lip and stood. "Am I?"

"You'll be no good to me all amped up." She made a fist in his shirt, pulled him close and whispered, "I'm betting you're out of your damn mind by now."

His throat worked. "I'm struggling, Mistress."

"We can't have that." Although, she liked his suffering. A lot. "Take my bra off."

Without breaking eye contact, Brady reached around behind her and undid the clasp. He pulled the straps until the cups fell away, and then his gaze fell, eyes darting to her nipples and up again.

"May I?"

Was it the way he was asking for permission, or the hungry look in his eyes that made her want to let him touch? For years, her breasts had been for nursing her children, not for pleasure. But not anymore.

"You may."

Brady's touch was almost reverent as he brushed his knuckles along the underside of one breast, then the other. Dropping her bra to the floor, he moved in close, and God did she love the sheer mass of him, big arms and hands to match. Her eyes fluttered shut as he skimmed a thumb over her nipples. They grew tighter, more puckered with every stroke.

Did he know what his worship did to her?

"I'm afraid you don't want this," Brady breathed. "Not the way I do."

"That's not true," she said.

She *wanted*—to take with abandon, to see how he reacted to the plug and the vibrating ring. But more than that, she wanted that tormented look on his face, to watch his head press back against the mattress, his muscles tightening as he begged and cried out in anguished pleasure.

"The way you want me, pet, I want you, too. The way you've been thinking about me, I've done the same."

Sam took his hands in hers and held them.

"You want to be on your knees, and I want to put you there. You want to be controlled. I want to control you. I'm as desperate for this as you are."

It was so clear now, how a hidden part of her had been starving for this. She loved pushing him into that place he got to as her pet, loved the place in *her* head it put her in. She wanted him there—she couldn't stop herself—and she didn't want to wait any longer.

She had power here. It was time for her to take it.

"You have one choice to make tonight, pet. The rest are all mine."

"What choice is that?"

Sam smiled. "How do you want to come?"

15

It was fun to watch Brady swallow as he thought out his answer.

"I only get to come once?" he asked.

Sam chuckled. "Greedy boy. You'll come again. But how it happens, the first time, is up to you. After that..." She got close enough to whisper, "I decide."

He licked his lips, worked his jaw a little. Then he stepped quickly over to the nightstand, fished out a condom and hurried back to her.

Sam laughed and took it from his outstretched hand. "I have a feeling this won't last long."

His face went red. For a moment, she wondered if she'd gone too far. But she'd seen it before—his relationship with being ashamed and aroused. They seemed to go hand-in-hand. And power coursed through her when she saw what it did to him.

Sam took off her panties, then sat on the bed and moved the toys and cuffs out of the way. "Well?"

He didn't need to be told twice. Yanking his crewneck over his head, Brady whipped off the rest of his clothes. Clumsy in a kind of schoolboy eagerness, he clambered onto the bed. Sam handed him back the condom. Letting him roll it on, she reached out to finger the silvery links of the chains surrounding them.

"I like these," she said.

"Yeah?" He was breathless. Hungry.

"Yeah. I like the way they're going to sound when you're trapped in them."

Another strangled grunt was her reply. Sheathed, Brady bent over her, his giant arms surrounding her like a cage, but he held himself still.

Sam wrapped one hand around his neck. "Go ahead, pet. We both know how much you need it."

She needed it, too. More than she was willing to say.

She watched as his tip pressed forward, and oh, that burning stretch. The sensation of being filled. Sam could feel him tensing, trying to move slowly when he couldn't. The effort made him shake.

"Don't hold back," she whispered. "Take what you need."

He answered with a soft moan, then started to thrust. She pulled him to her and drove her fingers through the curls at his nape. His mouth against her neck, he anchored one hand against the headboard, the other by her side. His massive shoulder eclipsed the room from her view.

Sam eased her free hand between them, eyes closing on a gasp when she found her clit. One circle. Two. Faster and then slow, 'cause *fuck* she wanted this to last. But it wasn't going to. Barely a minute later, Brady's breathing grew labored, his movements choppy.

"Gonna come," he said, his voice sharp and high.

She let him, putting aside her need for release and using both hands to dig into his back. He came with a startled sound, like he was surprised how good it felt, like he'd never done this before. Sam hummed into his ear as he gasped against her neck.

"Do that again?" he asked.

She hadn't realized she was doing it, half the time. But now that she knew he liked it, she held him close and did as he asked, dragging out the sound. He shook, hard.

He moved back, disposed of the condom. His smile was sheepish. "Sorry."

"Don't be. What you should be saying is thank you."

"Thank you."

"You're welcome," she said. "Now, my fun starts."

She sat up and pointed to the spot she'd just been in. Brady grinned and extended his limbs in a spread-eagled position, long legs and tremendous arms nearly taking up the entire bed. For the first time in a while, she was glad they'd bought this monstrosity of a mattress.

Restraining him was awkward, and it took a while. First she did the clasps wrong, and she needed his help figuring out how the O-rings worked, but seeing the finished product—his arms by his head, elbows by his ears, feet restrained at the ankles—was so pretty she almost wanted to take a picture.

"All mine," she said, dancing her touch over one thigh, then the other. "I want you to tell me if you start losing feeling anywhere. If your fingers start to tingle or your knee locks up. You're gonna be in this position awhile."

His mouth twitched into a smile. "Yes, Mistress."

She continued stroking, skating her touch across his skin. Having him leashed like this, his shaking limbs and strength tested against the restraints, was an incredible aphrodisiac.

"How does it feel?" she asked. "Being all tied up."

"I like it," he answered. "Feels safe."

"Safe how?"

He glanced up at one arm, tugged the restraints and then shifted his head again. "It's comforting. Keeps me tethered. Grounded." His gaze was steady. "Focused on you."

Sam shivered. Climbing onto the bed, she shimmied up his body, maneuvered herself over him until she'd fitted her knees on either side of his arms, the bottoms of her feet along his sides, thighs spread over his face.

"Are you focused now?" she asked.

He nodded, staring up at her, positively entranced. Sam braced her hands on the headboard for balance and lowered herself slowly until her clit grazed his mouth. His tongue came out in a gentle lap, then again, pointed right where she was the most sensitive. Her head sank back. As if he'd had them memorized, he mapped out all her spots, backing off and homing in on them, until her legs shook.

"I was going to fuck you, pet," she panted, grinding down on him. "But I think I'm gonna stay right here."

He moaned against her skin. The chains holding his arms pinged with the movement of his clenched fists—the only other sound of his eager assent. He angled his chin, worked it toward her pussy, facial hair rasping in a sharp tickle. Sam lifted up so he could drive his tongue inside. The sight of his face all wet and slippery was obscene, but fuck, who cared? Sam certainly didn't, not when her orgasm crested. Spreading her fingers wide against the wall, she arched back to get his mouth on her needy, swollen clit. He flicked his tongue *there*, that one sensitive spot that triggered her downfall. Christ, had it always been this good?

"Watch me." Her order was high-pitched, desperate, but she hadn't needed to give it. Brady's eyes were trained on her face as he worked her harder, desperate to see her tremble and give in.

Why was it that he paid attention to her here, but nowhere else?

Sam's release crashed over her, and her eyes slammed closed from pleasure. When she'd recovered, Brady was still watching her, a small smile on his face.

"Jesus," she said, barely able to catch her breath as she moved to the side. "How is it you can't remember where anything goes in the kitchen, but you remember that?"

Oh, God. Wrong thing to say. It broke through their roles, broke Sam and Brady into Mistress and pet. Why was she always fucking things up? But Brady didn't look unhappy. If anything, he looked amused.

"Good question," he said, lips shining with a goofy grin. "I guess it's because I want to know this. Because I was paying attention when you taught me."

She was so relieved not to have destroyed the moment she barely heard his answer.

She needed to recover her footing.

Sam crawled around his giant body, found a home for herself against the hollow of his hip. "I was paying attention when you showed me what you liked, too."

He hadn't shown her, not the same way, that first night she'd gone down on him eons ago. But she'd listened to his noises, catalogued the twitches and the hisses, and she knew his spots as well as he knew hers. She was looking for forgiveness now, when she took him half-hard into her mouth. Slow sucks, drawn-out movements with him hitting the back of her throat—that was what got Brady going. A few minutes later, he was standing at attention.

"Are you all needy and desperate again, pet?"

Her voice had taken on that taunting tone, the one that neared the edges of unkind. She didn't mean to do it—she was mad at herself for messing up here, not him—but Brady seemed to like it. He made a low noise of agreement, combined with a slow nod. He looked almost drugged, eyelids drooping despite the tension in his restrained arms and legs.

Reaching for the towel she'd stashed under the bed, Sam gently wiped his mouth, gathered the new toys and knelt between his spread legs.

"Well, you're gonna get more desperate."

The sound of his whimper was the most addictive thing she'd ever heard. She reworked the restraints on his legs, lessening the slack so he could move.

"Knees up," she told him, figuring he'd tell her if his old injury hurt, then reached for the cock ring.

His gaze zoomed in on the item in her hands—a matte silicone device that was thin and round on the bottom and flat on top.

"It's all charged up and ready to go," she said. "Just like you."

She stretched it open and fit it around him. It contracted snugly at his base, making him even more enormous. Her pulse raced in anticipation as she tapped the button on the side.

"This time—" she said, starting him up at a teasing murmur, "—you aren't allowed to come until I say so."

Brady jolted and his mouth dropped open.

"Like that?"

His hips swiveled and rose up into nothing. "Yes."

"I thought so." But she had to be sure. Sam found the bottle of lube, popped it open and drizzled it over him. "What was the other thing you said you liked the other day? My hands?"

She punctuated the question by slicking two fists over his stiff flesh. Brady's loud moan made her laugh. "Oh, yes. You do like that."

He gave her a quick, shaky nod, brows drawn together as he lifted up to meet her strokes. As much as he could anyway, chained up like that. Making sure her fingers were coated with lube, Sam kept one hand on him and dropped the other lower. Slowly, like she was approaching a scared animal. When he didn't flinch, she ran her thumb over his rear entrance in circles, first gently, then with more pressure.

"Fuck." Brady fought against the chains. His eyes were like blue fire, an incredible contrast to the ruddiness of his cheeks.

"What? You don't want this?" She circled a bit deeper. "Wasn't someone crying out while my tongue was here the other day that he wanted to use the butt plug?"

His cock kicked in her grip, swelling even more. It was all the reply she needed.

Carefully, so carefully, Sam switched to her pinky and edged it inside him, swirled it around the entrance. Brady's hips shot upward as he sought more of the feeling but was unable to move much with his powerful limbs so tightly tethered. She pushed past that first tight ring of muscle and smiled at his full-body shudder.

"Oh...*fuck*," he choked out.

"Such bad language." She thought she'd have to tell him to relax, but he gave in easily, his body eagerly taking her in. "Such a dirty mouth on my dirty boy."

When they'd gone a few minutes like that, she slowly switched fingers, turning up the intensity on the ring to distract him before pressing her middle finger inside. Curling it upward, she waited until she found that small, chestnut-sized ridge. Brady's body bowed off the bed.

"Is that it?"

He didn't reply, just moaned. She did it again and he shook hard, rattling his restraints. Sam grinned wildly, her heart racing. Such an incredible rush, to have this tremendous man at her mercy. She'd been mad at herself for not being better at this, but her aggravation washed away in the heat of his eyes, in the sweaty flex of his body.

"Tell me how much you like this."

Brady grunted in response, his brows pinched as if he was in pain. She would've preferred words, but it was all there, in his body language, his torso rolling like a wave. He pulsed between her fingers and whimpered again, head snapping up to look at her hands in both a plea and a warning.

"Oh, no you don't," she warned, easing off the stroking and slipping her finger free. "You're not coming yet."

Brady sagged against the bed, hips phantom-thrusting. "Please," he moaned.

"Please," Sam mimicked back, which seemed to only make him shake harder. It was cruel, to taunt him, to make him wait, but that fierce blush of his told her he was enjoying the torment. "Poor pet. Your whimpers are so delightfully pathetic."

Brady tensed, squeezed his eyes shut. Every muscle suddenly went taut, she assumed from the orgasm denial. He was practically convulsing in his need to come. She'd give him what he needed. But first, one more taunt. She turned the vibrations up a level and relished in his gasp.

"Should we put the horny little sub out of his misery?"

It was odd talking about him in third person, and in a tone she'd use with a child. She'd have hated talking to him like that in any other arena, but here, she loved it.

"Pet needs to come again, doesn't he? He needs to come all over his Mistress' hands."

He cringed, his eyes shut so tight creases appeared on his forehead. He turned his face to the side, hid it in the curve of his biceps. Sam hesitated, wondering if she should check in, but worried it would break the mood. He hadn't used his safeword. He hadn't said much of anything, actually, but if he couldn't tell her what he needed, she had to figure it out by watching him. All the physical signs of his pleasure were there, in the way he hissed and shifted up toward her touch, in the gleaming spot of pre-come at the tip of his cock. He was deep in what was happening in his body, and she wanted to drive him deeper.

She picked up the plug, thin and curved rubber with a solid flare at the base, and drenched it in lube. Teasing it against his rim, she wrapped her hand around his cock. Her fingers didn't meet her thumb. She'd never seen him this huge.

"You're so ready for this, pet. So ready to have your ass filled. I can't wait to see what this does to you."

He trembled, mouth firmly pressed against his arm. Sam took that as a sign of his assent and slid the toy forward, pumping it gently back and forth whenever she felt resistance. Brady's head jerked up, mouth open, brows slanted. She moved the toy in circles, and his head fell back again. His thighs jolted every time she swirled it around.

"I wish you could see yourself," she said on a firm, long stroke along his cock. "How helpless you are."

He made the most incredibly tortured sound. It was beautiful.

Filthy and dirty and fucking beautiful.

She angled the toy upward so it rubbed against his prostate. Brady thrashed against the chains. "Mistress," he moaned.

He swelled in her hand. Sam smirked.

"I haven't said you could come yet, have I?" She stroked him faster as she said it, fucked him with the plug. It was mean to admonish him when he was this close, but she couldn't help it. "Did you forget that you need my permission? Did I say you could?"

His head shot up again. "Oh fuck, *please.*"

"Please what?"

"Pleaseletmecome!"

The words mashed together so fast, his desperation clear in the tension of his body, the frantic movements of his hips. She paused for one last, delicious second, and then gave him what he needed.

"Come for me, pet."

His head dropped back, every tendon in his neck standing out. The chains jingled as his release tore through him, his moan guttural, liquid spurting hot and thick and getting everywhere.

Never in seventeen years had she seen him come like that.

With a smug grin, Sam gently slid the toy free and placed it on the edge of the towel. Shutting off the vibe, she wiped her hands and cleaned him off. "Feel better?"

He didn't answer. His head was mashed against the other arm, he was shaking and his breathing wasn't slowing down. This didn't seem right. Was it the ring? Was it hurting him? He was softening now, so she slid it off him and tossed it to the side.

"How's that? Okay?"

Still no response. Sam's heartbeat skipped a few times, then crashed together all at once.

"Are the straps too tight? Is it your knee? Hold on, I'll get them off."

Quickly, she fussed with the restraints, unbuckling them and freeing his arms and legs. He folded over onto his side and curled up in a ball.

Sam's gut clenched. Was this normal? She put a hand on his arm. "Brady?"

He flinched, then sat up, his back to her. "I need to...I can't—I'm sorry."

He got up, hastily grabbed a shirt and went into the bathroom. He slammed the door, leaving Sam in silence, confused and alone.

16

Brady didn't know what he was doing, other than that he needed to move. He had to get away from where he was, and the bathroom seemed the safest place to be.

The door shut behind him, he turned on the shower, dropped the shirt he'd grabbed for no reason and stepped inside the tub. The water hadn't heated up yet, and he startled at the chill before stepping back, crossing his arms and lowering his head.

What the hell had just happened?

He stared at his feet, at the water pooling there, and heaved in a breath. He'd loved everything in the moment, the chains, the way Sam looked above him—all of it. It was his wildest fantasy come true. So why did he feel like he was about to puke?

The shower stall steamed up. Brady doused his head, then washed off the dried jizz that was stuck to his pubic hair. Once he'd worked it out with this thumbs and forefingers, he turned around, widened his stance and pulled his butt cheeks apart. The stinging burn made him hiss, but he stayed put, letting the water course over him and trying to ignore the strange emptiness there—the result of being stretched and penetrated.

Penetrated. Christ. The reality of having done that sent a shudder through him and made him nauseous at the same time.

It didn't make sense. He'd been craving this. Asked for it. And Sam had given it to him. This should've been a no-brainer, like a math equation or line of code: pleasure plus fantasy-lived-out equaled happy. But Brady's skin was crawling, and he couldn't hack into his brain to figure out why.

Turning back around, he crouched under the nozzle. Stupid tiny shower. Except it was *him* who didn't fit, not the shower.

It was kind of hysterical. He was a six-foot-five giant ex-athlete who liked being demeaned and ass-fucked by his wife. Not that the ass-play bothered him. And bothered wasn't even the right word.

Something that bothered you was something you wanted to stop.

Not something that gave you the hardest orgasm of your life.

He'd never been overwhelmed by sensation like that. Even before it happened, he knew it was going to be intense. The pleasure was so startling he was almost scared to come. And what hit him must've been what a tsunami felt like. Dragged along by the most powerful force he'd ever experienced, he was helpless to do anything but give in.

Helpless. That's what he was. Completely and utterly. And she'd seen it.

He shook again, remembering the way Sam had mimicked him, the sharpness of her voice. She'd done it before, but tonight was different. Meaner. And the crazy part was he'd never told her about liking that. Hell, it was something he'd never said out loud at all. Having her laugh at his desperation—it was his deepest, most secret desire, and somehow she'd picked up on it like he'd blasted it across cyberspace, hacked it into every website known to man.

How many times had he had his dick in his hand and thought about being made fun of like that? Dozens? Hundreds? And why now, after living out the real deal, had he wanted to curl inward, to crawl under the blankets and hide away? He'd never felt his submission as deeply as he had in that moment. Chained up. Unable to escape. Body and mind caught in a battle between desire and shame.

If he was Luke and this was *Star Wars*, this would've been the scene when the Emperor tries to bring him over to the dark side with those electric jolts from his fingers. Except Luke liked it. And the Emperor would be a hot redhead instead of a creepy, wrinkly old guy.

Jesus, what was the matter with him?

He doused his head again.

Back when his submissive desires first surfaced, they were fantasies, nothing more. And at least he'd had football to even him out then, to make him feel like a man. Now he didn't know how to feel. He'd wanted this, but doing it in real life was different.

He shut off the water, got out and wrapped himself in a towel. He should talk to Sam, but he couldn't face her yet. He plunked down on the bathmat instead, balanced an elbow on his knee and rested his cheek on the heel of his hand. His fingers dug into the scarred ridge above his ear. Brady rubbed at it, wondering if he could sew some stitches over his desires so he didn't have to talk about them.

He didn't want to talk. He'd let her take him apart, and he was still like that, a big giant mess. He didn't feel like a man, a husband, didn't feel like anything strong at all. He was Humpty Dumpty, and he didn't know how to put himself together again.

There was a soft knock at the door. "Brady?"

Bile and anxiety swirled. He picked up his head. "It's open."

Sam came inside the room dressed in her robe. She twisted her necklace around, and if he'd been in a better mood, he would've joked that it looked like she was afraid the necklace would vanish if she let go of it.

But he wasn't in a better mood. And it was weird to see her unable to talk. It made him even more uneasy, to not know how to fix this. He was too big for this space, scrunched between the wall and the toilet. His legs filled up half the room, and yet he felt small and unguarded.

"Did I do something wrong?" she asked.

"Of course not."

"Is it because of what I said about the kitchen?"

"No, God no." That had been funny, actually.

"Then what did I do?"

"Nothing."

Her bottom lip quivered and her shoulders sank. She looked so damn *defenseless*, and suddenly everything between them reversed.

"Hey, c'mere," he said.

Before he could tack on a please, she was on the floor with him and in his arms. Having her looking to him for comfort, it felt right—felt balanced.

"You didn't do anything wrong," he breathed into her hair.

"Then why did you run out like that?"

He held her close, found something solid to hang on to in the feel of her body, even though the ground beneath him was still shaky. "Don't wanna say."

"Why?"

"Because I'm uncomfortable."

"About what?"

He didn't want to talk about it, didn't want to say anything that would make him seem weak to her.

Sam lifted her head. She shifted in his lap, reached up and touched his face.

"Trust me with your secrets," she said. "I'll keep you safe. I promise."

Jesus, wasn't that *his* job? To keep her safe, and not the other way around? That was what a real man did, what their wedding rings said. He was supposed to take care of her. This was why Brady liked things simple. Computer languages. Meat and cheese. Love your kids. Take care of your wife. But none of this was simple anymore, and her gaze was a tractor beam, forcing the honesty out of him.

"Do you still see me as a man?" he asked.

Sam's brows pushed together. She searched his eyes and caressed his cheek. "Of course I do. Why would you ask me that?"

Because she hadn't said she loved him in ages. Because he didn't fucking know how to navigate this place—how to be a husband and a father and a force to be reckoned with at work while spending as many evenings as possible begging his wife for mercy.

"Tell me," she said softly.

He bent forward and buried his face in her hair. He was terrified to show her this side of himself, but maybe getting it out in the open would chase these demons away.

"Because I'm supposed to be the man. The protector. Stronger, or whatever. How does this—" he waved his hand toward the bedroom, "—work when you're the dominant one? You're already so much smarter than me. Don't you see me as..."

His mouth went dry.

"...weak?"

"You're not weak. In case you haven't noticed, you're kind of huge. You could pick me up and toss me in the toilet if you wanted to."

She was trying to be funny.

He wasn't laughing.

"That's not what I mean," he said, acid churning like he'd eaten a bad burrito. Why was it so hard to talk about this? "I know you said you didn't like guys to be dominant in your books, and clearly you like it the other way around in bed, but I'm worried doing this makes you see me differently. That me being submissive makes me..." What was the word she'd used tonight? "Pathetic."

"It doesn't," she said. "And who cares what we like? It's just us. Just me."

"But it's *you* I'm worried about. That's why I never told you about wanting this."

"You don't trust me?"

"I do, it's..."

She waited and he swallowed. Good thing they were near a toilet, because what he was going to say was making him sick.

"I like it when you make fun of me," he whispered. "It's a kink I never understood—how being embarrassed sometimes turns me on."

"Embarrassed, by anyone?"

He shook his head, wrapped his arms around her. "Just you, like this."

"I embarrass you?"

"Sometimes."

"When?"

"In college. When you had to remind me about things." His mortification had churned and mixed with her smile, with her pride when he got things right, with the ridiculous heaven he found in her body. "When you'd show me off to your friends. And tonight, when you pointed out how turned on I was and asked me if I'd forgotten I couldn't come yet."

"I'm sorry." Her voice cracked on the words.

"No, no." He held her more tightly. How could he make her understand something he barely did himself? "It's not a bad thing. I mean, it's bothered me lately, when you get annoyed at me, but it's different when we're like this."

"It is?"

He hated that she sounded so unsure. "Very different."

"How?"

It made his body respond in ways he couldn't deny, gave her ultimate ownership over him, taking him to depths of pleasure even when he was fighting against it. "It's complicated. I hate it when you poke fun at me outside the bedroom. But when you provoke me, in there, as my Mistress—" he swallowed, "—it *does* shit to me."

"Good shit?"

He huffed out a breath. "Really good shit."

She smiled slightly. "I...think I knew that about you."

He was that cartoon character again, an anvil smashing his head. "You did?"

"I saw it, in college. And the last few weeks. Tonight definitely. I thought you just really liked it." She sighed and sagged against him. "I should've asked if it was okay to talk like that. I have no idea what I'm doing."

That was a shock. She'd felt like a practiced Femdomme to him from the get-go.

"If it helps, you're doing an amazing job."

"I am?"

"Yeah." He let his head drop against the wall as he said it. As exhausted and worn out as his body was, a heady pulse of desire for her was still there.

It had always been there.

He looked at her. She was still frowning.

"But you know," he said, "you're all I have to compare it with, so you could totally suck and I'd never know the difference."

Sam picked up her head, her eyes narrowed, lips twisted into something that was half a smile, half irritation. Brady laughed nervously until she shook her head and chuckled.

"Why do you do it?" she asked.

"Do what?"

"The jokes."

"'Cause it's easier."

"Easier than what?"

"The truth."

The half smile she'd been sporting melted away. Now he was the one to shake *his* head. "See? That's why I joke. I say something serious and you're not smiling anymore."

"Why do I always have to be smiling?"

"Because I love making you smile."

Sam's frown deepened. He was sure her brows were in danger of becoming permanently stuck together. "That's why you joke around so much?"

"Yeah. It's the best thing in the world when you smile. Even better when you laugh." It made his heart swell, made his stomach do flip-flops. It was his favorite damn sound in the world. "No matter how bad things get, how angry or distant we become, if I say something funny, and it makes you laugh, that's a win. You're happy, and I did that."

She put her hand on his cheek, stroked his beard and kissed him tenderly, lightly. He leaned into her. Inhaled her scent.

I love you, Sammy. More than anything. Don't you know that?

She pulled back and studied him with those deep brown eyes. "But you said the jokes were easier than the truth. What's the truth, then?"

Brady sighed and grinned. "Busted."

She didn't grin back. He looked away, but her hand was still on his cheek. She took his chin in her fingers, nudged his head up and made him look at her. "Tell me, pet."

It took a few beats before he could obey. Calling him *pet* was sexual. And what he was about to say wasn't. "You know sometimes it's hard for me to concentrate."

"I do." Her tone was gentle. Soothing. "Is it getting worse?"

"No. I've been dealing with it. It's not as bad as Allegra's."

It seemed strange, to mention their daughter's name, the struggles they shared, while they were half-naked on their bathroom floor. While Sam was Mistress and he was pet. It blurred the lines, made Brady even more confused about when their roles snapped into focus and when they didn't.

"It's just, you've gotten really mad at me for it lately."

Okay, now her brows were pinched so tightly together he was afraid she was going to hurt something. He had to keep going, though, to blurt this all out.

"I have issues. I accept it. I don't always...*get* everything you're saying. Not that I don't understand your words, I mean, of course I do. They're English words. I know what they mean." He was babbling. *Shut up, Brady.* "But sometimes you throw more at me than I can handle, and my mind is somewhere else, and then I forget things and disappoint you."

Her face softened. "You never disappoint me, pet."

"But what about when I'm not your pet? When you're not my Mistress but my wife?"

"Aren't I both?"

"I...guess?"

He sighed. This was why he never talked. He never felt like he was getting anywhere.

Sam stroked his cheek. "I get what you're saying. Sometimes I get frustrated, but that's all. And you *are* smart. You do things with computers I don't even understand. You built a business out of nothing, just what's up here."

She tapped his head gently as she said it, then stroked over the scar beneath his hairline.

"I'm sorry you feel this way, though." She turned in his lap and hugged him. "How can I help?"

That felt good—her cheek against his, her lack of frustration at everything he'd said. Her offer to help.

"That list you gave me today helped. So I could keep track of what you needed me to do." It worked at Helios—support tickets, emails, visual reminders. "That's what you used to do in college. You'd write me stuff on those little heart-shaped Post-it Notes."

She pulled back to look at him. "You remember that?"

"Yup."

Her big, beaming Sam-smile returned, bright enough to light up the room, to chase away his insecurities.

She leaned in again, kissed his cheek and hugged him. "Then that's what we'll do."

17

"You cleaned? There's definitely no more germs?"

Sam sighed into the phone. "Yes, Mom. I've sanitized every surface, and it's been days since anyone has coughed. You're safe."

"Did you close the windows?"

"I only had them open for a few." It had been Sam's attempt to enjoy the first semblance of nice weather they'd had. And to get some fresh air in a house that she'd cleaned this morning after having it shut up as a sick zone for the past two weeks. She'd cleaned the toys in her fancy UV cleaner, too, not that they'd gotten much use.

"Good. It's going to rain."

The sky was bright blue. Sam shook her head. Ever since her diagnosis, her mother believed she could predict the weather, and it was something Dad fed into. Sam was looking forward to their company, though, and not only because it was her father's birthday. They'd stuck with the food delivery service, so she hadn't seen them as often, only visiting intermittently to help clean.

"Get over here, then. Before the girls eat Dad's cake."

She'd gotten a store-bought one instead of baking like she usually did. There'd been no time for making anything other than chicken soup and tea lately. Hope had caught a nasty cold that managed to hit everyone in the house except Sam. As a family, they'd gone through about thirty boxes of tissues, any sexy-time with Brady halted because of the excessive amounts of mucous. He'd pushed her away with a joke at the worst of it, telling her to hide, to save herself.

She'd given birth twice, but for him a stuffed nose meant he was dying.

Sam rolled her eyes at his man-flu symptoms and enjoyed taking care of him. It helped alleviate how badly she'd felt since their talk in the bathroom. She'd had no idea his attempts at humor had been to see her smile. She'd thought they were to dodge responsibility. To blow things off instead of parenting alongside her.

Since then, she'd been determined to be extra nice, putting the Mistress aside to act as the doting wife, preparing hot chocolate while he played a football video game with the girls on the couch. Brady's eyes had lit up when they'd started asking questions about the game. It was the first time they'd shown an interest in anything he liked since he'd bribed them into seeing *Black Panther* and they'd all come home yelling, "Wakanda forever!"

It had been pretty damn adorable.

Sam closed the windows as her mother had requested. Spring had finally sprung, and the break from the cold was good for all of them, especially Allegra. Temperatures above freezing meant outside recess, and getting to play a bit had run some of the excess energy out of her.

Sam understood how her daughter felt. She'd been restless in the absence of her own workouts. She'd managed to hit the gym a few times, and once with Cassie and Lilly, the only chance the three of them had to catch up in a while. They talked again about a night out, but Sam had to push it off until she'd nursed her family to health again.

A short time later, Sam's parents' car rolled up the driveway.

"Okay, Allegra." She bent until she was eye level with her daughter. "What's the plan tonight?"

It was Sunday evening. Homework was all done, but the girls' rooms still needed to be cleaned, and tonight had to go smoothly. "To slow my tempo and say something if I feel out of control."

"That's right. Like in dance class." It was a new strategy her therapist had come up with—to connect Allegra's impulses to something she had power over. "What else?"

"Be nice to Hopey."

It was a nickname she'd started when they were both home sick, and Hope had responded to the new attention by copying everything Allegra did. Sam didn't know what had brought this new bonding on, but she didn't want to jinx it by asking. The doorbell rang, and Brady went to get it. "And what's your reward?"

She did a little quick-step. "To show Nana and Pop my routine in my pink shoes!"

Sam kissed her on the forehead and then Allegra was off, speeding to the doorway and running into her grandparents' arms. When it was time to eat cake, she didn't measure her piece against Hope's, too busy chattering about her birthday, still months away. And Sam almost fell over backward when she and Hope handed their grandfather his birthday present together.

"We have a gift for you, too." Sam's father pulled four small envelopes from his pocket. Allegra yanked them from his hand, then stopped herself and smiled at Sam with the same sheepish smile Brady often gave her.

"Good job slowing down," she said. "Go ahead and open one."

Allegra ripped open her envelope. "An airline gift card!" She pretended to be an airplane, running around the living room and then onto the couch next to her grandmother.

"It is," Sam's mom said. "So you can visit us in Arizona anytime you want."

When Hope curled up on the other side of her, Sam pulled her father aside. "Does that mean you picked a departure date?"

Another sheepish face, this one more guilty than gleeful. "The first weekend of April."

"As in, two weeks from now?"

"We decided it was time."

Months, they'd had to plan this out, and they suddenly decided. "Do you have a buyer?"

"No, but we've got a great Realtor, and everything is packed, so we're hoping you could do the rest."

They were *packed*? "When did you finish that?"

"Last weekend." He sighed. "You know how Mom is. She's convinced a rainy summer will make her hip worse."

Sam had to take a minute, take a breath. The sudden sense of loss was paired with a gut-clenching frustration. They were leaving and had given her zero time to prepare herself or the girls. Now on top of finding a sitter ASAP, it was going to be Sam's job to sell the apartment, as if she didn't have enough to do.

"We'll visit," Sam's father said. "I promise." He joined the girls on the couch, and Sam felt Brady's hand on her shoulder.

"We'll figure it out together," he said.

She wanted to believe him. She truly did.

She attempted to put it out of her head the rest of the night and into the next morning. She mostly succeeded, especially after running into Lilly and Gabe in the coffee shop near work on the way in.

"So, we're doing this?" she asked as they got on the elevator.

Gabe grinned. "Hell yeah, we are."

Sam looked around him to Lilly. "You're in, too?"

"Absolutely." She was texting as she talked. "And so is Cassie."

"What do I wear?"

Gabe quirked one dark eyebrow.

"Sweetie, it's a gay bar. There's no dress code. It's like Boston's LGBT equivalent to Cheers."

"So, Barrel 'n' Flask without the straight dudes screaming at the TVs."

"Basically."

"No biker leather then?"

Lilly wrinkled her nose as Gabe laughed. "Think more shabby chic," he said.

Sam didn't know what she owned that fell in that category. When she'd cleared out her plus-sized clothes, what remained in her closet was workout gear and old business suits. She'd already worn the few cute things she had.

"I feel like the only one here who has stretch marks and needs a babysitter."

"Some of us wish for that," Gabe said quietly.

"Stretch marks?"

He glanced at the floor. "No."

His comment caught Sam off guard, but she didn't know what to say. Lilly hadn't seemed to have heard it. "Speaking of a sitter," Lilly said. "Are we asking the boys to come?"

"I'm asking *my* boy!" Gabe replied, no longer melancholy.

Lilly rolled her eyes. "I know *you* are. But I don't think it'll be Jack's scene. Or Patrick's. Will it be Brady's?"

Sam didn't think so, but she didn't want to speak for him. "If Jack and Patrick aren't going, he probably won't want to either."

"God, our men are so boring," Lilly said. "Best to let them make their own plans."

Sam could say for a fact just how boring her husband wasn't. The elevator stopped at their floor and they walked through the firm's doors. "So, Saturday then."

"Saturday," Lilly agreed.

Gabe gave them both a thumbs-up, and then he and Lilly went in the direction of their offices. Sam walked toward her desk, surprised to find Reginald Pierce standing there.

"Mr. Pierce, good morning. Can I help you with something?"

And please don't be creepy, Mr. Creepy McCreeperson.

"I'd like to hope so, Mrs. Archer. Especially since it seems you've become indispensable here."

"Who told you that?"

"Everyone."

Sam couldn't help smiling as she took off her jacket and went to her seat. Indispensable was a term she liked. She'd quickly gotten on a first-name basis with all the vendors. The FedEx guy was eating out of her hands, she'd turned the previously messy conference-room schedule into a tightly run ship, and some of the clients already knew her by name.

"I'm free right now. What do you need?"

His gaze didn't slink toward her chest like she'd expected. Instead, he came around to her side of the desk. "Log in to your computer. I'm giving you access to the Choate file. I've already had the tech department lower the ethical wall for you."

"Ethical wall?"

"It's a screen that stops conflicts of interest or giving people access who shouldn't have it."

Fancy. Brady would think it was cool. Or he'd say he built stuff like that all the time. Maybe he'd built this one. It was staggering, to realize how little they talked sometimes.

She booted up her computer and started her email client. A message from Pierce was in bold at the top of her inbox.

"Read that," he said. "I'm sending you the login to the bank account, too."

"Got it. When do you want me to start on this?"

"Now." There was no irony to his words. "Start at the oldest file and work your way forward. We've only been doing this digitally since Hanna started so everything before then is already done and in storage." He started to walk away, then stopped. "Also, I see you've met Hanna."

She froze. Was that a problem? "I have."

"I'd appreciate it if you wouldn't mention this to her. She can get a bit...*possessive* over work she does for me."

Sam had noticed the pecking order here. The secretaries had their own social structure, a microcosm based around who they worked for. The ones who were assigned to the highest-paid attorneys, partners especially, ranked themselves higher than others.

Although Sam wasn't sure *possessive* was the word they'd use to describe it.

"She's also a bit disorganized," Pierce added with that toothy grin of his. "I wouldn't want her to know the receptionist is checking her work."

Sam simply smiled. "Understood, Mr. Pierce."

"Thank you, Mrs. Archer."

Sam got to work. By midday, it was clear Pierce hadn't been

exaggerating about the file. It was such a mess it reminded Sam of her house at the end of the weekend. There were subfolders for each year, more subfolders within for each month, and inside of each was a clusterfuck of downloaded invoices and scanned receipts. She got through the first few months and was able to match most of the checks to the bills she found in the file, however some were signed by Pierce and made out to cash. He must've been paying himself out of the Choate trust for the work he did, but the amounts weren't in an attorney's billable rate and were never the same.

She definitely needed a break.

It was generous for the firm to offer her a half-hour break on a part-time shift, but it wasn't long enough for her to go out like other people did. It was early, too, which meant the lunchroom was empty, and was a perfect time to pull out her iPad and read.

She heated up some leftover soup from last week's Flu-nami and sat. She wasn't trying to be sneaky or rebellious, reading smutty stuff here. Honestly, she was trying to figure out how to stop making mistakes with Brady. And if she was going to take things up a notch by adding the strap-on to their playtime soon—something she *really* wanted to do after his reaction to the plug—she needed to be sure she knew what she was doing.

She opened up to a pegging scene she'd read once and settled in. "That's a good one."

Sam whirled around. She hadn't heard anyone walk in, but there was Hanna, standing behind her at the coffee machine, a cup in one hand and her phone in the other.

"I—I'm just...." Sam shoved her iPad in her lap. "I'm so embarrassed."

Was this how Brady felt? Because this fucking sucked.

Hanna laughed. "Don't be. I reread that scene the other night." She lowered her voice. "Such a relief, I'll tell you. Most of the ladies here like the books where it's the other way around. I can't bloody stand that kak."

Sam wasn't sure what to ask first. "Kak?"

Hanna took a step closer. "Means shit."

"Oh." Her perfume smelled expensive. Chanel expensive. "What can't you stand?"

"The stories with the men on top." Hanna winked. Her hair was down and wild today, curls springing all over, her warm complexion standing out against a sultry wrap dress. A strand of long, thin diamonds hung from each ear. "Who'd want to read that?"

Sam laughed, completely flustered. "You read this...*exact* scene recently?"

"Yep. Good stuff, right?"

"Definitely."

Sam stared. She was dying to ask about Hanna's preferred line of cosmetics, but that wasn't the only reason she was enthralled. Hanna's rolled *R* had a tapped sound, like she put an *H* before it, and her *A's* were more like *eh's*. "I have to ask—where are you from?"

"Originally? South Africa. My full name is Hannaleen."

Sam had met a lot of people in DC, but only a few from that part of the world. "What was it like, growing up under Apartheid?"

Hanna threw herself into a chair. "Couldn't tell you. I was born after the ban on mixed marriages was repealed."

Sam did the math. That happened in the mid-eighties, so Hanna had to have been six to eight years younger than her. "So it didn't affect you?"

"It did, but my Dad got transferred back to the UK when I was twelve. He worked for AfrAsia Bank in London. I went to an international school there and then uni before coming here."

"You came to America for a job?"

She made a *pshaw* sound. "Made the stupid choice and followed a man. Wanker, he was." Hanna put her feet on the chair across from her, like she was right at home. "My parents hated my ex-husband, but I was in love. Two kids later, and that bastard's outta my life. Good riddance to that—"

"Piece of kak?" Sam finished for her, sensing the joke was the right way to go. Hanna didn't seem like the kind of person who wanted pity for her past.

"Hey, you catch on quick." She thumbed over her phone screen and turned it around. "These are my girls."

The photo was of two breathtaking children, skin a shade darker than Hanna's with slightly Asian features. "They're beautiful."

"They're a royal pain in my arse, that's what they are. But I love them." She locked the screen, then jutted her chin in the direction of Sam's phone. "Show me yours."

Sam found a picture she'd taken of them with Brady in a rare moment of no sibling rivalry.

"That your husband?" Hanna asked. When Sam nodded, Hanna leaned in more. "My God, he's massive."

Sam beamed. "He's a big guy."

"Lucky, too, I reckon."

"Oh?"

"Yeah." Hanna lowered her voice. "Got a gorgeous ginger wife reading about bangin' blokes up the bum. Bet he's not complaining too much in the bedroom."

Sam laughed so hard she had to cover her mouth. The kitchen phone extension rang—something Sam had learned was like a PA system when an attorney was looking for someone. She hurried over to it, seeing the call was from Pierce's extension.

"Hello, Mr. Pierce."

Hanna rolled her eyes as Sam mouthed the words, *He's asking for you.*

"Tell him I'm in the loo," she whispered. "Feminine issues. He hates that."

Sam had to swallow a laugh. "She's in the ladies' room, but I believe she'll be back shortly."

When she hung up, Hanna shook her head. "Can't get too far away from that one or he'll forget where he put his own ass."

"He certainly seems like a...handful."

It was the nicest way she could put it.

"Has been ever since his divorce. I'm like his work wife." Hanna stood, straightened her dress and grinned. "I've trained him, though. You've gotta know how to handle men like that. Put them in their place."

Something fluttered in Sam's stomach—a spark of connection.

"I should let you get back to your reading," Hanna said. "By the way, I love your hair. I'm so jealous."

"*You're* jealous?" Sam asked. "I'm jealous of your skin. It's flawless."

"It's all cosmetics, love. La Prairie, a line from Switzerland. I'm about out, too. Wanna go shopping with me tomorrow?"

"I don't get a long enough lunch to go anywhere."

"I could cut out for a bit if you've got some time after work." She nodded back in the direction of her office. "Tell Old Faithful that I've got a *female* appointment."

Sam laughed again, then thought it out. Allegra had dance practice tomorrow, but her parents could take her. After all, it was going to be the last time they'd be able to.

"An hour might be possible. I need to get something shabby chic for a gay club outing on Friday anyway."

Hanna paused, then blinked. "Okay, the hubby might complain a tad in bed."

Sam waved a hand. "No, I'm not...it's just for fun. With friends."

"Ah." Hanna looked Sam up and down. "Shabby chic isn't you. But we'll find something. Till then. Cheers!"

She walked off. Sam texted her mom to put the plans in motion, giddy like a teenager who'd found a new best friend. There was something about the other woman that intrigued her. Like her boss, Hanna acted like she owned the place, and that plus the scene she'd read told Sam Hanna might be a Domme. It was a stretch—reading dirty books didn't mean people did what was in them—but there was a chance something more was going on there.

And Sam wanted to find out.

18

Hanna had some seriously expensive tastes.

Their first stop was Saks Fifth Avenue. Sam hadn't been there since last year, when she'd gone with Cassie and Lilly on a shopping spree. She hadn't bought anything for herself; when she and Brady had money to spend, they spent it on the kids.

Hanna, apparently, didn't have that problem. The bottle of concealer she'd bought had actual caviar extract. She'd paid in cash for it, too, something Sam had no idea people did. Sam hadn't looked at the price, but it couldn't have been cheap. No wonder her skin looked so good.

As they emerged from the fancy department store, Hanna dug a hand into the bag of Lindor Truffles she'd picked up as a "shopping essential" and offered Sam one.

"Thanks, but I'll pass. I try to watch what I eat."

"Why?" she asked with a mouthful of chocolate. "You're positively tiny."

"I wasn't always."

Hanna leaned back and checked out Sam's backside. "Get out. With that ass?"

Sam had to laugh—was she actually *blushing*? "Baby weight. And then depressed-after-baby weight. And then the same thing again with baby number two."

"Good on ya for shedding it. I like food too much. Couldn't diet if I tried."

"It's not like you need it." The woman completely rocked her shape. "I doubt you're a slave to the gym like I am."

"Slave is an interesting word." Hanna popped another chocolate in her mouth and grinned. "I, personally, find other ways of sweating."

Okay, now she really needed to know more. As Hanna led her into Barney's and poked through a pile of Hermes silk scarves, Sam's inquisitiveness got the better of her.

"I guess the wanker's alimony payments are pretty good, huh?"

Hanna's expression darkened. "No alimony. No divorce. He just up and left one day."

"I'm sorry," Sam said. "I assumed..."

"It's okay. I'm the one who called him my *ex*-husband. Sounding divorced sounds better than sounding abandoned."

Sam felt sick. How could anyone leave their partner and children? She should let the thing lie, but then Hanna glanced up. Her lips were the color of currant today, and Sam would've been lying if she said they didn't make her stare.

"You can ask about him, if you want."

Sam blinked. "Him?"

"Washington, my ex-husband."

"That was his name?"

Hanna nodded, and Sam had to snort at the irony of it. They both had a Washington in their pasts. Hanna took out her phone and showed Sam a picture of a built, attractive man with black and Asian features.

"Good-looking wanker."

"Yep. We made some beautiful babies together."

"Do you still talk to him?"

"Nah. Pisser could be dead for all I know. Haven't heard a peep since the day I let the door slam behind him."

"Was there a reason he left?"

"He didn't want to be a dad anymore, or he couldn't take being with a real woman." Hanna shrugged. "Thing that pissed me off the most was that he proved my parents right. Not that I could talk to them."

Sam treaded carefully this time. "Are they no longer with us?"

"They're alive. They just don't speak to me anymore."

"At all?" Sam's parents were moving, but at least she knew she'd talk to them, FaceTime, see them again.

"Yeah. I miss them. Miss London, too. But I live here now. And they made their choice." She looked at Sam and sighed. "I'm dumping a lot on you, aren't I?"

"Not at all. I want to hear it."

A relieved smile cracked across Hanna's face. Sam wondered how many friends Hanna had. Hanna shifted her bags to one side and linked their arms together.

"There's a long story to it. You see, I was raised quite wealthy. I didn't say it before, because it's weird, yeah? But in Johannesburg we lived on an estate, kind of like the South African Beverly Hills, gated suburbs where the rich could hide their mixed-race kids. In London, we lived in Knightsbridge, really posh. I was groomed to be a debutante: piano lessons, French lessons—"

"You speak French?"

Because that was the important question to be asking.

"*Oui, madame. Je le parlé bien.*"

The translation of "*Yes, madame. I spoke it well*" took longer with the giddy flutter in her stomach. Okay, she was girl-crushing, hard. "I used to speak it, too. In college. At one point I was reading full-on French novels, studying literature and debating the state of American politics."

"Sounds like you were a bit of a superstar."

Sam laughed wistfully. "I was, I guess. Or I was gonna be."

Hanna's brows were raised in a look that said *go on.*

"I worked in DC for a while. Congress. But I had to come home to take care of family issues, and then I met Brady and the rest is history."

"We have more in common than we thought."

They'd wandered into the women's clothing department. Hanna flipped through a few tops, discarding each one as she moved them around on a rack.

"I was somebody, too. Had an education and a future, but I fell for a Blasian bloke who sunk me in a heartbeat, and I followed him across the Pond. He said he was a music producer, although the only thing he produced was the *product* he sold on the streets." She rejected the tops and turned around, head held high. "Now that prat's gone, and I'm making bank wiping the nose of one of the most powerful lawyers in Boston."

Hanna's history made Sam's past look like the epitome of First World problems. "Do you worry about your citizenship?"

The current political climate made even Sam nervous. But Hanna made that *pshaw* sound again. "Reg made sure I was okay. I've got a conditional green card, the 'condition' being that my marriage works out. Wash and I aren't divorced, so by legal standards that means things are working!"

Her smile was bright, but sarcastic. Sam had to laugh.

"In a year I'll be eligible to apply for citizenship," Hanna continued. "And I'm not worried about my kids' birthright citizenship, no matter what crazy shit we hear on the news or Twitter these days. As long as I don't commit any violent felonies, I'm good."

Sam was in awe. "You're a badass for making it on your own."

"I do it for my girls. And Wash's aunt lives next door to me, so she helps." She looked around, blew her hair off her face. "Come on, we're not gonna find what I want for you here."

"What *you* want?"

"Uh-huh."

Hanna led the way out of the store and down a side street. After a few blocks, they ended up at a blank storefront, with a keypad at the doorway. Hanna punched in some numbers and they were buzzed inside.

"Where are we going?" Sam asked.

"You'll see."

Drawn to the mysterious way Hanna carried herself, Sam

followed her up a narrow flight of steps, the lights above them fluorescent and blinking. At the landing was a door with a black placard sign on it that read "Molly's of Mercy." And behind it was the most elaborate lingerie and corset shop Sam could imagine.

"Hey, Molly. I got a new girl here," Hanna called out, then turned to Sam. "Much better than shabby chic, don't you think?"

Sam fingered a red bustier flocked in velvet. "You shop here?"

"I like pretty things," she said, then whispered, "And let's say I don't just *read* about things like you were yesterday."

"I knew it!" Sam felt like dancing. "Um, me, too."

"Then that giant hubby of yours definitely has nothing to complain about."

Was Sam blushing again? She was definitely blushing. "It's new though. I haven't had anyone to talk to about it."

"You don't know people in the lifestyle?"

She did, but they were all in Sam's inner circle, not people she could share this with.

Sam shook her head.

"Well, you do now."

It was like discovering they were sisters. She had to acknowledge that she found Hanna attractive—of course she did. But this was nothing more than a fast, furious and close friendship with someone like her. Sam had so many questions, she didn't know where to start.

"So, you've been doing—" she waved around the shop, "—*this* for a while?"

"You could say that."

"How do you keep up with it, while working and having kids?"

"Simple." Hanna's grin was gleeful. "I don't cook or clean much."

Skipping that would certainly free up some time. "And you're in a BDSM relationship? You're seeing someone?"

"Let's say my relationship status is permanently complicated."

Sam wanted to know why, but Hanna towed her over to a rack and lifted a hanger from it. "*This* is what I was looking for. It'll look stunning on you."

Sam took it from her. The corset was black, but completely untraditional. With steel loops and stays up the front, it had long chiffon sleeves attached to a bustier that came together under the bust. Buttons went up to a high neckline that could be left open to show a little, or a lot of cleavage.

"It's like a corset hidden in a shirt," Hanna said. "Like a superhero Domme outfit."

Sam laughed. Brady would like that. She flipped over the price tag. "Three hundred and fifty dollars?"

Hanna's eyes flashed. "It's very pretty."

"I don't need to buy my children birthday presents this year, right? Or pay my taxes?"

"Every Domme needs something that makes her feel sexy. Strong. Wanted. It's like armor. Something *more* to put us in that space. To boost us up, so we can be what they need."

Us. We. This was information she needed, the feedback she'd been lacking.

"You've sold me there." And Brady *had* said he wanted to see her in something like this, so that was another selling point. "But it's definitely not shabby chic. Not sure I can wear it this weekend."

"Fuck yeah, you can. And when you do, everyone's eyes will be on you."

Sam's heart got lodged in her chest. Wasn't that what she'd been longing for? To feel noticed and *seen*, in a way no one, including Brady, had in so long? She'd thought she'd lost that part of herself forever, and here was someone like her, someone she wanted to be more like, helping that part of her shine.

Sam took the corset off the hanger. "Does Molly sell any toys in here?"

"She's got a whole room of 'em in the back. I'll even make sure she gives you my frequent shopper discount."

Sam raised an eyebrow. "How much off?"

Hanna's head fell back on a loud, boisterous laugh. "Twenty percent, but I'm sure she'll work with you."

"You're gonna be a bad influence on me."

Hanna looped their arms together again. "I hope so, love. I hope so."

19

"**Y**ou're sure you've got this?"

Twirling a youth-sized football, Brady watched Sam move around the kitchen while they waited for her Uber to arrive. "I've got this."

Sam rummaged through her bag. "I wrote down the girls' bedtime routines—"

"I *have* put our children to bed before, you know."

"—I know, but—"

"But you thought I'd throw caution to the wind. Let them act like monkeys and hang from the ceiling."

Across the table, Allegra made monkey noises and Hope giggled.

Sam stopped rummaging and looked up. "Something like that."

Brady twirled the ball again and waited for her to smile. He appreciated the handwritten instructions she'd left upstairs, especially since it was the first time in a few weeks she'd done that, regardless of that talk they'd had. It was okay. She'd been busy taking care of everyone through The Great SnotFest of 2019. And he'd felt more capable lately. She had confidence in him and that had given him confidence in himself. He could handle things at home for a few hours—he'd been managing the mornings, so how difficult could bedtime be?—and she deserved a fun evening out.

Even if the two of them hadn't had a fun night *in* for weeks.

He put down the ball and walked over to her. "Don't worry. If anything goes wrong I'll have Patrick and Jack here for backup." They'd decided on a guys' night in since he had the girls, one that was hopefully going to include a few beers, a game on TV and absolutely no sex advice.

"And after we play some ball, we're gonna eat this amazing dinner Mommy cooked for us—" chicken and whole-wheat pasta with absolutely no potato chip or sugary deviations, he'd been warned, "—and have a pajama party. Right, girls?"

They lifted tiny fists. "Right," they said in unison.

"And Daddy's not gonna curse," Allegra added, then grinned at Hope. Brady made a face at them both. They'd bonded when they were home sick. He'd even caught Allegra reading Hope a book. It was awesome, and really freaking weird.

"Right," Sam said. "Or Daddy will be in trouble." She winked after she said it, and Brady willed himself to ignore his body's reaction. He didn't want to be in trouble with Sam tonight.

Well, maybe a little. If trouble involved the way she was looking at him now.

"Daddy," Hope said. "I want to be the line maker like you were."

"You mean linebacker."

Allegra bounced in her seat, legs swinging wildly. "And I want to be the wide retriever."

"Receiver," he corrected on a laugh. "A retriever is a dog. And you can be whatever you want."

He'd started to explain things when they were all sacked out on the couch blowing their noses. The video-game version he'd been playing had piqued their interests. Hope kept track of the score in her head while Allegra asked what a down and a drive were, and why it was called a touchdown when nobody touched anything.

It was basically the best day ever.

He turned back toward Sam. She'd pulled out her phone and was texting furiously.

"It's Gabe," she said. "He's pulling a Queer Eye for the Straight Girl and asking what I'll be wearing."

Brady wanted to know, too. Her hair was big and full, her eyes shaded, but she was still in jeans and a sweater. She'd gotten halfway ready here and was heading to Nick and Gabe's to dress up with Lilly and Cassie before they went out. She bent over, and Brady was hoping to get a glimpse of skin as her sweater peeled away from her chest. But it wasn't bare skin that caught his attention.

She wasn't wearing her necklace. She'd left her engagement ring off, too.

"No jewelry tonight?" he asked.

"I didn't feel like going out with a lot of bling," she said. "And the necklace doesn't match my outfit."

That made sense. It seemed like a dumb thing to bring up now that she'd told him. Besides, her wedding band was still on.

"Daddy, look." Allegra held up Sam's iPad. "I found videos of football players dancing."

Brady laughed, but Sam held up a hand. "Be careful with that. And remember, only an hour of screen time. Then it goes upstairs." She turned back to Brady with a frown. "Do you have to teach them football when I'm not here? Something could happen. They could get hurt."

"Sammy, relax. I've got this."

She searched his eyes, and his stomach pitched with nerves, like he wasn't supposed to call her that. Honestly, he wasn't sure what to call her. They hadn't played since that night he'd flipped out. Getting sick had been a factor, but his body had started turning inside out with edginess since, so he'd been working out a ton to compensate. And when that stopped helping, he'd tried losing himself in lines of code.

It hadn't worked. Part of him worried the last month was only going to be that—a brief escape from their humdrum lives, a dip into paradise never to be repeated again.

Then Sam's hand encircled his wrist. Her thumb stroked a line over the spot that hadn't been wrapped in her restraints in far too long.

"Okay," she said softly, and gave him her signature half smile. It lit him up, told him that no matter what name he called her, no matter what jewelry she was or wasn't wearing, she was coming home to him.

"Mommy, you look pretty," Hope said.

Sam's smile blossomed even more. "Thank you, honey."

"Yeah," Allegra agreed. "You look like a Disney princess but without the dress."

Sam opened her mouth to reply, but Allegra barreled through.

"Are you wearing a dress tonight? That bag doesn't look like it'll fit a dress. I think you might need a bigger one."

"No dress tonight, sweetie. Just jeans and a nice top."

Allegra rolled her eyes. "Boring."

Brady was sure nothing about Sam tonight was going to be boring.

"*We're* not gonna be boring, are we?" he asked. "We're playing football!" The girls cheered as Sam's phone buzzed, signaling her Uber driver's arrival. "Okay, say goodbye to Mommy and get outside. It's game time."

They hopped off their chairs. After careening into Sam for hugs and kisses, they made a beeline down the hall. Brady walked her to the front door.

"Will *I* get to see you in your jeans and nice top when you get home?" he asked.

She hadn't shown him what she'd purchased on her shopping trip with her new friend from work. She'd bought something else besides the top, and declared it off-limits, stashing it in their locked toy chest. The mystery was killing him.

She slipped on her jacket. "Is that a request?"

"It is." A small one he hoped she'd grant him.

"Then, yes." She kissed him lightly and whispered, "And if you're lucky, you'll see me out of it, as well as an extra surprise or two."

A thrill shivered through him.

"Have fun." *Love you.*

He waited until the Uber drove off, then went inside. He grabbed the kids' ball he'd had hanging around the house, hoping the girls would one day want to learn, and went out into the yard. It was a balmy day, the forty-something temperatures downright tropical after the bitter cold. The ground was wet with patches of leftover melted snow, but the sun was setting later, leaving them with another good hour of daylight. Baseball's opening day was last week, and it was one month until the NFL draft—the perfect time to educate his offspring about his favorite sport.

"Okay," he announced. "First rule is to keep looking at the ball."

Allegra, clown that she was, ran over to him, opened her eyes wide and stared at the ball in his hands. "Okay, I'm looking."

Hope skipped up and did the same. "Me, too!"

"That's not what I meant, but good start." Brady chuckled. "Here's the basics. There's eleven players on each team. Each player has a different role. Like the quarterback, for instance, whose job is to call the plays. There's also running backs, receivers—"

"We know this, Dad," Allegra said with another eye roll.

"Oh, do you, Little Miss Know It All?" She nodded and grinned. "I guess you already know how to throw the perfect spiral, too."

She shook her head and swung her arms around, the picture of innocence.

"That's what I thought, smartypants."

He gently bonked her on the head with the corner of the ball, then crouched to explain offense and defense. Their eyes only glazed over slightly when he talked them through theories on throwing motions, grips and the idea of "looking the ball" into their hands. Once he'd shown them both how to hold it, the real fun began.

"That's it, Hope. Dig your heel into the ground," he said, tossing the ball to her, then to Allegra. "Keep looking at the ball."

Hope was pretty good, her throw surprising for a seven-year-old. Allegra dropped the ball several times, but instead of having a tantrum, she stayed focused, picking it up and trying again. It made him wish he'd made time for days like this more often—that he'd been working less and been more present with the kids. Sure, they'd had fun days together, but he was always too overloaded, deferring to Sam for activity planning. Had that been an excuse? Maybe he'd avoided family time because facing Allegra meant facing what he didn't like in himself.

He'd caught up some at work, less distracted than he'd been when his thoughts were on Sam. It seemed like he could only be one thing at a time—pet, or husband. Boss or submissive. In order to be one, he had to put another on a shelf. They were all parts of him, yet he couldn't mesh them together to put all of his different pieces into one cohesive whole.

"Daddy?" Hope asked. "How come you don't play football anymore?"

Oh. Wow, he'd never told her this.

"Well, I got hurt." He put the ball on the ground, bent down and rolled up his track pants to show her the slightly translucent section of skin that ran a line from several inches below his kneecap to half a dozen above it. Allegra came over to join them. "You can't see it anymore, but the muscles here were all torn up."

The "unhappy triad" the doctors had called it—an injury to the anterior cruciate ligament, medial collateral ligament, and meniscus, one of the most feared sports injuries. The girls didn't need to know it wasn't during an actual game that it happened. He hoped they'd grow to live in a world where hatred like that didn't exist anymore. That it would be a story he'd never need to tell them. But if they were ever threatened the way Nick had been, he'd destroy every bone in his body defending them.

"Did it hurt?" Hope asked.

"A lot." He could remember the very *wrong* feeling of his knee changing direction, the pop he'd felt after his head hit the wall and his knee hit the concrete. Bones and hard surfaces didn't make a good combination.

She put her hand on his leg. "That's why you stopped playing?"

"One of the reasons."

"Does it still hurt?" she asked. He couldn't remember her asking that many questions in a single setting.

"Sometimes." He unrolled his pant leg. "But sometimes things hurt, and you've gotta get up, keep on going."

Brady stood as his phone buzzed with a two-word text from Jack: *"We're here."* He sent Allegra inside to get them. A minute later, his brother and Patrick were opening the back door.

"We're learning football," she told them. "Wanna play?"

Brady retrieved the ball and tossed it back and forth. "Uncle Jack doesn't play football. He and Patrick play *tennis*."

He made his voice high-pitched as he said it. His comment only got a laugh out of his brother.

"Tennis isn't an easy sport," Jack said as Allegra tried to drag him across the lawn. "Don't knock it."

"Yeah, because which requires more strength and agility?" Brady asked. "A game where you pass a little bouncing ball over a net? Or a full-contact sport where you need a helmet to avoid brain damage?"

He wasn't really ragging on tennis. It required some serious skill. But that sense of competition was strong between them. Brady had to take them down a few notches in whatever way he could.

Patrick crossed his arms. "You think football is more demanding, huh? Remind me why tennis players can play five sets every other day but footballers can't play for more than a few hours a week?"

"That's the networks' choices. Not the players'," Brady shot back. "And don't forget that football is played mainly in cold weather, while tennis is a summer sport. You know, to prepare you for your Florida retirement communities."

Patrick grinned. "I'd have no problems if Cassie wanted to move us down to Miami, my friend. None at all."

"Uncle Jack, are you gonna play or not?" Allegra was putting all her effort into yanking Jack's arm, her feet pedaling against the grass.

"Okay I'll play," he said, giving in. "What position should I be?"

"Wide retriever!" She let go of him at that and started barking, running around the yard in circles. So much for her focus, but she'd fall asleep faster tonight if she ran the energy out of her.

"I don't think Uncle Jack could be a wideout," Brady said as he tossed his brother the ball. "He'd have to run too fast every play. I'd worry about him having a heart attack."

Jack caught the ball and smiled. "Nice."

Brady's grin was smug in return. "Just speaking the truth. You're getting up there in years."

They threw the ball back and forth, the girls running between them, trying to grab it from the air. Patrick kept his arms crossed, standing off to the side.

"Not gonna join us, Patrick?" Brady asked. "Too afraid you're gonna mess up that pretty face?"

Facts were facts. Patrick was a good-looking guy, but he wasn't big or fast. There wasn't a single position he could play that wouldn't end in him getting beat on.

Patrick put a hand to his goatee, pretending to be deep in thought. "You know what else makes tennis harder than football? If you're tired or sick, you've gotta stay on the court, toughen up and get through it. You can't call in a *sub* to replace you."

The word meant substitute, but the way Patrick said it seemed intentional, meaning a different kind of sub altogether. It flustered Brady, had him looking at the ground as the girls jumped in between them. No matter how comfortable Sam had made him with his desires, he still didn't want that shit on display right now. And he *never* wanted Jack to know.

Frustrated, Brady spiked the ball without realizing Hope was running toward his side. Her head collided with his elbow, and Brady's heart stopped in the first awful moment of silence when the shock hit her, then she burst into tears.

"Shit! I'm sorry." He dropped to his knees, ignoring the sudden sharp sear of pain. Jack and Patrick bolted over to them while Allegra hovered a few feet away. "Shhh. You're okay. Can you tell me where it hurts?"

"My head," she hollered, then sobbed even louder. Damn it, this child never cried. The sudden outpouring of emotion was completely out of left field for her.

"I know your head, but where?" He put his hands in her hair and felt around. "There's a bump. Shit. Shit!"

"Daddy, you cursed," Allegra said. "Mom's gonna be mad."

Brady couldn't give a rat's ass about his language right now. "Allegra, enough."

"But Mommy said—"

"You're in a time-out."

"But—"

"Now!"

She cowered in fear, then ran inside. And Hope was looking just as terrified. This evening was quickly unraveling.

"I'm sorry, munchkin," he said, hands open like he was approaching a frightened animal. "Come on. Let's get you some ice."

He finally coaxed her inside. Once he'd gotten her an ice pack for her head, wiped away her tears and settled her in front of the TV clutching a stuffed animal, he went up to Allegra's room. She shouted at him to go away. Defeated, he returned to the kitchen and slumped over the table. Jack and Patrick sat there with their eyebrows raised, like the two old guys from the Muppets.

"You gonna call Sam?" Patrick asked.

"And tell her about my parenting fail?" Brady propped his head up in one hand and flipped his phone around with the other. He really was unprepared to parent in Sam's absence. "No. I don't want to ruin her night. It's her first time at a gay bar, after all."

Patrick's brow wrinkled as he looked over at Jack. Now he looked even more like a Muppet.

"What?" Brady asked.

"Brady," Jack said. "I don't think they're going to a gay bar at all."

Gabe opened his door and gave Sam a once-over. "I know I said shabby chic, but is *that* what you're wearing?"

Sam lifted her bag. "Nope, got a much sexier top and shoes in here."

"Good."

He took her hand and brought her inside his and Nick's Beacon Hill brownstone. Down the long hallway, she could hear laughter and music.

"What's this mysterious change of plans you texted me about?" she asked. Gabe's message had been cryptic, just that she should up her game clothing-wise, and it had made her glad she'd opted on the corset.

"We're not going to a gay bar," Gabe said.

"We're not?"

He led her into a kitchen that had been converted into half a beauty salon, half a photo studio. A light stand and white umbrella were propped up behind a wooden high-top table where Lilly and Cassie were doing their makeup.

"Nope. We're going to a dungeon."

"We're doing *what* now?"

Cassie's head fell back in laughter, and Nick snapped a quick photo. "Told ya Sam would flip out." She was dressed in head-to-toe leather and spiked leather ankle boots, looking like Catwoman minus the mask. "But, in a good way."

Lilly turned around to face Sam. She was wearing a schoolgirl outfit, complete with knee-high socks and her hair in pigtails. Her collar was clearly visible, too.

"I hope you're okay with this," she said.

"I am—"

Lilly squealed and clapped. "Jack gave me permission to go without him because there's so many of us." Her mouth dropped open on a pause. "Which is a thing with us..."

She cringed and Sam smirked. "I know."

Lilly's eyes went wide. "You know...what?"

"About you and Jack." Sam tapped on the padlocked heart hanging from Lilly's collar. "And why you need permission."

Her friend turned about twelve shades of crimson. "But, how'd you know?"

Nick stepped between them, camera in hand. "Everyone knows."

"They do?" Lilly asked.

He grabbed a grape from a bowl sitting amidst the makeup, popped it in his mouth and chewed happily. "Yup."

She turned back to the mirror. "Okay. I'm not completely humiliated or anything."

If *that* was humiliating, Lilly didn't have half the stomach Brady did.

Cassie propped a hand on her hip. "I didn't have to ask Patrick's permission. He knew I'd pummel anyone who gave me a hard time, including him."

Sam reached for a grape for herself. "I know *your* deal, too."

"And what's that?"

Chewing thoughtfully, she said, "I imagine it falls somewhere in the consensual non-consent category?"

"Damn," Cassie said. "Chica knows her shit."

Sam looked at Nick and Gabe. "And you two are vanilla and boring."

Nick cupped the back of Gabe's neck and squeezed. "So boring that we're thinking about moving to the suburbs, adopting a bunch of kids and getting a station wagon."

Lilly side-eyed him. "If you get a station wagon, I'm renouncing you as my brother."

"Okay," Nick said. "Make it a minivan."

Lilly threw a tube of lipstick at him. "That's even worse!"

Sam recalled Gabe's comment from the other day about wishing he needed a babysitter and wondered if Nick was joking. He took that moment to turn on her.

"And what about you, Samantha Archer?" he asked. "What's *your* deal?"

It was like truth or dare, like Washington, a politician hiding her dirty secrets. She thought about Hanna, about the enigmatic persona she put on in the corset shop, and smiled like Hanna would.

"A magician never reveals her secrets."

Sam reached down to pick up her bag. Nick leaned in close and grabbed it from her.

"I think you mean Mistress," he said quietly enough that no one else could hear.

"I plead the Fifth." Sam snatched her bag from him. "Where can I change?"

She got ready in the spare bedroom. The corset cinched her waist, giving her the kind of hourglass figure she thought only existed after a serious amount of photoshopping. She closed the top button of her shirt, then left several of the ones beneath open, creating a keyhole effect around her cleavage. This was why she'd left her necklace at home—it hadn't worked with the buttons. But going where they were headed now, it could've looked like a collar.

Still, it felt strange to not have it on.

Sam reached for her phone, took a selfie, and sent it to Brady with a text.

"Turns out we're going to a fetish club. But don't worry. I'm just a spectator."

His reply came a moment later—a simple, *"K."*

She frowned. *"You okay?"*

"Sure," his reply said. Then, after that, *"Have fun."*

His words were too clipped. There was no joking around, no normal Brady present. Why did he shut down like this? He was so hard to read sometimes. Was he overwhelmed with the girls, or was he mad? Did going someplace like this without him violate some kind of BDSM rule? Before they'd started this, tonight would've been just a crazy night out with her friends. She wouldn't have to clear it with him, and if she was the Domme, did she have to anyway?

But being a Domme didn't give her license to do whatever she wanted.

She frowned at her reflection. When was she Brady's Mistress, and when was she his wife?

Back in the kitchen, she received some flattering catcalls from her friends. They piled into Nick's car, and Gabe rattled off a list of protocols, things Sam had to remember before walking into the club. They'd already been vetted, allowed in on Nick and Gabe's behalf.

Maybe they weren't as vanilla as they let on.

"You don't have to participate in anything," Gabe said as he drove through darkened streets—an area of Lynn she'd never been to before. "We're all there to watch. And try not to yuck anyone's yum."

"What the hell does that mean?" Cassie asked.

Nick turned around in the passenger seat. "It means don't gawk if something grosses you out."

It was like cramming for a test Sam didn't know she had. They parked at a row of what could've been office spaces during the day and walked to where a small crowd had amassed in various levels of kink wear and costumes. The second floor of the building they were standing by had its windows blacked out, but a pounding bass could be heard despite that, loud and gravelly enough to get things outside rattling. A garage-sized door opened, and Sam followed behind as Nick led them in. Once their names were checked off a list, they were carted into an elevator that felt designed more for meat or freight than people. When it opened up on the second floor, the music was even louder, and they inched forward through a hallway in a single file.

Sam's nerves flew. She reached for her necklace, then

remembered it wasn't there. Maybe that was a grounding thing for her, too, to reach for Brady when she was uneasy. She wanted to text him again, but if he was unhappy about her whereabouts she didn't want to start a fight about it here.

Gabe was telling Cassie and Lilly something else as they neared the front of the line. Sam leaned in to listen.

"There's a wristband system," he said over the pounding beat. "It shows the level of play you're interested in. Green if you're actively looking, yellow if you're not but might consider it, and red if you don't want to get propositioned at all. Dungeon Monitors have reflective armbands—easily seen in the dark in case someone has a problem."

"Got it."

Sam stepped forward and got her wristband. Red, of course.

The others went into a room with a coat rack on wheels. She hadn't bothered with a jacket tonight, and everything else she needed was in her jean pockets.

"I'm gonna wander around," she told them, then stepped into the main room. Her breathing went shaky in a combination of exhilaration, feeling completely out of her element and right at home. Had she been folding laundry and cleaning snotty tissues and toys out of her purse a few weeks ago? Now she was at the holy grail of kinky communities, and her apprehension eased as people eyed her in her corset.

Hanna had been right; this *was* like wearing armor, and as Sam received more approving glances, she felt her former self return, the Boston Bombshell walking through a sexual playground.

The space was like a vacant office that had been converted overnight. The only lights were from several color-changing bulbs that swirled from one hue to the next, and throughout the room people grouped around different demonstrations.

First was a man in a lab coat in front of what looked like a medical table. He was passing a bright purple device over the pants-covered crotch of a writhing woman. Standing next to him was a woman holding a chalkboard that said, *"Violet Wand-gasms—23."*

The wand gave off an eerie glow and the distinctive scent of ozone, like the coming of a thunderstorm. A shower of electrical charge simmered off the tip, sparks coming off it as the woman on the table jolted and shuddered. The one with the chalkboard erased the number and wrote "24." Everyone surrounding them clapped.

"You wanna try?" someone in the group asked Sam.

The recently satisfied woman sat up, wiped her brow and smiled at the man in the coat. Sam held up her wristband. "I'm good. Thanks."

The person shrugged and someone else climbed on the table.

Sam kept walking, past a shelf where drinks were being served. In front of it, a man was on the ground and rolled up in a carpet like a burrito. A sign by his head said *"Ladies, please use your heels."* A woman in spiked shoes higher than Cassie's stepped on top of him, and he groaned.

Sam stifled a laugh, remembering not to yuck anyone's yum. She turned to the right and watched what had to be a fire-play demonstration, an older, wrinkly man in white briefs lying on a countertop while a young woman passed what looked like a stick with a flaming ball of cotton at the end over his chest. This was like Oz. If Oz was full of sexual deviance and Trance music.

In a room to the side, a ropes demonstration was going on. A woman in lingerie was dangling from the cords and trying to bite at her captor. Each time her mouth snapped, he tied another loop, making her swing in another direction. People were packed in that space, and Sam stopped to look at their faces.

It was amazing how they all showed their dominant or submissive inclinations so transparently. It didn't matter what their gender or orientation was—the behavior was the same. The submissives hovered close to their Dominants. Some sat on the floor beside them, either looking up lovingly or staring at the ropes display. The Dominants chatted amongst one another freely, some with their hands in their submissives' hair or...other places. In the back row, several couples were already going at it.

What would Brady have thought of all this? He'd probably have made a joke about wanting s'mores at the fire play, or pretended he was a bug flying helplessly toward a bug zapper at the wand demo.

Things he would've said to make her smile.

She frowned, thinking about their texts again. Why was it so hard to talk to her own husband? One of them had to push through this weirdness. It might as well be her. She took out her phone, typed the words *"I'm thinking about you,"* and hit send, but a guy who looked like Mister Clean with a silver armband appeared out of nowhere and loomed in front of her.

"No cell phones," he said sternly. "That's gotta go back in the coatroom."

Shit. That had to be the thing she'd missed Gabe saying. Powering off her phone, she went to the makeshift coatroom and got a ticket for her cell, then went down a long hall. The music got louder, the lights at the end more clustered together, leading to a packed dance floor.

People were cheering, dancing, writhing around one another. A feminine figure came away from the knot of pulsing bodies. Making her way through the crowd in sinuous movements, she curled through people like a snake through grass. She had golden brown hair pulled up in a sleek bun. Lashes you could see for miles.

Sam's heart skittered. "Hanna!"

Seeing her new friend and fellow Domme was like synchronicity, the most perfect coincidence, and Sam slipped around the bystanders to greet her.

"Hanna," she said again. They made eye contact a few feet apart. *"Bonjour!"*

Hanna blinked several times and quickly looked down. She laughed once, nervously, and then said, *"Bonjour, Madame."*

That was different. Hanna wasn't acting like the confident, brash woman Sam knew. She wasn't wearing any Femdomme armor either. She had on a white, midriff-baring top that set off the color of her skin, and a flimsy skirt. Her neck was completely exposed, and her wristband was green. The colored lights bounced off her flesh: brown, red, blue, purple.

Time seemed to slow and then stop. Sam's lips parted as Hanna stared at the floor. She looked shy, flustered and nervous.

She looked like Brady.

Like a submissive.

"Hannaleen."

Sam didn't know why she'd said her friend's name that way, other than it seemed to fit the moment. It got Hanna looking up, though, and when her eyes met Sam's again, they crinkled into a wince. She exhaled a short, sharp breath and shook her head, like something about it wasn't fair.

Sam felt the ground shift, the level playing field they'd shared before vanishing into thin air. Hanna reached a hand up, her fingertips soft as they came into contact with Sam's hair, just above her ear.

"So pretty," Hanna whispered, caressing Sam's hair with a feather-light touch.

It was a shock, a bolt of lightning, feeling this woman's hand in her hair. Sam was both rooted to the spot and swaying on her feet. It was a simple touch, but it made Sam shiver, and Hanna seemed reluctant to let go.

Sam was reluctant, too. Oh, God. What was happening?

Hanna rubbed the bottom of Sam's hair between her fingers, her eyes on Sam's face. Her expression was electrifying—drenched with lust and longing. Sam's scalp tingled, like Hanna's hand was the violet wand, like Sam was being set on fire.

Had this been simmering beneath the surface since they met? Had she been lying to herself all this time? Was doing this cheating? If so, she had to shut it down now. But she didn't, and as Sam stared at Hanna's lips, she remembered what it was like to kiss a girl. To feel the gentle press of a soft feminine mouth against hers and to want more.

She wanted more from this girl. She wanted lips and hands and bodies, wanted familiar and foreign, to touch and be touched by a body that was like hers. She wanted this gorgeous woman pliant beneath her alongside Brady, both of them subservient and willing.

Wanted to know what she could do that would make Hanna cry out in pleasure as loud as Brady did, and she wanted it now.

"I have to go," Hanna said.

"Wait—"

Before Sam could finish her sentence, Hanna dropped her hand. She turned away, vanishing quickly, disappearing into the crowd like a ghost. Sam stayed where she was, too stunned and shaken to follow.

21

Brady was half-awake when he heard the front door open. He rolled over in bed, his breath almost choking him in anticipation and dread. Tonight hadn't gone well, and Sam was going to be pissed.

He listened as she shut the door and put away her things. Her footsteps were first light up the steps, then louder as she went from the girls' rooms to theirs.

"Where the hell are our children?"

The question was loud, full of alarm. It was well deserved, but he hated the sound of it, like he'd lost their kids somewhere during the course of the night, forgotten about them and went to bed.

"At Jack and Lilly's," he said.

Sam flipped on a lamp. Brady pinched his eyes shut to shield them.

"Why?" she asked. "What the hell happened?"

He slowly blinked his eyes open. God, she looked incredible. The corset was unreal. He didn't want her angry at him looking like that. But he supposed he didn't have a choice.

"It wasn't a great night."

"Not great meaning what?"

"Hope got hurt. I was throwing the ball and she ran into my elbow."

"Brady!" She smacked her hand over her forehead. "That's exactly the kind of thing I worried about happening tonight."

"I know."

She dropped her hand and threw him a glare. "Is she hurt badly?"

"There's a bump."

"Jesus Christ. So you handed them over to your brother?"

"It wasn't like that."

Brady closed his eyes, not wanting to recall his parenting fail, or how Allegra had allowed her uncle into her bedroom and not him.

"I lost my temper and yelled. Allegra wouldn't talk to me. Jack finally got her downstairs, but she hid behind him and then Hope started doing the same thing."

And wasn't that a kick in the nuts. Jack had coaxed Allegra out to eat something by offering to show her pictures of Lilly's cat, and then stood there helplessly while his nieces cowered and asked to go home with him. His perfect big brother, who his own children felt safer with than him. Who'd known before he did what his wife was doing tonight.

"They wanted him," Brady said. "Not me."

"Why didn't you text me?" Sam asked.

"I did. Right after you messaged me but you didn't reply." He'd hoped the words *I'm thinking about you, too, but I need your help for a minute* would've merited a response. "I called but you didn't answer."

"I had to turn my phone off," she said. "Forgot to turn it back on."

That was weird, but whatever.

"Jack texted after he put them to bed. Even sent a picture." Brady reached for his phone and held it out to her as evidence. "We can pick them up in the morning."

Assuming either of them ever wanted to talk to him again.

Sam took the phone from his hand, sighed and sank onto the bed. Brady turned away. He'd promised her he could handle things, but he'd only made a mess, and now he wasn't sure if he'd disappointed her as her husband or her pet or both.

Both probably. And both sucked. Big time.

She tossed his phone on the nightstand. Good thing it had a case.

"They're safe?" she asked. "They have all their fingers and toes?"

"I didn't count, but I'm pretty sure all digits were still attached." He still couldn't face her. "Please don't be mad," he said quietly. "It's bad enough they wanted Jack instead of me."

He expected coldness. Distance. The same space they'd had between them before everything changed a month ago. But then her fingers were light on the back of his neck, trailing over to his ear.

"I'm not mad." She leaned over him, and then her tongue was sparking along his earlobe, teeth scraping. "I am something else, though."

What the hell?

A tremor raced through him, unexpected and sudden. It was a struggle to process, to catch up with her as her hands went over his back and down to his ass.

"I want you." Her nails bit into the flesh of his upper thigh as her lips found purchase on his neck and sucked. "Do you want me?"

Jesus, this was happening fast. He hadn't imagined *this* tonight. He'd thought she'd be mad, not horny—thought she'd be Mom and not Mistress. He never knew what version of Sam he was going to get, but if she could be this one for a little while, if she could—

"Oh, fuck."

She stroked over his ass, rubbing in circles, and suddenly he was right where she was. He spread his legs to allow for more of it, rocking into her touch.

"You and your filthy mouth," she said, amusement in her voice. "But that's not a yes, pet."

"Yes," he croaked.

As if he'd ever say no to her.

She hummed, then pressed inward on his entrance until he was hard and panting and rutting against the bed.

"I have plans for you tonight. Plans for right—" another circle, "—here. But first, turn over."

He did her bidding, twisting until he was on his back. Sam loomed above him, dressed like she'd been born to a wear a corset. Taking her in was like a sexy superhero costume reveal. The leather smelled new, like a clean pair of boots or a wallet store or a car fresh off the lot. The bow cinched below her breasts pushed them out and up.

"You look amazing," he said.

"Do I?"

Brady nodded. He was both grateful and dangerously turned on at the fact that she'd gotten something like this, like he'd asked. But he was a caveman when it came to her cleavage, and he needed to adjust himself.

She caught the move of his hand and smiled. "Good. I'll keep it on then."

Brady smiled back, albeit uneasily. She seemed different tonight in a way he couldn't place—wilder, more driven. He felt like he was spinning faster, too. Maybe the corset was sparking a leather fetish he didn't know he had. Or maybe it was the first time he was seeing her like this, every bit the fierce Domme of his fantasies.

"Please do," he said, then tacked on, "Mistress."

Her grin was sin and relief, like getting into a hot shower after a long day. Sam slid her fingers into the waistband of his boxers, pulled them down, tossed them aside. She coiled her hair over her shoulder and fit herself between his legs.

"Hard for me already. Good boy."

He made a noise, something thankful that died on a groan when she licked the sensitive area below the head. Over and over, just that one spot, a localized focused pleasure.

"Poor horny little sub," she said, and Brady couldn't contain his grunt. She mimicked the noise, but in a questioning way. "You want more?"

"Yes—" lick, "—*fuck*."

"You need it?"

His hips lifted on their own, his dick twitching. He couldn't come this way, but the feel of her pink tongue flicking over him was driving him crazy. "You're killing me, Sam."

She stopped licking. Everything went quiet.

"Mistress," he corrected.

Four loud thumps of his heartbeat passed before she hummed softly.

"I like killing you," she said. "I love it when you squirm."

Brady laughed nervously but fell into it, into the relief, the embarrassment, the pleasure when she started up again. He was safe here. They'd set up ground rules, safewords and limits. She wouldn't push him out of his comfort zone. She'd let him come eventually, and trusting her allowed him to give in, to simply hang in this space, in the ache between agony and bliss.

It felt good, to be here. To let her move and manipulate him, speeding him up and bringing him down as she saw fit. He grew lightheaded, and his eyes drooped closed. He'd felt like this before, the last time they played. It was the strangest sensation—writhing but floating, worked up but also totally Zen. Was this subspace?

The question faded away when she took him in her mouth—one, incredible, torturous suck. "Oh, God. Please don't stop."

He choked out the words, then gasped when she popped off him.

"Please?" She was using that teasing tone again. It revved him up. "Please."

She sat up, faked a pout—"Please?"—and unzipped her jeans. *"Please."*

She slipped off her jeans and panties, crawled to the edge of the bed and reached beneath it. She'd stashed the toy chest under there, and Brady's pulse spiked when he heard it pop open and she righted herself. The strap-on was in her hand, palm-up like an offering.

"Please?" Her voice was lower now. Seductive and chocolate-smooth.

Brady's throat worked. "Please," he whispered.

Sam smiled. "Hands and knees, pet."

Things went in slow motion. Fear and hunger tangled together. He turned over, faced the headboard, breath speeding up. The harness she'd bought was part of the anal training kit. Three different dildos came with it in increasing sizes. They'd already used the smallest.

"Which one are we using?" he asked.

"Which one are you ready for?"

The biggest one still scared him. The medium-sized one had a curved tip to stimulate the prostate. Shame and desire had his cheeks going hot. Was it possible to want something and still be terrified?

"The middle one," he ground out, and Sam's responding hum made the hair on his neck stand on end. He wanted this, he trusted her, but that knowledge was doing little to settle his nerves. She came up beside him, one hand stroking along his back, his hip, up to his shoulders.

"Knee okay?" she asked.

He tested it, moved his leg from side to side. "Yes."

"You know your safeword?"

"Mmm-hmm." The stroking felt good. He was getting drowsy again, like he was flying.

She made a fist in his hair, and he gasped when she pulled his head back to look at him. "Then say it, pet. So I know you remember what to say if you want this to stop."

His mind was sluggish. He had to close his eyes to think. Why had he chosen such a stupidly complicated word?

"Metamorphosis."

She released his hair, played with it. "Good boy."

The affectionate words had their desired effect, but Brady felt less like a beloved pet and more like the bug in Kafka's story—helpless, exposed. Sam pulled the wrist restraints up from where they'd been hidden, stuffed between the mattress and the headboard. Linking them together, she strapped his hands in.

"There," she said. "Something for you to hold on to."

He tugged once, to feel the pull. "Thank you, Mistress."

The sounds of her putting on the strap-on were strange and unfamiliar, metal clasps pinging. He couldn't watch, chained up the way he was, but heard another sound—a buzzing noise.

The ring?

A sudden vibration against his ass had him bucking forward. "Shit." He bucked again. "What is that?"

"A bullet vibe."

She circled his hole with it, buzzed once at his entrance.

"When did you...*shit*...get that?"

It was a shock, every time she used it. A good shock, though. "When I got the corset. It's your other surprise."

He cursed again, his whole body kicking forward and then moving back. She repeated the motion several times before rolling it over his balls.

"Fuck...*me*."

The vibe switched off. Her arms came around either side of him —not an easy feat considering his size. She managed to get her lips by his ear anyway and whispered, "Since you asked so nicely."

When she sat back, he heard the lube cap pop open, heard her hand slicking up the toy. Anxiety and excitement shivered through him when she lubed him up, too, first her hand around his erection, then thick liquid drizzling over his crack. He hissed when she eased her pinky inside him, and then his head was bowing, body arching. It was so intense, so immediate, and insanely good. She switched to her middle finger, testing him, stretching him. Getting him ready.

She pulled her hand back. His heart pounded when the dildo's wet tip rubbed at his back door.

Sam stopped moving and stroked his back in hypnotic circles. "Relax, pet. I've got you."

She did, he knew she did. So he closed his eyes and made himself go slack. Dropping his elbows to the bed and his head to his knuckles, Brady gripped the pillow with his strapped-in hands.

"Ready?" she asked softly.

His brain buzzed. His thoughts spun around. "Yes, Mistress."

The dildo nudged his ass, and Brady let out a hard, dirty exhale. Sam slowly thrust forward, the toy easing past the first tight ring of muscle. He was hit first with burning, then pressure that morphed into bliss.

"Fuuuuck." The word rumbled out of him in a moan.

Sam hummed, put her hands on his butt cheeks and gently

spread them apart. She got in a little farther, then palmed his hips as she started to thrust. He shook but held himself still, afraid to move, afraid to want, afraid to do anything that might change the waves of pleasure rolling through him. She swiveled her hips in that way that made him crazy when he was the one inside her, and Brady groaned, low and deep. She was fucking him, really *fucking him*, and he got lost in the slow drag and slide, sensations inside him he didn't know how to process. He didn't realize she'd picked up the pace or that he was rutting back against her until he heard the wet sound of the toy going in and out.

"Please," he moaned. He didn't know what he wanted—not faster or harder, just something more solid than his restraints to hold onto while everything in him spun out of control.

"You like getting fucked?" she said. "My dirty boy?"

Jesus. His shoulders hiked up, like they could hide him, like he could disappear if he jacked them up high enough. She laughed, and fuck if that didn't trip him up even more.

"Yes, you do," she said, singsong.

Brady moaned and mashed his face into the pillow. She bent over him and reached around, finding his dick with her fist and wrapping it around him. Brady jerked upright, head jolting back, his mouth open in a silent moan. Yes, he liked this. Fake cock up his ass, real cock getting stroked. Slick. Hot. Wet. His arms went straight and stiff in his efforts to hold himself up.

"Fuck, oh holy Jesus, fuck me."

"Brady Archer, your mouth."

"Can't help it." He didn't know how to handle pleasure like this.

She stopped stroking and a desperate shuddery noise came out of him. He slumped back down to the blanket.

"Did I tell you to move?"

He righted himself. "Sorry, Mistress."

"You don't have to apologize." She bent forward until her nipples brushed his back. Her arms came around him, bracketing his body. "But if you moved I couldn't do this."

She sped up her fucking, and Brady couldn't have moved if he tried.

"Ohhhh God, I'm gon—"

"No." She slowed down, slid out of him. He whined like a child.

"Not yet," she cooed. "Calm down. I want to make this last."

She stroked his back in reassuring circles, and he tried to catch his breath. He wasn't succeeding at calming down, though. His dick and balls ached with wanting, screaming for her to start again. This was torture.

She moved around, undid the restraints. For a minute he panicked, worried she was going to stop completely, that she was going to leave him like this, but then she got back into position and teased him with the blunt head of the toy.

"You trust me, pet?"

He nodded. "I do."

"Good. This time, I want you quiet. If you're about to come, grab my hand and I'll decide if I'm going to let you."

Brady whimpered, suddenly aware that he was her plaything, that his pleasure and his pain were equally in her hands. But he'd do anything to have her fuck him again, so he sank his teeth into his lower lip and made fists in the sheet as a reminder to keep silent.

"Ready?" she asked.

He nodded.

It was nearly impossible to stifle his moan when she pressed inside, even more so when she reached around and jerked him, fast and hard. He thought he'd die when she released him abruptly again, using both hands to push his hips forward and drag him back. It was like being a ping-pong ball, bounced from one extreme of pleasure to another. He rocked in time with her thrusts, and she went deeper, faster, making that damn humming sound until the convulsions of his body had his head knocking into the headboard. When she took him in hand again and he managed to smother his pleading with a squeak, her laughter drove him to the edge.

This wasn't fair. Wasn't fair for her to silence him, to scramble his brain this way. But it was too good for him to...it was too...oh, God. Too good. Too good. Too *fucking goddamn* good.

Brady reached back, grabbed her hand.

"Good boy. Come for me. Be loud, too."

That was it. He'd always thought it was bullshit that people could come on command in porn, but her permission was a trigger and he was the loaded gun.

His orgasm hit like a bomb.

Blinding pleasure crushed him from the inside out. He spurted over the sheets, moaning until his throat went raspy. When she'd wrung every last drop out of him and pulled back, he sagged to the bed. He felt strangely empty and open, like a sweater with its neck stretched too wide. He heard the sound of Sam unbuckling, the strap-on hitting the floor. Like last time, Brady wanted to hide. To curl into a fetal position, or run into the bathroom again and close the door.

Sam moved in beside him, touched his face.

"What do you need?" she asked.

Tell me you still love me.

"I don't know," he said instead. He still hadn't figured out how to ask that, and even if he did, it might not help untwist the lines in his head, the ones that told him he couldn't be this and Sam's protector, couldn't be a husband, a submissive, and a man.

She urged him onto his back. His naked body was slick and uncomfortable, his backside burned and the sheets were definitely soiled. But Sam didn't care. She drew the blanket up over them, took his hand and slid it between her thighs.

"Then focus on me."

Feeling her was grounding, watching her head tip back when he parted her folds even more so. Brady found his focus, touched her tender flesh until everything else gave way. Whatever piece of himself he'd lost, he found it again in the sounds of her release, in the worship of his Mistress, his wife, his Samantha.

22

*S*am clutched Brady's shoulder, gasping as her orgasm abated.

What a roller coaster tonight had been.

Getting home from the club, she'd been so keyed up and confused she wasn't sure how she'd be able to wind down. Then she'd crash-landed back into being a mom with an injured child she couldn't comfort, both of her daughters MIA. It was a nightmare, as was seeing how dejected Brady was, how upset he was at having disappointed her.

She should've turned on her phone when they left the dungeon. Should've not had her mind somewhere else. Shouldn't have been so turned on when the panic had abated and she'd realized they had the house to themselves that she'd blown off trying to talk.

She hadn't wanted to talk. She'd wanted to fuck.

Wearing the strap-on, controlling him, seeing him take what she wanted to give him, then shake and fly apart, was the highest power trip ever. She couldn't believe what he was willing to allow her, the trust he'd put in her hands. But even after that, even after the sharp, fast orgasm he'd given her and the slick pounding of his fingers after, she still wanted more.

Too much more.

She shouldn't have done it—she knew it was wrong, but while Brady was touching her, she'd imagined Hanna there, too, imagined each of them on either side of her, two pairs of lips and four pairs of hands, feminine and masculine and all of them wanting her.

God, she was so selfish. So greedy. She was addicted to the power of being wanted, of being sexually desired. She wasn't sure she was right about Hanna wanting her—wasn't even sure if what happened was real.

Real or not, she needed to tell Brady what happened. Tonight, and years ago.

"Can I talk to you?" she asked.

He propped himself up on one arm. "Sure."

"How would you…I mean, would you ever…"

Ugh. What was the right way to phrase this?

"Streak through Fenway yelling, 'Let's go, Red Sox'?" he asked. "Nah. Saw it on YouTube. It's been done."

Sam snorted, then shook her head. "Where do you come up with this stuff?" But it broke the tension, made it easier for her to talk. "Would you be interested in having another woman in bed with us?"

Brady's mouth dropped open. His brow furrowed and a shadow crossed his face. Sam's stomach clenched. She was risking whatever they'd found together here by asking and was about to say never mind when he reached over and drew a pattern on the blanket above her heart.

"I didn't know you were into that."

"That?"

He shrugged. "Girls. Threesomes."

Was it such a shock? She'd played the part of wife, of doting mother and homemaker for so long, it was hard to believe that was the mask and this was what she kept inside. "I was. In DC."

His drawing faltered, then started again. "Oh?"

Was he trying to sound casual? Or was this bothering him? She couldn't read his reactions to save herself. She wanted to, should've tried harder to figure him out, because he was the most important person in her world, but she never knew how much to push when he shut down.

"We never talked about my time there," she replied delicately. "I wasn't exactly an angel."

"I thought you didn't…"

"Have any relationships? I didn't. But I did do…" Why was it so awkward to tell him this? "Stuff."

"Stuff?"

Jesus, she sounded like a teenager. "I kissed a girl one night, at a bar. She wanted me to go home with her." Sam took a breath. "And the guy I kissed that night, too."

"Wow." A long, drawn-out pause followed. Then, "Why didn't you tell me?"

"I didn't know how you'd react."

He looked at her for a minute, as if he wasn't sure who she was. Then his lips tipped into a smile. "What was it like?"

"It?"

"The threesome."

"I didn't do it."

"But you *did* kiss a girl, right?"

"Yeah. You want, like, details?"

"Hell yeah!"

His emphatic response was too much. Sam turned into his thick shoulder, hid her face in his skin. He smelled like sweat and sex. "It was only for a minute, but it was…softer than it is with a guy. Wetter, somehow. Like we were melding together."

She glanced up. Brady was watching her intently.

"You enjoying this?" she asked.

"Are you kidding? This is the best story ever."

Sam laughed again, then groaned. It was a relief, to finally open up to him, to share this secret, but it seemed strange, too—to tell the man she was married to, had children with, and had known half her life something she'd never said. About wishing she'd slept with people who weren't him.

"Why didn't you do it?" he asked.

"It wasn't a good idea, professionally." That was the abridged version. "But I always regretted not doing it."

"That's a long time to want something. I know how it feels."

The guilt pricked, sharp at her chest. Sam kept her face tucked into Brady's shoulder. Here he was, getting what he'd finally desired from her, and she wanted more. His arm came around her, warm palm flat and comforting on her back. It almost startled her—the fact that he'd noticed her regret.

"It's okay that you didn't tell me, you know," he said. "It was years ago."

"Well...something sort of happened...tonight."

He froze. His hand was still on her back. "What kind of something?"

"Nothing like that. I didn't kiss anybody. I could've imagined the whole thing."

He pulled back. "Okay, it would be great if you could actually tell me now."

What was she doing? Why was she causing him stress? The look on his face was killing her. But she had to be honest. "My friend Hanna, from work. I saw her tonight and I think she's...interested in me."

"And are you interested in her?"

"Maybe?"

It was crazy to be having this conversation. And now Brady wasn't speaking. He went pale, then ashen. She might not be able to read his deepest thoughts, but she could read this. Sam took his hand, brought it up to her cheek. His eyes found hers.

"I'm not leaving. And I'm not interested in an open marriage," she said.

She had no idea how people did that. Not because she couldn't respect it, but she could barely manage taking care of the three people in her family, let alone add another person.

"I just want to have that experience I didn't get to have. To live out that fantasy. With her. And you."

His shoulders sank in relief. He moved closer to her again, curled up until his head was on her chest. "Okay, I might be into that."

"Might?"

"Your wife telling you she's into girls is pretty much the beginning of every porn."

"But this is different. We're different." She petted his head, ruffled his curls, so he knew what she was talking about. "And I think Hanna's different."

"Different how?"

Sam recounted the story for him, starting at what Hanna had told her when she'd found Sam reading and finishing with Hanna stroking her hair tonight at the dungeon.

"You told Hanna?" he asked. "About us?"

Sam cringed. "Just that I'm a Domme, too."

He didn't say anything. Sam suddenly felt both awful for violating his trust and frustrated with this constant gag order. "She doesn't talk to Lilly or Gabe. They run in different circles."

More silence.

"I needed to talk to *someone*, Brady."

"I get it," he finally said, then offered her a small smile. "So, she's a switch."

Sam frowned. She'd read about characters like that—ones who enjoyed switching roles, from Dominant to submissive, bottom to top. "But she seemed so strong. So capable and forceful." Passive didn't seem to fit Hanna.

Brady's expression darkened for a minute. "I guess it's hard for either of us to imagine being on the other side of the slash."

"The slash?"

"The line between Dominant and submissive."

"Oh. Right." Her frown deepened. "Why do you know so much about something neither of us have experienced in real life?"

His knowledge changed the balance, tipped the scales in a way she didn't like. She was supposed to be the one in the position of power. How could she do that when he knew more than her? But the comment seemed to bring Brady's smile back.

"I've just read about it in things that aren't fiction."

"You have?" she asked. "Where?"

"Chat forums. Other places on the Internet. I am still a geek under this manly exterior, you know."

She laughed and cuddled closer. "I like that about you. The geekiness."

"I'm glad." He breathed into her hair. "And touching someone's hair is PG-13 in my book, Sam. If it wasn't, I'd have wanted to kill your hairdresser ages ago."

She relaxed into him, into his warmth, his humor. Into the solidness of Brady. It was familiar. Safe.

Why did she need both? The safe, and the wild?

She questioned for a moment if she did—if this secure, comfortable, and lately exciting place she was in with Brady could be enough for her. It should've been, but Sam couldn't deny the electricity she'd felt with Hanna.

"It didn't feel PG-13," Sam said. "If a guy had done it, you'd have been pissed."

"Maybe. But I trust you. And if you haven't figured it out, you're kind of in charge here."

Sam held still. He put *that* much trust in her? That she could allow another person to touch her and he'd...stand by?

"I'm your wife, Brady. I made vows and I don't take them lightly."

Brady reached over, took her hand. Rubbed her ring with his thumb and forefinger. "I don't take them lightly either. I vowed to take care of you. I do that for you, you do it for me. End of story."

"Taking care of me means having a threesome?"

There was a pause in his breathing. "I guess, sometimes, taking care of you means giving you more of what you need."

Their eyes met, locked. Something clicked into place, something healing, mending a bit of whatever had gone wrong in the last few years. His blue eyes were bright, so bright, and for the first time in so long, Sam finally felt *seen* by him. She appreciated him, appreciated every deviant thing he'd let her do to him, was going to let her do. And there was only one way to explain how much that meant.

"I love you," she said.

Brady's smile was almost childlike. "You do?"

"Of course I do."

"I thought after how things had gotten, you didn't feel that way anymore."

Her heart ached. "Of course not. I love you. Never stopped."

"I love you, too." He leaned into her, his forehead against hers. "Never stopped."

A soft noise came out of her, something she couldn't name. She reached up, fanned her fingers into those soft curls of his, angled his head until his mouth met hers. The kiss was soft, slow and long. No tongue, just lips and breath and his beard brushing over her skin.

It might've been the sweetest kiss they'd ever had.

"This is what I need," he said.

"What's that?" she asked, still caressing his hair.

"After. When we're finished playing. I need you to tell me you love me."

"That's all?"

He nodded. "Yeah. That's all."

The simplicity of it stunned her. That was all he needed to pull him back to reality—her love. Brady gazed at her.

"Is that something you want to do?" he asked. "Bring Hanna here?"

"I don't know. Real life is different from a fantasy. And like I said, I could've been wrong about tonight."

"Do you think you were?"

No. But Hanna's desires weren't the issue here. Brady's were.

"If I wasn't, and Hanna is a switch, and is into this, what would you think?"

Brady shifted beside her. "If I said yes, what would you want?"

"Specifically?"

He nodded. What *did* she want?

"I want both of you touching me. Having both your pleasure at my domain." Her breathing went fast. She swallowed. "I'd want your praise. Your admiration. Your worship."

Brady's cheeks went pink. And his breathing had sped up, too. He seemed as into this as she was, but they were getting ahead of themselves.

"Let's not get carried away with details," Sam said. "I still haven't talked to Hanna."

Or thought out the implications. Sleeping with someone from work was not a good idea. That shit never stayed private. The too-close-for-comfort aspect was why she'd opted out in Washington. But it was too late now. Even if she and Brady hadn't talked, she and Hanna couldn't ignore what happened.

"Can we table this?" she asked. It was all feeling too crazy, too out of control.

"Sure."

Sam smiled and sat up. "Come on."

He got up without a word and followed her into the bathroom. Turning on the shower, she pulled him inside, rinsed them both off until their fingers went pruney and the water had run cold. When they were both clean, dry and in pajamas, she dug fresh sheets out of the linen closet. He helped her strip the soaked ones off the bed and remake it, then they crawled under the covers.

"Love you," she said again quietly. He tightened his arms around her.

Breathing in his scent, Sam drifted off to sleep.

23

$\mathcal{A}$t work on Monday, Sam was struggling to focus—half because she was on edge waiting to talk to Hanna. The rest was the fact that her clothes weren't fitting. A month out of her workout routine and her body was already rebelling.

She'd hoped to get to the gym but spent the rest of the weekend triple-checking Hope for signs of a concussion, and then spoiling both her daughters with a trip to the mall.

Because shopping was a great way to apologize for being a shit mother.

Maybe a shit daughter, too, since she hadn't gotten over to her parents' place. Then again, they were leaving soon and had hired a professional move management service to help organize their stuff. Not being needed saddened her almost as much as their impending move, but their absence would open her world a bit more, make time for things like her own groceries, which she hadn't had time to get to either. She'd have asked Brady, but he'd always buy the wrong thing or spend half the time calling to ask what brand of toilet paper or cheese or tuna she wanted, so they'd gotten takeout. Again. She could almost feel the grease coming out of her pores.

Fussing with the waistband on her skirt until she was comfortable, Sam forced herself to concentrate. She'd closed out several months of the Choate file bills, checking the statements in the digital file against the trust's online bank account. Mildred had no children, and trusted Pierce with every cent of her fortune—a large amount that would go to a few charities after she passed. Right now it was going toward paying her homecare providers, as well as her medical, electric and cable bills, all of which checked out. But Sam kept finding those extra checks, made out to cash and signed by Pierce. She could view images of checks for the last three years online, and the amounts on each one kept getting bigger.

Was Pierce skimming a bit off the top? He seemed slimy, but was it enough to do something like that? And if he was committing a crime, why would he ask Sam to double-check things? That didn't make any sense.

When lunchtime came, Sam grabbed her purse and light spring jacket and swung by Lilly's office. The young blonde's desk was covered in paperwork.

Sam knocked once on the open door. "Bad time?"

"Define bad."

"Bad as in you're drowning in work?"

"Then definitely bad. But I like it. What's up?"

Sam closed the door behind her. "Total hypothetical, but if someone were stealing from one of the firm's clients, what would happen?"

Lilly's eyes went the size of saucers. "Unless we're talking stealing paper clips, they'd probably get arrested."

Sam didn't like the feeling in her gut. It was the same hunch she'd had when she'd worked for Dawes and had figured out the shady dealings of that donor. "And how would someone go about proving that? Hypothetically, of course."

"*Well.*" Lilly dragged out the word, like she wasn't sure this was hypothetical at all. "Someone should be one hundred percent sure they're right first. And then talk to HR or the managing partners." Lilly frowned. "Am I missing something, or has working here made you start watching those legal dramas on cable?"

Sam smiled. "You caught me. I'm an addict."

"Those shows will make you paranoid."

"I know. I'll let you get back to work."

Sam closed Lilly's door behind her. She wasn't one hundred percent sure, and it wasn't a fair judgment call. Pierce might've been slimy, but that didn't mean he was extorting an old lady. She'd ask Hanna, but he'd specifically asked Sam not to talk about the project, and things with her were already dicey.

She had a feeling her friend was trying to avoid her.

Hanna was here today—Sam had seen her line light up on the switchboard, but they hadn't spoken or passed in the hallway.

Time to change that.

She walked around the office until she found Hanna by the copier. Her hair loose and curly, her lips a taupe color that matched her dress, she was talking to another secretary and laughing. The sight caused a spark of something Sam hadn't expected. Not jealousy. More like annoyance at being avoided. But if she'd figured this situation right, there was one surefire way to get Hanna's attention.

"Hannaleen."

Hanna froze and looked up. Sam smiled sweetly. Yup, that worked.

"Grab a cup of coffee with me?"

Hanna's mouth opened and closed, and she blinked, like she had at the club. A flare went off in Sam's gut—enjoyment at having gotten Hanna flustered again.

"Coffee sounds great," Hanna said. "Let me get my coat."

"Great, I'll meet you out front."

When Hanna joined Sam on the steps outside, her friend's gaze quickly dropped. There was a buzzing tension between the two of them.

"Let's find someplace to talk."

Sam led the way this time, heading around the green surrounding the Old State House, The Boston Massacre site she'd taken the girls to once to learn their history. Nothing had bloomed yet, but at least most of the snow had melted, the air filled with that crisp, clean scent of early spring. When they reached a little coffeehouse, Sam grabbed herself a muffin—bran, 'cause hey, at least she'd get some fiber this way—and found a table by the window.

Sam peeled the wrapper off the muffin. "Are we going to talk about it?"

"I guess it wouldn't work if I said talk about what."

"No. It wouldn't."

"Didn't think so." Hanna was quiet for a long moment. "I didn't expect to see you on Friday. It caught me off guard."

"And why is that?"

"I'm a Domme like I told you. And I'm bi. Well, I guess I'm more a chameleon. My inclination shifts depending on what gender I'm with. I bottom for women, top for men. With guys I'm less docile, more pushy. It's the real reason why Wash left, I think—he liked that I was into girls, but not so much when I took charge of him."

"And what does that have to do with me?"

Hanna clasped her hands together and twisted her thumbs, one over the other. A nervous habit, like Brady with his wedding ring, or Sam's tendency to reach for her necklace. "I'm attracted to you."

It wasn't good to be this turned on in public. Sam ate her muffin. Oh, the irony.

"But, you're married, and we're friends. There's zero chance of anything happening, so on Friday I was out hoping to scratch the itch with somebody else. And then there you were, in that outfit I helped you find. Kinda fucked up my night."

"I'm sorry."

"Don't be. How could you have known?"

They didn't speak for a full minute. All around them, the city spun, people walking, cars and taxis chasing through town like normal, like nothing was different, like Sam's life wasn't about to change. She was on a precipice, her life hanging in the balance between what she'd lived and what she wanted to live.

"I wouldn't say there's *zero* chance," Sam said.

Hanna's head turned so quickly in Sam's direction her curls bounced. "What does that mean?"

"It means you're not the only one feeling the attraction here."

Hanna blinked again. Several times. "So, you're bi, too?"

Sam wasn't sure what she was. How could she be, without ever trying anything? "I guess I'm more curious."

"About what?"

Time to put her cards on the table. "Having a threesome. Thought about it a lot more since Friday night."

"Does your husband know?" Hanna asked.

"About me being curious, or what happened with us?"

"Either. Both."

"Yes. To both."

"Damn, girl. That kind of honesty takes balls." Hanna crossed her arms on the table. "So, what does this mean?"

This conversation was like crossing a minefield. "I don't know. We work together. People gossip. I mean, this could be number one on the firm's 'do not attempt at home' list on the sexual-harassment policy."

Hanna laughed. "Seriously. Reg would have a field day if he found out. Or ask for pictures."

"Right. This is dangerous." And Sam did not want Gabe or Lilly finding out.

"I get it, but I'm very private. No one at work knows about my sex life." Hanna paused. "Except you."

"No one but my husband knows about *my* sex life. Aside from you," Sam said. "But why did you tell me about it when we were shopping?"

"I guess you felt like a kindred spirit. Like we had something in common."

Sam had certainly felt that all along.

"I think we can trust each other," Hanna continued. "You already know how much I spend on concealer. That's an epic amount of trust."

Sam did not, in fact, know how much she'd spent, but she laughed at the joke.

"I have a feeling your skin is beautiful, even without expensive makeup," she said, and a lovely rose color appeared on Hanna's cheeks. "But what could happen if things went badly? If feelings got hurt?"

"Don't worry about that. I don't get my emotions involved. That's why I said what I did about my relationship status."

"What do you mean?"

Hanna pointed at herself. "Biracial, queer, immigrant, kinky, single mom? Couldn't get more complicated. But all my energy goes into my girls. I need to get mine when I go out, but when I'm home, my life belongs to them."

Now it was Sam's turn to be caught off guard. She'd been bitter about her role, and here Hanna was, living the kind of life Sam had wanted and still managing to put her family first.

"I respect the hell out of you, you know?"

"The feeling is mutual," Hanna said. "Listen, I'm not looking for love, or to ruin anyone's marriage, but I'd love to be the first woman you're with, if there's room in your bed for me."

Sam's body tingled, from her chest to her clit. "We have a very large bed," she said. "I think we could make room."

That coy smile returned to Hanna's face. It was incredible, how she could shift gears like that. "I think we should all meet, first. The three of us."

They were doing this. Holy shit, they were doing this.

"Okay. I'll have to check with Brady." She checked the time. "Shit, I've gotta get back."

"Same here. Reg is breaking my balls today."

They stood and walked the few blocks back to the office.

"Let me know when you guys are ready to meet up," Hanna said.

Sam was already planning, eager to get home to Brady. This was going to be incredible. Or the biggest mistake of her life.

"I will."

24

*B*rady drove to his in-laws' apartment with his stomach in knots.

His in-laws' soon-to-be ex-apartment, actually. Sam's parents were moving in less than a day. It was weird to think he wouldn't come here anymore—he'd gone this way so many times the drive required zero concentration. Which was good, because he was mentally fucking shot.

The workweek had been grueling. That client they'd been creating the custom application for had decided they wanted a complete overhaul one week before launch. If that hadn't been bad enough, one database crashed and needed a total rebuild. Two sites migrated from the test server to live, he had three management meetings, and four new hires needed training.

And a partridge in a freaking pear tree.

He was exhausted, but he'd done his best to compartmentalize and things were stable at work, for the most part. But now on Friday night, in the driver's seat of his car, his wife beside him looking like a goddess, his children who still didn't seem to trust him in the backseat, and a plan to meet the woman they might invite into their bed, Brady felt like an old-school mainframe shutting down.

Last weekend had been the emotional equivalent of a rubber

223

band—first drawn out too far with the pegging, then whipped back into Sam's care. Snapped back out again with her surprise admission, then yanked in the other direction when she'd said she loved him. He hadn't realized how much he needed it until she'd said it, but even in the face of her words, he couldn't help being blown away at these new, or, he guessed, old desires of hers.

His wife was into girls.

It had shocked the ever-loving shit out of him. Yeah it was hot, and basically every guy's dream. But the life he'd once thought was simple had blown into epic levels of complicated, and this new information made him worry that he didn't know her at all.

"I still don't get why we're having dinner with Nana and Pop by ourselves."

Brady glanced in the rearview mirror. Allegra was pouting, her arms crossed. Sam had explained this to her several times, but it seemed she hadn't absorbed it. Seeing himself once again in his child, Brady tightened his hands on the steering wheel, anticipating Sam's irritation. But she only smiled.

"You and Hope are having a special granddaughter goodbye dinner while Daddy and I run errands. Then we're all going out for ice cream."

It was the truth, and also a lie. The girls were having a private dinner with Sam's parents, so he and Sam could go to a bar and meet Hanna.

They hadn't found a sitter, but they'd found time to work out a threesome.

It was weird, too. He would've thought Sam would want to spend her parents' last night here together, but he wasn't the authority on what his wife wanted at the moment.

"Where are we getting ice cream?" Allegra asked, already on to the next thing.

Clearly she didn't mind being shipped off again to yet another family member. Brady minded, though. Weren't kids supposed to *want* to be with their parents?

Maybe other parents didn't accidentally hit their kids in the head or forget to sign off on homework or buy the wrong kind of yogurt.

He'd grabbed some at Sam's request after work midweek when they'd run out and had ignored his instinct to call her and ask if it was the Yo-Kids or the Go-Gurt or the GoGo Kids SqueeZ Allegra liked more, afraid Sam would snap at him. Of course, he'd gotten the wrong thing. Allegra's meltdown had been epic.

Sam hadn't been thrilled, either, but she'd let it go.

"We'll go wherever you want," Sam said happily. "You and Hope decide."

Allegra rattled off places, and Brady tuned it all out.

Sam had come home from work on Monday buzzing with energy. She'd talked to Hanna, and things were a go, as long as Brady was still cool with it after they met. She insisted that it was his call. If he wasn't on board, she was out. Her arms around him, she'd said she didn't want to make him uncomfortable, and the intimacy they'd discovered was more important than her desire for wild experimentation.

He wasn't one hundred percent sure how he felt, but it puffed him up, knowing Sam would only be able to fulfill this fantasy because of him. It made him feel like he was taking care of her. And making her happy was an addiction, a drug he could never get enough of.

It wasn't just the old *"happy wife, happy life"* line. It was some kind of crazy chase, looking for ways to please her. To have her smiling at him instead of aggravated. To have her wanting him instead of that cold distance they'd felt for so long. He needed it like oxygen.

Brady pulled over across from Sam's parents' building. She turned to him and smiled.

"I'll take them up," she said.

"Okay."

Her hair was curly tonight, her eyes shaded in the sexiest way, and what she had on underneath her jacket was orange and white and flowy, cut in that way that left one shoulder bare. She'd said she wore it because it covered her belly now that she'd put a few pounds back on, but he sure as hell hadn't noticed. She could be heavy again, could be old and gray and wrinkled, and he'd still feel this way looking at her.

The girls climbed out of the car, and Brady's phone beeped with a text. He watched them go inside, then pulled it from his pocket.

Jack. He thumbed over the screen to unlock it and read the message.

"Everything okay?"

Geez. Did his brother have radar for the times Brady didn't want to talk?

Brady typed a quick reply. *"Yeah, why?"*

"You're not at Barrel 'n' Flask. Thought we were all meeting up tonight."

Crap, he'd blanked on that. Jack had left a voicemail about that midway through the week. So had Patrick. Nick had texted, too. He'd blown them off, too focused on Sam and work. He'd figured she'd be the one to tell Lilly, Cassie and Gabe they were doing their own thing tonight. Strange that she hadn't.

"Sorry. Forgot to tell you—we've got a thing with Sam's parents tonight. They're leaving tomorrow."

Good thing he wasn't face-to-face with Jack. His brother could always catch him in a lie.

"No problem. You sure everything is good?"

Brady dropped his head against the seat. He wanted to say no, that he wasn't sure what he was doing at all. He wanted to ask if being in a D/s relationship meant feeling like the ground beneath you was shifting all the time, if the drive to please your Dominant went so far beyond the bedroom you weren't sure it was even healthy. But talking about this was impossible. It would make him feel weak. It was bad enough that Sam had made that comment about Hanna not seeming strong, capable and forceful if she was a sub.

Didn't she see *him* as strong and capable? Hadn't she said that? Or was that only when she was his Mistress? Did she only love him as her pet, or as her husband, too?

Maybe all this hot sex was creating even more potholes in their marriage.

Maybe being Dominant and submissive wasn't fixing anything at all.

The building door opened. Sam stepped outside. Her smile was radiant, and it was focused straight on him, like he lit up her goddamn world. She'd said she wanted to parade him around tonight the way she used to in college—to show all the women there, Hanna included, that he was hers.

"Yeah," he typed back. *"Everything's good."*

They arrived at the bar a few minutes early. If Brady had thought his stomach was in knots before, now it was a fucking Boy Scout trying to earn a badge. He turned his ring furiously with one thumb in his pocket, hoping he didn't forget any of Sam's instructions. He didn't have to call her Mistress, but he should act respectful. Don't make too many jokes, but be himself. Try to relax, but tell her if he was uncomfortable.

Oh yeah. Totally easy instructions. No problem.

They sat at a high-top and ordered drinks. By the time the server returned with them, Sam was waving Hanna over. And holy goddamn hell, this woman was beautiful. Taller than Sam and a little more curvy, like a dark jaguar to Sam's pale lioness. And her skintight black dress hid nothing. Brady was stunned. Sam had mentioned Hanna's accent and how she looked, but he had no idea she'd be like *this.*

He was half proud his wife could get such a hot woman interested in her, half completely intimidated.

"Well, well," Hanna said, chin tipping up in the way he was used to when people first encountered his size. "Isn't he pretty."

Brady's cheeks went hot, and not in a good way. He didn't like being talked about like he wasn't there, but then Sam reached over and stroked his hair, beaming.

"He is, isn't he?"

Her smile and touch tightened that chain of ownership she had over him. It made him feel settled, safer and protected.

"For sure," Hanna said, waving over the server. "And you know how I like pretty things."

Was he a thing now?

"I appreciate the compliment," he said, finding his voice. Hanna was acting like she was the one in control, but Sam had made it clear —it was his call to say no.

It was strange, to have that decision on his shoulders. So much of him preferred it when Sam called the shots. And he had no clue how he was supposed to figure this out sitting in a bar. When the server arrived to take Hanna's order, Sam lowered her hand from Brady's hair. She and Hanna started talking about work, so he sat back and listened.

When Hanna was focused on Sam, her behavior was different than the brash and confident way she'd approached him. Was it just that she was a switch or was there more to it? He'd learned early on breaking into websites how to understand the inner workings of things and figure out how they functioned. It was all about getting past the user interface, looking for flaws in the armor. Hanna had armor on, but how did she function behind it?

Brady drew on his inner hacker, and watched. Hanna's drink arrived, and as she fingered the base of her martini glass and looked at his wife, she seemed almost innocent—girlish and shy. Maybe her vulnerability was that she did like Sam, and wanted to do this, but how could he trust there was nothing malicious behind it?

Sam's body language was easier to read. Her interest was genuine, and he already knew her insecurities. She was a little selfish at times, had a short fuse when she was overwhelmed. But she'd been upfront in wanting something that she'd kept hidden for so long.

Her eyes flicked his way. She reached under the table and squeezed his leg.

Sam wanted this. And he wanted to give it to her. But another rule of web development was if you followed an idea out of left field, you needed to set up some kind of control. A fallback, so if everything exploded, you could revert back to the first version without panic.

Brady sat up a bit taller. He'd thought they'd gone so far from simple it wasn't even funny, but things were getting clearer, and he had some questions to ask. And he might've been Sam's pet, but even a pet on a chain is its master's protector.

The two women paused in conversation. Brady took the shot and jumped in.

"I'd like to ask you something," he said to Hanna.

She turned his way with one dark eyebrow raised. A look that said, *I'm sorry, was I speaking to you?*

Brady ignored it and barreled through. "Have you done this before?"

"A few times," she replied. "Although the word *this* is kind of broad."

"*This*, as in had a threesome with a married couple in the lifestyle."

Mic. Drop. Couldn't get more specific than that.

Hanna grinned at Sam. "Cheeky, isn't he?"

Sam played with the straw in her drink. "He can be." But she was smiling, too.

Hanna turned back to Brady. "I haven't done exactly that, but I've had several different variations on the theme. And I've been in the lifestyle for several years."

"So you've been tested, then."

He didn't care if the question bordered on disrespectful. There was no chance that he was going to do this without being sure he was keeping his wife, and himself, safe.

"Yes, of course. I can give you the results if you want proof."

Sam and Brady locked eyes. She raised her eyebrows in a question, one he wanted to answer with an emphatic yes. He needed data, numbers to fall back on. Not someone's word. But he'd gone as far as he needed to go, and Sam was the one running the show here.

"If you have a copy on hand, that'd be good," she said. "Although Brady and I haven't been tested since before we were married."

Before he knew she liked girls. After she'd almost had a threesome. Once again, Brady felt strangely exposed. If he didn't like having Hanna know something that personal about him, how was he going to feel when they were naked together?

Hanna waved Sam's comment off. "It's fine. I trust you."

She trusted them? So easily? Sam seemed to need to push the issue, too.

"Are you sure? Neither of us have slept with anyone else since then, so I'm sure nothing has changed."

"Good on both of ya," Hanna said, raising her glass. "I don't know how you do it."

That got his stomach worked up again, got him tense wondering if she knew how big a deal this was for them, but he let it go. He'd said his piece.

They continued talking for a while more, small talk about nothing in particular, and when it was time to say goodbye, Sam took Brady's hand. She kept holding it while Hanna kissed her cheek, sweet and submissive.

It was a beautiful picture, and for a moment Brady let the image of the three of them tangled up together tiptoe into his head, but he abruptly cut the fantasy off. He needed things to slow down. To get off this spinning merry-go-round and stand on solid ground for a minute, to figure out their lives and their marriage and if their kids were okay.

Hanna's head was still close to Sam's when she gave Brady a look. "May I?" she asked Sam.

May she what? Kiss him? Give him a high-five? Dress him in drag and make him sing karaoke?

Sam gave Hanna a nod of permission, and Hanna leaned over. Brady remained perfectly still when she leaned in and kissed his cheek, too.

Her kiss was different. Longer. Lingering. A slow drag of her lips above the cut of his beard line. But it wasn't Hanna's kiss that got Brady hard. It was Sam's look over Hanna's shoulder. Her wild, ecstatic smile. The sudden need to serve her was intense, to see that look on her face as she rode him, her hands clasping his wrists, her slickness a scent he could wear. But they couldn't do that tonight, not with the girls to get back to, and Brady wasn't sure which one of them she'd be thinking about right now anyway, him or Hanna.

When they were in the car, Sam quietly asked, "So?"

He had to give her an answer now? It was hard to see clear between giving Sam what she wanted, and what Brady wanted for himself.

"I don't know if I trust her," he said.

"Why?"

His gut told him this wasn't a good idea, but he couldn't put his finger on the exact reason. "I don't *know* her."

Sam pinched her lips and exhaled heavily, and Brady's stomach took another beating before she shook her head. "That's fair. I don't know her that well either, but I guess I couldn't do this with anyone I did know, other than you."

He careened into relief and gratitude at being the one she felt comfortable with. Then she sighed, and it punched a hole through his chest.

"I still don't know what I'm doing," she said.

Oh, God. He hated seeing her that way. "It's not you. It's me not knowing."

She nodded quickly, offered him a tight smile.

"Can I sleep on it?" he asked.

Her smile softened. "Sure. No problem."

* * *

The next day, Sam's parents moved to Arizona.

Most of their personal things had been packed up and shipped. A moving van came to collect the furniture they were taking, although they were leaving some to help stage the apartment, something Sam would be responsible for now. The place was still on the market—they'd rejected the lowball offers they'd gotten, and their new townhome came fully furnished. Sam took the keys without blinking and seemed less upset than he thought she'd be when they said goodbye at the airport. The girls, however, were snot-faced from crying, and they stopped at the park on the way home in the hopes of cheering them up.

Allegra's sadness seemed to subside when they got out of the car, but Hope hovered close, pressed tight against Brady's side.

"You want me to carry you, munchkin?" he asked.

Hope nodded. He picked her up without a word, his relief

palpable. She, it seemed, had finally forgiven him, and clung to him like a monkey as they approached the playground.

"What if Allegra doesn't want to play with me?"

Geez, had he passed on his attention issues to Allegra and his fear of rejection to her?

"Maybe you'll make a new friend." It was a sunny day, too, so the tree-lined space was packed with other kids, parents standing around by the park benches.

And one of those parents was Hanna.

"Hey," Sam said when they approached her. "I didn't know you lived around here."

They were considering sleeping with this woman, but Sam didn't know where she lived?

"I don't," Hanna replied, giving Brady a casual wave. "We live on the north side of the Pike. I take my kids here because it's nicer than the playground by us."

She was in jeans and a hoodie, a completely different look from last night. Less threatening, more...normal.

"You have kids?" Allegra asked. Not the slightest bit shy, as always.

"I do. Two girls. You want to meet them?" When Allegra nodded, Hanna cupped her hands around her mouth. "Aliyah, Imani! Over here, now!"

It wasn't the Hanna he'd met yesterday. This one had the voice of a mom—one who took no shit. Allegra went up on the balls of her feet, chomping at the bit to meet new friends. Two children darker than Hanna bolted from the playground and trotted obediently to her side.

"Girls, say hello to Mommy's friends."

They both waved as Hanna introduced them. Aliyah's hair was in two braided pigtails, and she eagerly bounced toward Allegra.

"You wanna play on the swings?" she asked.

Allegra nodded, and then they took a hard run toward the rubber mats of the playground, shouting over who could get there first. Imani hung behind, looking up at Hope.

"You wanna play with her?" Brady asked his daughter.

Hope nodded and he let her slip to the ground. Imani was younger, and Brady watched in relief as Hope asked her quietly where she wanted to play. Holding hands, the two went to the slide.

"You don't have to worry about keeping an eye on all of them." Hanna pointed to an older Asian woman standing at the corner of the playground. "Mimi is like a guard dog."

"Mimi?" Sam asked.

"Wash's aunt."

Sam didn't explain, but she didn't need to. What little he knew about Hanna was that her husband was a deadbeat dad who'd skipped town, and she had some extended relatives who lived nearby. They started talking then, and once again, Brady stood to the side and watched.

He'd had his guard up about Hanna, but looking at her now, she was no different than them. She was a person with a family. Yeah, she was someone kinky who wanted to play, but they were all still just parents. Just people.

Sam glanced over at him. Smiling, she reached for his hand and rubbed her fingers over his wedding ring.

And that was all he needed.

Out on the playground, Allegra started laughing—a boisterous sound he'd know anywhere. Hope was standing at the bottom of the slide waiting to catch Imani. For a moment, Brady finally felt like a superhero, like he was making all his girls happy. He couldn't ignore the feeling that so much was changing, that life as he knew it was swiftly getting left behind, but giving Sam what she wanted was the overriding thing.

He could give this to her. After all, she'd given him everything he'd wanted so far, and it was every guy's dream to have a threesome. He was just getting a different version of that dream. And like Sam said, it wasn't like they were opening their marriage. He was the recurring character. Hanna was the guest star.

He pictured how the night could go, allowed himself to imagine Sam ordering Hanna around in that way that got his skin prickling. Imagined Sam commanding them both. Him and Hanna pleasuring Sam together.

Yeah. Fuck. They were gonna do this. There was no reason not to. She'd gotten him this far, taken him safely through butt plugs and pegging and humiliation. She'd take him safely through this. And he'd do the same for her. He'd stand in traffic for her, and she loved him. Nothing was getting in the way of that.

What did they have that huge bed for, if not to do shit like this?

When they left the park, they let the girls run off to the car ahead of them. Under the cover of the trees, Brady walked close to Sam.

"Hey," he said. His stomach flip-flopped when she looked up at him.

Brady nodded over his shoulder in Hanna's direction.

"Yes."

25

Sam's phone rang when she was halfway home. There was traffic on the Pike, jamming up two full lanes and making Sam worry she was going to be late for the bus, but she couldn't do anything about that, and she didn't want to ignore Cassie's call.

She hit the button on her dash.

"Hey," she said. "Sorry about last weekend."

"No worries." Cassie's cheerful voice came through on her car speakers. "We missed you."

Sam grimaced. She'd ignored both Cassie's and Lilly's texts about going to the pub, then made up excuses about being busy with the kids. "I missed you guys, too."

"How's work going?" Cassie asked.

"Good." It was, mostly. Aside from finding more checks for the Choate file that didn't line up. They all pointed to Pierce, but she couldn't prove it. "Busy, but good."

There was a sound in the background—a voice that didn't sound like Patrick's, then the noise of a phone getting muffled.

"You guys suck at subterfuge, you know that?"

"What do you mean?" Cassie asked.

"Lilly, you can talk," Sam said. "Or should I pretend I didn't hear Jack talking?"

Lilly made a sound of exasperation. "You really would make a good attorney."

There was a small break in the traffic, a few yards of movement that had Sam looking at the clock, calculating how long it would take at this rate. "So what's the reason for this intervention?"

There was a short pause before Lilly said, "We're worried about you."

"Worried I'm watching too many courtroom dramas?" She was pulling a Brady here, using humor and sarcasm to divert the conversation.

Now she got why he did it.

"Neither you nor Brady are talking to any of us," Cassie added.

Sam didn't know what to say. She'd kept her distance from her friends since things started up with Hanna. Stopping talking to them wasn't intentional—she just had a thousand balls in the air.

It wasn't the only thing she'd stopped doing.

She hadn't been to the gym or updated her Instagram profile. Previously posting to it daily, now it remained untouched, like one of the girls' toys left behind when a shiny newer one arrived. She missed her workouts but didn't have time for them, missed her parents, too, but they'd left, and it was something she needed to accept. Now instead of looking after them, she was looking after the apartment, fielding calls from the Realtor in between everything else. She was on a constant high, running from work to home to dance lessons to doctors' appointments to texting with Hanna, who'd emailed her test results. The house hadn't been cleaned either, the dishes piled up, laundry unfolded, her vacuum gathering dust.

It felt like things were unraveling a little, and there were moments when Sam asked herself what the hell she was doing. But she'd been waiting to feel like this. She didn't want off this ride.

"We're both super busy," she said

"Are you sure?" Lilly asked. "Jack's texted Brady a bunch and he barely even answers."

She didn't know what was going on there. They hadn't talked about Jack taking the kids that night. Sam had avoided it, because honestly, she felt rotten about the whole situation. "I appreciate the concern, but we're fine."

"Okay," Cassie replied slowly. "But let us know if you need anything. To talk. A girls' night. We can do a potluck at your house so you don't need to find a sitter."

"Actually, I might've found a sitter."

It was something she and Hanna had chatted about during the week. Mimi loved looking after her grand-nieces, and Allegra and Aliyah had gotten along so well. Hope had liked Imani, too, so having all the girls together in one place seemed like the perfect scenario for their upcoming night.

"That's...great!" The forced enthusiasm in Cassie's voice was obvious.

Sam sighed. She was being a sucky friend. "I promise, we're good. We'll plan something for when life calms down a bit. Okay?"

They'd said goodbye by the time Sam reached her exit. She put on her blinker, got off on a side street and booked it home.

Later that night, she and Brady were lying in bed. The girls were asleep, and Sam's phone was hot in her hands from texting Hanna. Now that the mechanics were set—it was happening this Saturday, here, with the girls staying at Hanna's with Mimi, something Allegra and Hope were super excited about—they were negotiating who did what.

Figuring this out in advance was smart. Much more responsible than what she'd almost walked into in DC. This was how consenting, level-headed adults behaved.

Besides, it gave her time to clean the house.

"What's she saying now?" Brady was on his side, his head next to hers, his beard tickling her shoulder. He hadn't put on a shirt after his shower and was only wearing pajama bottoms. His massive arms were crossed over that beautiful chest, the rest of him hidden beneath the sheets. There was something so intimate about him in nightclothes, under the covers of their bed.

A place they were about to share with another person.

"She said she loves my ideas and can't wait to do them."

She'd worried her fantasy of having both of them touching her, both of them submissive and making her come together, was too boring for her worldly and experienced friend. Knowing Hanna liked it was like the most delectable, sinful icing on a decadent cake. But she had to be careful with Brady, with the power she wielded. Dawes had said power was the ability to influence or outright control the behavior of people. To manipulate others and have superiority over them. She didn't want that. From him or from Hanna.

Which was why she had to be delicate when it came to Hanna's other comments.

"Hanna was wondering if I'd be willing to go down on her."

His brows shot up. "Hot."

Yeah. No duh. "She'd also prefer, when she's in that space, to only be touched by me." It seemed unfair, and Sam was at once wildly turned on by it and guilty as hell. "She only bottoms with women. Is that okay?"

Brady was quiet for a moment. "Yeah, I get it."

Sam looked at him. "You do?"

He nodded but didn't say anything more. She never knew how much to push. These silences of his mystified her. It worked better when she asked him questions.

She turned on her side to face him. "Why doesn't it bother you to watch me with a woman? Would it be the same with a man?"

"It's a total double standard, but no."

"Why?"

He grinned. "'Cause it's hot."

Sam laughed. He was such a man. Her phone beeped again. She thumbed over the screen and no longer felt like laughing. "Hanna wants to know if you're okay having sex with her."

"She wants that?"

Sam flipped the phone around so he could read the message. *"I'd love to ride that giant husband of yours."*

Brady made a face Sam couldn't decipher, but he didn't look comfortable. "And *you're* okay with *that*?" he asked.

Sam fiddled with her necklace. She wasn't okay, and for a moment wanted to shut this whole thing down. But he was giving her this night. She couldn't say she was allowed to do things with Hanna, but he wasn't.

"I know I *should* be," she said, then sighed.

"Should be?"

Sam dropped her necklace, put her phone down and covered her face. "I'm selfish," she said behind her hands.

"Why?"

"Because I feel like Allegra, not wanting to share my toys."

Brady snickered. "I'm a toy now, am I?"

"You know what I mean!"

His fingertips came up along hers, gently prying her hands away from her face. When she opened her eyes, he was smiling. "You're allowed to be possessive of me."

"I am?"

"Yeah."

"You don't think I'm selfish?"

"I didn't say *that*," Brady teased. Sam swatted him away. He laughed. "It's okay to be selfish. This is complicated."

"It is," she said, thankful for his analytical thinking. "Do *you* want to have sex with her?"

"I'm not sure, honestly. But...I wouldn't mind having her watch *us*."

She could feel the wideness of her own smile, the height of her brows lifting. "Really?"

There went that blush of his, bright pink and stealing across his face. His eyes were positively glowing. Sam snuggled in close to him. "My big bear of a husband is an exhibitionist."

He tucked his chin into the pillow and groaned.

Why did she like it so much, rubbing in his face how turned on he was? It was lucky for Sam that he'd lit that particular spark in her, and she couldn't wait to see what Hanna did with it. She'd mentioned it earlier in the week, and her friend had practically rubbed her hands together with excitement.

Sam picked up her phone again. "So should I tell Hanna no?"

Brady went quiet for a long time. "No to sex," he finally said. "But I'm okay with oral if you are."

That might be hot to watch. "Maybe both of us can do that to you at the same time."

His lashes lowered. "You'd do that?"

"Yeah." She moved in close, brushed his cheek with her nose. "After all, I'm the one who knows how to tease my pet into a frenzy."

He stiffened and grunted.

"Would you like that?" She nuzzled his ear, sparked her tongue along it. "Two tongues on you?"

Brady shuddered out a breath. "Fuck, that's hot."

Lord, she loved having this kind of power over him. But she'd watched enough superhero movies with him to know that with this kind of power came a whole different level of responsibility.

"Is there anything you *don't* want?" she asked. She would not fuck up another night together. Especially not this one.

He was silent for another moment. "No anal with her. At all."

That was fair. And, selfishly, another part of Brady she wanted to keep to herself. "Okay. You both have your own safewords—" Hanna's was *Pierce*, which Sam found hysterical, "—but I think for this night, let's have red as the general word, instead of two different ones."

"Smart," he said. "Red. Three letters. Should be easy to remember."

"Are there any limits you want to change?"

"Is scat or golden showers suddenly on the table?"

Sam snorted. "Erm. No."

"Then I think we're good." He glanced up at her. "Are you not going to wear your necklace?"

"Do you want me to?"

He shrugged. "I like it when it's on you. I feel connected."

She didn't like that shrug. But at least he was saying what he was feeling.

"We're already connected." Sam reached out and touched his ring. "I take care of you, you take care of me."

He smiled. "End of story."

Two soft knocks sounded at their door. Sam texted Hanna that she had to go and locked her screen.

"Whichever one of you is knocking," she yelled, "you're supposed to be in bed."

The door opened. Allegra and Hope were both standing there in their pajamas, holding hands. "We're sad that Nana and Pops are gone," Allegra said.

Sam's stomach bottomed out. She'd been so caught up in this, so focused on checking in with Brady and Hanna that she hadn't remembered to check in with her own damn children. What was wrong with her?

She patted the space between her and Brady. "Come here."

Allegra and Hope climbed onto the bed. Hope curled into Brady. The image was sweet enough to make Sam's heart melt.

She'd been so unhappy she'd forgotten the good times, the times when he *was* there. Times when he'd helped. When he'd taken both girls out for a drive after work so Sam could get an extra hour of sleep. Sure, they'd come back with sticky faces from the ice cream they weren't supposed to have before dinner, but he'd done it. He'd been there.

Why had she been so hard on him?

"I know you're sad," she told Allegra. "But we'll go visit them in Arizona soon, and we'll FaceTime with them tomorrow. We'll do it every day if you want. I'm sure they'll love that."

"Okay, but I wanna spend the weekend with you and Daddy."

"This weekend?" Sam's breath got lodged in her chest. "Honey you're going to Aliyah and Imani's on Saturday."

Allegra didn't answer. Sam waited. She wouldn't put her desires in front of her children again. There'd be other weekends, they could reschedule...

"Okay," Allegra said. "Next weekend then?"

The relief and the mom-guilt descended even as Sam inhaled a fresh breath. "Next weekend. You'll have us both to yourselves, I promise."

She wrapped Allegra up in her arms, wanting to live in this bubble of happiness forever. A foot away, Brady gazed at her, Hope's head tucked under his chin. He smiled. Mouthed the words, *"I love you."*

Sam felt lit up from within.

"Hey," Brady said. "You two want to see us dance?"

The girls cheered, and he untangled himself from Hope. Sam groaned but smiled as he stood, picked up his phone and queued up a love song. Then he put it back down and held out his hand. Sam rose from the bed and put her hand in his. They started slow-dancing, the girls smiling like idiots on the bed.

"Mom," Allegra said, "you never told me you could dance."

Sam let Brady twirl her around. "This is how we danced on our wedding day."

"And Mommy looked even prettier than Aunt Lilly did," Brady said. "She was the prettiest woman in the world." He dipped her, then whispered, "She still is."

Sam tucked her face against his chest. It was like her romance novels—the moment when you know everything is going to be happy, when the heroine gets a perfect ending with the husband and the home and the kids, the job and the kinky sex.

She couldn't believe how lucky she was.

The song ended. Sam picked up Hope, squeezed her and twirled her around the room. Brady bear-hugged Allegra and tickled her until she squirmed out of his grip.

"Come on, you two monkeys," Sam said. "Let's get you back to bed."

26

On Saturday night, Sam drove the girls to Hanna's while Brady finished setting up at home. Hanna lived ten minutes north, and Sam rehearsed Allegra's plan with her as they drove. Sam was a mix of excitement and nerves, doubts whispering defiantly in her head. She was bringing her children to a near-stranger's house. Bringing a near stranger into hers.

Her doubts got louder when they reached the two-family house that Hanna and Mimi shared the rent on. It wasn't rundown as much as it was old. And inside it was a mess.

Now she knew why the Choate file was so disorganized. Clothes were piled on top of chairs, toys spilled out of tipped-over boxes and ran rampant on the floor. Mimi was frying food in the kitchen, and Sam had to resist asking if the fire extinguishers worked.

They got the girls settled, watching a movie, and Hanna smiled at Sam.

"They're playing happily," she said quietly, dressed in a black floor-length coat. "I'd like to play now, too, if it pleases you."

Sam swallowed. Her doubts melted away. "Let's go."

Hanna followed Sam in her own car. Sam had said she was welcome to stay the night, but Hanna preferred to have her own transportation. Sam hadn't argued. She'd need to pick up the girls

243

midmorning anyway, after she made sure the Realtor had everything ready for tomorrow's open house.

They stepped inside the house. Sam was too excited for small talk, and from the tension rolling off her friend, Sam knew Hanna felt the same.

"Lose the coat," Sam said.

It was electrifying when Hanna obeyed, revealing bare shoulders and the luxurious red velvet corset Sam had seen at the shop. Sleeveless, with hook-and-eye fastenings running the length of the front, it was traditional and hot as hell.

"When did you get that?" she asked, stroking a finger along the flocked edge.

"I went back and bought it," Hanna replied. "After I saw you liked it."

"Hmmm." She had on dark jeans, too. Sam reached out, toyed with the zipper. "Do you have on other things I'll like beneath these?"

"Oui, Madame."

The French words and polite, demure behavior from Hanna made an exquisite combination.

"Good." Sam ran a nail along the teeth of the zipper. Hanna sucked in a breath. "Follow me."

Hanna followed her silently up the steps. Brady was in the bedroom, and everything had been set up as she'd asked. The lights were dim. The bed was turned down, towels stacked up at the foot of it, toys on the nightstand. And Brady looked like a bodyguard. He was shirtless and barefoot, nothing else on but jeans.

Sam strode to the closet, knowing they were watching as she removed her jacket and hung it on a hook on the back of the door. She'd worn her corset top again, without her necklace or her rings. Brady seemed okay with the lack of jewelry, especially when she showed him what was beneath her pencil skirt: nothing but a garter belt, thigh-highs and boots.

She looked the part of a Domme. Cinched at the waist. Wound up as tight as they were.

And she wanted to unravel them both.

Sam turned around, hands on her hips. "Hannaleen, you may call me Madame tonight. That will please me."

"Merci, Madame." Hanna's eyes were full of lust, and so, so green. "You look incredible."

Brady's eyes were on Sam, too. "She always does."

Sam smiled, preening under their praise. "Thank you, pet." She walked over to where he stood. "Shall we show our guest how *pretty* you can get?"

His chin lowered, but his eyes stayed on her. "Pretty, Mistress?"

She stroked from his cheek down his arm to the waistband of his pants. He was already pretty. But that wasn't what she'd meant.

"Pretty, as in big—" Sam unzipped him, "—thick—" She pushed the denim aside. There were no boxers beneath, just as she'd requested, "—and hard."

His cock leapt forward, not fully erect, not as big as he was going to get, but close. She took him in hand, gave him several long, unhurried strokes. Brady shuddered through an inhalation as he thickened the rest of the way.

Sam smirked. "Good boy."

His chest rose and fell. He watched her, hands limp by his sides, obedient, breathless. Even when she stopped stroking him, palmed the tip and then scratched both her hands up his torso until they scraped over his tight, small nipples, he didn't protest or move.

Sam tugged on his jeans. "Take these off. Then wait for me on the bed."

"Yes, Mistress."

It was almost too much, having them both at her mercy.

Almost.

She turned around and paced over to Hanna. Sam reached up and threaded her fingers through all that silky, golden hair. Hanna closed her eyes, her head sinking back, lips parting.

"Have you been thinking about kissing me?" Sam asked.

"If I say yes, does that mean you'll do it?"

"Oh, you're a little brat, aren't you?" Sam hadn't been expecting that. But she wanted the kiss more than she wanted to impart discipline. "Say you're sorry."

Hanna's eyelids fluttered open. She looked at Sam, pleading and hungry.

"*Je suis désolée, Madame.*"

"That's better." She gripped hard, one hand tight at the nape of Hanna's neck as she kissed her.

It was like she remembered, but better. Hanna's lips were pillow-soft and pliant. They gave way beneath Sam's, and Hanna exhaled, sighing into Sam's mouth. She inched her tongue out, wet and eager. Sam allowed Hanna one tiny flick of their tongues before she broke off the kiss and turned over her shoulder to glance at Brady. Naked on the bed, he was watching them. His cock stood at attention, and even from here, she could see the redness of his cheeks.

"Unzip my skirt," she told Hanna, then watched Brady's face as the fabric slid to the floor.

Now you're watching, aren't you?

Smug, she turned back to Hanna, whose gaze had dropped to Sam's bare thighs. "See something you like?"

Hanna nodded slowly. Sam nudged the skirt away with her foot.

"Me, too." One by one, she undid the clips on Hanna's corset, revealing beautiful bronze skin as the fabric fell away. She skimmed a finger along Hanna's breast, thumbed over her nipple until it went taut.

"Jeans off," she ordered. "Leave the panties on. Then you may join us."

"Yes, Madame."

Sam climbed onto the bed and straddled Brady. She nestled his cock against her clit, slid it up and down. His startled gasp was like rocket fuel. Pleasure simmered through her with each rock of her hips. Brady moaned but stayed pressed against the bed, all that masculine power shackled with only her words.

"Undo my garters."

"Yes, Mistress." He was clumsy in his efforts to unclip them, fingers too big and his hands trembling, but he got through them all. Sam tossed the belt to the side as Hanna got onto the bed beside them.

Sam's heart was positively galloping. This was it—what she'd been waiting for. And these two beautiful people were going to give it to her.

Climbing off Brady, she settled onto her back between them and undid the top stays of her corset until her breasts were free. Her nipples were stiff, pointy and begging for attention. Sam stretched her arms out and looked to both of them.

"Come here," she said, arching her chest. "I want to feel both your mouths on me."

Brady reached in first, brows slanted in the most beautiful appetite, like he'd been starving for this. One big warm hand came around her left breast, and she inhaled a sharp breath when his beard gently scraped her skin, then again when his lips closed over her nipple. Sam felt a line ricochet from her breast to her clit.

That line got even sharper when Hanna's mouth found her other breast.

The sensation from her friend's mouth was different. Hanna tongued a slow circle around Sam's nipple, then flicked the tip of it over and over until Sam's hips were rising off the bed.

She searched through the pleasure for the French words she was looking for.

"*Comporte-toi,*" she hissed. *Behave.* "No teasing."

Hanna smiled before she took Sam's nipple into her mouth. Brady paused, then resumed his ministrations, and Sam closed her eyes. After years of never feeling like her breasts were something sexual, now having mouths on them was intensely erotic. Her legs winged open wide, soft skin going slick. Hanna bit down lightly, and Sam tipped her head back. A pulsing ache started between her legs, and they'd barely even begun.

"Stop," she said.

They both behaved in tandem. The cold air was a shock against Sam's puckered, wet skin. She pulled Brady close, letting him rest his head on her shoulder and drape his arm around her middle. Then she did the same to Hanna. Her friend looked up at her, expectant.

"Touch me, Hannaleen."

Hanna's smile was pure deviance. "With pleasure, Madame."

Sam tried to stop shaking as Hanna placed a hand on her belly, then moved slowly down. She locked eyes with her husband, body shaking at the light tickle of her friend's touch. Hanna caressed her trimmed strip of hair, and Sam held on to them both and closed her eyes as Hanna's fingertip danced across her clit.

"Oh, God."

Hanna's pointer finger was slim. Warm. Different than Sam's own finger and somehow the same. She drew a pattern over Sam's flesh, slow circles around Sam's most sensitive spot. She didn't mind Hanna avoiding it though—she liked the torture of dragging this out, and she was sure, the second Hanna's fingers met that one sensitive button, she would explode.

"How does it feel, Madame?"

Sam could barely answer, lost to the pleasure. "Amazing."

Brady let out a short breath, and Sam found a way through the cloud of pleasure to press a hand to his back, to try to say, *I'm here* and *thank you* without words.

He tightened the arm he had around her in response.

Hanna drew a wider circle. "I meant how does it feel to have two people who want you so badly?" She punctuated the question by giving Sam a few caresses in rapid succession before returning to those slow, measured loops.

"Fuck, do that again."

Hanna obeyed. Sam's head lifted off the bed. Her friend's touch was shocking.

"Again."

Hanna drew it out this time, adding a few more hurried up-and-down strokes. Sam jolted at the feeling, dropped her head back to the pillow. This wasn't the same as it was with her and Brady. No emotion—just sex. It felt more like Hanna was running the scene, too, but Sam was too worked up by the hand on her clit to care.

She searched her mind for the word she was looking for.

"Rapide."

No, that wasn't right. It was a close translation, but not correct, and Hanna didn't obey anyway. Sam opened her eyes and glared at her friend. Hanna's grin was sly and cunning, like she knew exactly what she was doing.

"Faster," she instructed. "Or I won't touch you at all."

Hanna pouted falsely, looking for all the world like a misbehaving child—one who knew she'd still get a toy no matter what she did. *"Pardon, Madame."*

She did as she was told, though, and Sam was instantly breathless at the astonishing pleasure. She dug her nails into Brady's back.

"Touch me, pet. Touch me now."

He followed her request without question, lifting his hand to dip below Hanna's. Sam let out a wild cry when his big middle finger slid inside her.

"It feels incredible," she said, finally answering Hanna's question as Brady added another finger to the mix. "You both feel incredible."

Her hips rocked in time with their movements. Hanna's fingertip was a millimeter off from the spot that would send Sam into overdrive. She didn't know how Brady knew—maybe it was the look on her face, the strain in her body or the noises she made, but he lifted his head and said, "She's more sensitive on the right."

Hanna edged her finger the tiniest bit over, and Sam made a fist in Hanna's hair. She'd wanted it to last, but there was no stopping this now. Fuck, she hadn't counted on this, hadn't imagined their worship would drive her to the point where she lost all sense of being in command.

"Gonna come," she moaned, and then she was clutching both of them, gasping through waves of crippling bliss that stole her ability to think, to talk, to do anything at all except thrash and shake. She didn't feel sated when they both pulled back though. Her hips were still surging when she heard Hanna speak.

"What does she need after she comes?"

Sam opened her eyes. Brady's gaze was right on her, loving and hungry.

"Simple," he said. "She needs more."

27

_B_rady wasn't misbehaving when he reached for a condom without Sam's instruction. He knew what she needed, and he needed to prove it.

He hadn't expected to need to prove himself tonight.

He hadn't liked it when Sam and Hanna were speaking in French. He'd felt excluded. He hadn't liked the way Hanna called Sam _Madame_, sharing her as their Domme but also alienating him at the same time. It wasn't a big deal, though, not big enough to use his safeword on.

And none of that mattered when Sam nodded and reached for him.

It was like a reboot to his system. He stopped thinking about anything else. He sank into that place in his head where her ownership was all he felt, her satisfaction all he craved.

Hanna moved away, giving them space. Brady vaguely registered her action. He didn't want her out of the bed—there was enough room for the three of them—but he needed a glimmer of his confident Sam, his Mistress. The woman who'd quirk an eyebrow at him if it looked like he was going to step out of line and lay down holy hell if he did. He wasn't seeing that version of her. She seemed lost in all this, so he sheathed himself quickly, climbed on top of her and guided himself inside.

Sam whimpered, and God, she was so tight. Too tight at this angle, he needed to change it, but Sam reached up, put her hands on his face and pulled him down roughly until she was kissing him. They were fast kisses, like they were drinking each other in, each using the other for air.

This wasn't how they kissed—it didn't feel like *them*. There was a hunger from Sam she didn't usually show. He came up for a breath to look at her, but she rose up into the next kiss, the next thrust, grabbing his back and trying to pull him harder onto her.

"I'll crush you if I do that."

"Don't care," she said. "Closer. Kiss me."

So he did. She was more desperate than he'd ever seen her, and he needed to fill that abyss. He moved until they were skin to skin. Kissing her slowly, he deliberately measured his thrusts, using his body to show her how much he loved her, like there wasn't someone else in the room.

But there was, and that someone needed to see what he and Sam had.

He wasn't an exhibitionist like Sam had thought. He wanted to show Hanna he was the only person who could have Sam like this.

He was more jealous than he'd realized.

It wasn't a fair thought to have, not now, not when they were doing this, when Hanna hadn't done anything wrong. He felt Hanna's hand trace over his back, and he liked it. Liked the quiver that coursed through him when she used her nails.

"So pretty," Hanna said. "What a good boy you are. How well you serve her."

Brady laughed and smiled, felt his pleasure spike and his cheeks heat as he turned his face away. Who knew the embarrassment from unexpected praise would crank him up higher, too?

Sam moaned, a soft, needy noise. Brady's eyes were back on hers in an instant. She brought her hands to his shoulders, body undulating beneath him.

"Shhh," Brady whispered.

He stopped thrusting, long enough for his arms to quake from the effort of holding still and know she felt him shaking, too. This would've been the moment, if they were alone, that he would've thrust fast and hard. But he didn't want to fuck. He wanted to make love to his wife, to be selfish and possessive and feel the ownership only *he* could have of *her*.

Staring into those deep brown eyes, he eased even deeper inside her. One inch at a time.

"He never takes his eyes off you, does he?" Hanna asked.

Sam shook her head, her gaze gentle and amazed.

He wasn't going to say it, not with Hanna here, but he hoped Sam knew he'd never taken his eyes off her. Not once in seventeen years. He'd seen her when she was in college, when she came home from DC disappointed and depressed. He'd seen her pregnant and heavy, when she'd shed the weight, too, and every single minute he'd been in awe of her.

He was still in awe. Of how she commanded him now, without a single word.

Brady spread his legs wider, expanding his stance with his knees farther apart. Sam rose up again and kissed him, dug her hands in his hair. She broke the kiss and pushed him up until he hovered above her.

"Make me come again." Her voice was rough. Abrasive. "Get the bullet vibe."

It wasn't until she glanced to the side that Brady realized the order was for Hanna.

Hanna retrieved the vibrator from the nightstand, then moved in close. The visual as Hanna's darker arm crossed the midsection of his wife's pale body was hot as hell. This was what he'd pictured when he'd agreed to this—to fuel Sam's lust along with her friend. Her knuckles bumped against Brady's pubic bone as she fit the vibe against Sam's clit and turned it on. It was strange and arousing, and the jolt of Sam's body as she gasped and went slicker startled him toward his own release.

"Mistress," he groaned.

"Not yet," she said, and Brady barely bit back a cry of protest.

"We're working on his control," she said to Hanna, who turned the vibe up higher. Sam choked on a moan.

"He's not gonna make it," Hanna teased. "I bet it feels too good, fucking into you like that. I bet you're so soft and wet he can't hold back another second."

Brady grunted and pinched his eyes shut. That was the shit that got at him. Talking about how close he was, putting his face in his own pleasure nudged at that weird space inside. Like he was the toy nestled between them, nothing but a plaything with a flicked switch.

He tried to slow down. To hold off.

"Can't," he gritted out. "Sammy, please."

The name slipped out, and for the first time, he didn't try to swallow it. She was his Mistress and his Sammy, his wife and the mother of his children. She was everything to him, and he belonged to her, no matter what name he called her.

"Yes. Now, fuck yes, I'm coming, too."

He gripped her tight, lost it, groaned into the sweaty hollow of her neck. Sam bucked up against him a moment later, until they were both shivering messes, raspy breaths panting to quiet.

"So pretty," Hanna said again.

Brady turned to look at her as Sam reached up to stroke her cheek. "Yes, you are."

Hanna blushed, and Brady knew it was his turn to give them space, to watch Sam dominate a woman. He wasn't sure how he was going to feel about it, but by the time he'd slid out, disposed of the condom and turned back to them, they were already kissing. Hanna had moved onto her back, and Sam was hovering over her, running her fingers over the other woman's legs.

"I was right," she said. "Your skin is gorgeous everywhere."

Brady positioned himself at the edge of the bed to watch, and he had to admit they were beautiful together. He was worried he'd be jealous, that he'd feel like less of a man watching this, but he was enthralled with the way Sam touched Hanna's breasts, playing with and twisting her nipples. Sam dragged Hanna's panties down her thighs. His mouth went dry when Sam leaned forward. Ass in the air, corset still laced, thigh-highs a dark sheen against her white skin, she snaked her tongue out against Hanna's clit.

"*Oh, oui. S'il vous plaît, Madame.*"

Brady knew enough French to translate. And even if he couldn't, he'd be able to figure out what Hanna wanted from the roll of her body, the way her hands gripped the sheets.

Sam hummed—that infuriating, intoxicating noise, and the other woman's eyes slammed shut.

Brady felt a funny kind of kinship with Hanna, watching Sam lick her clit the same way she'd licked his cock that night after the dungeon. Quick, short laps with the pointed tip of her tongue, over and over, until Hanna mewled and squirmed. Did it feel the same for her as it had for him?

Had he looked as helpless as Hanna did, right now?

Sam did something that made Hanna squeak, and then Sam was laughing. She stopped, went up on her knees, then flipped Hanna over onto all fours. He watched Sam's arm move, then heard the skin-on-skin sound of fingers parting soft flesh. Brady watched Hanna's face contort in pleasure.

"*Mon Dieu, Madame.* Feels so good."

"I know it does, you greedy girl," Sam said with a smirk. Brady watched her arm move faster. Heard those sounds speed up. "I'd spank you, but I wouldn't want a handprint on that beautiful skin."

Sam stopped stroking, palmed Hanna's hips, drew the other woman upright until they were chest-to-back. "So instead let's hear what you sound like when you come."

Sam wrapped one arm around Hanna's middle, hooked her chin over Hanna's shoulder as she reached for the vibe and placed it between Hanna's spread thighs. She turned it to the highest speed, rubbing it in a ruthless way that made Brady sure Hanna had no choice but to come. When the other woman's body jolted, Sam looked at Brady, her smile wild, liked she'd reached into that box of Lucky Charms and found a marshmallow clover on the first try.

Gasping, Hanna leaned against Sam. They stayed like that for a few moments. Then Hanna turned one sweaty cheek toward Sam.

"Merci, Madame," she said, then glanced in Brady's direction. "May I play, now?"

Sam's eyes met Brady's. His heart rate sped up.

"You may," Sam said, one devious brow slanting. "He's all yours."

Wait, had they agreed on this? He'd consented to oral, but was something else happening?

"I haven't played with such a big toy in a long time," Hanna said as she crawled toward him. "Your Mistress is lucky."

"Thank you—"

Shit. What was he supposed to call her? They hadn't discussed it, so Brady left it at that. Hanna stroked her hands up his legs, scratched her nails down them. His body reacted, his dick going from soft to semi, but his head wasn't in it.

"Oh yes, such a pretty slave."

Brady looked away, mashing himself against the pillows. He didn't like her calling him that. If he was Sam's slave, it was in their own private moments when they were alone. But Sam would catch that, right?

He waited as Hanna stroked up his thighs. Sam said nothing.

"Such powerful legs," Hanna said. "I liked watching them move. But you did something naughty just now, didn't you?"

"What's that?"

"You called Madame the wrong name."

Brady's stomach clenched. Oh, no. That wasn't fair. He tried to see around her, to catch Sam's eye, but Hanna got in his line of sight. *"I'm* talking to you now, slave. Apologize to your Mistress."

Brady closed his eyes. "Apologies, Mistress," he whispered, but he didn't want to be sorry. Not for that. Not when those blurred lines had solidified into one he could understand, one he'd finally felt good about.

"That's better," Hanna said. "Always remember to treat your Domme with respect."

"I will," he croaked. He thought he had. He tried to curl away, tried to sink into himself, especially as Hanna moved closer to his dick.

"Good. Time to reward the little subby."

Brady flinched. He felt small again, while somehow massive, an ex-linebacker's body with a mind that didn't match. He didn't want to feel this way, not in front of her. Suddenly he didn't want this at all.

But Sam didn't notice. She watched from the foot of the bed, smile mischievous, her eyes shining. He pleaded for her to figure it out, prayed she'd see him squirming away as Hanna kissed his inner thigh. He was getting hard at her unfamiliar touch, his traitorous body reacting beyond his control.

"Don't," he said, but Hanna didn't stop because that wasn't the safeword. Neither was metamorphosis. Shit. What had they decided to change it to?

"Don't what?" Hanna asked. "Don't do this?"

Hanna held his hips down, opened her mouth, and Brady searched his stupid, useless, forgetful brain for whatever word he was supposed to say, but it wouldn't come and he needed to get out of here.

"Stop! Seriously, get the fuck off me."

Brady sat up, pushed Hanna off him, and she pitched assbackward onto the bed. Sam's expression went from a grin to disaster.

"Brady—" Sam began, but he talked over her.

"No, I can't do this. I'm sorry."

But he wasn't sorry. Not then and not when he stood, grabbed a towel and quickly wrapped it around himself. He didn't want anyone else, didn't care if not wanting it made him a real man or not. He didn't want to get disciplined by a stranger either, no matter how much his wife liked her. He didn't know how to say no to Sam, and God help him, he never wanted to, but he'd been on this roller coaster with her thinking she'd keep him safe.

She hadn't.

Brady walked out of the room. And he didn't look back.

28

By the time Brady heard Hanna drive away, he'd showered, dried off and was sitting in the bathtub. It seemed like a good place to put himself, even though he'd had to shove another towel under his butt when the one he'd wrapped around his waist got wet, then thrown another over his shoulders for good measure. He looked ridiculous, covered in towels too small for him and trying to fit his giant body in here, but he didn't care. He didn't feel like leaving this room.

His legs bent, he balanced his elbows on his knees and waited.

For what, Brady had no fucking clue.

He tensed when Sam came upstairs. He had no idea what was going to happen. He hoped they could hug, that she would tell him she loved him and they'd put this whole thing behind them. Didn't seem likely, though.

Sam knocked once—one quick rap of her knuckles. "We need to talk."

Brady didn't want to talk. He never did, but being angry always made him fuck up his words, trip over them and say stupid shit. But unless he planned on living in his bathtub, there wasn't another option.

"Come in."

The door opened. Sam's brows were hunched and her arms were crossed over her bathrobe.

"Why did you do that?" she asked.

Seriously? She was pissed off at him? "Why did I do *what*?"

She shook her head quickly, like she'd been hit with something and needed to clear it. "Why *what*? How about why'd you shove Hanna and curse at her?"

Oh. He hadn't realized it came off like that. "I didn't like what she was doing."

"Then why didn't you use your safeword?"

Brady turned away, stared at the wall. "I forgot it."

"You *forgot* it?"

"Yeah. We changed it and I couldn't fucking remember what the new one was."

"Did you need a reminder?" she spat. "Should I have put it on a Post-it Note?"

He cut his eyes back to her and matched her glare. "You know, you can tell me what to do up to a certain point, but you just fucking passed it."

Sam recoiled, her mouth open. He wasn't often as mean as she was, but she'd pushed him too far.

"Yes, I forgot the damn word," he said. "But you forgot me, what I wanted."

"What did I forget? What part of what we negotiated did I not follow through on?"

He looked at the opposite side of the shower again, let his head fall back against the wall with a thump, because the answer to that was confusing and too fucked up for even him to figure out.

"She shouldn't have made me apologize for saying your name," he said. "It wasn't her call."

"*That's* what you're upset about?"

No. "I didn't like the French either. When you were talking, when she was going to do stuff to me, it made me feel—"

Like less of a man. Like he couldn't be what she wanted. Like he was never going to be enough for her.

"Like what?"

He gritted his teeth. His faced burned. Couldn't she tell him she loved him? Isn't that what he'd said he needed after? This didn't feel like a Domme comforting her sub, though. It felt like his wife scolding him, felt like the old them all over again. But this wasn't him missing what she was saying or buying the wrong damn brand of yogurt. This was something much more private, and if she didn't realize that, then there was no point explaining.

"Nothing. It doesn't matter anymore."

"Of course it *matters*, Brady. It matters that Hanna said two things and you shoved her. I was worried you were going to hurt her."

"It's *her* you're worried about?" he shouted, shooting her another glare. "You didn't think it would bother me when you fucking rented me out, handed me over for Hanna to use? Jesus Christ, Sam. When would you ever think I'd be okay with that?"

"You think I rented you out?"

"I think saying 'he's all yours, have fun,' counts as renting me out."

"That's not what I did," she said coldly. "That's not fair."

Brady looked away from her again.

"Oh no," she said. "You don't get to shut down. I asked you what you didn't want. I stood by those requests."

She was right, but he wasn't going to take the fall on a technicality. "I didn't think I had to explain that I didn't want her to humiliate me."

"I told her you liked that! You said provoking you in the bedroom does shit to you. You didn't say it—"

"Bothered me?" Brady looked straight at her. "Yes, I did."

It was here in this room. He'd told her he liked it when *she* made fun of him. Just her.

"You didn't say you didn't want Hanna to do it."

He thumped his head against the tile a few more times. Where was the delete button on this whole conversation? Could he safeword out of this, too? Maybe other submissives didn't feel this way. Maybe being into humiliation required having tougher skin.

Maybe he was weak, after all.

"I don't understand," she said. "I asked if there were any other limits or things you wanted to change. You said we were good." She narrowed her eyes. "Is there something I'm missing, Brady?"

"No, there's nothing you're *missing*," he snapped back. "Except the fact that I didn't want to do this in the first goddamn place."

"Then why did you agree to it?"

"Because it's impossible to say no to you!" he roared. It was that drug, the make-Sam-happy drug, the thing he wanted above everything else. "Because I'm so fucking desperate to please you, to keep feeding these *needs* of yours, that I do whatever you want even if it's not good for me or what I want."

They stared at each other. Her hands were clenched by her sides.

"So you didn't want to do this," she said. "Ever. At any point."

"I thought I did. But then it started and I didn't anymore."

He wasn't being fair. He *had* been turned on by the idea, because he was turned on by anything when Sam was worked up, and there were moments he had enjoyed.

He hadn't known where the line was until they crossed it.

Sam sank onto the closed toilet seat lid and looked at the wall. "But you said nothing to me."

Her voice was quieter now. He sighed. "I don't know when I'm supposed to act one way or another with you. When I'm your pet and when I'm allowed to speak my mind. I don't know how to be everything you want, Sam. I don't think I can be."

They were the scariest words he'd ever said. But it was the truth. The simple, serious, not-joking-around truth. This felt hazardous, though. Like if they weren't careful, they were going to break something important.

"I don't think I can be everything you want, either," she said quietly. "I'm supposed to do everything right. Read you when you don't talk. Figure out your needs when you're silent. I can't do it all. I can't be that and the person who finds everything in the house and be a halfway decent mother, and hold down a job and..."

She broke off into a sob. Panic took hold.

Tell me you love me. Just say those words and everything will be okay.

"This isn't working," she whispered.

Brady felt the color drain from his face.

"I'm not a mind-reader, and you weren't honest with me," she added. "We shouldn't do this if we can't talk to one another. If you can't trust me, then this is all a house of cards."

Sam didn't move, so Brady stared at the wall along with her. The ugly-ass blue tile wall he imagined one day he'd fix up for her, back when he thought he could give her everything.

"I thought things were getting better," she continued. "That we were fixing things. But we've been using sex to stitch together a broken marriage. Trying to build it on top of something that was falling apart."

Brady twisted his ring until it went hot between his fingers. It wasn't helping him figure out how to gulp in a fucking breath, though.

Sam stood, facing away from him as she crossed her arms tightly around her body.

"I think we should take some space," she said. "I'll go to my parents' place tonight."

"Okay," he said.

He should've said *don't go*.

He should've said *please stay*.

He should've said *I love you*.

But he wasn't sure any of that mattered anymore. Sam sniffed one more time, then squared her shoulders. Brady stared at his ring, this metal band of promises he'd thought meant forever as she opened the bathroom door and shut it behind her.

Brady closed his eyes. He always knew letting this part of himself out would break them.

He hated knowing he was right.

29

Sam awoke to unfamiliar surroundings. Lumpy couch. Bare walls. Right, she was at her parents' apartment, and her marriage had fallen apart last night.

She turned on her back and stared at the ceiling.

How had everything gone so horribly wrong?

She'd watched Hanna talk to him. All the signs of Brady's pleasure were there: flushed cheeks, chin dipped. He looked like he always did when he was turned on. He was a little on edge, but she'd chalked that up to the newness of the situation. Not that he felt like he'd been loaned out for someone else's discretion.

She rubbed her hands over her swollen eyelids and sighed. He was right—it did seem like that was what she was doing, but if he didn't want that then why hadn't he said something? Was she supposed to figure it out the way she knew how to load the dishwasher or find a lost pair of gloves? She'd been trying to read Brady, but she couldn't possibly know everything when he locked shit away in his head.

He hadn't trusted her, hadn't told her how he felt. He'd made her feel like she'd forced him into this.

Had she?

In her excitement to do this, had she ignored unease on his part? He'd said it was impossible to say no to her, that he had to keep feeding her needs. But she'd given him a million chances to speak up, given him time to think and told him it was his call. If he couldn't cough out the words, how much was she to blame?

Maybe she should've figured it out. Maybe she was a sucky Dominant. She had no idea how Hanna felt, or if she'd even enjoyed the evening. She'd stated she didn't get emotions involved, and maybe that was the problem. Sam hadn't felt anything last night, just got carried away in the sex. She'd been turned on, but it was nothing but body parts and sensation. The connection she usually had with Brady was missing, and she'd been too lost in what was happening to focus on either of them.

The phone rang—the ancient landline her parents had kept running. Sam sat up and picked it up off the end table. "Hello?" she asked, then coughed through the grit she had in her throat from crying.

"Sweetheart?"

"Oh, hey, Mom." She was happy to hear her mom's voice, but a part of her had hoped it was Brady on the line.

"We were wondering why you weren't answering your cell. Is everything set for today?"

The open house. Oh, *shit*.

Sam raced into the bathroom to wash her face. "Yeah, I just got here."

"Oh." There was a beat of silence. "Is everything okay?"

Sam stared at herself. Puffy eyes, splotchy skin, hair like an ad for cheap shampoo. Mascara and dry tears crackled in the corners of her eyes. Staging the place meant no hairbrush or toothbrush hanging around, so she splashed her face, brushed her teeth with her fingertip, then tried to work out all her tangles and knots.

The mirror told her she was doing a shitty job.

"Sure," she said. "Why?"

"We called the house first," her mother said. "Brady didn't sound good."

Sam's heart lurched. She didn't have the energy to throw on her *I'm fine* mask anymore, for all that it made her mother sad. "Things are bad right now."

"You know, honey. Sometimes people get lost in a marriage. They forget the things that attracted them to their partners, what made them want to be there in the first place." Sam didn't say anything, so her mother sighed. "Just, remember the history you two have."

Yes, they had a history. But maybe all spending years with another person meant was that you knew how to cut deeper, how to hurt them more.

When the Realtor arrived, Sam booked it out of there and plugged her phone in to charge in the car. She'd turned it off to save battery overnight, forgetting a wall plug for it. But there were no messages. From anyone.

She'd been overextended for years. Grabbed at and needed by everyone. Now no one needed her at all.

She drove to Hanna's place in a fog. Her friend let her in and pulled Sam aside. "You okay? What happened after I left?"

Sam had felt lousy, watching her friend drive off in the middle of the night, but Hanna had insisted she was fine. She looked fine now, too, just as perfectly done-up as always. Sam, however, was not.

"Sorry." She shook her head. "I need to just...*not*...for a while. Can we talk later?"

Hanna nodded, concern clear on her face. "Sure."

Inside, Mimi was making pancakes slathered in cheap, fake maple syrup, full of food dyes and God knows what else. Running on instinct and very little sleep, Sam snatched Allegra's plate from her.

"What did we say about junk food?" she snapped. "What did we discuss?"

Allegra pinned Sam with the kind of glare she hadn't thought her daughter was capable of. "You never let me do anything!"

Anger in eyes that matched hers reflected back at her, Hope copying Allegra's expression by her side. Sam was about to lash back when a sharp *"Shhh!"* from Mimi quieted them both. Sam whirled around to find the tiny Asian woman smiling and offering Allegra a bagel with butter.

Sam nodded once. "Finish up," she said robotically once the plates had been swapped. "We have to go."

When they'd gobbled down their breakfasts, Allegra smiled at Mimi and dutifully brought her plate to the sink.

Great, a veritable stranger was a better mom than she was.

Terrible Domme. Terrible wife. Terrible mother.

Sam managed a thank-you to Hanna and Mimi for letting the girls stay overnight before ushering her children out the door. Neither of them spoke to Sam on the drive home, matching sullen faces in the backseat. Back at the house, Allegra went up to her room and slammed the door while Hope joined Brady in the living room where he was watching TV. He didn't greet Sam either.

Now she understood why he let the kids go to Jack's that night.

She went up to the bedroom and sat on the stripped bed. He'd cleaned up. The toys were put away. But it seemed mechanical, almost spiteful, not done in deference or love. He probably thought she was the most awful, selfish person on the planet. Maybe she was. She'd gotten so swept up in this that she'd felt in control even when things were spinning into chaos. And she was the cause of it.

She didn't know how to fix this. She didn't know if she could.

What she did know was that she needed some space.

They all did.

A few hours later, Sam closed the pantry door and tucked some protein bars into her suitcase. Brady finally surfaced, standing at the kitchen entryway. His eyes were bloodshot, and his hair was a mess, curls standing every which way. He needed a haircut, and Sam couldn't help but think she should make an appointment for him.

One of the many things she'd done for him, things a grown man should do for himself. Things she might never do for him again.

He looked at the bag, then at her.

He said nothing.

"Girls," she called out, still holding Brady's gaze. "Come here. Now, please"

They appeared behind Brady a few moments later. Like their father, they saw the bag by her feet and stopped.

"I'm going to stay at Nana and Pop's. To take care of it, and make sure it gets sold."

Brady barely moved, other than his eyes. Sam felt it when his gaze hit the floor.

"Why do you have to stay there?" Allegra asked.

"The Realtor needs someone there to set up showings—"

"What's a showing?"

"It's when people who might buy it come see it. And someone needs to be there to make sure that happens."

She waited for Brady to call her out on her lie. She didn't need to be there. She'd given the Realtor a spare key, and even if she hadn't, she could've used a lockbox, or had Brady set up a home automation system so she could let them in from her phone.

"But you're coming back...right?"

That question came from Hope.

"I'll be here to pick you up from the bus, to help with homework, take you to dance and your doctors, and then go back when Daddy gets home."

Sam had rationalized this out. She couldn't take the girls with her. Having their stuff at the apartment would mess up the staging, and she'd have to wake them at an ungodly hour to drive them to school, then double back in the other direction to get to work.

"You won't tuck me in?" Hope asked softly, and it broke through Sam's composure.

Sam knelt in front of her. "Not for a few days, but I will on the weekend. You can come stay with me at Nana and Pop's."

Hope started to cry. How could Sam explain that this was the right thing? That she needed to do this for herself and was certain she wasn't good for any of them right now. Sam picked Hope up, surprised by the tightness as her arms curled around Sam's neck.

"Don't cry, honey. You'll see, it'll be like a big sleepover party, sometimes with Daddy, sometimes with me. Daddy has been putting you on the bus in the mornings anyway when I go to work. It won't be that different."

"Yes it will," Allegra snapped.

Sam looked over Hope's shoulder to Allegra. Her daughter's gaze could only be called furious.

"You're lying. You're leaving and everything is going to be different."

She bolted into the hallway with her back to them before whipping back around. "What about my birthday?" she hollered, then slapped her sides. "Oh, I get it, my parents are getting divorced for my birthday. Great. Thanks a *lot*."

It was the first time she sounded like the pre-teen she was about to be.

"Honey, no one's saying that's—"

"No, don't lie. I hate you!"

As Allegra ran up the stairs, Hope slithered out of Sam's embrace and sprinted after her sister. The door to Allegra's bedroom slammed, and Sam pinched her eyelids shut.

Divorce—the word sounded like a death sentence.

She took a breath, wiped her face and opened her eyes. Brady was slumped over the countertop, head bent.

"Why are *you* the one leaving?" he asked. "Shouldn't I be the one to go?"

Because that was what men did, right? Men like Hanna's ex.

Was Sam as bad as he was?

"It's your house," Sam said. "Your parents bought it. It's not mine."

It wasn't the real reason—not completely. She needed to get away from him, from herself, from the person she'd become in this space. Whether he believed her or not, though, he didn't reply. Sam walked over to her suitcase and pulled out the handle.

"You can heat up frozen chicken tenders for dinner. And corn. Microwave that, though. Make sure it's not too hot."

No response.

"It's supposed to be nice out tomorrow. Allegra will want her yellow spring coat. I brought it up from the basement last week. It's in the coat closet."

A silent nod.

"I know we still don't have a sitter," she added, because she had to keep talking. "Maybe we could use Mimi. Until we figure things out."

He visibly stiffened. "Sure," he said. "Whatever."

She glanced to his ring. He wasn't rubbing his fingers over it, and she wasn't wearing hers. Her engagement ring and wedding band were on the dish on her nightstand along with her necklace where she'd left them last night.

So much for taking care of one another.

Maybe Allegra was right. Maybe this *was* the way their story ended.

Sam started toward the door, then stopped. "It's better this way, Brady."

"No," he said. "It's not."

* * *

Friday morning felt like a month later. Allegra had called Sam every night crying, then yelling. Hope had become even more withdrawn. And Sam had no idea how Brady was.

Or how she was, herself.

She couldn't figure anything out, so she'd focused on work instead. Staring at the computer screen, she tried to reconcile bills for the Choate file. She'd closed out everything except this past month. This time, the checks made out to cash didn't match anything at all—a check had been written on March 26th for two hundred and thirty dollars, one upwards of five hundred a few days later. Pierce was stealing in bigger and bigger chunks, almost like he wanted to get caught. She should tell someone, but her head hurt, and Sam was in too much of a daze to make sense of anything.

She automatically reached for her necklace, but it wasn't there, and her hand felt bare without her rings. It was uncomfortable not wearing them, but she didn't know where she and Brady stood right now, and she'd felt too awkward to go into the house to get them during the week anyway. She'd hadn't wanted to go inside at all, resorting to taking the girls to the library and coffee shops to help with homework before dropping them off when Brady got home.

When Lilly and Cassie walked in, Sam could barely find the energy to smile.

"Hey, lady," Cassie said. "I had a meeting in the area and figured I'd pop up and say hi. How are you doing?"

I'm in complete crisis. I've failed at everything.

She didn't want to say that, but she didn't have the capacity for pithy conversation either.

She looked at her friends, the ones with hot relationships and great jobs and who seemed to have it all. "You know what I said about romance novels, how it wasn't possible for women to have everything?"

Cassie nodded, and Sam felt the pressure of every parent blog-writer, the condescending, superior looks from the stay-at-home mothers at the gym. The PT assistants she'd met during her mom's recovery, working women who'd said they'd chosen "less competitive" lives, too, and how smart it was, the people who said it was such a pity she had to leave Washington.

"I was right."

Happy endings were a myth. And if they weren't, they weren't for her.

Her friends glanced at one another and frowned. "Do you want to go to the gym with us over the weekend?" Cassie asked.

Sam hadn't gotten to the gym in weeks. She'd been eating low-calorie frozen dinners at her parents' place to compensate, but the extra sodium had made her feel bloated and disgusting.

"Thanks, but I can't." She'd have the girls this weekend. Discussing that was the only conversation she and Brady had in the last few days, over text messages of course, and she didn't want to tell her friends just how bad things had gotten.

"Is there anything we can do?" Lilly asked.

She wanted to ask them how they made it work. How their kinky relationships didn't screw up their lives.

She shook her head instead.

Cassie checked her watch. "I've gotta run. Call me if you need anything, okay?"

"Okay," Sam said, but even if she did reach out, she had no idea what to say.

At lunchtime, Hanna came around with her purse slung over her arm.

"Up you go," she said. "I've found you coverage for a full hour. We're having lunch."

Sam was too exhausted to say no.

They went to a fancy French and Italian fusion place. It was noisy, but they sat at a kitty-corner table and ate way too much, which Hanna insisted was her treat.

"BDSM is supposed to be about openness, right?" Sam asked when they were waiting for the bill. "Aren't a submissive and a Dominant supposed to be honest with each other?"

"Starting that kind of relationship is like the discovery phase in a trial. You should always go in with as much knowledge as possible. Neither party should keep secrets. But it doesn't always work that way."

"That's what the congressman I worked for said. Trying to hide things can turn a secret into a scandal."

Hanna's expression grew distant, but when the server returned with the check, her usual smile returned. She reached for the billfold and fished her wallet from her purse.

"By the way, Mimi loved the girls," she said. "She'd be happy to pick them up after school if you need some time to yourself. Take a nap or a bath or something."

"Do I look that bad?"

Hanna pulled out some cash. "Of course not, love. Just trying to help."

Sam was considering her suggestion when Hanna's phone rang. Hanna glanced at the screen and frowned.

"It's Mimi." She put down the billfold and stood. "I can't hear a thing in here. I'll be right back."

Sam hoped nothing was wrong. Wanting to help out the friend who was so eager to help her, Sam reached for the check. She could at least pay the tip. But as she was pulling it toward her, she accidentally knocked Hanna's wallet to the floor. Dozens of receipts fell out of it in a mad cluster, and Sam cursed. Crouching by the chair, she started snatching them up. She stuffed half of them back in Hanna's wallet, then caught a glimpse of one from Saks Fifth Avenue.

No matter what had happened in the last week, she was still a curious person. And she wanted to know how much that concealer with caviar cost.

She picked up the receipt. Two hundred and thirty dollars.

On March 26th.

No. Oh, no.

Sam glanced up. Hanna was still standing out in the hall. Grabbing her own phone, Sam drew up her calendar, and looked at that date. The same day that check had been written from the Choate file was the day she and Hanna went shopping.

Sam's gut sank. This couldn't be happening. She had to be wrong. Keeping one eye toward Hanna, she rifled through all the receipts until she found the one from Molly's of Mercy.

Five hundred and ninety dollars. Two days later.

By the time Hanna returned, Sam was seated again, receipts and wallet back in place. "Everything okay?"

Her voice came out smooth, despite the fact that inside, Sam was shaking.

"Mimi is sick." Hanna grabbed her wallet like it was a burner she'd left on too long and pulled out some cash. "I have to cancel that offer for her to take the girls today. Turns out I'll have to leave work early."

"It's fine. I covered the tip, by the way."

Hanna smiled. "You're a doll."

Sam forced a smile back.

They walked in relative silence back to the office. When Hanna left for the day, Sam emailed her personal mail the login to the Choate online bank account. She needed to go through everything, to be one hundred percent positive that Hanna was stealing. Gathering up her things, she passed by Pierce's office. He was slamming file drawers shut, moving from one to the other as he searched for something Hanna could've purposely misplaced.

Suddenly, he no longer looked like a sleazy attorney embezzling funds. He looked like a toothless lion, lost without the secretary who was possibly duping him.

Brady had been right not to trust Hanna. He'd held back, not wanting to be intimate with someone he didn't know, but he'd done it anyway, for her. Now look where it had gotten them. She should've trusted him, but instead she'd put her faith in the wrong person.

And she had no idea what that was going to cost her.

30

"Dude, where's your head at?"

Brady glanced up. The conference area was set, screens ready for today's big meeting. Months of work had gone into prepping for today's launch. And Myles and Wendell were staring at him.

"I'm sorry, what?"

Wendell cued up the presentation on the flat-screen. "I asked if you were good to go."

"Totally good," Brady said, nodding a few times for emphasis. "Just tired."

It was an understatement. He was exhausted. This week had been hell.

Sam had avoided him every day. She'd never come in the house, just dropped the kids off. He had no idea how long she planned on crashing at her parents' place. Allegra was barely speaking to either of them, sullen as fuck and shutting herself up in her room. Oddly enough, Hope was the one talking now, quietly crying when he'd tried to read her a bedtime story and whispering that she missed Mommy.

Yeah, he did, too.

He'd barely managed to get them onto the school bus every

morning. There was so much crap to keep organized it was insane. It made him painfully aware of how much he'd relied on Sam, the stuff he didn't know. Where the Band-Aids were. How she was able to cram everything into the dishwasher. Even his own goddamn schedule. He'd tried to set up a system for himself to compensate, but shit was still a mess.

Maybe some of what he'd been doing was selective defiance—a new term he'd Googled recently after Allegra's doctor had emailed him and Sam an article about ADHD in teenagers and what to expect. Maybe he hadn't helped out as much at home because that stuff wasn't his wheelhouse, and he knew she'd pick up the slack. Or maybe it was because he'd always rather have fun and make everyone happy than figure out what tasks needed to be done.

Whatever it was, he barely remembered everything when Sam *was* there. Without her, it was impossible, especially given how overloaded he was at Helios. At least he hadn't forgotten to put on a suit today.

"You sure you're gonna make it through?" Wendell asked.

"We can hold it down without you," Myles added. "Better that our lead Dev guy is absent than here and checked out."

He *had* been checked out. For weeks. These guys had always been cool, but there was a splinter of tension in their tones, a clear sense that if Brady wasn't going to knock this one out of the park, he should go the fuck home. Paul sat on the other end of the table, munching on a slice of pizza and darting glances around like an air hockey puck.

"I'm sure." Brady picked up the second slice he'd piled onto his own plate, then dropped it in disgust. He missed Sam's healthy kale chips and zucchini fries.

Screw that. He didn't miss the food. He just missed her.

"Cool. But maybe go home after that," Wendell suggested. "Take the weekend off."

"Yeah, all right." Although his empty house wasn't where he wanted to be this weekend. He reached for the salad that came with the pizza and ate that instead.

After the meeting ended and they had a happy client on their hands, Brady gave them all fist bumps before gathering up his things. Paul hung around with a sheepish smile.

"Thanks, Brady."

The guy was finally calling him by his first name. "For what? You did the work."

"For having faith in me. Now I get why everyone looks up to you so much here."

Brady paused, closed laptop in hand. He would've joked that everyone looked up to him because he was the tallest employee, but he didn't feel like being funny, or like he was the kind of person anyone should look up to right now.

Not knowing what to do with himself, Brady left and drove around. He didn't want to go home, so he put himself on the Pike and headed east. Before he knew it, he was weaving through the streets of Allston, heading toward the B.U. campus. He turned down Babcock Street, his old dorm on the left, Nickerson Field looming over Rich and Sleeper Halls on the right.

He pulled into a spot on the street. He didn't get out, though—just cut the engine and rolled the windows down. Lacrosse and soccer were played here now, but Brady remembered the feel of the AstroTurf, the russet of the rubber track that surrounded it. The sound of plays called, of pads and helmets smashing into one another, the lights shining on the field. The short yards and long touchdown passes, the speed of the game.

The feel of cement against his skull. Of his knee hitting concrete.

He palmed his phone, dialed a number and threw it on speaker.

"Hey," Nick said.

"Hey." What was he doing? Why was he poking this bear? "Can I ask you something?"

"Fire away."

He stared at the stadium wall. "You really don't ever miss football?"

A few moments and one long exhale passed before Nick answered.

"No, but it was different for me. I never felt that same

camaraderie. I was in the closet, and hiding who I was made me feel like I didn't fit."

Brady let out a laugh. He got that.

"I know *you* miss it, though," Nick continued. "I never forgave myself for that day."

"You? You didn't do anything."

"That fight ended your career. You sacrificed it for me."

"It was the right thing to do."

"That's what makes you such a hero. You did it without thinking."

Was that what made a hero? Doing things without thinking? 'Cause he certainly did that often enough.

"I could've died that day," Nick added. "I probably would've, if it weren't for you."

Brady was quiet for a minute. They both were. A bus pulled up in front of the athletics building. Brady watched a bunch of the lacrosse team members pile out of it. It was still a gut-punch for him, what he'd lost, but what must it have been like for Nick in that locker room years ago? How much had that day cost both of them?

"Why do you think they did it?" he asked.

"Because some guys are threatened by anything they see as weak or feminine."

That threw him for a loop.

He'd looked at football as something that evened him out, the thing that made him the most masculine. But thinking about it now, the homophobic culture that still existed, football players tweeting anti-gay comments, the pressure to be a man—maybe it made him worry that being submissive would negate his masculinity. Because some guys were so threatened, they were willing to kill for it.

It also made him wonder if Nick had known that about him all along.

"How'd you get through it?" Brady asked.

"Forgiveness, for one."

"You *forgave* those jerks?"

"Not right away," Nick said. "But eventually, yeah. It took a while to get there. I had to talk to people."

"Talk?"

"Yeah, you know. Like healthy people do, instead of covering it up with jokes?"

Brady snorted. "Cheap shot."

"True shot."

He'd always thought jokes were easier. Simpler. Maybe they weren't. Not talking certainly hadn't helped with Sam. If he'd told her half the things he'd been feeling, maybe they wouldn't have ended up in this shitty place.

"Look," Nick added, and Brady knew what was coming next. "I know you have your issues when it comes to Jack, but talking to someone who understands the kind of relationship you're in—"

"Oh, dude. Why do you know that?"

"Because I do."

Fuck. Was it possible to hide under his steering wheel? "I really wish you didn't."

"Too bad. And talking to someone who also happens to care about you—"

Brady made a face. "Gross, man."

"—isn't a bad thing."

He sighed. "I know." Nick was right, it was time to stop hiding who *he* was, but man his buddy was annoying.

"And it was Jack's birthday the other day."

"Oh, shit." He'd completely forgotten. It was the kind of detail Sam always kept track of.

"It's cool. Lilly said they were keeping it small. No fancy parties like Patrick had last year."

Patrick. Brady hadn't talked to him since the football incident. Turning the ignition, he banged a uey straight across Babcock, earning him a loud honk. Whatever. "Thanks. I think I'll still stop over there."

"Hey, good idea," Nick said. "I wonder who came up with that?"

Sarcastic fuck. "Some pain-in-the-ass friend of mine did."

"Smart guy. Talk to you later."

Brady doubled back through Allston and up across the river. Rolling along Mass Ave, he drove through the pristine streets of the

Harvard campus until he turned onto Jack's street. It was a long shot if his brother would even be home, but Jack's car was sitting in the driveway. The huge Victorian with a massive porch wasn't something their parents had to buy for Jack. He'd paid for it with his own money. Probably paid the mortgage off by now, too.

Brady cut the engine and walked up the steps. He had no idea what he was going to say but rang the doorbell anyway.

Jack opened the door with a surprised smile. "Hey. Since when do you wear a suit to work?"

"Oh. Yeah. Big meeting today," Brady said. "Can I come in?"

Lines appeared in Jack's forehead. Brady's brother possessed many skills but keeping a poker face wasn't one of them. "Of course. Come in."

Inside, he plopped onto a stool at the island in Jack's tremendous kitchen. Shiny copper pots hung from the ceiling. Brady wondered if Jack made Lilly scrub the place on her hands and knees.

"You want something to drink?" Jack asked from the fridge.

"You got whiskey?"

"You're asking me for hard liquor at three in the afternoon?"

Yeah, wrong question to ask. It wasn't long ago that Brady had been the one worried about Jack, who'd spent most of his nights lost to alcohol after Eve passed away.

"I was joking." *Mostly.* "Water is fine."

Jack brought him a glass. Brady drank a few sips, then looked at his brother.

"So, Sam left."

"Left, as in...*left*?"

"She's been at her parents' place all week. It's kind of a disaster."

"I didn't know things were that bad." Jack sat on the stool next to him. "What happened?"

Ugh. He didn't want to go here. But he had to.

"For a while it was normal fights. I thought it was 'cause she was cooped up in the house all the time, but it was partly my fault. I wasn't there, mentally. I was working constantly, and trying to do too many things at once makes my brain crash." He looked at the countertop. "I think I have some of the same issues Allegra does."

"Can you do anything about that?"

There was no shame from his brother. No judgment. Just legitimate concern.

Brady shrugged. "Probably. I've avoided it though. And I got used to Sam doing everything because it was easier that way."

Just like it was easier not to talk. Easier to bury himself in work.

"That happens in relationships," Jack said. "Sometimes you need to change something to make it work."

"We tried to change things. It didn't work."

"What things?"

Brady twisted his ring under the island. How did people do this? How had Nick?

"I was always jealous of you," Brady said, not bothering to explain the subject change. "I was always in your shadow, always felt inferior."

"Inferior?" Jack asked. "You are aware that you design databases while Lilly still has to explain Google Docs to me."

Brady would've laughed, but for the first time, he didn't want to joke around.

"Doesn't matter. I wanted to be like you, still do. But when you told me about you and Lilly, I realized I'm nothing like you at all. I'm your opposite."

Jack frowned. "I don't understand."

"You and Lilly. Me and Sam. You told me what you are. I'm your opposite."

Come on, brilliant big brother. Figure it out.

It took a few seconds for Jack to reply. "Oh. Wow. Okay." That line in his forehead deepened. "That's why Sam left?"

Not exactly. "She left because we tried something and it fucked everything up."

"And I'm guessing the thing you tried was a BDSM thing."

"Basically."

"How did it fuck everything up? Did you guys not communicate or something?"

Of course it had taken Jack all of two minutes to hit Brady's critical error on the nose. "I wasn't honest about what I wanted."

Jack smiled, slightly. "We're not mind-readers, Brady. As good as Dominants are, we can't figure out what our submissives need by osmosis."

Wasn't that what Sam had said? That she couldn't read his mind. Brady tried not to let the weirdness of the moment overwhelm him. "I have a hard time telling her things that won't make her happy. It's like I have some kind of mental wall against it."

And that wall acted like a gag, stopping him from saying, or even from figuring out what he felt. He put her happiness first because he dreaded the withdrawal, scared of doing anything that didn't make Sam smile.

"What did you struggle to tell her, if it's okay to ask?"

Brady cringed. "I like being submissive with her, but...when we had someone else—"

Jack's eyebrows shot up.

"—with us, I freaked out." Jesus. He was actually saying these words. "Does that make sense?"

Jack's brows stayed raised. "Well, someone can enjoy getting spanked sexually by their partner, but it doesn't mean they want to get smacked by anyone else, or even by that same person in another situation. That's why you create limits."

Brady hadn't seen his submission as a limit. It wasn't a toy he didn't want to use, it was something deep in him. But it clicked now, putting it that way. He didn't want to submit to anyone but Sam.

Next question.

"Is it normal for a submissive to want to make their Dom so happy it eclipses everything? Even your own doubts and reservations?"

"I think it happens, but that's when you speak up. Say how you're feeling."

"I kind of suck at that." Brady stared at his hands. At his ring. "I kept a lot hidden from her, being submissive especially. I was worried it made me weak."

"*Weak?*"

Brady had to look up. That was how shocked Jack's voice had been.

"Do you have any idea how strong you have to be, to do what you do?" Jack asked. "Submissives put their faith, their bodies, their *lives* in the hands of their Dominant. Do you know how difficult that is? To give in and allow someone else to control you? I couldn't do that."

He'd never thought of it that way—that it took strength to hand over his own power like that. And it was a bit of a boost, to know he was a natural at something his brother wasn't.

"Was this ever...hard for you?"

"You're joking, right?" Jack asked. Brady shook his head. "I hid this for *years* from Eve before finally opening up. I was terrified she'd reject me or divorce me."

"Seriously?"

Jack nodded. "Lilly and I fell into it quickly, but that was because we knew who we were going in. Still, that doesn't mean it's easy for us. Half the time I'm scared shitless that I'm going to hurt her."

"Wow." Man, it was scary as hell, to accept who you were.

"I think everyone grapples with some part of this when they realize it's who they are," Jack continued. "But there's no stronger or weaker half. The submissive might be the bottom, but the bottom is the bedrock. You're the one who holds the Dominant up, who lets them be in that top space they need to be in. The submissive is also the mirror—you help the Dominant see who they are when they can't see themselves. But you both have to be present, when you're in role and when you're not. You have to talk. Trust, openness and honesty, that's what this is all about. Not sex."

Things snapped into place and fell apart at the same time.

"I should've told Sam. I should've said something sooner instead of worrying she wouldn't accept me." Even worrying about her not loving him was partially his fault. After all, he'd stopped saying it also. "I should've told her a lot of things."

"Can you talk to her now?" Jack asked.

"I think it's too late. We might be too broken now."

"Broken things can be mended. I don't think you're broken beyond repair."

"Why not?"

"Simple. Because my little brother happens to be a rock star at problem solving." He smiled. "And because you still love each other."

It was simple. It was the simplest answer of all.

"Thanks. That helps. And sorry I flaked on your birthday, by the way."

Jack clapped him on the shoulder. "We'll celebrate again when Sam comes home."

Brady headed out, starting toward home, then got off the Pike and went to Sam's parents' place. He'd done her wrong by not being honest. By letting her take on too much. He'd been hiding at work, making it the place he felt like a superhero, when it was his excuse. He was avoiding things, sleepwalking through his marriage, hiding pieces of himself and thinking that was the right way to keep Sam, terrified to lose her for real.

He reached the apartment, found a spot and got out, but no one answered when he buzzed in. Brady stepped back and looked up to the second-floor window. The lights were off—she must've been out with the girls, but he stared anyway. It was where she'd been all week, where she'd slept and maybe cried and felt terrible about what had happened because she thought it was all her fault.

It wasn't. He was as much to blame for things falling apart as she was.

He didn't know if he could keep up with her—she might want more experimentation than he could handle—but then it was his job to speak up. He couldn't fix the past, but he could change things going forward. It was time to take ownership over his struggles with communication, to stop hiding and step up to the plate.

It began to rain. He got back in the car, headed in a different direction. He wasn't going to let this be their ending. Their love was special—a once-in-a-lifetime thing, and that kind of connection didn't crash and burn in a week after seventeen years. He could be her bedrock. Her mirror. Her lucky charm and her hero.

She was his Sammy. And he was going to figure out a way to get her back.

31

"I still don't get why we can't go inside."

Sam sat in the driver's seat, too shell-shocked to answer Allegra's question.

She'd taken the girls to get ice cream after school, and after she'd allowed Allegra to play a game on her phone and started Hope on her homework, she'd logged into the Choate trust bank account on her iPad. It had been painstaking work, going back transaction by transaction, but she'd separated the legitimate expenses from what she was pretty certain were bogus ones.

"Mom?"

"Because it's raining and I don't have an umbrella. So let's wait for Dad."

Allegra huffed out a dramatic sigh and mashed her head against the seat. Oh, the teenager she was about to become.

It was a dumb excuse, though. They wouldn't have come back to the house at all except Sam had been so distracted she'd forgotten to have the girls pack their bags for the weekend. She should put on her big-girl panties and go inside with them, but she'd seen a moving van parked down the street and it had freaked her out, like it was some kind of omen. Plus, it was pouring—the kind of rain that fell in sheets and forced green out of the brown grass, drenching the pavement until it ran in rivers. But the truth was, she was stalling.

She needed more time to think.

Back at the ice cream shop, she'd zoomed in on the images of the cashed checks. There was no discernible difference in the signatures, except that the ones made out to cash had a slightly different tilt to the *G* in Reginald. It wasn't enough of a smoking gun, but the Saks and corset shop purchases were. She'd been sure Pierce had been the one stealing, but it was Hanna, to the tune of eight grand.

She couldn't prove it, though. Not without those receipts. So what was she going to do?

She could tell Hanna to come clean, but Pierce had told Sam not to say anything. Would doing so put her job in jeopardy? She could go straight to Pierce, but Hanna was her friend. At least, Sam thought she was.

She stared out the windshield and watched the rain run rivulets along the glass.

Hanna had talked about discovery, about not keeping secrets, but she'd been lying. And Sam had been so caught up in everything, so blinded by the excitement and flattery of Hanna's attention, that she hadn't examined the situation. She'd wondered how Hanna afforded her lavish life, but pushed it to the side. And now she'd been intimate with, allowed her children to be around and possibly ruined her marriage over, someone who'd committed a crime.

It stole her breath, the idea of losing Brady for good. How had she been so horribly, completely wrong?

"Daddy's here," Hope said from the backseat.

Her stomach leapt as she watched Brady's car pull into the driveway. She hadn't seen him in almost a week—the longest they'd ever been separated. He unfolded himself from the front seat, stood up to his full height, and landing her eyes on him was like getting in a deep breath after holding it, like a good spring rain after a long, cold winter. He was wearing a suit, too. Not the one he'd worn to the wedding, but a softer one—a gray blazer with a baby-blue shirt beneath it that picked up the color of his eyes.

She wanted to run to him—to throw herself into his arms in the rain like a scene from a cheesy movie or one of her books, but she stayed where she was. Brady squinted in the rain, curls getting doused, then held up a finger and went into the house. He emerged a minute later with a giant umbrella they'd bought after Hope was born. It was impractical and bumped into everything, but Brady had thought it was funny and named it Godzillumbra.

He neared the driver's side, and Sam lowered her window.

"Somebody call for an umbrella?" he asked. He was smiling, too. Not a big, goofy Brady smile—his eyes weren't sparkling—but that silliness was there.

"Yeah," she said. "Thank you."

But then he was looking at her and frowning. "What's wrong?"

Months ago, she would've had to yell for him to even realize it was raining. Now, not only had he brought out an umbrella, but he knew something was up without having to ask.

"Um..." She nodded at the kids, then shook her head. Brady's brows pushed together, his frown deepening beneath his beard. God, she wanted to bury her face in that beard, to go back in time and tell herself to realize what she had with him.

"You wanna come in?" he asked.

Such a small offer, and yet she was flooded with relief. Sam nodded, and he opened the back door. "Come on. Everyone under Godzilla."

"Godzillumbra," Allegra corrected happily.

They got out of the car and squished together as the rain suddenly came down harder, and booked it toward the house.

When they were safely inside and a little breathless, Brady waited on the doorstep and shook out the umbrella. He'd changed the storm door for the screen, something she'd always had to remind him about before, and Sam could smell his cologne mixed with spring rain through the mesh panel.

"Mom, do we have to pack now?" Allegra asked.

Sam and Brady exchanged glances. "Not yet," she said without breaking eye contact. "You can go play for a bit."

The girls scampered off in different directions. Brady smiled through the screen.

"Hold on a sec, okay?" he asked. "I'll be right back."

"Okay."

Sam treaded slowly into the kitchen. Her mouth fell open as she looked around. It wasn't the off-kilter placement of everything that had her putting a hand to her chest. It was the Post-it Notes dotting dozens of different places. *Cups* over one cabinet. *Bowls* over another. A list of the girls' favorite snacks on the pantry door.

On the counter, Allegra's prescription, and on a note in all caps: *MORNING DOSAGE.*

She walked into the living room. Another Post-it with Allegra and Hope's favorite TV shows written on it was stuck to the remote. One was slapped on the coat closet door that said *yellow jacket— Allegra's fave.* Another beneath it said *Bring down scarves and hats. Bring up bicycle helmets.*

Tears sparked in Sam's eyes, hot and painful. This was what he'd done in her absence—tried to keep track on his own with the system she'd shown him years ago. How cruel she'd been, not helping him get things right the way she'd promised.

Sam was still standing like that when Brady came inside, his arms full of grocery bags.

"You went shopping?" she asked.

He dropped the bags on the table. "Yeah." His hair was sopping wet. Even his lashes had drops of rain on them. "Tried my best to remember everything."

She wanted to take a towel and dry off his hair.

"I see your notes."

He gave her a small, sheepish grin. "Not the most technical system, but it works."

He took off his rain-spattered suit jacket. The dress shirt beneath it barely contained his arms and shoulders, arms that were once hewn for football, not hugs or housework or holding or their children. When they met, she'd wanted to protect him. Shelter him. To tuck him away from anyone who'd dare hurt him and keep him safe. She'd never thought about what it must've been like for him to need protecting.

She gestured toward his suit. "You had something important today?"

"A meeting with a big client. We've been working on the site for months."

"Oh." They never talked about Helios, other than her being annoyed by how much of his attention it took. She never appreciated how hard he worked, all he'd done to keep this family afloat.

He began unpacking. "You wanna sit? Tell me what's wrong?"

"How do you know something's wrong?"

He put a container of milk in the fridge. "Because of how you looked in the car. I know you, and this is more than just us."

Warmth spread over her, from her shoulders to her toes. All that time she'd felt invisible, but maybe he hadn't stopped seeing her at all.

Maybe *she* was the one who'd stopped seeing *him*.

"Something is going down at the firm," she said as she made her way into a chair. "Something with Hanna that could be bad."

He froze. "With Hanna?" he asked. Sam nodded. "What is it?"

She started talking, and telling him felt normal. Comfortable. Like they hadn't been living separately for six days. By the time she'd told him everything, Brady had his hands braced on the back of a chair, his expression grim.

"Why didn't you tell me when it started?" he asked.

Sam shrugged. "We haven't been talking much."

"True."

Strange how he acknowledged it without making a joke, but it was nice, too. "So, what do you think?"

Brady pulled out the chair and sat. "First off, the girls are *not* going over there again. I don't want someone who broke the law around our children."

It seemed harsh, but Sam agreed. And she liked this fierce, protective side of her husband.

"That's fair, but what about work? If I tell Hanna, Pierce could know I talked to her and I could get fired. If I tell Pierce, Hanna could go to jail. And what if she finds out I told him? She could expose what the three of us did together."

"You think she'd do that?" Brady asked.

"I don't know. People do stupid stuff when they're angry."

This time, she meant herself. Brady reached out, like he was going to take her hand, then put his hand on the table.

"First off, I don't see why she'd do that," he said. "Exposing you exposes her, and you said she's super private, so that doesn't make any sense."

"Right." He'd always been good at analyzing things. Something else she hadn't recognized enough.

"And second, even if she does get mad, I don't think she'd be mad at *you*. She might get scared and feel trapped and not know where to go, but I don't think it's you she'd be upset at."

Sam gazed at him. "Are we still talking about Hanna?"

He smiled faintly. "Mostly."

Maybe he was trying to tell her he wasn't mad at her, but it seemed too precarious, too soon to make this conversation about them. Sam crossed her arms on the table to stop herself from reaching for him. "And we were so close to having a new sitter."

"I might've found a few options," Brady said. "Two B.U. students answered our ad. So did a retired grandma, and a high school student who moved in down the street."

"Is that the moving van I saw?"

"Yeah. I met her and her parents the other day when we were waiting for the bus."

She looked around the kitchen, at this room she'd fed her family in. She'd hated having to clean it, felt powerless in it and overrun by the chaos in her home, but now it was the only place she wanted to be.

"I don't know what to do, Brady."

He leaned in again, and Sam felt that draw. The need to close the gap between them, and not as his Mistress, but as his wife.

"You'll figure it out. I have faith in you."

Sam swallowed hard. He believed in her? Even after everything that had happened?

She'd fucked up as a Domme, a wife, a mother. She had a husband she thought didn't see her anymore, and maybe he hadn't in many ways. Maybe her mother was right: sometimes in a marriage you stop seeing the other person, forget the reasons you fell for them and stuck with them.

Sam remembered it now, remembered Brady's gentleness, the way he'd made her feel in college, and when she'd come back from DC. He'd been there for her when she was at her lowest, sitting next to her at a bar with those eyes and smile and love that had never dimmed.

She didn't deserve him.

Brady smiled again and stood up. "I'll get the girls ready."

He left the kitchen, and Sam felt her pulse race. She wanted to be back here, to fix them. In her romance books, the character who'd messed things up needed to do something huge to make things up to the other one. She hadn't done anything like that yet. She couldn't come home without getting out of the mess she was in, the one she'd gotten *them all* in, first.

Her children's chatter got louder as Brady herded them down the stairs. Sam stood and went to the door.

"Ready?" she asked the girls.

"Ready," they replied without enthusiasm.

Brady held up a hand. "Wait. I got you something."

He went into the kitchen and returned with a box of Lucky Charms.

"Here," he said as he held it out to her. "Thought you might need it."

Sam's heart pounded and her eyes went hot. She took the box from him and stared at it. "Thank you."

Sam turned toward the door, then stopped. Her feet felt glued to the floor.

"I don't have any milk at my parents' place," she said as she turned around. "You think we could eat this here tonight?"

She was asking him permission. Flipping the roles.

She didn't care.

His big, baby-faced smile was her entire world. "I think that would be okay."

32

n Saturday morning, Sam sat on a bench in Newton Center Park.

She'd gone back to the apartment last night with the girls, after they'd all had cereal for dinner and she'd decided what to do. Now Allegra and Hope were running across the playground while Brady sat in the car nearby. A public spot was the safe place to do this. She knew what she was risking here. But it was the only option she could handle.

"Hey, love."

Sam jolted when Hanna appeared from behind her. Aliyah and Imani were with her.

"Thanks for inviting us out."

"No problem."

Hanna patted her daughters on the back. Mimi wasn't with her —still sick, maybe. "Go on. Go play."

They ran to join Allegra and Hope. Hanna sat beside her, and Sam tried not to visibly stiffen.

"How are you?" Hanna asked.

Devastated. "I'm okay."

She was so sad this was happening. It was like a different person was sitting next to her. The attraction was still there—there was no denying that—but what Hanna had done eclipsed everything.

"You look more than okay," Hanna said. "Like you've figured things out."

Maybe she had. For the first time, Sam really *looked* at Hanna. She was wearing skinny jeans in butter-soft denim, a white T-shirt with a designer name on the front, a linen jacket with the sleeves bunched up, and stilettos. Inappropriate for a playground, and a stark contrast to Sam's sneakers and sweats. And too expensive for a single mom on a secretary's salary.

"Are we going to talk about it?" Sam asked.

"About what?"

"The Choate file."

Hanna's eyes went cold. Her jaw worked as she looked out at the playground, as if she were on the lookout for danger. "What do *you* know about the Choate file?"

"Pierce put me on it. To clean up the files."

"So?"

She'd hoped Hanna would at least play innocent. But her answer wasn't a question. It was defensive. And borderline hostile.

"I know you've been stealing, Hanna."

Her friend's laugh was almost a hiss—a sharp, short exhale. "Why would I steal from an old lady?"

"I don't know, but you are."

"That's why you invited me out here? To accuse me of—"

"Hannaleen."

Hanna froze. It was so clear now—how powerful a name could be. It quieted her, changed the dynamic, told Hanna she was under Sam's control. How often had Sam done that to Brady, calling him pet outside of their play? When she did that, he stopped being in control of himself, too. It was a flicked switch, tethering him to her, to her authority—not a good thing when they were outside the bedroom.

She shouldn't have done that to him. Maybe it wasn't right to do it to Hanna now either, but Sam needed to take control of the situation.

"You told me that people who got involved the way we did shouldn't keep secrets."

Hanna tensed, but didn't reply.

"I know you've been writing out checks to cash from Mildred Choate's trust. And you've been doing it for a while."

"You can't prove that."

But she wasn't saying she didn't do it. "Your wallet fell on the floor when we went to lunch. I saw the receipt for the corset. And the Saks one. They match checks written from the trust."

Hanna's lips pursed. Sam stared at her.

"Why'd you do it?" She couldn't hide the hurt in her voice. "I brought you into my house. My bed. I *trusted* you."

"You act like it has something to do with you." Hanna's gaze snapped back toward hers. "It doesn't."

She looked at her daughters again and was quiet for a long moment.

"You don't know what it's like," Hanna finally said. "To try to take care of your kids and feel like you're doing a miserable job. That you're not providing a good life for them."

Sam gazed at her own children. "I might know a thing or two about that."

"You don't. You *can't*. You're white. A citizen. Middle class. With a husband who takes care of you. I'm mixed, I'm an immigrant and I'm alone. You don't know what my life is like."

Her words were needles, piercing into everything Sam took for granted.

"You're right. I don't. But I do know what you're doing isn't right."

"And what *is* right?" Hanna barked. "Mildred Choate—she has nobody, no kids, no one who needs her after she's gone. Her money's going to charity. I want my babies to grow up the way I did. With nice things. Nice clothes and jewelry they can use as their armor when people look down at them because their daddy left them or because of the color of their skin."

The clothes, the jewelry, the makeup—it was more of Hanna's armor. For her and for her kids.

"But Hanna," Sam said gently. "You're not just taking money for them. You're spending it on makeup with caviar in it, and a six-hundred-dollar corset."

Hanna threaded her fingers together. "You could've taken the receipts to Pierce. You could've told him."

"But I didn't. I'm telling you."

And what was the fallout going to be from that? What price would Sam have to pay? One cost was clear as she watched Allegra and Aliyah twirl around and laugh.

This sucked. This all just sucked.

"At first it was only to pay a few bills," Hanna admitted. "Stuff when money got tight. Then I rationalized it out. Told myself Mildred wasn't missing anything. I only stole for things I couldn't afford but made me feel..." she sighed heavily, "...better."

Sam didn't have an answer for that. What could she say that wouldn't make her sound like she was on some kind of high horse? She had privileges Hanna didn't, ones that went beyond the color of her skin. She had parents who checked on her despite the fact that they'd moved across the country, and a husband who wouldn't think of walking out the door, no matter what she'd done.

"They're going to press charges," Hanna added, and only then did Sam hear the fear in her voice. "It's fraud and forgery. I could lose my green card or go to jail. They'll take my babies."

"Maybe Pierce won't do that if you talk to him."

"Then what? At the least he'll fire me, and I won't get another job like that, not without a recommendation."

"Could you call your parents?"

"They won't care. Not after all this time."

Movement to the left caught Sam's attention. Brady had gotten out of the car. Leaning against it with his arms crossed, he was watching them, stealthy and silent, her own personal secret service. Her giant knight in a shining T-shirt and jeans.

"In my experience, people who care about you will still care, no matter what you've done, if you talk to them."

Hanna glanced in the direction Sam was looking. "Things better with you two?"

Better didn't seem like the right word to explain it. Healing? On the path to it?

"Maybe," she said, hoping it was true.

Sure, Brady drove her crazy sometimes, but she'd married a good man. She'd gotten disconnected from that, blinded by her own desire to experiment, looking for something exciting when she'd had that right in front of her. The sexual connection she'd been craving, she already had. She'd just lost track of it somehow, and even when she found it again with him, she hadn't been careful with him. His submission was a gift, and she hadn't honored that.

They locked eyes across the grass, and Sam didn't want to break that contact. She didn't know what lay ahead of them, wasn't even sure they'd return to a totally monogamous lifestyle if they were able to work everything out, but there were two things she did know:

One, she wanted him. And two...

She looked at Hanna. "Whatever happens, we can't be intimate anymore."

"I get it."

Hanna stood and waved Aliyah and Imani over.

"Please do the right thing," Sam said.

Hanna didn't answer. She took her kids' hands in hers and walked away.

* * *

Brady kept his eyes on Hanna until she was out of sight. Then he walked to the bench where Sam was sitting. Allegra was practicing dance moves on the grass, and he was still several yards away when Hope ran up to him.

Brady paused, but when she silently reached her arms up to him, he picked her up, ignoring the way his knee bitched about it.

"Are you and Mommy talking again?"

"What makes you think we're not talking?"

She looked at him but didn't say anything. Of course she'd picked up on what was going down with him and Sam. Kid barely spoke at all. She'd notice when other people were doing the same.

"Okay, you're right," he said. "Mommy and I had a fight."

"About what?"

"Sometimes grownups fight. They say things that hurt each other. And they have to stop talking for a while, so they don't hurt each other more."

"You told me sometimes things hurt, but you have to keep going."

Jesus, was this kid seven or forty? "I did."

"So do you and Mommy then."

"You're pretty smart for a munchkin, you know that?"

She giggled. They neared the bench, and Brady lowered Hope to the ground.

"You two can play more," Sam said to her and Allegra. "Daddy and I are going to hang out here, okay?"

The question was directed at him. The girls ran off, together it seemed. Brady put a hand over his pocket, checking that what he'd put there earlier was still inside it, and asked, "How'd it go?"

"Not great. We'll have to see what happens at work." She pulled her legs up, the bottoms of her sneakers on the bench. "Thank you for being here."

"You're welcome."

He hadn't known what could happen with Hanna, but he was ready to run in if Sam needed him.

"Sit?" she asked.

He sank on the bench beside her. Sam wrapped her arms around her legs, rested her chin on her knees and looked up at him.

"We never talk about it, you know," she said.

"Talk about what?"

She reached up, stroked a finger over the scar line on his head. He closed his eyes at her touch.

"These healed, so I felt you were, too," she said. "We never talk about what you lost that day."

Her hand fell away. Brady opened his eyes.

"I don't know if we *need* to talk about it," he said, and he wasn't blowing it off. There was a simple answer to this. "I lost football, but then I found you."

Sam's smile was sad. A breeze lifted her hair off her shoulders, a red halo framing her face. "You said the other day that you didn't know how to be everything I want."

"I did."

"You already are, though."

His lungs got tight. Sam lifted her head and moved closer.

"You're strong, honest and decent. Kind and sweet. Your bravery, your goodness, your tech skills—it's like being married to Superman *and* Clark Kent. A superhero geek."

It was the best compliment she could've given him. "You're definitely more Wonder Woman than Lois Lane," he said.

"I don't know about that. I've made a lot of mistakes. It's hard to figure this out."

"This?"

"Marriage. Parenting. Dominance and submission," she said. "Life."

Brady chuckled. "I'll drink to that."

"I got wrapped up in things. I thought I was rediscovering this part of me I'd lost. But I was hurting you. Hurting the kids. I got selfish and fucked everything up."

"Samantha Archer," Brady said with a smile. "Language."

A small laugh bubbled out of her. Suddenly he could breathe again.

"I'm sorry for not taking better care of you when you were always taking care of me," she went on. "I didn't see you, or what you needed. I'm sorry I made you feel rented out, or like I didn't value you. I promise I won't ever be that blind, or hurt you like that again."

He hated the look in her eyes, the sadness and regret.

"You're not the only one who fucked up, Sam."

"I'm not?"

"No." It made sense now. She couldn't see herself, like Jack said. A Dominant needed to be lifted up by the submissive sometimes, to be shown who they were. And the submissive needed to be the solid ground their Dominant stood on from time to time. "I wasn't being honest. I didn't tell you how I felt. I've felt inferior about all this for a while. Jack helped me figure out that being submissive doesn't make me weak."

"You told him?" she asked. "You know he's…?"

"He told me, last year." Cue the squickiness. "Wait, how do *you* know?"

"Lilly's kind of textbook. Her collar gave it away, too."

"That necklace is a collar?" he asked. Sam nodded.

They all knew way too much about each other's sex lives.

"Anyway, I realized I've been thinking about this all wrong. I wasn't picking up the slack at home, either." And man, five days without her showed him how much he'd taken advantage. "I had no idea how much you were juggling. That wasn't fair, especially since you gave up your career because of me."

"That's not true," she said. "I came back for my parents. I stayed because of you. Giving up my career was my choice, and I never should've made you feel badly about that. You're a good man and were there for me, and I love you."

Brady's breath caught. He hadn't been sure he'd ever hear her say that again.

"I love you, too."

They moved closer, bent their heads together until their foreheads were touching. On the playground, Allegra shouted, but not in anger. Brady angled his head to see her pushing Hope on a swing. "Are they…getting along?"

"Looks like. But Allegra's gonna be a teenager soon, so we shouldn't expect it to last."

They both laughed, and it was the sound of relief. "I want us back," Sam said.

"You never lost us."

She shook her head. "I'm the one who's supposed to make the grand gesture. You're making this too easy for me."

"The grand what?"

"In the romance books. The character who messed everything up is supposed to do something impressive and apologetic to the other one. To prove their love."

He reached for her left hand, touched the spot where her wedding band should sit. Putting his other hand in his back pocket, he fished out her rings and necklace.

"You don't have to prove anything," he said. "Not to me."

She let out a shaky breath and nodded. Brady slipped her rings back into place, then held out the clover pendant for her.

There was a sigh of relief from both of them when she put it back on.

Sam put her head on his shoulder. Her eyes were shining, but she looked happy. "So what do we do now?"

Brady had plans on what to do. He didn't tell her what he was thinking though. Things had been put in motion but nothing was solid yet. "Know what I do when things go wrong?"

"What's that?"

"I reboot. Shut things down. Figure out what I want to do better and start over."

"Start over, huh?"

He nodded and beamed. Who'd have thought his hacker and computer skills would help him fix his marriage.

"Okay. I don't want to stay at my parents' place anymore." She paused. "What do you want?"

"To go to Vegas?"

She rolled her eyes and laughed. A real, happy Sam laugh.

Brady looked out at their girls, then back at her. There were lots of things he wanted. To work less. To be present for his family. Maybe go to a doctor, see if there were meds that could help his concentration after all, take this seriously and figure his shit out before he turned forty. But there was one simple thing Brady wanted most.

"I want you to come home."

33

Midway through Monday morning, Sam was usually through that day's mail and the weekend pile. Today, however, she was distracted, her eyes darting toward the closed conference room door. Hanna had been in there with Pierce and Johnson Phillips for over an hour.

She didn't know what was happening, whether Hanna had initiated the conversation or something else had gone down, but the fact that HR was present was not a good sign.

At least there were no authorities or immigration officers present.

She finished with the last envelope when the door finally opened. Hanna came out with Phillips behind her. He remained at the door as she walked toward the reception desk.

"I only have a minute," she said. "I turned myself in. They gave me an hour to clean out my desk."

"Are they pressing charges?"

"Amazingly, no. I have to pay back the money, but Pierce didn't want a criminal investigation." She laughed. "I'm not sure if it's because it's better for me or if a lawsuit would be bad press for the firm."

Sam saw a different person in front of her. Hanna's hair was twisted up in a half-finished bun, and she didn't have on any makeup at all.

"Did I…" Sam could barely get out the words. "Ruin your life?"

Hanna gave her a tired, sad smile. "No. You told me to do the right thing, and I did. I almost didn't though. I could've quit my job, left with the money and disappeared. But I need to take responsibility for what I did. And I didn't want to take off the way Wash did."

Sam smiled back. Maybe she wasn't so terrible at wielding her power after all.

"You also reminded me what I wanted in my life," Hanna added. "Watching you and Brady, it reminded me what it was like to be loved. To be a part of a family. I want that again."

Sam's heart skipped a few beats. "You called your parents?"

"Last night. They told me they'd come here if I needed them, but I think I'm gonna take the kids and go back to London, once I sell my stuff and repay the firm."

Sam had too many emotions to process. She hadn't destroyed her friend's life. Hadn't destroyed her marriage. Maybe everything was going to be okay.

A throat cleared. "Mrs. Clay," Phillips said.

Hanna turned around. "One more minute." Then she put her arms on the hutch and leaned over. "Do me a favor?"

"What's that?"

Her face had an odd expression to it, remorse and a bit of shame. "Apologize to Brady for me?"

"For what?"

"I think I might've taken some things out on him that weren't meant for him. Old Wash issues. He'd never address me properly, refused to use a title. When Brady didn't do that for you, I got upset. It was my baggage, not his." She smiled again, and Sam had a feeling it was the last time she'd see her friend. "You've got a good one there, Samantha. Hold on to him."

I intend to.

Hanna walked toward Phillips. "Samantha," he said.

Sam's gaze shot toward him.

"Mr. Pierce would like to speak with you."

Yeah. She'd been expecting that.

Taking the envelope she'd prepared from her purse, Sam rose and made her way around her desk. She'd worn her interview suit today, the same skirt and blouse she'd worn when she'd first walked through the doors.

It seemed like a good way to bookend her time here.

Pierce had the bridge of his nose pinched between his thumb and forefinger when she entered the room.

"Mr. Pierce?"

"Close the door."

Nice greeting. Sam followed his instruction and sat down across from him.

He lifted his head. "I specifically told you not to mention the Choate file to Hanna. You went against my wishes."

"I did." She didn't feel the need to reach for her necklace, even though it felt good to have it back on. Her Boston Bombshell confidence had returned.

"Why?"

"Because it was the right thing to do."

Pierce narrowed his eyes, then shook his head. "I'm glad you did."

Sam blinked. "I'm sorry?"

"Hanna never would've come forward on her own. Who knows how long she would've been doing this, or what other clients she would've stolen from."

"She told you I figured it out."

"No. But I imagined someone had to be holding something over her, and you were the only other person with access." He shook his head. "I gave you this project because it was a mess and I wanted you to organize it. I never expected you to discover forgery."

"Honestly, I thought it was you."

"I'm glad you were so diligent." He chuckled out a laugh, then sighed. Sam felt bad for judging him wrongly. "What a mess. I don't suppose you'd like a job as a legal secretary."

"Actually, Mr. Pierce—" she slid the envelope across the table, "—I'm offering my resignation."

"You're what? Why?"

"I don't think I belong here."

She'd taken Brady's suggestion to heart. She needed a reboot. Not just at home. Everywhere.

Pierce frowned at her. "I had a feeling you weren't long for that job."

"It wasn't the right fit. And I appreciate your offer, but I don't feel right taking Hanna's place."

He looked hard at her, swiveled back and forth in his chair.

"There might be another opportunity for you," he said. "We're opening up a new arm for the firm. A new subsidiary. FS&P Government."

"Government?"

Pierce nodded. He was watching her. Carefully.

"It'll provide legislative and regulatory counsel to public and private sector clients on a wide range of both federal and state policy issue, ranging from lobbying to building grassroots coalitions." He swiveled back and forth again. "Interested?"

Sam must've looked like a cartoon character, her mouth had fallen so far open.

"Hell yeah, I am." She wanted to take the words back as soon as she'd said them, but then Pierce laughed. Cursing in front of her boss. Brady was going to be so proud. "What would the job be?"

"It'll be a new position, but I see it as a legal assistant-slash-government consultant. We've got some good attorneys on the team but no one with any government background. They could use someone with your skills."

This was too good to be true. "But you said *federal* government."

"I did. The job will require some travel to Washington, but the main offices are here in Boston." He gathered his files, then glanced up at her. "It would be full time, too."

Shit. That was the catch.

"Thank you, Mr. Pierce. I'll need to talk to my husband first."

He stood and extended his hand. "Let me know what you decide."

When Sam left the office a few hours later, it was a warmer day than usual for late April, the magnolia trees starting to bloom pink and white. It reminded her of the DC Cherry Blossom Festival, of new starts and fresh possibilities.

She wanted this job. But whatever she and Brady decided about it, she needed to stop looking backward and start looking to the future. To let go of what she'd once had and imagine what her life could be.

Brady greeted her at the house with a smile.

"What are you doing home?" Sam asked, although she wasn't upset to see him there.

"I took a half day," he said. "So what happened?"

She filled him in on everything, first about Hanna, and her apology to him, then about the job.

"That's perfect for you," he announced, jubilant.

Sam wasn't on board yet. "But the hours, the travel. How do we work around that?"

He crossed those huge arms of his, muscles barely contained under a lightweight long-sleeved shirt. "Why be the CTO of a huge company if I can't change my hours?"

Sam stopped staring at his chest long enough to absorb his words. "What aren't you telling me?"

"I told Wendell and Myles that I was burning out and needed to be more available to you and the girls. I can do a lot remotely, so three days a week I'll leave midafternoon and work from home. I'll have to switch it up if there are any meetings, but it means I can get them off the bus instead of a sitter every day. And you can take this awesome job."

Sam threw her arms around him. It always annoyed her when this happened in her romance novels—when everything worked out into that perfect, sappy, Hallmark Channel Christmas movie ending. But it turned out in real life, she didn't mind so much. She sank into him, into his scent, into the safety and certainty of her husband.

"Thank you," she said.

"For what?"

"For loving me."

"I always have," he said. "I take care of you, you take care of me. End of story."

Sam smiled. It wasn't the end. It was a beginning.

The girls wanted to stay outside when they got off the bus. Sam unearthed a box of sidewalk chalk, which Hope used to do math problems on the driveway. Allegra asked to borrow Sam's phone, turned on some music and practiced the dance routine she'd be doing at her party. The highschooler who'd moved in down the street came to check out Allegra's moves, and before Sam knew it, both her daughters were asking to go to her house.

"My parents are home," the young girl said. Sam had met her parents the evening before, a quick hello when they were all taking their trash out. They'd invited her in for a few, and they were waving now from inside the window.

"Okay." But Sam didn't agree just to placate her children. She had her own agenda. She took down the girl's cell number. "Bring them back by five."

When she and Brady watched their daughters disappear safely into a house down the street, Sam took her husband's hand. "Take me inside?"

He turned to look at her. His eyes had gone turquoise.

They went into the house, past the pile of Post-it Notes they'd pulled down, agreeing to find a better way to manage responsibilities together.

"There's one more thing we haven't discussed," Sam said, stopping at the stairs. They needed to talk about this first, before they went into the bedroom and things got foggy. "For the past few months, we've had this overlap. There was no line between how we were in bed and how we are in the rest of the world."

"Okay," he said. Sam inhaled steadily.

"See, this is what I don't want—to always be the one in charge while you wait for instructions. Inside the bedroom, I like that. But outside it, we're equals. No more pet and Mistress out here. I want your input. And your help."

"Oh," he said, and got quiet for a second. She waited, knowing it took longer for Brady to get his thoughts out, that if he was trusting her with them, she had to be patient and listen.

"That line got messy for me, too. I got upset when Hanna told me what name to call you, but the thing is, she was right. I want to be a dad and a boss, a husband and a man, your hero and your pet, but I can't be all of them at once. I need some separation. Times when I'm your pet and when I'm definitely not."

"I need that, too," she said. "I don't want to always be your Mistress. I like calling the shots in bed, but outside it, I need there to be times when I don't have to tell you what to do."

He grinned. "So you're just the boss in the bedroom."

Sam glanced around at the house. It was a disaster. "And maybe sometimes a little bit in other rooms, too?" She was going to need a tub of disinfectant and pitchforks to wade through this mess.

"Fair," he said. "But we're partners first, kink roles second."

She liked that. "So, you still want it?" Sam asked. "You said you wanted a reboot. I thought maybe you wanted one with the kink, too."

"I don't want to undo *everything*," he said. "But I want to back up. Start slow. Still be where we are, but figure us out first. Make sure we're solid before anything or...anyone else comes into the picture."

"Anyone?"

He shrugged, chin dipping with his smile. "I know what it's like to stifle something. I did it for too long. You're gonna want something like what we did with Hanna again, with someone else."

Sam tried to protest, but he quieted her softly, one finger gentle against her lip.

"I'm okay with it. We can leave things open to a possibility in the future, but I'm not anyone's sub but yours. That's my hard limit going forward."

Her heart beat furiously. She wanted to kiss him, to show him how grateful she was, to let him see all the possibilities they could have with just the two of them, right now.

"So I'm only going to call you pet when we're playing," she said.

"And that balance of power between us, it only shifts when you let it."

That furious blush of his appeared. "Could we shift it...now?" he asked.

Sam exhaled, a quick, hard shudder. "Take me upstairs."

Brady grinned, then picked her up quickly, flipping her over his shoulder like a caveman. Sam laughed, watching the first floor disappear. When he'd laid them both out on their bed, Sam turned and rolled their bodies until she was on top of him. He gazed up at her, supplicant.

"You know," he said, "I never asked what *you* needed, after."

A tight breath shuddered out of her. "I need you to see me."

He kissed her then, softly, and Sam didn't mind that he'd done it without permission. But she didn't have the capacity, or the time, to be gentle. Their kisses turned heated, and then Sam was grappling with his shirt. Their clothes came off between scrapes of teeth and heavily panted breaths.

"I love what you let me do to you," she said. "Things you won't let anyone else see."

"Just you."

Just her. Sam hummed and ground her hips in tantalizing circles, until his eyelids drooped and his shoulders shook. "There's nothing sexier than watching a strong man go weak with hunger."

His eyes fluttered open, a hint of insecurity in them. "You like me weak?"

"Yes," she said, then bent down and kissed his neck. "But only when you're weak for me."

He hissed. Cursed. Rose up to kiss her, but she wouldn't let him yet.

"You remember your safeword?" she asked.

"I do."

"Good. Because I want to push you to that dirty, desperate place only I can get you to."

She pitched her hips in a circle again, and Brady groaned. "You're getting me there, now."

"Oh, I know," she said with mock-ridicule. She loved watching him struggle through that mix of discomfort and enjoyment. "My poor pet can't help himself."

Brady's eyes flew open on a growl, but he held himself still. Tethered. Obedient. Waiting for her.

"I was right." She drove a hand into the curls at the base of his neck and cleaved him to her. "You can't help yourself. Not when it comes to me."

"Never could."

Sam reached for a condom, the urged him up and shimmied herself beneath him.

"I want to feel you," she said. "All your weight. All of you."

They both moaned when he pushed inside. It wasn't slow, but it wasn't hard either, not until after Sam broke apart, and he knew what she needed without being told—hard. Fast. *More.* Sam clenched against a surprising rip of sensation when another release tore through her, then allowed Brady his own. When he rested his sweaty cheek to the hollow of her throat, Sam kissed his forehead.

"I love you," she said.

He looked up, caressed her hair, moving the locks off her face, his eyes the brightest blue she'd ever seen.

"I see you, Sammy," he said. "Always have. Always will."

Sam exhaled and held him close.

She wasn't disappearing. Even when Brady wasn't looking at her, he saw her.

34

*B*rady woke up in bed without Sam next to him. Smiling at the heart-shaped Post-it Note she'd left on her pillow, he reached for his shiny new phone.

"Okay, Google. What's on my agenda today?"

"You have an appointment at the YMCA at ten in the morning," the electronic voice answered. "Allegra's birthday party is at two p.m."

"Right." The mobile upgrade had been a splurge, especially after paying off the bill with the sex toys on it, but it was worth it, as was the Google Home kit for the house.

He sat up in bed, tucked Sam's *Happy Saturday, Sexy* note into his nightstand drawer, then stuck his head in the hallway.

"Hope? You ready for today?"

"Ready!" she hollered back.

Brady grinned and got in the shower. The last two months since Sam accepted that job had included a lot of changes, not the least of which was his plan to renovate this bathroom and finally put in that tub. Jack and Patrick offered to help him, which he'd accepted, knowing he needed the extra hands. It seemed silly, now, to have felt the way he had around them, but his therapist had said it was normal—that a component of ADHD was shame.

He'd finally gotten evaluated and found out he indeed had the same issues as Allegra, plus some difficulties with processing. He'd had to come to terms with the fact that he'd passed this on to her, but instead of feeling shitty, he was finding ways of helping them both deal with it. He'd started a med that was actually helping, and he was learning more about the way their brains worked. They weren't bad or weak, just needed different tools to succeed in life.

For him, that meant setting reminders at home and downloading an app for grocery shopping, one that included a space for photos so he didn't worry about incurring Sam's wrath over the wrong kind of yogurt. She didn't get angry as much anymore, but that was because she was happier, and because he was putting systems in place for himself. Like Allegra, he didn't focus when he was faced with something he didn't want to learn. He hadn't wanted to learn stuff like the cabinets or the dishwasher, and couldn't follow Sam's system of order. They'd reorganized things so he was part of the process, and now he'd learned where everything in the kitchen went the way Neo knew kung fu.

A short time later, he'd piled Hope into the car and fired off a quick text to Sam letting her know they were on their way.

"You excited?" he asked Hope as he drove.

She bopped her head. "You?"

"Hell...ck yeah," he said, then glanced in the rearview mirror at his daughter. Her grin was as goofy as his. "Don't tell Mom I said that."

"I won't."

At the Y, there were lots of other kids in the parking lot, Hope's age and older, running around in the warm weather. Brady went inside with her and up to the front desk.

"I'm here to sign my daughter up for youth flag football," he said.

It seemed the head injury of this spring hadn't deterred her, and he couldn't have been more thrilled when she'd asked if she could learn to play. He'd finally attended a family therapy session with Sam, and the doctor had said they needed to take seriously what Allegra's disability might be doing to Hope. He was glad to see his younger daughter coming out of her shell and finding her place in the world, a place that allowed him to step more into his role as a father. Not that he couldn't have done that if she'd chosen another sport or hobby, but football, he knew. He'd even stood back proudly while she'd picked out her own Patriots hat—in hot pink to match everything Allegra owned, of course.

The employee gave Brady the forms. "Anything else I can help you with?"

"Actually, I'm hoping to sign myself up, too. As a coach."

Another way to step up to the plate as a dad, and find a way back to the sport he loved. He and Hope sat at a table together, and he filled out the paperwork.

"You know," he said. "Football and coding aren't so different. With both you have to think quantitatively and be fast on your feet. Make a decision between this or that. See a problem and find a workaround."

He looked up at her to see if she understood.

"You're weird, Dad."

He laughed. They handed in the papers, met some of the other kids and practiced throwing a few passes before heading across town to Allegra's dance studio. His baby girl was turning eleven. Hard to believe she was almost a young woman already. There was even, apparently, a boy here she liked, and when the kid showed up Brady shot him his best *don't mess with my daughter* look as he gave Allegra a big embarrassing hug. Sam was bustling around with cake and presents, looking frazzled, and Brady immediately jumped in to help. He didn't catch every instruction—she had to repeat a few— but it all got set up. When the instructor started some kind of dance game, Sam sat in the audience with Hope on her lap while Brady stood in the back of the room. Lilly quietly came over to him.

They didn't speak for a minute, just watched Allegra getting jiggy on the stage until Lilly leaned in and whispered, "I'm here if you ever need to talk."

"That's gross," he whispered back.

"Totally gross."

"Insanely, completely, nasty-ass weird."

"Yup."

"But I appreciate it."

He might never take her up on it, but that was more because he was feeling confident with who he was than any discomfort he had with her. He'd discovered he could feel good as his Mistress' protector while still being himself.

In the audience, Sam turned around and smiled. Brady smiled back at her. He didn't have to fit into one or two boxes—football player or geek, boss or father, husband or submissive. He could be more than one thing. He could be all those things.

Just as long as his Sammy was with him.

* * *

"So how's everything going?"

Sam put the finishing touches on her tray of veggies and smiled at Jack. "Work is great. And Allegra is doing well, too."

It was Memorial Day, two days after Allegra's dance show, and Sam and Brady had invited their friends over for a summer kick-off barbeque. Loud music was playing in the yard and Allegra was running around. She was a little out of control, but Sam let her be. She'd been fighting against her daughter's frenzied nature, constantly worried she was messing her up, but it was time to accept who Allegra was. She was different from Sam and Brady but was wildly energetic and creative—her own little brand of awesome—and Sam was incredibly proud of her.

She was proud of all of them.

"And how is everything *else*?" Jack asked.

Sam felt what he was asking in the calm steadiness of his eyes. They weren't in-laws now, they were talking Dominant to Dominant. But the sound of a hard smack against siding interrupted them.

"Sorry!" Brady jogged toward the open windows and bent to retrieve the football that had punched against the house. "It's Nick's fault. He throws like a girl."

"Hey," they heard Nick yell. Sam laughed.

"We're gonna start cooking soon," she told him. "Ten minutes."

Brady pulled his phone from his pocket. "Hey Google, set a countdown for ten minutes."

He went out to the lawn where Nick, Gabe and Patrick were standing. Sam turned to Jack.

"Everything," she said, "is going really well."

The phone was a smart investment they'd made while developing a better understanding for Brady's issues, and were looking into a similar one for Allegra. The Google Assistant had been a nice replacement for the Post-its, although Sam still had a soft spot for them. Working at home had made Brady take on more, and Sam finally felt like she had a partner. He'd even made an effort to watch his language in front of the kids.

Not today, though. She could hear his curse through the windows when the football sailed over into the neighbor's yard. Allegra and Hope's new babysitter ran off to get it.

"Glad to hear it," Jack said. "If you need to talk, though, about anything..."

Yup, still awkward, talking to your brother-in-law about being his baby brother's Domme. Nick and Gabe had hooked her up with some people in the lifestyle, impartial people not related to any of them. It felt more comfortable.

"I'll let you know," she told Jack. "Promise."

They went outside. Jack carried a tray of raw meat for the grill. Low fat, of course. Sam placed the veggies on the patio table and stood back for a minute to take it all in. The warm weather, the laughter, the feeling of being surrounded by friends and family. She hugged Cassie and Lilly, these friends who had been there for her even when she hadn't been ready to see it. She'd taken them both out for drinks after the dust settled and thanked them. Although she'd never mentioned what Hanna had done.

"You ready for your trip?" Cassie asked.

Sam could barely contain her excitement. Next week she'd be heading to DC for the first time. "I can't wait to get back there. And to show the kids next month."

They'd planned a family vacation to Washington after school was out coinciding with Sam's upcoming travel. Two more trips were happening after that: one with Lilly and Jack to see Brady's parents in Maine, and another at the end of the summer, to Arizona.

She'd had a lot to think about when it came to family and had finally found peace about it. Sometimes you don't get the life you thought you wanted, and sometimes your kids or parents or partners have challenges life didn't prepare you for. But that's when you love them harder. She'd done that for her parents, and now they were healthy and happy someplace else. Their apartment had sold, and that chapter of Sam's life had closed.

Another chapter had ended. Sam had gotten an email from Hanna, settled now in London along with Aliyah, Imani and her parents. Sam was still a bit wary of Hanna's decision-making and her own inability to see things clearly, but she didn't regret the experience they'd had together, and was glad they'd both moved on.

Nick caught Brady's next throw and put the ball down. "So, we've got an announcement," he said, standing next to Gabe.

Allegra was still dancing. Sam turned down the volume on the Bluetooth speakers. Allegra stopped her routine and folded herself into Sam's side.

Nick pulled a photo from his pocket of a fair-skinned baby girl with dark eyes and a shock of black hair. "We're adopting."

Lilly squealed and ran over to them, along with Allegra and everyone else.

Sam leaned toward Brady. "I totally called that."

"How?"

"They've been dropping hints for ages. Just took a little observing."

He looked at her. "You sure you're not the hacker in the family?"

Hacker. Lawyer. Receptionist. Politician. Who knew what Sam was? What mattered was that she was happy. They congratulated the new parents-to-be, and when Brady put his arm around her, Sam couldn't help but think maybe her romance novels were right.

Maybe it was possible for everyone to have it all.

"Can I talk to you for a minute?" she asked Brady.

"Sure."

With everyone occupied and plenty of adults to supervise the kids, it was a good time to pull Brady inside. She'd ordered something special for him—the grand gesture she'd never given.

They hugged Nick and Gabe, then excused themselves and went in the house.

"What's up?" Brady asked. He was wearing a Superman T-shirt, a cobalt gray that offset the color of his eyes. He'd trimmed his beard short for the summer, and they'd started lifting together at her gym. It was nice, to do that as a couple, and to see the stay-at-home moms gawk over her husband's physique. She wasn't sharing him with them, though, or anyone else anytime soon.

"I have something for you."

They went to the bedroom. Sam reached under the bed and unlocked the toy chest.

"There are people outside, you know."

Sam grinned. "It's not a dirty gift."

She handed over the soft cotton bag with a drawstring tie. Brady pulled on the cord. The smell of fresh leather hit Sam's nose as soon as the bag opened and the custom-made wristband fell into his palm. It was mahogany brown, wide with grooved edging and hand-stitched bands. A silver four-leaf clover was in the middle of it.

"Is this what I think it is?"

She nodded. Instead of a collar, it was a submissive cuff. "Something for you to wear when we play." And something to solidify their bond. "It's only for then, though. When you put this on, we're Dominant and submissive. The rest of the time, we're equals."

"I love it."

Sam took it from him, turned it over and handed it back. "Read the inside."

He flattened the cuff and looked at the word inscribed on the inside.

"Metamorphosis." He gave her his signature goofy grin. "Is that in case I forget my safeword again?"

Sam had to laugh. "No."

"Is it because if I put this on I'll turn into a giant cockroach?"

"Oh my God."

She held one end of the cuff, ran her thumb over the word, and thought about the story she'd helped him understand years ago. "Metamorphosis is the process of transformation, of changing from one thing or person into a completely different one."

Sam closed the snaps, liking the sound of it clicking shut.

She was going to like it even more when it closed with his wrist inside it.

"It's seeing what happens when people let each other change." She looked at her husband, at his baby face, at his arms, eyes and smile, at the man who was her pet and her protector all wrapped up in one. "Thank you, for letting me change."

"You're welcome," he said. "We changed together."

She tucked the cuff back in the bag and pulled the drawstring. "I'm still not sure why you're so good to me."

"Simple." He turned her hand over, rubbed his finger along her wedding band. "I take care of you. You take care of me."

Sam kissed him and smiled. "End of story."

THANK YOU!

I hope you enjoyed *Their Discovery*! Brady and Sam made my heart ache to write at times. I'm so happy they finally get their happily ever after.

Maybe you loved them too? Maybe you didn't? Either way, I want to hear about it!

As you might know, reviews aren't easy to come by, and you, my darling reader, have the power to get others interested in my books. I'd be super appreciative if you took the time to leave me a review. If you're so inclined, you can leave one wherever you purchased the book from, and on Goodreads.

ALSO BY REBECCA GRACE ALLEN

Legally Bound:

His Contract

Her Claim

Portland Rebels:

The Duality Principle

The Hierarchy of Needs

The Theory of Deviance

Shakespeare in the City:

Taming Sugar

Hunter Pains

Decades Duet:

Find the Cost of Freedom

Smells Like Teen Spirit

EXCERPT FROM TAMING SUGAR

The rumble of Hunter's truck was easy to catch in the otherwise quiet evening. Roxy waited eagerly until he reappeared beside her, holding a bottle of wine. A very expensive and rare bottle of wine, judging by the name and vintage on the label.

"Was your quick errand to a winery?"

He smirked. "No. This is from my own personal storage."

Whoa. She hadn't imagined him to be a wine connoisseur, but Roxy was starting to think she'd imagined Hunter Finn all wrong.

He produced a corkscrew from his pocket and uncorked the wine.

"There's a few things I've learned to appreciate since I moved here," he said. "Things that don't involve money or fame. Hard work. A beautiful sunset. A meal made from scratch."

He sat down in the chair next to hers and poured a single glass.

"Some things get better the more you wait for them. Like wine."

Roxy rolled her eyes and picked up the empty glass, holding it out in his direction. He didn't fill it.

"I don't need a lesson in wine from you," she told him. She knew enough from the time she'd spent in her father's bars.

"Don't you?" He nodded toward her glass. "Put that down."

She frowned, but did as she was told.

"Now close your eyes."

Again, Roxy obeyed, willing to play his game. The chair beside her scraped over the patio, and then he was by her side, one hand brushing her face, knuckles skimming over her ear. A shiver coursed through her as he moved her hair to settle on her opposite shoulder. Then his hand was on the back of her neck, thumb solid at the base of her head.

Her next inhalation brought the scent of wine into her nostrils. She didn't dare open her eyes to check, but she guessed he was holding the glass in front of her.

"What do you smell?" he asked. "Explain it."

His touch was making her too fuzzy-headed to think clearly, but Roxy tried anyway. "It's a woodsy scent. Like the air out here, but with a fruit flavor. Cherry."

He didn't tell her if she was right or wrong, but the scent vanished as he moved in closer and brushed his lips over her ear. "Do you want a taste?"

Hot breath washed along her cheek. Roxy twisted in her seat. "Yes."

"Say please."

Roxy almost growled. Just like when he insulted her, being made to beg hit some previously untouched chord inside her. It pushed her deep into a place of obedience and held her there, a place that both repulsed and enticed her at the same time.

She gritted out the word, "Please."

Hunter ran his lips along her earlobe, then down her neck, nipping gently. The rasp of his beard over her skin made her every nerve ending tingle and come alive. He was making her wait, torturing her, and she gripped the armrests of the seat.

Returning to the shell of her ear, he whispered, "Say please, may I have a taste of wine, Sir?"

Roxy froze. She knew what the word *Sir* meant. Men had asked her to call them that before, and she'd complied, even when saying it felt like nothing more than a memorized line. But this...this didn't feel like acting. No, this felt *real*.

Hunter pressed his thumb harder against her neck. "You haven't spoken, and your body's gone stiff, but you're not frightened. You know how I know that?"

She fought to find her sarcastic side. "Because you're secretly psychic?"

Hunter laughed. Tightened his hand a little more. It was a move just shy of threatening.

"No, sugar. But there's another thing you didn't know about a man like me. I didn't only date for money. I dated for power, and not just in politics. More women than I can count have fallen to their knees for me. I assume you know what that means?"

She swallowed. "I'm guessing that was what you were talking about when you said you got what you wanted."

"Pretty much." His laugh sent another warm breath over her skin. Since when did warmth make her shiver?

"Am I about to become another one of those kneeling women?"

He found the juncture between her neck and shoulder with his teeth and bit down until she yelped. "If you're good."

Roxy tried to recover, tried to find something crass to say, but her head was spinning too much, her thighs pushing together in an attempt to stifle the ache between them.

"You pissed me off from the minute I met you," he said. "But I haven't stopped thinking about you since. No one has kneeled for me in ages, and it's an itch I needed to scratch." He licked over the spot he'd injured. "I think it's an itch for you too, isn't it?"

She was panting now, body straining in the chair. "I think it might be."

"I think so too. So, let's try this again." The scent of wine drifted by her nose once more. "May I have. A taste. Of wine. Sir."

Rebecca lives in southern Florida with three cats who firmly believe they are the main characters. When she's not immersed in fictional love stories, she can usually be found chasing strong coffee, good workouts, and the kind of books that balance heart, heat, and humor. She writes romance for readers who like their happily ever afters earned, their characters flawed, and their love stories a little messy in the best possible way.